"COME HERE. . . ."

Dane's fingers tightened on Jacqui's, drawing her against him . . . so close she could feel his breath on her lips.

"I've wanted to know the taste of your mouth from the first moment I saw you," he murmured huskily.

Jacqui's heart gave an involuntary leap.

"It's what you want as well, Jacqueline."

He slid his hand beneath her heavy silken mane, lightly stroking her nape. Jacqui made a soft sound of pleasure and protest, unconsciously leaning into his touch.

"Tell me," Dane commanded. "I want to hear you say the words." His grip tightened. "This has to be both of us. Tell me this is where you want to be. In my arms. Against my body. With my mouth on yours. Jacqueline," he breathed, running his hands across her shoulders, his thumbs skimming her throat where her pulse beat frantically. "Tell me to kiss you. Tell me . . . and I will."

Books by Andrea Kane

Dream Castle
Masque of Betrayal
My Heart's Desire

Published by POCKET BOOKS

Masque of Betrayal

Andrea Kane

POCKET BOOKS

New York London Toronto Sydney Tokyo Singapore

An *Original* Publication of POCKET BOOKS

POCKET BOOKS, a division of Simon & Schuster Inc.
1230 Avenue of the Americas, New York, NY 10020.

Copyright © 1993 by Andrea Kane

ISBN: 0-671-75532-3

First Pocket Books printing June 1993

10 9 8 7 6 5 4 3 2 1

POCKET and colophon are registered trademarks of
Simon & Schuster Inc.

Cover art by Gregg Gulbronson

Printed in the U.S.A.

To Brad and Wendi . . . I love you both!

Brad, your unfailing faith in *MASQUE* and your unending love for its author gave the book life.

Wendi, your hours of patience, moral support, and enthusiastic input . . . not to mention our shared fascination for Alexander Hamilton . . . gave the book heart.

Acknowledgments

To all who were instrumental in the writing of *MASQUE OF BETRAYAL:*

The Philadelphia Historical Society . . . my thanks for the stacks of books and the wealth of information.

Gisou et Chris . . . merci beaucoup.

Clare . . . many thanks for sharing your vast feline wisdom.

My two feline friends . . . Dusty, for your coloring; Alex, for your heritage.

Helen W. . . . with appreciation for helping me bring the Philadelphia Dance Assemblies to life, and for the numerous other odd facts unearthed.

Marge . . . your artistic genius is surpassed only by your open heart. Thank you for both.

And finally, my deep, heartfelt gratitude to a support system like no other:

My agent, Alice Orr, for her confidence and integrity;

My editor, Caroline Tolley, a partner in the truest sense;

And my critique partner, Karen Plunkett-Powell, for relentlessly pushing me to be the very best I can be.

Masque of Betrayal

CHAPTER
1

Philadelphia, April 1794

The voices grew louder.

She stopped dead in her tracks.

The warm April night was cloudlessly clear . . . too clear, lit by a full, glittering moon. The footsteps became more distinct as the strangers approached, and her eyes widened with fear.

It was two men. She could see them . . . but they had yet to see her. Thus far she was safe, her drab attire blending in with the shadows. But in a moment escape would be impossible, all she had worked for lost.

The sounds of heated conversation drew alarmingly close, knotting her stomach with trepidation. Where could she hide?

She looked furtively toward the row of poplar trees that cloaked the cobblestone street. In desperation, she darted for their protective shelter. Perspiration beaded on her nape and trickled down her back, making the dark muslin gown cling to her slight figure. She willed her breathing to slow, praying she could make it to safety before she was spotted.

But it was already too late.

Jacqueline *had* been spotted . . . not by the two men she feared, but by another.

He was studying her through glowing emerald eyes. Instinct told him exactly where she hid. He could stalk her, hunt her down in an instant. But he had no interest in doing so . . . not yet.

With keen anticipation, he watched his quarry approach. With taut apprehension, so did she.

"Damn, but you're restless tonight, Dane." The complaint came from the leaner of the two men, as he lengthened his strides to keep pace with his tall and powerfully built companion. "Are you upset over tonight's topic of conversation? Is it that blasted newspaper reporter again?"

Dane Westbrooke shrugged, pausing for the first time since leaving the City Tavern ten minutes earlier. Silently, he contemplated the whiskey in his bottle, then brought it to his lips for a deep, satisfying swallow. While he *was* troubled by the fervent political debates that had dominated the discussions of the prominent men who frequented the tavern, he didn't believe that they alone were the source of his growing unease. No, it was something far more deep rooted.

He shifted uneasily, unable to shake the ominous premonition that had been with him all evening. It sounded a clear warning: Danger.

"Dane?" His friend studied him speculatively. "What the hell is wrong with you?"

Dane lowered the bottle and turned, regarding Thomas Mills through eyes of pure, piercing silver. "I'm not certain. Yes, that reporter's scathing columns infuriate me. It's damned mysterious the way he seems to know everything that transpires within the inner circles of our government . . . and has a negative opinion on every Federalist stand." He hesitated. "But it's more. I can't put my finger on it exactly. . . ." He broke off, unable to describe the heightened awareness that plagued him. He had long since learned to heed his intuition, for it was the manifestation of a sixth sense that was Dane's since birth and had served him well for two and thirty years. It had been instrumental in making him what . . . and who . . . he was today. A rich, powerful, respected shipping magnate. And incomparably independent.

Dane's penetrating stare searched the deserted street, the darkened line of trees and buildings. All was still. He could see nothing. And yet . . . someone was out there. Suddenly he tensed, grabbing Thomas's arm. "We're being watched."

Thomas stiffened. After five years of close friendship, he had seen the accuracy of Dane's uncanny instincts countless times. Too many times to dispute. He waited for Dane's direction.

So did the silent observer. He crouched, ready to strike.

Dane gestured for Thomas to follow. Cautiously, they continued down the road.

The assailant struck.

In one fluid motion, he sprang through the air, knocking Dane and Thomas off balance. Then he went for the kill.

Furiously, he lapped up the contents of the broken bottle, purring victoriously while he drank. Quickly, before Dane and Thomas could retaliate, the kitten licked his lips and dashed off into the concealing trees . . . and straight into the face of the open-mouthed young woman who hid there, flat on her belly on the cold ground.

Nose to nose, female and feline gaped silently at one another.

As the irony of the situation sank in, it took all of Jacqui's willpower not to laugh aloud. She resisted, sobered by the fact that she was still very much at risk. Instead, she concentrated on listening to the continuation of the unexpected conversation she was overhearing.

She was not disappointed.

Thomas broke the silence with a hearty chuckle. *"That* was our fearsome adversary?" he managed, righting himself and brushing the dirt and droplets of whiskey from his waistcoat. "You must be losing your touch."

Dane cursed as he rose, dabbing at his damp shirt. "Apparently," he agreed. "What the hell was that?"

3

A cat, Jacqueline Holt mouthed, as she stared into the black kitten's glazed green eyes. He looked equally startled, neither of them entirely sure of the other's intent. However, with the common goal of avoiding discovery, neither dared move.

Jacqui watched the kitten sway on his feet and instantly decided that he was far too sluggish to do much harm. That conclusion did little to ease her fear. For she sensed the real threat came from the deep-voiced predatory man named Dane . . . the man, she knew, who simply *felt* her presence. Just as she felt his. Acutely.

There was not a doubt in Jacqui's mind that it was *she,* and not the untimely kitten, who had actually triggered Dane's unerring suspicions. She couldn't begin to imagine what he would do if he actually found her . . . especially if he learned of her mission. Nor did she have any desire to find out. She licked her dry lips and flattened herself more firmly on the cold ground.

"That," she heard Thomas taunt, "was merely a very thirsty, very agile kitten." He sounded highly amused that his astute friend had been outmaneuvered by a scrap of an animal. "But don't worry, Dane . . . I think you are out of peril. Obviously, the little beggar got what he wanted."

Dane gave up on the soggy shirt and shot Thomas a look. "I'm pleased that you find this so humorous," he said dryly. "But I still think . . ." Abruptly he paused, his penetrating stare probing the narrow roadway, the still trees, searching for something he was not ready to dismiss.

Jacqui's heart began to race, though she was certain he hadn't spotted her. And yet, as he stood silhouetted in the night, rigid and unyielding in his perusal, it seemed his omniscient stare was fixed on her, exposing her to his blatant scrutiny. Relentlessly assailed by the pungent odor of earth, moss, and whiskey-drenched fur, Jacqui fought the reflex to gag, lest she give herself away. She lay totally motionless, her nails dug into the ground, her gaze riveted on her foe's daunting form.

He was but a menacing shadow, looming dark and indistinct before her. Still, it did nothing to diminish the effect of his commanding physique and the primitive sort of power generated by his very presence. A power he would not hesitate to use. More than that, his instincts were obviously as well honed as her own, making him a formidable enemy. A tingle ran up her spine, one she recognized as a mixture of fear and exhilaration. She had to elude this man . . . and she would.

The next move was his. Jacqui held her breath, waiting. Thomas spoke.

"Dane, there is not a thing out there except the wind and your imagination," he complained. "I think you've been working too hard. It's time for a diversion . . . preferably a female one."

With a roguish grin, Dane relaxed. "You needn't worry on that score, Thomas," he assured his friend. "I've not been lacking in female companionship." He gave one final glance into the darkness. "But perhaps you're right about my being wrong. *This* time, at least. It is late and I am tired."

Thomas looked quickly down at his timepiece. "Speaking of women . . ." he began.

"Were we?" Dane baited. "Funny. I don't recall that we were speaking of women. But, evidently, you have one on your mind."

"I do. One I would rather not disappoint. And, if I don't hurry, I'm going to be late for our . . . visit."

Dane digested this piece of information thoughtfully. "Are you ever going to tell me who this mystery woman is?" he asked.

"No, thank you," Thomas declined, holding up his hand to ward off Dane's request. "I need no competition from you, my too-charming friend. This is one lady I plan to keep all to myself." His eyes twinkled. "Good night, Dane."

Good-naturedly, Dane accepted the evasion. "Yes, good night," he returned. "Although I'm certain you've already planned to have one."

"And what have you planned?"

Dane flexed his arms in front of him, stretching his powerful muscles. "I told Alexander I would stop in to see him by nine o'clock."

Thomas hesitated for a minute. "Fine. I won't repeat myself by telling you that you're working too hard. But you are." He gave Dane a mock salute. "Not I, however. *Adieu.*" Whistling, he took his leave.

Whoever Thomas's lady was, Dane reflected with a chuckle, she was good for him. Dane hadn't seen his friend this happy in months . . . not since his textile-import company had begun to lose money, a situation that only promised to worsen as the months progressed. Especially if Hamilton prevailed in raising import duties to bolster America's fledgling industry. Then things would become even bleaker for poor Thomas.

Turbulent political issues confronted their country. America's government was, in many ways, like a new colt, still wobbly on its legs, its fiber being molded by the brilliant minds of its leaders. Tension with England was peaking again, badly needing to be diffused. The last thing the States could withstand was another war. It had to be prevented.

Purposefully, Dane strode toward his destination: The office of the Secretary of the Treasury.

Jacqui watched him go and released her breath on a sigh. Slowly, cautiously, she stood, waiting until Dane's booted footsteps had faded down the cobblestone walk before she emerged from her hiding place. Then she crept out and peered after him. Thank goodness . . . he was gone.

A rustle from behind made her jump and spin about in alarm. A small, weaving ball of fur plunked down on the road beside her, the sound of the unceremonious plop magnified by both the night's absolute stillness and the frantic pounding of Jacqui's heart.

With a delicate lick of his whiskers, the inebriated kitten gazed up at her cross-eyed.

This time Jacqui relaxed into muffled laughter. She squatted down beside the small cat and gently stroked his wet fur.

"You are a terribly untidy and pathetic bandit, you know," she murmured, scratching his ears lightly. Greeted by the suffocating smell of liquor, Jacqui wrinkled her nose. "Not only did you practically give us both away, but you've managed to cover yourself with whiskey as well. Whatever will your owner say?"

The kitten did not answer, his eyes closed with ecstasy as he soaked up the attention he was receiving. Nearby, the branches of the trees whispered in the wind, and Jacqui's head shot up, her petite body tensing. It was always possible that a late-working merchant would still be about. Or worse . . . a menacing thief or a drunk. Hastily she stood, backing away from the kitten, who looked startled and bereft at his sudden abandonment.

"I must go . . ." Jacqui muttered, smoothing her hands rapidly up and down the sides of her gown, while scanning the deserted street. The immediate danger might have passed, but she couldn't rest until she was where her father would expect her to be . . . at home, in bed.

She hurried off, her slippered feet moving soundlessly on the road, then through the rows of elm trees. She ducked down a narrow, unpaved alleyway and bolted across the next street. She had but a few more blocks to go. Now only one. There, at last . . . home. She could see the graceful two-story brick house at the road's end. Her job was done . . . for tonight.

It was then she heard the noise.

Her face drained of color, she whirled, nearly tripping over a small black lump at her feet. The lump moved.

"You!" she hissed, staring at the kitten dumbfounded. "What are you doing here?"

The kitten merely gazed up at her with a haunted expression that tore at Jacqui's nearly impenetrable heart.

"Why don't you go home . . . where you belong?" she

asked, with a sinking feeling in her stomach. "Home," she repeated, knowing full well that it was to no avail. Clearly, this poor creature was an orphan.

The kitten blinked its huge green eyes and answered with a sound that curiously resembled a hiccup, while rubbing itself insistently against Jacqui's gown. Then it opened its tiny pink mouth and let out a not-so-tiny meow that could have awakened the dead.

"Hush!" Jacqui looked about anxiously, convinced that at any moment the entire neighborhood would descend upon her, demanding an explanation for her unseemly conduct. And *that* would be the end of all her carefully laid plans.

No other recourse in sight, Jacqui scooped the forlorn little fellow into her arms, carrying him around to the side of her house, where she stopped. "How shall I manage that old oak while I'm holding you?" she demanded, half to herself. "It was hard enough when I had only myself to hoist." She chewed her lip thoughtfully, then shrugged. There appeared to be no other choice but to attempt it . . . unless she was willing to concede defeat. And the word *defeat* was not in Jacqui's vocabulary.

Raising her gown and tucking it between her legs, she placed the kitten upon her shoulder. "Hold on," she instructed softly, praying that the animal would understand. She winced as he dug his claws into her gown . . . and her skin . . . for better traction. Then she proceeded to shimmy up the endless, winding oak tree that led to her bedroom.

Ever so quietly, she eased back the shutters, exposing the open window that was her gateway to safety.

With a surge of relief, Jacqui climbed inside and dropped onto the hardwood floor. Her gown was ripped in three places, she noted, wiping beads of perspiration from her brow. How was she going to explain that?

The answer climbed hesitantly down from her shoulder, shook out his whiskey-scented fur, and gave an unfocused blink at his new surroundings.

A smile tugged at Jacqui's lips. "Yes, little whiskey thief,

8

you just might be my savior after all," she acknowledged. She studied her rent gown closely, then nodded. The tears could certainly have been caused by a cat. She studied the gaping window. Cats could definitely climb trees. Her smile widened. Yes, it would work, all right. No one would doubt her.

Not when the explanation was right there for all to see.

And to smell.

Jacqui waved away the pungent fumes and stifled a cough. "Cat, you need a bath even more than I do." She fetched her washing basin and placed it on the floor, glancing at her reflection in the large oval mirror as she passed. Her thick, mahogany tresses lay in tangled disarray down her back and stuck in damp tendrils to her smudged forehead and neck. "Upon closer examination, I retract that statement," she muttered, seeing the additional smears of dirt on her cheeks and arms. She gathered up the porcelain pitcher by her basin. "So I shall heat water for us both. You wait here."

Quietly, and with as little fuss as possible, Jacqui managed to heat a small amount of water, which she carried back to her room. A trifle awkwardly, she cleansed the dirt from her face and body with a cloth and a bar of soap. She didn't dare drag the heavy tub up the stairs for fear of awakening the household. Tomorrow was soon enough for a real bath; for now, this would have to do.

After she had slipped into a clean nightrail, she proceeded to douse the squirming, protesting cat in soapy water. "It serves you right for smelling like a distillery," she scolded, avoiding his claws. She dried him off, her lips twitching at his wet spikes of fur, his scrawny appearance. "Whiskey, you are quite the thing," she praised. "And just as bold as I. Why, I do believe that we are going to be great companions."

The kitten, thereby christened "Whiskey," hiccuped his agreement. Then, with an exaggerated yawn, he leapt onto the beckoning softness of the bed, curled up on the plump feather pillow, and fell fast asleep.

"A wise decision," Jacqui concurred. The harrowing

9

events of the night were taking their toll, and she was possessed of a sudden, ringing weariness. Yawning, she climbed into bed, snuggled beneath the bright patchwork quilt, lay her head next to Whiskey's, and closed her eyes.

Sleep did not come easily. Nor had she expected it would.

She always had trouble falling asleep after completing her weekly mission, for her mind was filled with the ramifications of her actions . . . and the importance of her cause. She therefore assumed that tonight would be the same.

But instead of her night's activities, all Jacqui could see was the dark, towering man that had come within a hair's-breadth of exposing her secret.

All was still at the corner of Third and Chestnut streets when Dane rounded the bend. Only a snatch of light came from beneath the solid door that led into the two-story brick office building. Dane gave a brief rap, then opened the door and strolled in.

"I'm here."

The handsome man with the powdered auburn hair looked up from his desk, put down his quill pen, and acknowledged Dane's presence with a faint smile. "So I see. Rather disheveled, are you not?" He indicated the whiskey stains on Dane's shirt and breeches.

Dane didn't smile back. "I had an unpleasant encounter with an inebriated cat," he answered shortly, with a dismissive wave of his hand. "It's late, Alexander," he began without preliminaries. "You should be home with Betsey, not here working until all hours of the night."

Alexander Hamilton leaned back in his chair. "Good evening to you, too, Dane."

Dane strode across the room with purposeful familiarity and lowered himself into a chair. "It has been mere months since you took ill . . . an illness you've scarce recovered from," he staunchly continued, assessing Hamilton's pallor and visible weakness. Dane couldn't forget how he had

10

almost lost his friend to an epidemic of yellow fever that had spread like wildfire through Philadelphia last fall. "Have you so quickly forgotten your close call with death?"

Hamilton made a steeple with his fingers and rested his chin upon it. "I haven't forgotten. However, I have regained my health. And there is much I need to do before I retire from office."

Dane nodded his understanding. He knew how much Hamilton wanted to separate himself from the political upsets of the past few years, how much he wanted to go home to New York with his family and resume his law practice.

How much the country would lose with his departure.

"Thomas and I were at the Tavern tonight," Dane said at last. "The talk was of Laffey's latest column in the *General Advertiser*. He all but stated that war with England was imminent—"

"President Washington has asked John Jay to go to England to negotiate for peace," Hamilton interrupted quietly.

Dane bolted to his feet. "Damn it, Alexander! You're the one who should be going, not Jay!"

Hamilton sighed deeply, his astute gaze holding his friend's molten silver one. "Despite our individual beliefs . . . or our passions," he added pointedly, "we must do what is best for the country. For me to serve as the American envoy right now would be foolhardy. We both know it, Dane."

"You told that to President Washington?" Dane persisted.

"I did."

"What was his reaction?"

Hamilton did not hesitate. "He was greatly relieved."

Dane slammed his fist on the desk in frustration. Hamilton was right. There was too much controversy surrounding his handling of Treasury funds. It was a lot of nonsense, but it diminished his credibility nonetheless.

"I wanted to tell you first . . . before the information was made public," Hamilton was continuing.

"Or before Laffey makes it public."

Hamilton frowned. "Laffey . . . yes. He is a real thorn in the side of our government." He raked his hand through his neatly queued hair and stood, hands clasped behind his back. "We have enough to deal with, without his scathing columns. They incite too many people by prematurely revealing information that is better kept undisclosed."

"Not to mention his unique ability to obtain the information before it becomes public," Dane added. He shook his head angrily. "But the problem is, no one knows who he actually is."

"I can think of many people who would attack my philosophies," Hamilton returned dryly, staring at the floor but not seeing it. "Especially in the *General Advertiser*. But none of those people would dare go so far as Laffey has, particularly in light of the volatile situation with England. It is not only that Laffey labels me and the entire party as monarchical, but that the information he imparts could only have been obtained in closed social functions, and from men who are far too shrewd to publicly state opinions they realize should remain private."

"What are we going to do about it?" Dane demanded, recognizing the dawning, decisive light on Hamilton's face. The Secretary of the Treasury had an idea.

Hamilton grinned, a boyish grin that made his elegant good looks even more striking. "I'm going to host a small gathering of prominent politicians and businessmen in the Long Room. And *you,* my charming friend, are going to flit about, as you do so well, speak with all our guests . . ."

". . . and see what I can learn," Dane finished, chuckling at Alexander's uncustomary, exaggerated praise.

"Precisely."

"Next Friday?"

"Eight o'clock."

"Done." Dane turned and headed for the door. He paused for a moment, his expression one of stark determination. "By next Saturday you and I will know exactly who Jack Laffey really is."

Hamilton's jaw clenched. "And when we do, we will make certain that his pen is silenced for good."

CHAPTER
2

~~~

"You look radiant, my dear." George Holt, dashing in his own fashionable black evening attire, beamed at his elegant, mahogany-haired daughter as he assisted her in alighting from their carriage.

Jacqui glanced disdainfully at the City Tavern. "I don't feel radiant, Father," she retorted, adjusting her satin cloak. "I feel cantankerous."

He chuckled. "Perhaps, but no one would know it. You conceal it well." He took her gloved arm, giving it a gentle squeeze. "I do appreciate your decision to accompany me to Secretary Hamilton's ball."

"Even if it was on such short notice," she reminded him with a sidelong look.

George's smile faded. "It is hardly Monique's fault if she became ill, Jacqueline."

Jacqui recognized her father's warning tone and fell silent. When it came to *la très belle* Monique Brisset, George Holt was unwavering, unheeding, and hopelessly besotted. It had been that way from the start, since he'd first laid eyes on her at Oeller's Hotel a year ago February, during the annual ball given on President Washington's birthday. Nothing was going to alter George's feelings . . . not even

14

Jacqui's carefully masked dislike, a dislike that rivaled her great relief that, at last, after ten lonely years of solitude since her mother's death, George had finally found another woman to love.

Silently, Jacqui passed beneath her father's arm and glided into the Tavern's dimly lit front entranceway. To her left, merchants gathered in the Coffee Room, drinking mugs of whiskey and discussing their latest business ventures. Farther down the hall, pairs of handsome, influential men and expensively dressed women headed toward the staircase that ascended to the ball above. Jacqui barely noticed them. Instead, she inched her way to the right, absently smoothing the silk folds of her vibrant lilac gown.

Her father wasn't fooled for a minute.

"Not tonight, Jacqueline." He took her elbow firmly and steered her away from the Subscription Room, where she had been intent on overhearing the talk among the different newspaper and magazine reporters.

Jacqui followed along resignedly, casting a reluctant look over her shoulder. "But, Father, I was only wondering if there were any news of impending war or discussion of the tax imposed on whiskey. Surely you wouldn't mind if . . ."

"But I would." He guided her through the milling crowd and up the heavy wooden staircase. "We are guests tonight, and this is a *social* event. Let us attempt to keep it that way."

"Yes, Father." Jacqui had no recourse. The infuriating thing was that this time her normally indulgent father was right. And while she would greatly prefer being part of the heated debate on what to do with those few distillers who stubbornly refused to pay the excise tax on whiskey, she knew that it was an honor to be invited to the Hamiltons' ball, and she owed it to her father to be gracious.

The Long Room was brightly lit, its polished floors gleaming, its grand walls lined with notable people. Soft strains of violins playing a Mozart minuet drifted amid the perfume-scented air and mingled with the women's soft laughter and the men's deeper-voiced conversations. Garbed in brocade gowns of rich silks and satins and adorned with headpieces boasting ribbons and feathers, the ladies clustered together in groups of four and five, chatting gaily and nibbling delicately at their *hors d'oeuvres*. As if sensing Jacqui's presence, they looked up, assessing this new and unknown addition to their circle.

A small, dark-eyed woman in a dove-colored gown broke away from the others and approached Jacqui and George. "Mr. Holt, 'tis a pleasure to see you again." She gave him a radiant smile.

George Holt bent over her hand with a bow. "The pleasure, Mrs. Hamilton, is mine. I am honored that you thought to include me this evening." He stepped away, drawing Jacqui forward. "May I present my daughter, Jacqueline?"

Another charming smile. "Miss Holt, you are every bit as lovely as your father has boasted. Welcome."

Jacqui smiled back, taking an instant liking to the serene-faced, gracious lady who was her hostess.

"Thank you, Mrs. Hamilton. I, too, am honored to be here tonight." Feeling the curious stares of the other women, Jacqui glanced boldly into the room, blatantly challenging their scrutiny.

Betsey took her arm. "Come. Let me introduce you to our other guests." She turned back to George. "My husband will be delighted to see you. He is with those gentlemen in the corner." She gestured toward a large group of men, several of whom Jacqui recognized as senators whose political views were closely aligned with Hamilton's.

"Thank you, my dear. I shall find him." George caught the appealing look Jacqui shot him and swallowed a smile. "Mrs. Hamilton, I wonder if you would object to *my* introducing Jacqueline to the guests?" He leaned forward conspiratorially. "My daughter is not quite twenty and still somewhat shy."

16

Jacqui nearly choked over the barefaced lie. She . . . shy?

Betsey nodded instantly. "Of course, sir. I understand perfectly." She took Jacqui's hands in hers. "Please enjoy yourself. If I can be of any help to you, do not hesitate to ask."

"You are very kind, Mrs. Hamilton," Jacqui answered softly, feeling almost guilty over the small betrayal. *Almost.*

"Thank you, Father," she said instantly, when they were alone. "I don't think I could have withstood an evening of idle chatter."

"So I assumed." He looked across the room. "Actually, I see our host is deep in conversation right now. Why don't I present you to a few of the other guests and we can find Hamilton later."

Following her father's gaze, Jacqui could barely make out Secretary Hamilton's profile and could see nothing of the men with whom he spoke. She nodded eagerly, and she and George strolled in the opposite direction.

"All the guests appear to have arrived." Alexander Hamilton spoke in low tones. "All but Thomas," he added. "Will he come?"

"I doubt it, Alexander," Dane replied honestly. "He has been working every night, trying desperately to find a way to recoup some of his losses." Seeing the pained look on Hamilton's face, Dane broke off. He knew his friend felt deep regret, as well as a twinge of guilt, over Thomas's business losses. Thomas had served under Hamilton in the War for Independence, had fought beside the Secretary in his brilliant siege against Cornwallis at Yorktown, and Hamilton held a special fondness for Thomas. No amount of personal sentiment, however, would deter Hamilton from his call for higher import tariffs, for he believed them essential toward making America self-sufficient.

Hamilton scanned the room. "I assume you were unsuccessful in convincing your mother to attend?"

Dane's jaw tightened. "You know she feels awkward attending parties without my father, Alexander. And, as it is highly unlikely that he shall ever stray from English soil, there is little hope for that situation to be remedied. In any case, she sends you her regards and her regrets."

Hamilton nodded his understanding and tactfully dropped the subject. "If we hope to accomplish our goal of unmasking Laffey, you will have little time to dance and less time to spend with but one lady, Dane. Therefore, I have arranged for lots not to be chosen pairing you with a partner for the evening. It will make it easier for you to circulate." He gave Dane a meaningful look and concluded, "I hope the gathering proves fruitful."

Dane finished his Madeira and placed the empty glass on a passing tray. "There is only one way to find out, isn't there?" With a self-assured smile, he strolled into the crowd.

"Good evening, Westbrooke. Join us." The greeting came from one of Hamilton's congressional allies, Senator Rufus King of New York.

"Gentlemen." Dane walked over to the small group of politicians. He had known most of them for years now and was hard pressed to believe that any of them was, in fact, the man he sought. Still, no one was above suspicion.

"We were just discussing Laffey's latest column in the *General Advertiser.*" It was as if King had read Dane's mind. "Rather scathing, was it not?"

Keeping his expression carefully blank, Dane replied noncommittally. "No more so than any of his previous ones. I, myself, give very little credence to his ramblings. And I have to believe that many others share my opinion."

Six shrewd pairs of eyes studied Dane's reaction. His close personal relationship with Hamilton was a well-known fact.

"So you don't believe there is a real threat of war with England?" Richard Hastings, a wealthy Philadelphia merchant, fired the question at Dane.

Dane folded his arms across his broad chest. "Of course the threat exists. We are all well aware of it. However . . ."

But Hastings wasn't finished. "What if there should be war . . . does that present you with a conflict, Westbrooke?"

Ice-gray eyes bored into the pudgy, middle-aged man. "I think it would be the worst thing for our very new, very war-weary country."

"True. But, should America falter, you still have your heritage and the titles and land that go with it awaiting you at home in England."

"Philadelphia is my home, Hastings." Dane's tone was deceptively quiet, masking a core of barely leashed anger. England and his noble heritage had been cast aside more than a decade ago. He had never looked back.

Hastings saw the muscle flex in Dane's jaw and abruptly dropped the conversation, sauntering off in pursuit of more Madeira.

Dane turned back to the other men, feeling more than a little irritated. He was determined to find out what he could and then get the hell out of here. The party had, quite suddenly, lost all its appeal.

Jacqui was downright disgusted.

The only conversations she had been privy to thus far had been those of the prominent businessmen who were her father's friends or competitors. And, since she already had a thorough understanding of the Holt Trading Company, she had no desire to listen to endless hours of praise regarding its profits.

The alternative was even more disconcerting.

Each time she strayed from her father's side, she was immediately accosted by one of the ball's available gentlemen and asked to dance. "Gentleman," she quickly learned, was a complete misnomer, and "dancing" could be loosely defined as lewd and flirtatious advances under the guise of harmless frolicking about the room.

"They would welcome a conflict between us and England, despite the rivers of blood still flowing from their own revolution. Nothing would please the French more than America allying with them against their common enemy, the British."

Jacqui's ears perked up at the sweeping statement, which originated from a small cluster of pro-Federalists. Slowly, nonchalantly, she sidled over to their closed circle, stopping just near enough to hear what was being said, but not so near as to be observed.

"That is a certainty." Jacqui recognized the second voice as that of William Larson, a prestigious Philadelphia banker, who was avidly pro-English. "Is it not, Mr. Secretary?"

"Welcome seems a rather strong choice of words." Alexander Hamilton spoke in measured tones, seeming to consider his answer carefully before he spoke. "I do not believe they would welcome additional bloodshed, regardless of the benefit to their cause. Every day ships from the Continent bring word of another series of beheadings on the *Place de la Revolution.* I would think that restoring order to their own country would be the priority of the French."

"I agree." Jacqui saw her father join the group in time to respond to Hamilton's cautiously worded reply. "But I cannot blame France for expecting our sympathy. After all, it is the English who—"

"Hopefully," Larson interrupted with a disgusted snort, "our government knows better than to align itself with the French." He raised bushy brows, shaking his head adamantly from side to side. "We have nothing to gain from supporting a country whose own government is in shambles. We should be concentrating instead on strengthening our trade with England . . . a far more advantageous goal."

"Even in light of their seizing hundreds of American ships in the Caribbean?" George Holt sounded stunned.

"Indeed," agreed Horace Benson, a business associate of George's and one who shared his more moderate political beliefs. "The English did flagrantly violate our neutrality.

Why, over three hundred American ships and their cargoes have been taken!"

"We need England," Larson shot back. "We do *not* need France."

Jacqui stiffened.

"The fact is," Larson was continuing, "that England is doing what it must do in order to prevail. We must do the same. If that means making concessions to the English"—he shrugged—"then that is what it means."

Jacqui's feet were carrying her forward, moving with a will of their own. She was just on the verge of exploding into a fierce verbal tirade when her father turned in her direction. Catching her eye, he gave her a warning scowl and a quick shake of his head. Although he said not a word, Jacqui could feel his thoughts as tangibly as if he had spoken them aloud. *Do not create a scene, Jacqueline,* his expression cautioned. *Don't even consider it.*

Jacqui halted in her tracks. Her respect and love for her father warred with her rage and she inhaled sharply, counted to ten under her breath. Then she spun on her heel and stalked off. Her tolerance was gone.

As the strings fell silent, Dane extricated himself from the clinging grasp of the woman with whom he'd been dancing. She raised appealing green eyes to him, staying his exit with a touch of her hand.

"Please, Dane . . . I have scarcely seen you all night . . . all week, for that matter. Must you go?"

He was about to reply when a flash of lilac caught his eye. It was a woman . . . a beautiful, visibly indignant woman . . . who hovered, for but an instant, in the doorway, then disappeared from the room. Fascinated, Dane wondered who she was and why they'd never met before this night . . . an introduction he most assuredly would recall. He stared after her, pondering the reasons for her obvious upset, eagerly awaiting a second glimpse of her captivating loveliness.

21

The doorway remained empty.

Unable to resist the compulsion to do so, Dane went in search of his answer.

"Dane?"

Belatedly, Dane recalled his dance partner. "Forgive me, Amelia," he said with a regretful smile. "I am not terribly good company tonight." He glanced restlessly toward the door. "I have pressing matters on my mind."

"Business matters?" She pouted, unwilling to so easily relinquish him.

Dane frowned, wondering where the deuce the unknown woman had gone. "Uh . . . yes . . . important business matters." He continued to inch away. "But I shall pay you a visit just as soon as they have been resolved." Without further explanation, he strode off.

The hallway was deserted. Dane checked each of the smaller rooms on the second level, but both were empty. That left only the lower level. His curiosity growing by the minute, he descended the staircase two steps at a time. Then he came to an abrupt halt.

She was just outside the Subscription Room, a mere twenty feet ahead, her back turned toward him. She appeared to be absorbed in the process of adjusting her bodice.

Quietly, he came up behind her.

"May I be of assistance?"

Intent on overhearing the conversation from within, Jacqui was totally taken aback by the deep baritone interruption. Not to mention the outrageousness of the question. Quickly recovering, she spun about, meeting the wicked gleam in his eye with unleashed fury.

"I beg your pardon?" she spit out.

Dane felt as if he'd been dealt a fatal blow. Never had he been so struck by a woman's physical appearance . . . but never had he encountered a woman whose beauty equaled that of the stormy vision that stood before him.

Masses of curls the color of rich, deep chocolate tumbled down her back, tendrils of which framed a flawless face and crowned a still more breathtaking body that even the impediment of a gown could not disguise. But what really drew him were her eyes. From beneath thick, sooty lashes, they blazed at him, the deep, intense blue of a midnight sky, filled with the golden sparks of a thousand distant stars.

And, at the moment, as lethal as death.

"Are you quite finished?" Jacqui demanded, acutely aware of his scrutiny.

A slow smile tugged at Dane's lips. "I don't believe I am. In fact, I've barely begun."

Jacqui started. Whoever this scoundrel was, his behavior surpassed scandalous. "If you will excuse me, sir, I was on my way out for some air." She gave him a meaningful look. "Which I require now more than ever." With a last reluctant glance at the Subscription Room, she stalked out of the tavern.

Second Street was deserted. Jacqui took several deep breaths, shivering, wishing she had her cloak with her. She was suddenly and inexplicably chilled to the bone.

"Would you like my coat?"

The low-pitched masculine voice brought her up short.

"No," she retorted without turning around. "I would not like your coat. Nor your company."

He chuckled. "There are many who find my company quite pleasant. But, be that as it may, you should not be out here alone at night. It isn't safe for a lady."

"Oh really?" She spun about to face him. "Just what makes you think that I am a lady?"

Dane's silver gaze smoldered, taking in her expensive clothing and jewelry, then lingered on the expanse of creamy skin above her bodice. "Your appearance tells me so."

"Appearances are often deceiving," she countered.

"So they are," he agreed in a husky voice. "Very well then, if you are *not* as you appear to be . . ." Without warning, he lowered his head and brushed his lips against the fragrant pulse at her throat.

Jacqui wrenched away, drew back her hand, and slapped him resoundingly across the face. "You lecher! If the streets are *unsafe* for ladies such as myself, it is because *gentlemen* such as you make them that way!" With all the regality of a queen, she raised her chin, lifted her skirts, and swept past him. The tavern door slammed shut behind her.

Dane rubbed the smarting edge of his jaw, reeling from the impact of her blow. He was stunned by his own impulsive actions. Whatever had possessed him to take such outrageous liberties with an obviously well-bred young lady? He considered the question with bewildered amusement. Well-bred, yes, but unlike any young lady he'd ever met. Forthright, independent, and disturbingly immune to his charm. All of which added up to one thing: a challenge. Something Dane Westbrooke could never resist.

Grinning roguishly, Dane reentered the tavern and headed for the stairs. It was time to discover the identity of *both* his quarries: the elusive Jack Laffey and the equally mysterious little spitfire with the face of an angel and the tongue of a shrew.

In the Long Room entranceway, he scanned the crowd, admitting to himself that it was not Laffey he sought but his rare and evasive hellion.

There was no sign of her. Undaunted, Dane made his way among the guests, never pausing in his search. Finally, he caught a fleeting glimpse of lilac and eagerly went in pursuit.

He was but an arm's length from his destination when he was waylaid by William Larson, who was, by this time, so intoxicated that he could barely stand. "Westbrooke! Where've y'been?" he demanded, grabbing Dane's arm. "We needed your opinion . . . 'specially if we're going to war like Laffey says."

Dane winced, seeing the flash of lilac disappear into the crowd. He wanted nothing more than to shake his arm free and sprint after her, but the name Laffey reverberated in his mind like a discordant note. He had a job to do . . . one he had promised Alexander would get done tonight.

He inhaled deeply. "I was out getting some air, Larson. What did you say about Laffey?"

Magically, a group of curious men materialized around Dane.

"We were discussing Laffey's assessment of the English, Westbrooke," Dr. Lawrence Harigan informed him. "And whether he's right that their treatment of our ships will result in a war."

"It is a grave possibility," Dane returned candidly, looking from one face to the next, seeing everything from complete approval to wary skepticism. "One we had best pray we can avoid. Our country is not prepared to defend itself against the English. Nor are we able to do without her trade. Thus our course is obvious. We must find a peaceful resolution to this problem."

"This problem, as you describe it," Paul Jabot, who was of French descent, argued, "involves blatant, unprovoked aggression on the part of the English. Is it not enough that they are at war with France, representing, yet again, a threat to liberty? Do we lack the courage to stand up for what is right? After all, the French—"

"Have every right to expect our support."

All eyes turned toward the clear, feminine voice that broke into their heated discussion. Flushed with anger, Jacqui stalked boldly into their closed circle, her head held high. "Well?" she continued, hands clenched into fervent fists at her sides. "Were the French not present to show us support in the time of *our* revolution? Or have we so quickly forgotten the desperate need to free ourselves of a monarchical rule? What of our quest for freedom? Is everyone not allowed that same right?" She glared at each man as if daring him to contradict her. Finally, her blazing eyes met Dane's composed expression. "Apparently, principle is far less important than profit. How very sad." She walked around Dane, being careful to avoid any contact with him. "Pardon me," was all she said before she was swallowed up by the crowd.

Dead silence prevailed as all the men gaped after her, stunned that any woman would be so forthright.

"Good Lord . . ." Dr. Harigan breathed, turning to Dane in amazement.

"Who is she?" Dane demanded, watching Jacqui's exit.

"I have no idea. I have never seen her before tonight."

"Nor I," admitted Jabot.

Dane's lips curved into a hint of a smile. "The lady," he said at last, "does have a point, does she not?"

"But . . ."

Dane interrupted Harigan with a shake of his head. "Gentlemen, I need a drink. If you will excuse me?" Purposefully, he moved away, helped himself to a brandy, and tossed it down. Through narrowed eyes he surveyed the room, more determined than ever to stalk his prey.

"Good evening, Dane." George Holt acknowledged Dane with a courteous nod.

"Oh . . . George. Good evening." Dane blinked at his ofttimes business associate, whose trading company frequently contracted with Dane's ships to transport its cargo to and from the Continent.

George raised inquisitive brows. "You look a bit perplexed. Is something amiss?"

"Amiss?" Dane echoed, still searching the crowd. "No . . . but perplexed . . . yes. Earlier this evening, I met the most intriguing woman. She is extremely beautiful, uncommonly intelligent, and more opinionated than any female I've ever known." He chuckled ruefully. "I have yet to learn her name, for she keeps escaping me. However, twice tonight I have been lambasted by her searing tongue."

"Ah," George commented dryly. "I see you've met my daughter."

CHAPTER
3

~

Your daughter?"

George nodded, scanning the room. He found Jacqui without too much trouble. But then, he knew where to look. While Dane had probably been searching among the ebullient dancers, George sought out the groups of debating politicians. Sure enough, just alongside them, eagerly listening, was Jacqui.

"Come." George gestured for Dane to follow him. "I can rectify your problem by providing you with a proper introduction." They weaved their way among the guests and across the room, pausing behind Jacqui, who was oblivious to their presence. "Jacqueline," George murmured, taking her arm.

Jacqui whirled about, guilt staining her cheeks. If her father had heard of her earlier actions, he would be incensed. "Yes, Father?" she asked tentatively.

George moved aside to allow Dane to step forward. "I'd like you to meet Mr. Dane Westbrooke. Dane . . . my daughter, Jacqueline."

Dane? The name crashed through her in huge, biting waves of memory. By his towering height and powerful build, Jacqui had no doubt that the man who stood before her with that cocky grin and penetrating silver gaze, the man who had accosted her that night, was the same *Dane* who had nearly discovered her secret the previous week. Ignoring her trembling legs, Jacqui schooled her features, determined to appear as normal as possible.

Jacqueline. Dane had to bite back his laughter at the expression on her face, which was a mixture of stunned chagrin and fury. She said nothing, merely stared at him with those incredible dark blue eyes.

"Miss Holt." He took her reluctant hand in his and brought it to his lips. Her skin was soft, and the scent of fresh flowers clung to her. Dane inhaled deeply. "I am charmed." He pressed a warm, caressing kiss upon her knuckles, lingering as long as he dared. He felt the quiver that went through her and raised his head, trying to decide if it was anger or pleasure she was feeling.

"Mr. Westbrooke." The ice in Jacqui's voice erased any doubts Dane might have had about her reaction. She tugged her hand, but Dane would not release it.

"Dance with me." It was a request, an invitation, a command. Remembering himself, Dane half turned to George, holding fast to Jacqui's unwilling grasp. "George, may I have permission to dance with your daughter?"

"Certainly," George replied.

"No," Jacqui blurted out simultaneously, then shot her father a beseeching look. "I apologize, Mr. Westbrooke," she added hastily, having no idea what excuse she could give, "but I . . ."

"Go ahead, dear," George broke in. He was not anxious to see Dane Westbrooke insulted, and besides, he would be grateful to see his headstrong daughter occupied. It would keep her out of trouble. "Go and enjoy yourself."

There was little Jacqui could do but allow Dane to lead her onto the dance floor.

"So . . . Jacqueline . . . at last we meet." His voice was laced with amusement as he led her into a minuet.

She lifted her chin. "Did you seek me out to chastise me for my earlier outburst?" she demanded.

Dane shook his head slowly, utterly taken by her fiery beauty. "To the contrary, I wanted to congratulate you on an argument well stated."

For an instant she looked unsure. "Oh . . . I see."

He chuckled. "Have *I* succeeded in shocking *you*?"

"No. But I will admit you have surprised me. I assumed you would be appalled by my behavior."

"Consider it the first of many surprises between us," he promised. He spun her about and brought her closer to him, keeping her there for a long moment before he eased her away.

Jacqui tensed at the suggestiveness of the remark, though not for the reasons Dane presumed. She cocked her head to one side and studied her partner from beneath thick, dark lashes, wondering if the pointed comment implied that he had, in fact, witnessed her flight home the other night. She had to find out.

"Tell me, Mr. Westbrooke," she baited sweetly, "why else did you seek me out? Was it to apologize for *your* scandalous behavior in the street tonight?"

Dane flashed her a wicked grin, his teeth white and gleaming in his tanned face. "Oh no . . . never that. I would simply like the opportunity to rectify your opinion of me by demonstrating my charming self to you."

"Your charming self," Jacqui repeated, chewing on her lower lip, which threatened to curve into a smile. "Now, why do I not believe that is possible, Mr. Westbrooke?"

"Dane," he corrected.

Jacqui raised her slender brows. "Really, Mr. Westbrooke. We hardly know each other well enough for that."

"Something else I intend to rectify."

Jacqui shook her head in disbelief, smiling in spite of her best intentions. "You surpass scandalous."

"Among other things . . . yes." He stroked her hand with his thumb. "But then again, so do you."

29

Jacqui trembled. He didn't suspect . . . hadn't seen her escape that night. Why then was her heart threatening to beat its way right out of her chest?

She licked her lips, making a concerted effort to bring herself under control. He was just a man . . . an ordinary man like any other. Immediately, her mind negated that fact. Dane Westbrooke could be described as many things, but ordinary? Never. Unlike the other men in the room, Dane's hair was cut short at the nape and was an unpowdered raven black. His features were hard, carved in granite, which, combined with his imposing height and build and piercing silver eyes, made him even more formidable up close than he had been from a distance.

"Like what you see?"

Jacqui lifted her startled gaze to meet Dane's teasing look, and she blushed scarlet. "I don't know what you mean. . . ."

"Yes you do." Dane spoke softly so only she could hear, his words a warm whisper in her hair. "And I'm pleased that you find me appealing. Because I happen to find you exquisite."

For the first time in her life, Jacqui was speechless. She stepped away, attempting to break the magnetic pull of this powerfully enigmatic man. Caught up in sensations she had never before experienced and did not understand, she could do no more than stare up at him, wishing only for this dance to end.

The music complied with her prayers.

The strings fell silent, leaving only the laughter of the guests and the clinking of the crystal in its wake. Yanking her hand free of his, Jacqui uttered something indistinguishable and turned away. She was desperate to be alone.

Dane caught her arm. "It is useless to try, Jacqueline." Her name was a resonant caress. "You cannot escape me . . . not again." His choice of words made Jacqui dizzy, as she once again pondered their meaning.

Watching her unsettled reaction, Dane captured a strand of her hair and rubbed it between his fingers, giving Jacqui a slow, meaningful wink. "Until later, my blue-eyed enchantress," he murmured. He brought the tendril to his lips, then released it. "Until later."

Jacqui stared at his retreating back, feeling her throat constrict. Whatever Dane was, he was trouble. Handsome as sin and cunning as the devil himself . . . and well aware of both . . . Dane Westbrooke was a complication to be avoided at all costs.

"Don't leave."

Thomas propped himself up and reached for the beautiful, blond-haired woman who was easing out of his bed.

She turned and gave him a dazzling smile. "I must go, *mon amour*. After all, a lady does need to consider her reputation, does she not?"

Thomas didn't answer but watched her stretch gracefully and begin to dress. She paused, the moonlight glistening on her half-naked body, and picked up the documents that had been sitting on the nightstand. Reverently, she stroked her fingers across the pages. The first step toward her future . . . and the future of the brilliant man she adored.

"We must arrange for copies of these papers to be sent to England immediately," she stated adamantly. "Then you must find a way to restore them to Secretary Hamilton's office so they will not be missed."

"It will be taken care of, love." Thomas had come up behind her, looping his arms about her waist and nuzzling her neck. "Tomorrow." He bit lightly on her soft earlobe. "But, for tonight, let us just enjoy each other."

She sighed, leaning back against him, watching a patch of moonglow illuminate the pages in her hands. "Very well, Thomas. How can I deny you after you have done so fine a job?" She turned in his arms. "How did you manage to get the papers so easily?"

He buried his face in her hair, wondering which meant more . . . the money or holding her in his arms. Five months had passed since their chance first meeting on the

31

grassy banks of the Schuylkill, and still his craving for her was incessant. "Hamilton is hosting a party tonight. I knew his office would be empty. It was simple enough."

She kissed his shoulder. "But how did you get in?"

"I borrowed Dane's key. He did not take it with him tonight."

The woman tensed. "But won't he notice?"

"No, my love." Thomas was lost in her scent. "I slipped through Dane's kitchen window and returned the key. I knew he wouldn't be home. . . . He is attending Hamilton's ball, so he will never suspect a thing."

She smiled against his lips. "You are very clever."

"Yes." He gathered her to him. "I don't wish to discuss Hamilton or Dane any longer. In fact, I don't wish to talk at all."

She gave a throaty laugh as he carried her back to the bed.

Dane was whistling as he strolled into the office of Westbrooke Shipping Monday morning. Hearing himself, he stopped short, shaking his head bemusedly. In truth, he had nothing to whistle about. The party Friday night had proven to be an abysmal failure. Despite hours of intense probing and equally intent listening, neither he nor Alexander was any closer to learning the true identity of Jack Laffey than they had been before. Dane was convinced the man was invisible.

But then, Dane knew his good humor had nothing to do with Laffey.

The smile returned to his face as, for the hundredth time since Friday, he thought of Jacqueline Holt.

A vision to behold, with eyes that could bring a man to his knees and a tongue that could tear him to shreds. And a lightning-quick mind that few could rival. Ah, Jacqueline.

Dane chuckled. She was more than merely beautiful and intelligent. She was fascinating as hell.

After their first dance, she had stayed as far from him as possible, consenting to his persistent requests to dance only when it became impossible to refuse without making a scene. Even then, the bright red spots on her cheeks had told Dane how furious she was at being coerced. She had spoken very little as he whirled her about but concentrated instead on demonstrating in no uncertain terms that she did *not* care for his attentions, nor for him. But Dane hadn't been fooled. For, while her every gesture spoke of annoyance and refusal, her body spoke to him in a language all its own. And what it said was exciting and forbidden and explosive.

No, Dane was not deterred. He had every intention of seducing the lovely and bewitching Miss Holt. The only question that remained was when.

Preoccupied with thoughts of Jacqui, Dane crossed the room and lowered himself into his chair. Idly, he glanced down at the newspaper on his desk. The *General Advertiser* . . . a stark reminder of the more pressing problem at hand.

Frowning, Dane skimmed the pages, suddenly coming to his feet like a bullet. "What the hell!" he exploded, startlingly confronted with a shocking, day-early edition of Laffey's column. Furiously, Dane reread the words with frustrated disbelief. In concise terms, Laffey wrote of Hamilton's "monarchical gathering at the City Tavern," then quoted several specific snatches of conversation that Dane clearly recalled hearing at Friday's party.

"How did he know that?" Dane barked aloud, flinging the paper onto the desk and pacing the room with long, angry strides. "I spoke to every blasted person in the Long Room. He wasn't there! He couldn't have been there! How could I miss him?" Stopping abruptly, Dane forced himself to be practical. "How would Laffey know those things if he hadn't been at the party?" Dane shook his head in denial, already knowing the answer. He wouldn't. There was no way Laffey could have directly quoted the words that had been exchanged over the American dispute with England, nor could he have penned a word-for-word account of the various opinions on the possible outbreak of war, without having heard it himself. Silently, Dane cursed. The miserable bastard had been there all along. Right under their noses. He had eluded them again.

"Mr. Westbrooke?" Dane's clerk, John Edgars, poked his head into the office. "Pardon me, sir," he added, flustered, "I did knock, but I don't suppose you heard me." He waited, shifting from one foot to the other.

Dane blinked, the red haze of anger clearing. "Hm-m? I apologize, John. What did you say?"

Seemingly encouraged by his employer's controlled tone, Edgars stepped a bit further into the room and continued, "It is Monday, sir, and I do have several contracts and a huge pile of correspondence for you to look over." As he spoke, he held up an impressive stack of letters and documents. "But if I'm interrupting . . . I can come back at another time. . . ."

"No, John, that won't be necessary." Dane spoke briskly, gesturing for his clerk to take a seat at the opposite side of the carved walnut desk. Edgars complied and Dane leaned forward, reaching out his hand. "What do you have that requires my attention?"

Edgars began at the top of the pile, where he'd placed the most important papers. "Well, sir, there are several confirmations . . ."

"And did the shipments in question arrive on schedule?"

"Yes sir." Edgars nodded, giving the confirmations to Dane, who scanned them quickly, then put them aside.

"What else?"

"None of the correspondence is urgent. But the contracts need to be reviewed and signed."

"Contracts with whom?" Dane wanted to know.

"There are two. The first one is with Holt Trading, and the second one . . ."

But Dane was no longer listening. He sat up straight, snatching the contract from his surprised clerk while muttering, "Holt Trading . . ."

Edgars cleared his throat uncomfortably. "I'm sure the

papers are in order, sir. But if you will check them, I can have a messenger deliver them to Mr. Holt later today."

"That won't be necessary."

"Pardon me, Mr. Westbrooke?"

"I said, that won't be necessary. I will read the contracts and bring them to Mr. Holt myself." Ignoring the stunned look on Edgars's face, Dane continued, "I have some business that will take me out of the office this afternoon. I'll stop by Holt Trading and deliver the contract."

Edgars schooled his features and wisely refrained from commenting on Dane's decidedly odd behavior. "Yes sir."

"Good." Dane squinted at the document in his hand. "Then, if there is nothing else, John . . ."

Taking the hint, Edgars hurriedly rose. "Very good, Mr. Westbrooke." He placed the remainder of the papers in a pile at the far corner of Dane's desk. "I'll be getting back to work now."

Dane grunted his agreement, but, in truth, he hardly heard his clerk's words, nor did he hear him leave the room. His mind was racing to the very pleasant prospect that had, unexpectedly, been handed to him.

Scanning the contents of the contract, Dane grinned. Nothing out of the ordinary. He came to his feet. Why wait for this afternoon when the morning would do just fine? His grin widened. Further, why take the papers to Holt Trading when he recalled George Holt mentioning that his residence was on Spruce Street, which was but a short jaunt away? With that thought, Dane left his office the same way he had arrived less than one hour past . . . whistling.

CHAPTER
4

Jacqui was dreaming.

It was a different dream than the one she usually had. Usually, she was standing before a roomful of men, demanding to be heard, protesting her innocence—or, rather, the true reasons behind her guilt. The men would never heed her, but instead insisted that she be punished. And she was.

She would always awaken at that point, frustrated and angry and . . . yes . . . frightened. But not enough to be deterred from her goal.

The past three nights, however, the dream had taken another turn. This time she was fleeing, trying to escape, and everywhere she went, her hiding place would be discovered by a tall, disturbing man. A man who wanted her.

It didn't take a scholar to know who that man was.

With a soft moan, Jacqui rolled onto her back, flinging her arm above her head. Her defenses lowered, she lay, still half asleep, still on the outskirts of the dream. The dream about Dane Westbrooke.

A warm tongue stroked her lips, then her cheeks and her nose. Is that how it would feel to be kissed by him? Jacqui wondered vaguely. She sighed, a strange lethargic warmth flowing through her veins.

Something soft and silky brushed against her shoulder. Is that how his hair would feel to the touch? Like handfuls of black silk . . .

Something cold and wet rubbed against her face.

Jacqui came awake with a start. Cold and wet?

A pair of emerald-green eyes were staring directly into hers. The moment Jacqui lifted her lids, a soulful meow filled the room, shattering the silence . . . and Jacqui's sensual dream . . . into earsplitting awareness.

"Whiskey, for heaven's sake, you scared me to death!" Jacqui pushed herself to a sitting position, unseating the mournful kitten in the process. Determined not to be ignored, Whiskey scrambled up the canopied bed and climbed purposefully back onto his mistress's shoulder. Then, lest his message still be indistinct, he put his mouth to Jacqui's ear and emitted another plaintive cry.

"All right! All right! You've made your point!" Jacqui caught the small black fur ball in her hands. She raised her knees and placed Whiskey atop them. "Although I have still to understand how so small a creature as yourself can have a voice twice its size."

Whiskey ignored the insult. He was just where he wanted to be: on Jacqui's lap. With a contented purr, he stretched across her legs and licked his lips, squinting lazily as the bright morning sunlight warmed his fur.

Jacqui glanced toward the windows. "The sun is high. What time is it?" she wondered aloud.

In answer, her bedroom door swung open and a big-boned, matronly woman stomped in, looking none too pleased.

"Awake at last, are we?" She crossed the room and threw apart the drapes, letting the brilliant sunlight stream in. "I thought for sure you were planning to sleep away the day."

Calmly, Jacqui regarded the scowling housekeeper with

the severe gray bun. "And when have you *ever* known me to do that, Greta?" she asked.

The older woman grunted. "Well, you'd best get up and have some breakfast. It's nearly ten o'clock."

Agreeably, Jacqui nudged Whiskey off her lap, slid out of bed, and stretched. "Very well, Greta. I'll be down in a few minutes."

"Fine." And, with a disdainful glare in Whiskey's direction, Greta was gone.

Only after the door had closed behind her did Jacqui allow herself to smile. Greta had been with the family for as long as Jacqui could remember. Born of strict German stock, she was as stiff and efficient as an army general and as warm as an iceberg. But her bark was far worse than her bite. For, in her gruff and exacting way, she cared. About both the Holts.

Twenty minutes later, Jacqui was washed and dressed in a lemon and white muslin gown, her luxuriant hair tied back with a yellow ribbon. "Come, Whiskey," she instructed. "Let's have some breakfast and see what today's newspaper has to offer, shall we?"

As she descended the stairs, Jacqui could hear Greta arguing with a man at the front door.

"Herr Holt is not at home, sir." Greta's tone was adamant. "Therefore, you can either leave the papers with me or take them to his office."

"I see," the deep baritone voice responded. "Well, may I come in and leave Mr. Holt a note explaining my visit? Then I'll be on my way."

Greta blocked the door with her ample body. "I'm sorry, sir. I am *not* in the habit of allowing gentlemen callers in . . . especially those I don't know."

His reply was a husky chuckle. "I am a business associate of Mr. Holt's, madam," he told her, "and, I can assure you, I am quite respectable."

"Now, *that* is a questionable assessment," Jacqui returned from behind Greta's imposing figure. She placed her hand on Greta's shoulder. "It's all right, Greta. I know Mr. Westbrooke. You can let him in."

Greta moved away from the doorway, surprise and distrust still evident on her face. "Are you certain, Fräulein?"

"Yes, Greta, quite certain."

Unconvinced, Greta lingered a moment longer, her sharp gaze narrowed on Dane in a bold and thorough assessment. Then, mumbling under her breath, she stalked toward the kitchen.

Amusement in his eyes, Dane watched her go. "A real charmer, isn't she?"

"Charm is not everything, Mr. Westbrooke," Jacqui said in a crisp tone. "What can I do for you?"

Dane turned his full attention to Jacqueline. If possible, she looked even more beautiful by daylight: younger, more vulnerable, fresher. Her sharp tongue, however, was unchanged.

"You can let me come in, for one thing."

Jacqui gestured for him to enter. She closed the door behind him, then turned to face him. "Now, what was it you wished to see my father about?"

Dane never took his eyes off her. "I have a contract for him to sign."

"Do you always deliver your own papers, Mr. Westbrooke?"

He grinned. "No."

"I see. Well, my father is at his office. Surely you know where that is? Especially since you do quite a bit of business together?" She walked toward him with a challenging look.

"Oh, I know where it is," Dane replied smoothly, placing the contract on the low table in the hallway. "But it was not your father I wished to see. It was you."

Jacqui stopped short, unused to such blatant candor.

Dane closed the remaining distance between them. "No scathing reply, my very beautiful Miss Holt?" he asked quietly when they were but inches apart.

Unwilling to raise her gaze to meet his, Jacqui stared at

his waistcoat. Damn him. The man had the most unbeliev-able effect on her.

"Well?" He brushed her fingers with his.

"I have nothing to say," she managed at last.

Dane chuckled, curling his fingers around hers. *"That* I refuse to believe." He brought her hand to his mouth. "I've missed you, Jacqueline."

Jacqui snatched her hand away. "You don't even *know* me!"

"Don't I?"

The intimate allusion found its mark. Jacqui's head snapped up and she met Dane's burning silver gaze in a staunch attempt to unearth the hidden meaning of his words. What was it that he knew about her? she asked herself again.

She licked her lips, visibly shaken. "You'd better go, Mr. Westbrooke."

Dane's mouth curved into a forbidden smile. "Dane. And I'm glad I've been in your thoughts, sweet. Because you haven't left mine." He lifted his arm and brushed her chin with his thumb, marveling at the midnight splendor of her eyes. "May I stay for just a while?" he asked softly. "All I require is some coffee and conversation."

Jacqui's unease faded somewhat, and she felt a strange quiver rush through her. "Only coffee and conversation?" she quipped, desperate to retain her composure. "Rather meager requirements, Mr. Westbrooke."

"I'll take whatever you offer."

A suggestive silence hung in the air.

"Fräulein Holt has not even eaten breakfast." Greta stomped by them and entered the dining room, slamming a tray down upon the table. "There are strawberry tarts and coffee," she announced a moment later when she emerged, her cool gaze once again sweeping Dane in a precise, albeit brief, perusal. "I have brought enough breakfast for you as well, Herr Westbrooke," she barked, then stalked off with-out awaiting a reply.

40

Jacqui looked after her, blinking in surprise. "Well . . . I must say I've never seen Greta behave so graciously before."

Dane chuckled. "That was gracious?"

"For Greta? Yes."

Another silence.

Dane kept his hands purposefully by his sides. "The choice is yours, Jacqueline. May I join you . . . for breakfast?" he hastily added.

"I should say no."

"But you'll say yes?"

"Just coffee."

"And conversation," he reminded her with a twinkle.

"And conversation," she conceded. She turned away quickly and preceded him into the dining room, trying not to recall the way his dark breeches hugged the contours of his body, accentuating the powerful muscles of his thighs, and the way his coat fit smoothly, but snugly, across his massive shoulders, the collar just brushing the silky edge of his raven-black hair. He was too handsome and charming for his own good . . . and hers. Not to mention that damned magnetism he emanated that intrigued her and unsettled her all at once, rendering her completely off-balance. It was a novel feeling . . . and one Jacqui did not welcome. However, she reminded herself, swatting Whiskey off the dining-room chair, she owed it to herself to determine exactly how much he *really* knew about her.

"How do you take your coffee, Mr. Westbrooke?"

"Dane," he reiterated firmly. "And black." He hadn't missed Jacqui's brief, but admiring, appraisal. The tantalizing Miss Holt was more interested than she wished to allow.

Jacqui gestured for Dane to sit, then handed him a cup of coffee and a plate with two of Greta's mouthwatering strawberry tarts on it.

"Thank you."

They ate quietly for a few minutes.

"How is it we never met before Friday?" Dane finally asked.

41

Jacqui delicately licked a crumb from her forefinger. "I was merely a substitute for my father's"—she hesitated—"companion. Unfortunately, she fell ill and was unable to accompany Father to Secretary Hamilton's gathering. Otherwise, I assure you, I would not have been there." Seeing Dane's amused, questioning look, she added, "I don't attend many such parties, Mr. Westbrooke. I am not terribly fond of them."

"Of parties in general, or only of those hosted by politicians whose views you do not share?"

"Parties of *any* kind," she qualified, raising her chin in a defiant gesture that Dane was beginning to recognize. "Quite simply, I dislike being ogled and pawed."

Dane's lips twitched. "I see." He leaned back in his chair thoughtfully. "Tell me what you *do* enjoy doing."

Jacqui took a sip of coffee, regarding Dane cautiously over the rim of her cup. "Are you asking what my interests are?" she questioned carefully. "If so, I must warn you that they are not the conventional things you would expect."

"From you I would never expect the conventional."

"Very well." She placed both hands flat on the table and leaned forward as if readying herself for verbal battle. "I like to read and I have an extensive library, filled mostly with the classics. I am also superb at both whist and chess." She shot Dane a challenging look.

"All admirable pursuits," he answered smoothly, refusing to be baited.

Jacqui smiled sweetly. "I am also fond of placing an occasional wager, if the horse in question seems promising enough."

Dane swallowed a chuckle. "As am I."

It was time to best Dane Westbrooke. "And I keep the ledgers for Holt Trading."

Rather than looking appalled, as Jacqui had expected, Dane looked positively fascinated. "Now I *am* impressed. You are involved with your father's business?"

"I am my father's daughter, Mr. Westbrooke. The name of the company is *Holt* Trading, which is my name as well."

"Your father is a very lucky man," Dane said in a voice that was a husky caress. He covered her hand with his. "He has a daughter who is not only beautiful and captivating, but loyal and intelligent as well."

Jacqui's bewilderment showed on her face. It was not the compliment that confused her, for she had received many that were far more flowery. But they had all been delivered by men who, though handsome and effusive, wanted nothing more than to possess her and squelch her spirit. How then was she to deal with this charming rogue's undisguised admiration, not only of her physical attributes, but of her mental ones as well? Oh, she was not naive enough to believe that she could trust him, nor that his intentions were honorable. He meant to seduce her; of that there was no doubt. But he seemed to want more . . . although what it was he wanted, she still didn't know. She only knew that, whatever it was, he had not been put off by her revelations.

Staring down at their joined hands, Jacqui swallowed convulsively.

Dane Westbrooke might feel unthreatened. But Jacqui did not.

"Jacqueline is a beautiful name." Dane began to stroke her fingers in a slow, circular motion. He watched her stare, entranced, at the movements of his hand, saw her breath coming a bit faster, and it took all his control not to stand up and drag her into his arms. "Your name is lyrical and captivating and elegant. It suits you."

"It is French. My mother chose it." Jacqui could barely concentrate past the heat of his touch.

Dane traced the smooth skin of her knuckles. "Your mother has excellent taste. Is she of French descent?" He raised his dark brows as a sudden thought occurred to him. "Was that the reason for your impassioned plea on France's behalf last Friday?"

43

Jacqui shook her head. "*Au contraire, monsieur.* My mother was French Canadian . . . from Quebec. Her people were hardly sympathetic toward France. Even the English were preferable to them. No, sir, my beliefs are my own."

"You said 'was.' Is your mother no longer alive?"

A shadow of sadness crossed her lovely face. "My mother died ten years ago," she replied shortly.

"I'm sorry, Jacqueline."

He sounded sorry, too, his deep, resonant voice filled with something curiously akin to compassion.

For the first time, Jacqui raised her eyes to Dane's, wondering at his reaction and simultaneously hoping that, by focusing on anything but their joined hands, she could break the sensual spell he had cast. It was a mistake. The moment her hesitant gaze met the tenderness of his, the tingling sensation in her body intensified and a warm, heavy ache began deep inside her.

It spread like a narcotic, demanding control of her body, and she fought the feeling. Not because it was unpleasant, for, in truth, it was wildly exciting. But because it was overwhelming and left her vulnerable and unsure. She would tolerate neither.

"Come here."

Dane's fingers tightened on hers as he stood, and before Jacqui could even think to protest, he had drawn her against him, lifting her face so close to his that she could feel his breath on her lips, inhale his masculine scent.

"I've wanted to know the taste of your mouth from the first moment I saw you," he murmured huskily, gliding his fingers through her hair.

Jacqui's heart gave an involuntary leap.

"It's what you want as well, Jacqueline." He slid his hand beneath her heavy silken mane, lightly stroking the nape of her neck. Jacqui's eyes slid closed and she made a soft sound of pleasure and protest, unconsciously leaning into his touch. "Tell me," Dane commanded. She stared up at him slumberously, her eyes registering confusion and apprehension and untried sensuality. "I want to hear you say the words," he whispered, tightening his grip in a definitive gesture. "This has to be both of us. Tell me this is where you want to be. In my arms. Against my body. With my mouth on yours. Jacqueline," he breathed, running his hands across her shoulders, his thumbs skimming her throat where her pulse beat frantically, "tell me to kiss you. Tell me . . . and I will."

Physical pleasure stormed Jacqui's senses, the skin where he'd touched her alive and tingling. Exhilaration warred with uncertainty, and control was cast to the wind. She stared up at him helplessly, knowing, as the keen silver of his eyes darkened to a deep, smoky gray, that he understood exactly what was happening to her. And yet he waited. Breathing became difficult and speaking impossible.

"Jacqueline . . ." he whispered again.

"Yes . . ." she managed, unable to say more.

But Dane was relentless. "Yes . . . what?" He cradled her head in his hands, tugging her closer.

"Yes . . . kiss me."

Her words were swallowed by his mouth as it covered hers, possessing her in a kiss that was unlike anything she had ever experienced, or even imagined. Dane molded his lips to hers, moving against her mouth with deliberate, insistent pressure until she parted her lips to the more intimate penetration of his tongue. He delved into the sweetness of her mouth with deep, rhythmic strokes, felt her small hands glide up his shirt and wrap around his neck, urging him closer. With a masculine sound of triumph, Dane enveloped her, crushed her to him, until she was surrounded by the hard wall of his chest and the powerful strength of his arms. His mouth slanted across hers again and again, branding her, seducing her, demanding that she do more than merely receive his kiss, but that she respond to it with a fervor that matched his own.

Jacqui gave him what he wanted.

She returned his kiss with a newly born passion that astonished her, accepting the lusty strokes of his tongue and giving him her own.

The kiss blazed out of control.

With a low groan of need, Dane lifted Jacqui from the floor, fitting her against the full length of him and tightening his hold so that she could feel every hardened contour of his aroused body. He wanted her. More than even he had known. More than he wanted his next breath. More than he could bear . . . he wanted this woman.

For Jacqui, the world and everything in it faded into nonreality, as she allowed her yearnings free rein, reveling in the first-time experience of pure, potent physical desire. She threw herself into it with the same utter abandon that she did each of life's adventures . . . totally and without inhibition, thrilling to the sensual awakening. The discovery in itself was enthralling.

For Dane, it was not nearly enough.

His hands roved restlessly over her back, finding the buttons that separated him from the promise of beauty beneath. His control was fast evaporating, fueled by her wildly exhilarating response. The taste of her mouth, the feel of her in his arms, was intoxicating enough, but the way she pressed her soft, lush body against his, returning his openmouthed kisses with an innocent, unrestrained ardor, was more than he could withstand. Her passion rivaled his, but he knew that she lacked the experience to control it. It was up to him, and he was fast approaching the point of insanity. In mere seconds he was going to carry her to her room and make love to her until neither of them could move. Hell, he thought, inhaling her perfume, he would take her right here, right now, were he not certain that it was her first time.

Her first time.

That intrusive thought forced reason to return in a rush.

46

Dane raised his head, his chest heaving with the strain of slowing himself, and stared down at her with eyes still burning with hunger. "Jacqueline."

Her lids fluttered, then lifted, and she stared up at him, still in the throes of dazzling sensation. Her midnight eyes were dazed and far away, and she blinked, trying to understand the reason for Dane's abrupt withdrawal.

Seeing the honest play of emotions flash across her beautiful, flushed face, Dane experienced a queer surge of feeling in his chest. With aching restraint, he lowered her to the floor, cupping her face tenderly between his shaking palms. "I know, sweetheart. But not now . . . not this way. For you, it has to be perfect."

Reality descended upon Jacqui with a resounding crash.

She pressed her hands to her hot cheeks, her breath coming in short pants, her lips still throbbing from his consuming kisses. "Oh . . . my." She inhaled sharply. "I can't believe I just . . ."

Dane covered her hands with his. "No, Jacqueline. *you* didn't just. *We* did." His eyes twinkled, despite the insistent throbbing in his loins. "In fact, we would have done more than *just* if your charming Greta were not in the kitchen."

Jacqui gasped and glanced over her shoulder. "Greta! Oh, Lord." She closed her eyes, mortified . . . then enraged by her behavior. When her lids lifted, Dane immediately saw the warning lights that glittered at him.

"Am I to be slapped again?" he asked, grinning. "I have not yet recovered from your first assault."

"What is it you want of me, Mr. Westbrooke?"

Dane chuckled at the belated formality. "To begin with, I want to hear you use my given name. Surely, that is not too much to ask after the intimacy we shared?"

Jacqui flushed anew. "Very well . . . Dane. But you have not answered my question."

Dane was stunned by the impact of simply hearing his name on her lips. "What question, sweet?" He was already impatient for the next time, the right time, the time when he would actually make love to her, make her his. His body throbbed its agreement.

"What do you want of me?" she repeated, trying to disengage herself from his embrace.

"I believe that is obvious, Jacqueline." He refused to release her. "I want you."

"But I *don't* want you," she said, raising her chin defiantly, knowing, even as she spoke, that, in light of the past five minutes, her statement was absurd.

Dane's lips twitched. "I am sorry to hear that, love. But I'd like the chance to change your mind."

Before she could reply, he bent his head and kissed her again. But this kiss was totally unlike the first. Soft, coaxing, teasingly light, it was a butterfly caress against Jacqui's feverish mouth, over as quickly as it had begun.

Jacqui clutched his arms.

"Let's finish our coffee, sweet," Dane suggested mildly, releasing her only when he was certain she could stand by herself. "And our conversation," he added in a teasing tone.

How could the man turn his passions on and off like that? Jacqui wondered dazedly, lowering herself into her chair.

"Are you all right?" Dane's gentle question reinforced her observation . . . and her annoyance. If he could have such blasted self-control, then so could she.

"I am fine, Mr. Westbrooke. Dane," she amended, seeing the amused lift of his brows. "I assure you, I am not so fragile as to shatter from a single kiss."

What had happened between them far surpassed a single kiss and they both knew it. But all Dane said was, "I'm glad to hear you've recovered, love."

Jacqui took a gulp of cold coffee. It was time for a much-needed change in conversation.

"You are English," she blurted out, saying the first thing that came to mind. She recalled the name Westbrooke appearing frequently in the company ledgers, vaguely remembered her father telling her that the owner of the company hailed from England.

Jacqui's choice of subjects was apparently not to her guest's liking. Angry sparks flashed in Dane's eyes, and Jacqui had a glimpse of the predatory man she'd seen that dark night last week. A chill ran up her back.

"I'm American." Dane's tone was as forbidding as his expression.

Every one of Jacqui's instincts warned her to leave it alone, while her curiosity compelled her to investigate further. "But you are English by birth."

A muscle worked in Dane's jaw. "By birth . . . yes."

"When did you come to America?"

"Over a decade ago."

The more evasive he grew, the more intrigued she became. "You were educated in England?"

Dane gave her a measured look. "I attended Oxford."

"Oxford! Your father is a Tory?"

"My father is a marquis."

It took a moment for Dane's words to sink in. Then Jacqui sat up straight, a look of stunned horror on her face. "Your father is a marquis?" She might just as well have called him an ax murderer. "That makes you an *earl* . . . an English nobleman."

Dane slammed his fist down on the table, rigid with an anger he fought to control. "I've said it once, Jacqueline, and I do not plan to say it again. I am an American . . . as much an American as you. Who and what my father may be is irrelevant. In case you failed to notice, I am very much my own person. I would appreciate your remembering that in the future, since I do *not* wish to discuss either my father or his titles again. Am I making myself clear?"

Jacqui considered arguing, saw the furious light in the steel-gray eyes, and thought better of it. "Perfectly clear."

"Good. Now, do you have any other questions pertaining to my upbringing?"

Jacqui's own temper flared. "I have no intention of allowing you to bellow at me, Mr. Westbrooke. Perhaps you should go. We seem to incite one another despite our best attempts to the contrary." She stood, ready to show him the door.

Dane stood as well, catching her hand and tugging her back to him. "Honesty and forthrightness work both ways, my love," he said in a dark, perceptive tone. "If you want to be candid and speak your mind to me, I demand the same right of you." His expression softened and he kissed the inside of her wrist. "As for our effect on one another, it cannot be avoided, my beautiful Jacqueline. That is the way it will always be between us. And, *mon chaton colereux,* my fiery little kitten, you wouldn't want it any other way."

Jacqui considered smacking that damned knowing smile from his magnificent, arrogant face.

"Such a look, sweet!" Dane chuckled. He released her hand. "Before you do me bodily harm, I believe I shall take my leave." He strolled toward the door. "Thank Greta for the delicious breakfast. I shall return to enjoy many others." He turned in the doorway and winked. "Until next time, my lovely Jacqueline."

"I am not *your* Jacqueline," she retorted, knowing she sounded like a petulant child and not giving a damn.

Dane surveyed her tousled mahogany curls and soft, swollen mouth with a look that said otherwise. Then he gave her a slow, devastating smile. "Ah, but you will be, *mon chaton colereux.* You will be."

CHAPTER
5

That was a wonderful dinner, George, and a welcome change from dining at home. Thank you." Monique Brisset gave George Holt a brilliant smile, placing her half-finished cup of coffee firmly in its saucer and sitting back in the inn's beautifully carved walnut chair. "I could not manage another morsel."

George smiled indulgently, his heart in his eyes. "I'm glad you enjoyed it, love. You deserve only the finest in everything: food, wine . . ."

". . . and men?" she teased, her blue eyes dancing. "For, in that case, I already have the finest. You." She reached across the table and took his hand.

George lifted her fingers to his lips. "I don't see you often enough," he murmured. "I missed you terribly at Secretary Hamilton's party last week."

Monique stroked his cheek. "I'm dreadfully sorry, *mon amour*," she answered with a pout she knew George found irresistible. "But I simply could not gather the strength to attend a ball. Not after having been abed for two days."

"Certainly not, my dear." He gave her an anxious look. "But you are feeling yourself again, are you not?"

A shadow of a frown crossed her face, then was gone. "Of course, George. I am splendid."

But, as she intended, George had seen the flicker of sadness, heard the hesitation in her voice. Triumphantly, she noted the transparent concern on his face and silently congratulated herself. He was so very easy to manipulate, she thought smugly. As was Thomas. Two stupid, smitten fools, both perfect for her purposes. But then, she had carefully selected them many months ago for those very reasons. George . . . lonely, vulnerable, owner of a busy trading company . . . just the access she needed to France. Thomas . . . young and greedy, predictably susceptible to seduction, closely connected with Hamilton and his Federalist government.

Yes, her two liaisons were ideal.

George was leaning forward, his heart in his eyes. "Monique . . . are you unwell?"

"No, darling, of course not," she assured him, sighing deeply.

He searched her beautiful face for signs of illness but could find none. "You are telling me the truth?"

She gave him a soft half-smile. "I wouldn't lie to you, *chéri*. You know that."

"But there is something," he guessed astutely. "Tell me what it is."

Again, Monique hesitated, lowering her lashes in heart-tugging indecision. "I don't like to trouble you with my problems, George."

"Anything that troubles you, troubles me as well. Tell me," he urged.

She regarded him silently for precisely the right amount of time. "Will you be sending a shipment to the mainland this coming week?"

"A shipment?" George inclined his head in surprise. Whatever he had expected, it hadn't been this. "No. Not for a fortnight. Why do you ask?"

Monique's voice trembled. "It . . . it is my sister Brigitte."

"Your sister? In Paris? Is she ill?"

She shook her head, chewing on her lip thoughtfully. "Not physically, no. It is only that I am so worried about her, George. She has lost so much since the revolution began. Her husband has been arrested and imprisoned in the Carmes and her home has been ransacked countless times for evidence that might incriminate her as well. I am afraid that if things do not improve soon she might do something drastic." Tears filled her luminous eyes and slid down her cheeks. She wiped them away with the edge of her napkin. "The only thing that seems to bring her any solace is my correspondence. I know it sounds silly, but I have a small present that I wished to send her in time for her birthday next month. I was hoping that you might be able to . . ." She broke off, lowering her head. "Forgive me. I did not mean to lose control."

George took her hand between both of his. "Why did you not tell me any of this sooner?" he demanded.

"I did not wish to burden you," she whispered.

"You are never a burden, my love. Never." He thought intently for a moment. "Give me your package. I will speak to an associate of mine and arrange for it to be aboard the next ship headed for the mainland. Your sister shall have her gift on schedule."

Monique's eyes glistened with tears and hope. "Oh, George, is that really possible? How can I ever thank you?"

"You can smile for me," he answered softly. "That would be all the thanks I need."

Her smile illuminated the inn and warmed George's heart. At five and forty years of age, he had never expected to love again. For nine years after his beloved Marie's death, there had been no one in his world but his precious little Jacqueline. But now Monique had come into his life, and once more he felt like a man. A man who was hopelessly, totally in love.

"Come, my love," he suggested, an intense look on his handsome face. "Let's take our leave."

Monique smiled. "Yes, darling. Let's." Delicately, she placed her napkin on the table and rose, slipping her arm through George's and reaching up to touch his smooth-shaven cheek . . . a promise for the evening to come.

Early Wednesday morning, Dane headed for Hamilton's office and the unavoidable conversation that he knew would take place.

Since Dane's visit with Jacqueline two days past, he had been submerged in his business dealings, unable to break away. This morning was, therefore, his first opportunity to answer Hamilton's rather definitive summons. He knew Alexander wished to discuss the results of Friday night's party. Not that there was much to say on the subject, Dane thought disgustedly. For there had been *no* results. But by now Alexander had seen Monday's *General Advertiser* and was no doubt livid, both at Laffey and at himself for being unable to discover the rebel's identity.

Dane had fared no better. So, knowing how his friend loathed failure of any kind, Dane braced himself for a less than pleasant chat.

He was stunned to instead find Hamilton tearing his desk apart, drawer by drawer.

"What in the name of heaven are you doing?" Dane demanded.

Hamilton looked up, visibly upset. "I am beginning to fear that I have lost my mind," he replied. "I was certain that I had placed those papers in my upper desk drawer, and yet they are gone."

Dane frowned. "Papers? What papers?"

"The ones containing my notes to Jay. He'll be leaving for England in a fortnight and I've outlined what I believe should be our negotiating strategy in the current crisis."

"And those papers are missing?" Dane's expression grew dark.

"It would appear that way. Should the British get their

54

hands on these documents, they would know our tactics before Jay even begins to negotiate. They would be prepared to counter each of our terms, and Jay would be unable to extract any concessions from them. His entire mission would be a failure." Hamilton banged the drawer shut in agitation. "As I said, I thought I'd placed the notes in my desk on Friday and, truthfully, I haven't looked for them since." The word *theft* hung between them, but was not spoken. As was his way, Hamilton refused to speculate before the obvious answers had been thoroughly explored.

Quickly, Dane scanned the office. It was sparsely furnished, with little in the way of hiding places. If the papers were still here, there were only a few spots where they could be located.

Beginning with the obvious, Dane checked the open compartments in the hutch above Hamilton's desk and the exposed writing area on its surface. From there he moved to the drawers of the low tables and then to the cushions of the chairs. No papers were found.

By this time, his concern was escalating. It was not like Alexander to misplace things.

Intending to conduct one final search, Dane headed across the room and was about to join Hamilton in a thorough inspection of the desk, when his friend made a triumphant sound and rose. "Here they are."

Dane relaxed. "Thank goodness. Where did you find them?"

"They were caught between some other documents. Apparently, I placed them in the middle drawer and not the upper one as I had originally believed." With a deep sigh, Hamilton shook his head. "I am becoming forgetful in my old age."

Dane snorted derisively. "You are far from old and anything but forgetful. What you are, is exhausted. You are merely a man, Alexander, not a god. You expect too damned much of yourself."

"And of you?" Hamilton's eyes twinkled, his good humor restored now that the missing papers had been found.

Dane sank into a chair. "Ah, we arrive at the real reason you asked to see me. The identity of the ever-annoying Jack Laffey."

"Which you do not know."

"No, I don't have the vaguest idea."

"Nor do I." Hamilton leaned back against the disheveled desk. "Did you learn anything of significance at the party" —he gave a meaningful pause—"other than the accomplishments of George Holt's daughter, that is."

Dane shot Hamilton a look. "Nothing escapes you, does it?"

"One could hardly miss your obvious fascination for the lady." Hamilton lightly baited his friend. "So much for my attempts to keep you from the clutches of one woman throughout the evening. As it turns out, you would have preferred the drawing of lots." He studied Dane's closed expression. "She is quite beautiful."

"I noticed."

Hamilton hid his smile. "So did every other man in the room. Not that you gave them much opportunity to pursue her."

"Nor do I intend to," Dane returned, scowling.

Hamilton chuckled. "So that's the way of things, is it? Shall I inquire as to *your* success with the very spirited Miss Holt?"

"Merely a modicum better than my success with Laffey."

Hamilton's smile faded. "The contents of the *General Advertiser* refutes our original conclusion that he was not in attendance on Friday night."

"Obviously."

Hamilton slammed his fist on the desk. "Then which guest was Laffey? Which of my supposed *friends* pens that damned column?" He made a sound of anger and frustration. "Without knowing Laffey's identity, we cannot begin to think of a way to still his pen."

"The matter of stilling his pen needn't concern you. I've already devised a plan to secure Laffey's ruin."

"You have?" Hamilton swooped down on Dane's announcement. "Why didn't you tell me this?"

"What would have been the point? My plan cannot be implemented until we know Laffey's identity."

"Nevertheless, I'd like to hear it." Hamilton glanced past Dane to verify that the door was carefully closed, ensuring total privacy. Satisfied that they could not be overheard, he turned expectantly back to Dane. "Tell me your plan."

Dane nodded. "Once we know which of our supposed colleagues is Laffey, we isolate him, feed him highly confidential but volatile political information, and wait for him to disclose it in his column."

Hamilton stared. "But in the process of baiting Laffey, we will be endangering our country."

"Not if the facts we give him are false."

Slowly, a smile of comprehension spread across Hamilton's face. "So we provide Laffey with inflammatory but inaccurate data and wait for it to appear in the *Advertiser*."

"Yes. Then we step forward and reveal the information as totally false, discrediting Laffey and his column before all of Philadelphia." Dane spread his hands in a triumphant sweep. "In short," he concluded, "Laffey will hang himself. But in order to do that, you and I must first determine who he is."

A tentative knock interrupted Hamilton's reply. "Yes?"

John Edgars entered the office, rubbing his hands against his breeches in a nervous gesture. "I am really sorry to intrude, sir," he began, looking at Dane.

"John? What is it?" Dane was curious. His clerk never sought him out unless something required his immediate attention.

Edgars cleared his throat. "You received an emergency package from George Holt this morning. He requested that

57

it be dispatched on our ship leaving for Europe today. I didn't know how you wanted me to handle it. . . ."

Dane frowned. "That is highly unusual for Holt. Customarily, he makes his shipping arrangements several weeks in advance."

"I know, sir." Edgars nodded. "But he was insistent. Shall I tell him no?"

"I suppose not. If Holt needs to send something to the mainland, I imagine we can oblige him. Go ahead and make the necessary provisions."

Hamilton remained silent throughout the exchange. Interestingly, this was the second time in minutes that George Holt's name had come up in conversation. First, in connection with his daughter, Jacqueline, and now, because of a deviation in his normally precise business procedure.

Hamilton tapped his chin thoughtfully. While he himself had little direct contact with the successful owner of Holt Trading Company, he knew that Dane dealt with him often and well. He also knew that Holt traveled in powerful political circles and had friendships with both Federalists and Republicans alike. Personally, Hamilton had always found Holt to be an affable enough fellow, though a bit too pro-French to suit the Secretary's tastes.

Now, it appeared, Holt had done something quite out of character.

"Evidently, George Holt is a bit on the impulsive side," Hamilton mused aloud once Edgars had scurried off.

Dane shook his head in puzzlement. "Anything but. The man is painstakingly well organized. He generally supplies me with his schedule weeks in advance. This conduct is highly unusual."

"Really." Hamilton's own tone was speculative. The timing of Holt's mysterious action nagged at him. Perhaps, he reflected, he was growing overly suspicious, for there was no tangible reason for him to dwell on the incident—other than the fact that, by nature, Hamilton despised unresolved questions. That, together with his own unsettled state of mind, were probably the true culprits. He was plagued by anxiety over America's plight with England and agitated by Laffey's inflammatory columns. The combination had left him on edge. Still . . . he tucked the episode away to ponder further when he was alone.

Had Dane not been so preoccupied with the earlier subject of their conversation, he would have recognized the contemplative look on his friend's face. But, as it was, Dane's thoughts had already returned to Laffey and the problem of exposing his identity.

"What now?" he demanded.

"Pardon me?" Hamilton's brows rose in question.

"How do we proceed from here? How do we determine which of Friday's guests was Laffey?" Dane answered, exasperated. He paced the length of the room, hands clasped behind his back.

"Give me a few days to think, Dane," Hamilton answered evasively. "The solution might show itself."

Dane stopped short, eyes narrowed on Hamilton's face. "I thought you had no direction for your suspicions."

"I don't," Hamilton assured him. "However, I think each of us should carefully review Friday night's guest list. It is a starting point."

Dane fell silent, wondering what was going on in the Secretary's brilliant mind. "All right," he said at last. "But I don't plan to give up, Alexander. As far as I am concerned, Laffey is a man without scruples, which is little better than a traitor. He should be dealt with accordingly . . . which I intend to do," he added grimly. "That wily scoundrel is not going to best me."

"I'm certain he won't," Hamilton agreed mildly. "I have not the slightest doubt that you will unmask Laffey in no time at all."

Endless weeks later, Dane was no closer to learning the truth about Jack Laffey than he had been in Hamilton's office. He had discreetly questioned every conceivable person on the guest list, and still . . . nothing. Baffled and angry, Dane was forced to acknowledge that now, more than a month after the ball, Laffey's identity still eluded him.

Worse than that, so did Jacqueline Holt.

And if his lack of success in exposing Jack Laffey left Dane peevish, his lack of progress with the beautiful Miss Holt left him as testy as a caged tiger.

After five pointedly unanswered messages and a dozen lame excuses delivered at the Holts' front door by an adamant and ever-vigilant Greta, Dane came to the unprecedented conclusion that, for the first time, a young woman he was ardently courting was blatantly rejecting his attentions. The irony of the situation was more staggering than the realization itself.

For never had Dane desired a woman the way he did Jacqueline. She was a consuming fever in his blood, the obsession of his days, the haunting of his nights. Despite his thriving business and the political concerns that plagued him, Dane found his thoughts returning time and again to Jacqueline . . . the luxuriant masses of her rich, dark hair, the bottomless blue of her eyes . . . even the continual challenge of her caustic tongue.

The way she'd responded in his arms.

That one shattering kiss they'd shared, more than anything, replayed itself over and over in Dane's mind. It was just as he'd known it would be. Once he'd held her, tasted her, nothing could deter him from having her. And, even then, it wouldn't be enough. It would never be enough.

Not for him, nor for Jacqueline.

Dane understood only too well what his stubborn little hellcat was trying to do. In her naiveté, she was hoping that, by avoiding him, by pretending he didn't exist, she could forget what had happened . . . what *was* happening between them. But Dane was neither naive nor inexperienced.

He knew better. He and Jacqueline were far from finished . . . in fact, they'd barely begun.

It was time that Jacqueline knew it, too.

The May sun was high overhead when Jacqui stepped out of her house, an impatient Whiskey slithering past her ankles to scoot out into the daylight. Jacqui paused, raised her face to the sky, and inhaled deeply, reveling in the fragrant scent of the air. Spring was in full bloom, the gardens alive with the smell of lilacs, and bluebirds singing merrily as they soared about.

"Oh, Whiskey, I keep forgetting how very much I love the springtime," she murmured, tucking a stray curl behind her ear. She knew she should be wearing a bonnet, but the sun felt so good upon her bare head and it had been so long since she'd allowed herself the freedom of a daytime walk.

Lost in thought, Jacqui strolled through the garden and across the lush green grass. It was not like her to be a coward, she admitted to herself. She had faced far more threatening challenges than Dane Westbrooke, and had not permitted herself to be intimidated. Yet . . . she had never felt so out of control as she had when they'd kissed. Sentimental weakness was an emotion Jacqui abhorred. And, if avoiding Dane was the only way to rid herself of the unwanted feeling, then so be it.

She hadn't expected him to be so persistent. It was only the two days past that his endless flow of notes and visits had ceased, allowing Jacqui's life to resume as it was before Dane Westbrooke exploded into it. She'd won, she congratulated herself. Finally, he'd given up.

She despised the disappointment that her realization elicited.

"Good afternoon, *mon chaton.*"

The low-pitched male voice made her start, spin about in surprise. Just as she had at their first meeting.

Leaning negligently against the tall elm tree that had

shielded him from Jacqui's view, Dane grinned. "It is a lovely day, is it not?"

"What are you doing here?" she snapped, berating herself for allowing him, yet again, to catch her off-guard. Inadvertently, she stepped away from him. Or was it from herself? Damn the swooping sensation in her stomach! And damn Dane Westbrooke for causing it!

"I am waiting for you, sweet. Since it would seem that you have not received any of my messages nor been told of any of my visits." He straightened, his probing silver gaze locked on hers. "Pity that your faithful Greta is not as efficient as you had originally thought she was."

Jacqui felt herself color at his pointed sarcasm. She gripped the folds of her gown, feeling uncustomarily off-balance, a state that only Dane Westbrooke seemed to reduce her to. "I—I—I have been busy," she managed lamely, knowing she sounded like a fool.

Dane's gaze dropped to her mouth, then lower, raking her hungrily, seeming to see clear through to the internal turmoil raging inside her. "I never thought of you as a coward, love." His voice was husky . . . knowing . . . erotic.

"I am not a coward!"

"Then why have you been avoiding me?" Dane stalked her slowly, his broad shoulders eclipsing the sunlight, leaving nothing in Jacqui's vision but his advancing, magnetic presence.

"Nor am I a fool."

He stopped. "Meaning?"

"Meaning that I do not intend to be seduced. Is that clear enough for you, Mr. Westbrooke?"

Dane chuckled at her intentionally formal address. "Very clear. Miss Holt," he added with a twinkle. He closed the space between them, placing his hands on her narrow shoulders and stroking his thumbs over the fine material of her lime-green gown. "You are frightened by what is between us. I understand. But you have no cause to be afraid. I have no intentions of harming you, sweet. Not ever."

Jacqui could feel his words, his touch, burn a path straight through her to an unknown place deep within. "But you do plan to seduce me," she clarified in a guarded whisper.

"No." Dane cupped her face tenderly between his hands, wondering at the ferocity of his craving for her, aware, on some level, that it transcended the mere physical. "To the contrary, love. I plan to allow you to seduce me."

Jacqui caught his wrists and shoved them from her face, nearly sputtering with indignation. "You plan to . . . what?"

Dane wrapped his fingers around hers, holding her still so she was forced to hear his words. "I won't let you go, Jacqueline. I want you too much. What's more, you want me too." He ignored her furious protest. "But I do not intend to take what you don't willingly offer. So you see, love," he freed one of her hands to bury his fingers in the soft masses of her hair, "you have nothing to fear. I won't coerce you into my bed. However, if you choose to come to me on your own, I could never turn you away." He brushed her lips with his. "And you will come to me, love. I promise you, you will."

Jacqui jerked free of his iron grasp. "You are the most arrogant, conceited, contemptible blackguard I have ever had the misfortune to meet!" She massaged her wrist, trying to eliminate the tingling that was a result, not of pain, but of Dane Westbrooke's touch.

Dane smiled slowly. "But I excite you."

"You infuriate me," she shot back.

"That too." He lifted her hand and gently kissed the wrist she had been vigorously rubbing. "Did I hurt you?" he murmured.

"You insulted me." She snatched her arm away.

Dane's dark brows rose. "By telling you that I want you? By saying that you are, by far, the most breathtaking, desirable woman I've ever known?" He raised her chin with a strong, tanned forefinger, forcing her to meet penetrating silver eyes that branded her with burning possession. "By confessing that I actually dream of making love to you?" he added softly, brushing her lower lip with his thumb. "No, *mon chaton*, that is not an insult, but the highest of compliments."

Jacqui swallowed, caught between the heat of her fury and the telltale truth revealed by the accelerated beating of her heart. She loathed the fact that Dane's words alone could affect her so powerfully; still she drank in the excitement accompanying the stirrings of her newly awakened body. The conflict tore at her, clouding her reason, yet she could no longer deny that Dane forced her to feel things she'd never before experienced. But was it desire she was feeling? Or was it simply anger coupled with the clever manipulations of a very charming, very experienced man?

Only one thing was certain . . . Jacqui was in way over her head.

Dane felt a wave of sympathy at the utterly bewildered look on her expressive face. He was pushing her too hard, too fast, and he knew it.

Reluctantly, he released her chin. "You were on your way out?"

"O-Out?" Jacqui stammered. The man's technique for dropping her from the height of an emotional precipice to the mundaneness of a casual conversation was incredible.

"Yes, sweetheart," Dane repeated gently, "out."

Jacqui licked her lips, battling her way back to reality. "I was just going to get some air. I haven't strayed from the house since . . ." She broke off, flushing, as she realized that he knew exactly how long it had been since she'd left the house. He also knew why.

Seeing her discomfort, Dane resisted the urge to taunt her. "Then may I join you?" he asked instead.

She sighed. "Dane . . ."

"At least you recall my name," he teased. "So there must be hope after all. I am, indeed, a fortunate man."

She tried, unsuccessfully, not to laugh. "You, sir, could charm a serpent into sacrificing its prey."

"In that case, can I charm you into taking a simple walk with me?" he pressed, grinning a sly, devilish grin. "Think carefully before you refuse. For if you do, I shall have no choice but to convince you in the only way I know how . . . to continue where we left off scant weeks ago." His grin widened at her blush. "This time, however, we will not be able to savor the privacy your dining room afforded us, but be forced to . . . enjoy each other right here on your front lawn," he made a sweeping gesture with his hand, "in plain view of the whole neighborhood." His look was pure innocence. "The choice, my love, is yours."

Jacqui shook her head in amazement. "You would do it, wouldn't you?" She glanced up and down the quiet street, nearly giggling aloud at the thought of the reactions she would receive if the neighbors saw her passionately kissing a man in broad daylight.

"I would." Dane watched her, fascinated. "And it wouldn't bother you in the least, would it?" he asked incredulously.

"The fact that you kissed me or the fact that others might witness it?" Her eyes danced with mischief.

Dane chuckled. "I *know* my kiss would bother you. I was referring to the latter."

"Not particularly." Jacqui shrugged. "If I spent much time worrying about what people thought of me, I would be as most other women I know: totally bored and utterly tiresome."

Dane threw his head back and shouted with laughter. "What a delightful description of the female sex."

"Not delightful, but accurate."

"And you, of course, are the exception."

She gave him a dazzling smile. "Of course."

Without warning, her smile invaded his heart and exploded in his loins, igniting a passion so fierce that it staggered him. All humor vanished from his handsome face. "Walk with me."

Dane's words, their implicit meaning, washed over Jacqui like a tidal wave. There was no fighting the primitive, raw sexuality he effortlessly exuded.

Jacqui walked.

With each step, she assured herself that it was curiosity and not desire that made her agree, that it was their challenging banter and not his overwhelming magnetism that made Dane Westbrooke's company so intriguing.

Then she was in his arms.

Sheltered by the tall pines beside her house, they came together with an urgency that was as fervent as it was natural. There was nothing even remotely tentative or teasing about this kiss. It was hot and hungry and out of control before it began.

"How I've missed you," Dane breathed, lifting her off the ground, fitting her against him, pressing her close enough to feel her full length.

Jacqui wrapped her arms about his neck, welcoming everything he'd taught her the last time . . . the intimate probe of his tongue, the blatant hardness of his body against hers. She kissed him back, gliding her fingers through the silk of his hair, opening her mouth to deepen his presence within her body.

Dane tangled his fingers in her thick curls, bending her backward so his mouth had access to the bare skin of her neck, her throat. He nuzzled the fragrant pulse behind her ear, whispering her name, then biting on the soft lobe until she moaned aloud. He kissed his way down the side of her neck to her shoulder and lower, to the top of her breast. "I want you," he whispered against her racing heart. "I want all of you." He lifted his head, met the fathomless midnight of her eyes and felt triumph surge through him at the longing that was so clearly revealed to him. "Jacqueline . . . I have to have you." Dane was stunned to realize that he was actually shaking.

Jacqui couldn't quite catch her breath. "No," she managed.

Dane kissed her flushed cheeks. "Yes," he contradicted softly, struggling to master his rampaging desire. "But not yet. Not until you want it as badly as I do. Not until the moment is right." He lowered his head briefly and pressed a lingering kiss on the upper slope of each breast, murmuring, "Your first time has to be as wildly intoxicating . . . as magnificently unforgettable . . . as thoroughly exquisite as you."

Jacqui fought the flash of heat that shot through her at Dane's explicit words, his intimate caress. She licked her swollen lips, still clutching his shoulders for balance. "How do you know it will be my first time?"

He raised his head and looked at her tenderly. "I just know."

"Damn you, Dane Westbrooke," she whispered, unconsciously caressing the nape of his neck. "Damn you to hell."

"Anywhere, as long as you're with me." He tugged her to him for another kiss. Running his fingers up and down her back, he stroked the fine material of her gown, soothing her and arousing her all at once.

"Stop," she ordered, her arms still locked about him, her eyes heavy-lidded with passion.

"Soon," he promised. He continued to kiss her for long minutes; deep, drugging kisses that left them both breathless, hungry for more. When he lowered her to the ground, he kept his arms about her, her head pressed against his chest. "Don't be afraid, sweet," he repeated softly into her disheveled hair. "I'll never hurt you."

"You confuse me dreadfully." Jacqui's confession was muffled against his coat.

"I know I do." He kissed the top of her head. "But that won't be forever."

She looked up at him. "You are so sure of yourself, aren't you?"

Absently, Dane rearranged her tousled curls in the hopes that Greta wouldn't notice her mistress's rather rumpled state. Even if Jacqueline cared nothing for her reputation,

Dane was determined to spare it. At last he shook his head. "It has nothing to do with being sure of myself, love. What I'm sure of is that you will belong to me. That is innate knowledge, not conceit."

"But only if I come to you," she reminded him.

He grinned. "Yes, *mon chaton colereux.* Only if you come to me."

"That is quite a challenge you are issuing, sir," Jacqui said, silently promising herself that he would never win, then assuring herself that she would pull free of his arms . . . in just a moment.

Dane kissed the tip of her upturned nose. "But one I do not plan to lose." He eased her away from him, keeping one arm locked about her shoulders.

Jacqui glanced down at his gesture. "I assume you believe that by continuing to hold me you will influence my decision?"

Dane chuckled. "No. I believe that by continuing to hold you I will keep your knees from giving out and tumbling you to the grass."

Bristling, Jacqui slapped his arm away and promptly teetered unsteadily, forced to grab hold of his forearm to regain her balance.

"Better, love?" Despite his resolve to the contrary, his lips twitched. He tucked her hand through the crook of his elbow. "I shall assist you to your front door."

He took a step forward, only to trip over a solid object in his path. Looking down in surprise, Dane saw a small black ball of fluff that sprang to life, hissing and arching its back in response to the unappreciated assault.

"Who is this?" Dane appeared unintimidated by the less-than-pleased kitten.

"This is my cat." Jacqui leaned over and scooped Whiskey into her arms, kissing his soft fur with an uncharacteristic warmth Dane had never seen her display. Deeply touched, he watched, fascinated.

"It's all right, little one," Jacqui murmured, her customary guard lowered. Unaware of Dane's tender scrutiny, she spoke softly into Whiskey's fur. "I know he is quite large and the impact of his feet must be painful, but he did not intentionally harm you." She stroked the tiny length of the kitten, which began to purr contentedly.

"I most assuredly did not mean to hurt you," Dane solemnly concurred, bending over to scratch Whiskey's ears. "Next time I shall be more—"

Dane never finished his sentence. The moment his hand touched Whiskey's fur, the kitten sprang into action, leaping forward with an angry hiss and slashing his claws across Dane's cheek. Ignoring Dane's furious expletive, he bounded to the grass and raced off, like a naughty child who did not intend to remain for his punishment, and disappeared around the front of the house.

"Whiskey!" Jacqui called after him, appalled.

"Bloody hell!" Dane cursed again, pressing his fingers to the deep gashes now covering his left cheek.

Jacqui went to him, still stunned, staring after her now-vanished pet. "Dane, I apologize profusely for my cat's actions." She removed Dane's hand, standing on tiptoe so she could see the ugly wound. "Whiskey has never done anything like this before. He's always so friendly with people."

"Well, he obviously does not feel friendly toward me," Dane grumbled back, feeling the sharp sting of the cuts.

An image flashed through Jacqui's mind . . . an image of the night she'd adopted Whiskey. She fought back a smile, remembering. This was not the first time Whiskey and Dane had met . . . nor the first time Whiskey had attacked Dane.

"What the hell is so funny?" Dane demanded, further irritated by Jacqui's amused reaction.

"Nothing," she assured him. She frowned at the blood now trickling along Dane's jaw. "Come into the house and I'll treat those scratches."

Instantly, Dane's irritation vanished. "All right."

He allowed himself to be led into the Holts' spacious

sitting room, leaning back and closing his eyes as Jacqui tended to his cheek. The brush of her hands was heaven.

"Am I hurting you?" She paused, assuming that his tightly closed eyes implied pain.

"No, sweetheart." Dane gave her a slow, devastating grin. "If this is the only way to convince you to continue touching me, it was well worth the price." He opened teasing silver eyes and caught her hand in his. "In fact, I only wish that your wretched little cat had done his minor damage to those portions of my anatomy that *truly* require your attentions."

Jacqui flushed and yanked her hand free. "You are not supposed to say such things to me," she informed him.

One dark brow lifted in amusement. "Really? And why not? You obviously liked hearing them; your face is flushed and your eyes are sparkling." He dragged her hand back to his face, this time bringing her fingers to his warm, open mouth.

She didn't deny his words, nor did she reclaim her hand. "That is not the point."

"Then what is?" He kissed each of her fingertips, then her palm, letting his tongue stroke her soft skin. "You have already informed me that you are nothing like other women, nor do you care what people think of you."

"Yes . . . but . . ."

"But?" he prompted, feeling the pulse in her wrist throb frantically.

"But this is totally irrational," she tried, tingles running up her spine as Dane's warm breath caressed her arm.

"This?" he questioned softly.

"Yes, this." She gestured from herself to him. "What is occurring between us. We hardly even *know* each other." Her token protest was uttered in a small, bewildered voice.

Dane kissed the delicate veins on the inside of her wrist, then lifted his head, giving her a look of tender understanding. "Some things, my beautiful little scholar, defy logic. Our attraction"—he frowned at his own choice of words—

"our mutual fascination," he corrected, "is one of those things."

"But it is only a physical fascination," Jacqui qualified.

Dane pressed her hand to his cheek. "Is it?"

For a long moment there was silence as he held her gaze with his.

Acutely aware of Dane's warm skin beneath her hand and mesmerized by the intensity of his probing silver stare, Jacqui could barely remember what they'd been talking about. She licked her lips nervously. "Would you like a drink?" she blurted out.

Taking pity on her, Dane released her hand. "A drink would be splendid, both for pleasurable and medicinal purposes." He moved his jaw gingerly. "Not only will I be able to enjoy your exceptional company, but perhaps a drink will take my mind off my injuries."

Jacqui rolled her eyes heavenward. "It is only a scratch, Dane, not a fatal wound." Seeing his disappointed expression, she smiled. "You will find that my sympathy is not so easily attained."

"Nor is your affection," he noted with a mock sigh. He leaned forward, catching a soft fold of her gown and using it to tug her closer to him. "Tell me then," he asked, tracing the contours of her slender waist with teasing, suggestive fingers, "what will you offer me, if not sympathy or affection?"

"*I* will offer you a glass of brandy," Greta announced loudly, stalking into the room and thrusting a drink at Dane. She stood, glaring, until he had released Jacqui's gown and taken the proffered glass. Then, without waiting for thanks, Greta slapped a newspaper down onto the table beside Dane and placed a small tray of food next to it. "Your newspaper, Fräulein Holt," she barked. "Also some homemade white gingerbread, still warm, for you and your guest." She shot Dane a pointed look. "The refreshment should appease both your pain *and* your voracious appetite,

Herr Westbrooke." With a reproachful sniff, she left the room.

"I believe I have just been duly chastised," Dane said dryly. "Also put in my place by yet another female in the Holt household." He took an appreciative sip of brandy and reached for a slice of gingerbread. "Ah, well, at least this offending woman feeds me."

Jacqui couldn't argue his point, and its truth astounded her. Greta, who *never* doted, who rarely even smiled, had for the second time indulged a flagrant, notorious rake who was a stranger in their home and who was taking unprecedented liberties with Greta's mistress. It was nothing short of astonishing.

Unaware of Jacqui's bafflement, Dane took another sip of brandy, then placed his drink on the table. The newspaper caught his eye.

"The *General Advertiser,*" he murmured. "Now why doesn't that surprise me?"

Instantly, Jacqui retaliated. "What does *that* mean?"

"It means that I should have expected it would be Bache's Republican newspaper, and not the *Gazette,* that would appeal to you."

"Just as I would expect it to be the *Gazette* that you advocate and not the *Advertiser,*" she returned. "After all, it is your friend, Secretary Hamilton, who kept the *Gazette* alive and in business this year past. Without his financial support, it would have collapsed, and with it much of the Federalists' influence."

Dane looked incredulous. "The influence of great men does not depend on the survival of one newspaper, Jacqueline. Alexander's voice would be heard with or without the *Gazette.*"

"But not nearly as loudly," she countered. "Are you going to deny that Hamilton uses the *Gazette* to promote his own ideas?"

"Are *you* going to deny that Jefferson does any less in the *General Advertiser?*" Dane shot back, coming to his feet.

"My God, Jacqueline, Jefferson has tried for years to influence the country into a pro-French stance."

"He has a definite point," she defended hotly. "Perhaps we can all learn something from the revolution that is taking place in France right now. The majority of our countrymen are not wealthy businessmen such as yourself and all your friends who are pro-English, but poor farmers who rely upon their land and their crops to sustain themselves. We cannot build a country that only benefits the rich!"

"Nor can we build a country without the necessary foundations: a strong central government and an effective financial system."

"I have no argument with that. But must those foundations ignore the needs of the masses? Where is our national unity? Does that not count as well?"

"Unity?" Dane bit out. He tore open the *General Advertiser,* scanning the pages with fury in his eyes until he found what he'd been seeking. "Tell me, Jacqueline"—he thrust the paper in her face—"is this the writing of a man who wants to *unite* our country?" He stabbed a finger at Laffey's column, which that day dealt with America's concessions to the British as demonstrated by Jay's recent departure for England. "Tell me, Jacqueline," Dane repeated, furious at her immature idealism, "is this opinion meant to enlighten, or is it meant to provoke? And what, in truth, does Jack Laffey hope to accomplish by further inciting one sector of our country against the other?"

Jacqui stared at the column without speaking. Then she swallowed and raised her eyes to Dane's. "You've never before mentioned your obvious loathing for this . . . Jack Laffey."

Dane shrugged, a furious light burning in his hot silver eyes. "It never came up. But loathe him I do. And when I finally discover the dishonorable blackguard's actual identity"—he inhaled sharply—"I shall deal with him as he deserves."

The underlying threat was not lost to Jacqui. "It might not

73

be a question of dishonor, Dane," she replied quietly. "Sometimes one must incite in order to enlighten. Maybe you are confusing hostility with patriotism."

Dane gave a harsh laugh and tossed the newspaper aside. "I fail to see your logic."

"Wasn't it you who told me that some things defy logic?" she questioned in an odd tone.

Perhaps it was that odd tone, or perhaps it was her uncustomary pallor, that snapped Dane out of his tirade. He took a deep, calming breath.

"Jacqueline . . . forgive me. I didn't mean to upset you."

Jacqui shook her head. "You didn't upset me. It's just that our views are so very different." She paused. "Too different."

"I don't think so," Dane refuted quickly, taking her hand. "We are both loyal, concerned Americans who want our country to prosper. We just have different ideas about how to make that happen."

Jacqui met his gaze. "I will never stop expressing what I believe in," she told him. "No matter what the cost."

"Fair enough," he agreed, kissing her fingers. "If you think the prospect of your forthrightness and your honesty will send me away, you had best think again, love." He rubbed her knuckles lightly across his lower lip. "Have you not yet guessed that those are the very traits of yours that intrigue me so?"

She remained silent, her expression veiled.

He was about to press her when a crash resounded from just behind them.

Whirling about, Dane saw pieces of his brandy glass fly all about, spilling the contents into a small puddle on the floor. From atop the table, Whiskey watched the results of his handiwork, then leapt lightly to the floor and began to rapidly lap up the liquor with his tongue. That done, he raised his head, licked the last few droplets of brandy from his whiskers, and stumbled out of the room.

"What the hell . . ." Dane's eyes narrowed, memory

returning in a jolt. "Jacqueline, do you let your cat run free?" He turned toward her, stunned to see her struggling to restrain her laughter.

"No," she managed. "Why do you ask?"

"Because last month—"

"Whiskey just happens to enjoy his liquor," she interrupted hastily. "That is, in fact, how he got his name."

Dane stared after the kitten thoughtfully. "Interesting," was all he said. Then he turned back toward Jacqui. "Do you enjoy the theater?"

"Yes, of course, why?"

"Because that is where we are going Friday night."

Jacqui scowled. "Isn't it customary for you to *ask* me and not to *inform* me?"

He grinned. "Probably. But I think we should continue to be unconventional, don't you?"

Again, Jacqui grew quiet. "Dane, I don't think . . ."

"But I do." He drew her to him and kissed her softly, possessively, for a long, dizzying moment. Then he released her slowly, caressing her with his eyes. "I'll be here at eight o'clock. Don't keep me waiting, *mon chaton.*"

Jacqui watched him go with a dazed expression on her face. The situation between them had grown even more complicated than it had originally been. Wandering back into the sitting room, she picked up the scattered pages of the *General Advertiser* and stared down at Laffey's column, forcing herself to view the contents through Dane's eyes. Once again, she could hear his bitter threat, see the predatory gleam in his eyes.

A chill ran through her.

In truth, Laffey's tone was most scathing with regard to America's concessions to England. Brutally so. But with good reason, she defended to herself silently. For his words had merit. But she could not deny Dane's accusation. . . . The article was indeed provoking.

Jacqui frowned. She hadn't intended it that way when she had penned it.

CHAPTER
6

The weeks that followed were fraught with indecision.

Each time Jacqui and Dane were together—the evenings at the theater, the dinners at the inn, the dances at Oeller's Hotel, the verbal sparring matches in her sitting room . . . the few but exhilarating moments in his arms—every one of Jacqui's instincts cried out its warning, cautioning her that to continue an association with Dane Westbrooke would be altogether foolhardy. Despite the enjoyment she experienced in his company, the danger he represented was simply too great to ignore. She had worked far too hard to risk losing everything at the hands of a man.

It was not her virtue that Jacqui guarded so fiercely.

It was her well-hidden alias.

As a woman, Jacqui had learned quite young that the only man to give credence to her opinions, political or otherwise, was her beloved father. Time after frustrating time she had been put in her place by a man, beginning with her father's friends and associates, culminating with the few beaus she'd had the misfortune to entertain. Finally she'd decided to take drastic measures.

Thus, Jack Laffey was born.

Laffey could do what Jacqui could not. He could give

voice to her well-thought-out though controversial opinions and be assured that, whether read by concurring Republicans or scornful Federalists, the words were met with respect, interest, and, most important of all, credibility.

Once every week, under cover of darkness, Jacqui stole away to an unlit alleyway and handed Jack Laffey's column over to a handsomely paid messenger. The lad then delivered his parcel to the *General Advertiser*, answering no questions and providing no information about the column's source. Least of all the fact that its creator was a woman.

It had been nearly a year now, and no one in Philadelphia suspected that Jacqui was Laffey. But then, she deliberately kept her distance from others, allowing no one close enough to surmise the truth.

Not until that fateful spring night when her weekly excursion had flung her into Dane Westbrooke's dynamic path.

Jacqui knew she was playing with fire, that she should sever their relationship before it even began. The problem was that she didn't want to. Dane made her feel vibrantly alive, brimming with anticipation. He challenged her mind, accepted . . . no, reveled in her intelligence, respected her opinions, her forthrightness, even her bold tongue.

And he kindled a fire in her blood that nothing seemed to extinguish.

The truth was that, deep down inside, Jacqui *wanted* to experience every new and tantalizing sensation Dane promised with his raw masculinity and blazing silver eyes. If she could only keep her other life a secret, what harm would there be in exploring the world of dazzling physical pleasure with him? After all, why deny her body its first taste of passion, especially since she knew her heart to be immune?

Besides, it wasn't her heart Dane Westbrooke was after.

Dane knew precisely what he was after, and Jacqui's heart was only part of it.

What Dane wanted was Jacqui.

His relentless need for her grew stronger each time they were together, stronger still when they were apart. And as his craving intensified, his patience ebbed and his reason vanished. Come hell or high water, he *had* to have her.

But how was he to make his need a reality?

Sexually, Dane sensed that it was only a matter of time before Jacqui relented and came to his bed. But the only thing her physical surrender would bring was a temporary salve for the ache in his loins and a newer, greater complication.

To indulge in an affair of endless duration was out of the question.

With both pragmatism and tenderness, Dane recognized that Jacqueline Holt was simply *not* a woman one kept as a mistress. Not because she would swoon at the unorthodox suggestion, he mused with a grin. Knowing Jacqueline, she might be intrigued. But even if, in all her unconventional splendor, she were amenable to the idea, her father would most assuredly not be.

Besides, Dane determined with a fierce surge of protectiveness, a role of secondary import was beneath her. Jacqueline deserved better. She deserved marriage.

He was just the man to give it to her.

His uncharacteristically respectable decision was not wholly unselfish, Dane acknowledged honestly. The truth was that the idea of marriage to Jacqueline appealed to him immensely, which was indeed a surprise. Marriage had always seemed a faraway goal to Dane, something to be considered only when youth was gone, leaving in its stead a yearning for the complacency offered by one mate and the feeling of immortality fulfilled only by the siring of children.

The ironic thing was that the woman he wished to wed had never mentioned either marriage or children, and had a personality that would offer him about as much complacency as a captive eagle straining to soar.

But she was such a challenge, such a beautiful, untamed bundle of contradictions, such a bewitching, infuriating little hellcat. Dane wanted her fire, her spirit, her newly born passion. He wanted her brilliant mind, her exquisite body, her carefully guarded heart. He wanted her love.

Because, in truth, he was already half in love with her.

It was midmorning and Jacqui was deeply engrossed in the new edition of the *General Advertiser*. Since Dane's tirade the month before, she had been very careful to keep Laffey's columns straightforward . . . at least as straightforward as she could without compromising her beliefs. She nodded, satisfied with the day's results, and tucked her legs beneath her on the settee.

The newspaper moved in her hands.

"Whiskey, stop it!" Jacqui scolded without looking down at her lap. She could feel the kitten's sharp claws as they penetrated the fine material of her gown and dug into her skin—Whiskey's ploy to get his mistress's attention. When it proved unsuccessful, he lifted his head and yowled.

Jacqui tossed the paper aside. "I was trying to read!" she said in exasperation, ignoring his forlorn look. "You are dreadfully annoying. What is it that you want?"

Whiskey responded by licking his lips.

Jacqui sighed, glancing out the window at the bright June sky. "Yes, well, it is warm today and you have been running about for hours. Are you thirsty?"

Whiskey's eyes widened in anticipation.

Jacqui fetched a small bowl of water from the kitchen and placed it on the sitting-room rug. "Here."

Whiskey fairly flew to the bowl, leaned over, and lowered his tongue eagerly to drink. All at once he froze. Lifting his head, he gave the water a look of utter disdain, turned about in a most haughty manner, and stalked away. He paused beside the table that boasted two decanters of wine and turned to Jacqui hopefully, blinking his huge green eyes.

"Absolutely not." Jacqui refused, shaking her head emphatically. "That is Father's finest Madeira and it most definitely is *not* for cats!" She pointed to the untouched water. "I'm afraid it must be the water, my little friend. Either that or nothing. It is your choice."

Not one to readily accept defeat, Whiskey sauntered over and rubbed up against Jacqui's legs, issuing his most beguiling meow.

"No," Jacqui repeated, unmoved.

With an arrogant, disgusted expression, Whiskey gave in, taking but one reluctant lick of the detested liquid. Then, in order to convey the full extent of his indignation, he lifted a small black paw and, with one strategic motion, flipped the still-full bowl over, splashing water every which way.

"Whiskey . . . you miserable wretch!" Jacqui exploded as the copy of the *General Advertiser* she had been holding grew soggy, the contents unreadable.

Whiskey glared back brazenly. Then, having made his point, he lifted his nose, turned his tail in the air, and sashayed out of the sitting room.

Jacqui was about to dash after him when she saw him pause in the hallway, then stop, a predatory gleam in his eye. Arching his back, he began to hiss loudly, his body poised to spring. Whatever he was staring at, Jacqui could see that he was about to attack. Suddenly Greta charged through the hallway, chastising Whiskey rapidly in German and shooing him into the kitchen.

A moment later the explanation strolled through the sitting-room door.

"Good morning, sweet," Dane greeted Jacqui cheerfully, glancing behind him to see Whiskey's hasty retreat.

"Hello, Dane." Jacqui accepted the now-familiar flutter in her stomach that his presence elicited.

He reached out and drew her to him. "I didn't care for that greeting at all." He took her arms, wrapping them about his neck. "Now . . . again."

Jacqui felt herself smile. "Hello, Dane." She stood on tiptoe and brushed her lips across his chin.

"Hello, Jacqueline," he said in a husky voice. Before she

could move, he brought her against him and covered her mouth with his own.

"Dane . . ." she protested, "Greta . . ."

". . . is occupied with your vicious cat," he answered against her lips. "Kiss me."

"But . . ."

"Kiss me." He stole her final protest away with a warm sweep of his tongue, feeling that incomparable instant when Jacqui let herself go and became his. He drank in her lush softness, feeling his body blaze instantly out of control. "Yes, love, like that," he murmured, taking her mouth in a primal rhythm that made them both tremble. Months before, this would have been enough. To hold her, to kiss her, to tease her with what was to be . . . it had sustained him these endless weeks. But no longer. Dane wanted her . . . *needed* her, with an urgency that could no longer be squelched. "Jacqueline. . . ." He breathed her name, unconsciously lifting her to meet the instinctive motion of his hips.

Jacqui made a soft sound deep in her throat and tore her mouth from his. "Dane . . ." There was no fear in her voice, only reluctance, matched by the anxious expression on her beautiful, flushed face. "We can't . . ."

"I have to be inside you." He stared down into her haunting eyes, unable to retain his hold on sanity.

Jacqui felt his words unfurl within her like scalding ribbons of fire. "Not now. Not here. Not yet." She shook her head in total bewilderment. "Dane, please. I can't think when you're holding me."

"Perhaps I don't want you to think."

"One of us has to."

Dane chuckled, despite the relentless throbbing of his body. "And that someone, of course, has to be you. My ever-thinking Jacqueline." His hands slid to her hips. "Just tell me that you want me," he commanded.

Jacqui licked her lips. "I believe that's obvious."

"Say it." Fiercely, he crushed her lower body to his.

"I want you."

"Now tell me when."

"I can't, Dane. I don't know." She could actually feel him pulsing against her, feel the answering response within herself. Weakness pervaded her limbs, and with the weakness came fear. "Put me down."

Dane heard the vehemence of her words, but he also recognized the strangled tone characterizing her order. For a long moment he did nothing, still holding her to him, staring deeply into her wide, midnight eyes. He read her internal struggle . . . but not its cause. She was unafraid of their impending physical union . . . of that he was certain. Nor did she give a damn for public opinion concerning her conduct. Then what?

He watched Jacqui catch her lower lip between her teeth and chew on it nervously . . . a typically feminine gesture. The realization hit him that, unconventional or not, Jacqueline was indeed a woman, with not only a woman's needs but with her sensibilities as well. Perhaps what she required was the very thing Dane intended to offer her. A commitment.

Slowly, he lowered her feet to the floor, keeping her in a loose embrace. "We have to talk."

Jacqui stepped back. "Talk? Is *that* what we were just doing?"

"No. But it *is* what we are going to do now."

She studied Dane quietly. "All right." Moving out of his arms, she sank down onto the settee, gesturing for him to do the same.

"Jacqueline, you're nineteen years old," Dane began, sitting beside her.

"Actually, I'll be twenty next month," she put in, wondering where on earth this was leading.

"I stand corrected." He stared at the polished tip of his boot, aware that he was searching for words he had never before spoken, determined to say them first to Jacqueline before he even approached her father. "In any case, you are no longer a child, but very much a woman."

Jacqui gave a deep sigh, folding her hands purposefully in her lap. "Yes, Dane, I know. I can well imagine what you plan to say."

"Can you?" The deep timbre of his voice was a caress.

She nodded. "Yes. You are going to remind me that you cannot . . . *will* not . . . go on as we are indefinitely. I do understand. As you just said, I am not a child, but a woman grown. I recognize your needs. I am also fully aware of my own needs . . . probably more so than any other woman you've encountered."

Something in her tone gave Dane pause. "Meaning?"

"Meaning that, no matter what should occur between us, you must clearly understand that the only person I will ever truly belong to is myself. Regardless of whether I share my thoughts, my beliefs"—she paused—"even my body with another, it will not alter that fact. My identity," and she smiled softly at her own choice of words, "is my own."

Unreasonable anger began to churn inside Dane. "And where will your husband fit into all this?" he demanded.

Jacqui looked at him as if he had lost his mind. "My husband?" She uttered the word as one would a profanity.

"Yes, your husband," he snapped back. "The man you eventually marry."

Jacqui laughed. "Whatever gave you the idea that I planned to marry?" she asked in an incredulous tone. "I would never even consider the idea."

"Why the hell not?" Dane came to his feet in one fluid motion.

"Because, my arrogant sir, if you study the marriage vows you will learn that when a woman marries she must relinquish her thoughts, her opinions, her very soul to the man she weds." Jacqui was becoming angry as well. "She becomes nothing but a piece of chattel—a belonging, an acquisition of her husband's. None of which I intend to be." She glared up at him, almost angry enough to blurt out the truth. Almost. "There are . . . aspects of my life that I would be unwilling to change . . . for anyone," she said instead.

"And if you fall in love?" Dane's thoughts were centered on but one thing. His voice was deadly quiet, his jaw clenched.

Jacqui rose, her chin stubbornly set. "I would never have expected such a fanciful, romantic question from you. But since you've asked, here is my answer: I hope I am never weak or foolish enough to succumb to love, but if I should, it would change nothing. Were I to marry, force myself to be a dutiful wife, my love would soon turn to hate. So, in the end, I would be alone anyway."

Something flashed in Dane's eyes, a distant, pained memory, that was gone as quickly as it had come. He knew firsthand what happened when marital love deteriorated into resentment and finally into dust. "I understand," he said, his tone odd, flat.

Jacqui gave him a curious look. "Have I *so* shocked you with my opinion?"

"No. You haven't shocked me." Dane replied curtly. He glanced down at his timepiece. "I must be leaving, Jacqueline; I have an appointment in less than an hour."

"All right."

Dane studied Jacqui, his eyes hooded, his expression dark, brooding. She looked to be on the verge of questioning his strange mood shift, then abruptly seemed to change her mind.

Without a word, he went to her and tugged her to him for a series of long, thorough kisses. He didn't release her until she was kissing him back with the same ferocity that burned inside him. Even then, he kept her in his arms, tightly held to his chest.

"We are going to the Binghams' party on Saturday night," he told her when their breathing had returned to normal.

Jacqui stiffened. "Oh no, *we* are not!" she shot back, adamantly shaking her head against him. "I refuse to go to one of their garish balls. Why, Mrs. Bingham is nothing more than a flaunting, haughty extension of Hamilton's Federalists. . . . She and her husband are little better than English nobility!" She paled as she realized what she'd just said.

But Dane's only response was a deep, lazy chuckle. "Try to keep that opinion to yourself on Saturday, *mon chaton,*" he advised, nuzzling her hair with his lips. "Although I do believe it has been said before."

"Didn't you hear me, Dane? I said I'm not going!" She pushed ineffectively at his massive chest.

"I heard." He continued the caressing motion of his lips. "Have I told you how much I love the scent of your hair?" he breathed. "So sweet. So soft. So beautiful." He felt her inadvertent shiver and smiled against the satiny tresses. "Think of it as an opportunity to reinforce your hatred for the cursed aristocrats of our fair city. Or think of it as an evening to accumulate more ammunition for the Republican cause. Or just think of it as an opportunity to spend the night dancing in my arms."

Intrigued by the prospect of spending an entire evening eavesdropping on the Federalists who frequented the Binghams' parties, and aroused by the subtle images conveyed by Dane's words, Jacqui could feel herself weaken. "Even if I agree to go, there is little chance that we'll be dancing together," she managed faintly.

"Why is that?"

"Because I assume lots will be drawn. And with the number of people who attend the Binghams' balls, I fear I shall be relegated to another man for the duration of the evening." She raised her head and gave Dane an impish smile. "So you see, sir, that final argument is not a convincing one."

"Do not be so certain of that, my love." He gave her a cocky grin.

Jacqui's hands curled into fists. "Even *you* cannot tamper with the lots!"

"Accompany me and see," he invited, a challenging gleam in his silver eyes.

"You're incorrigible."

"Absolutely," he agreed. He bent his head and nibbled lightly on her lower lip. "Not only staunch Federalists will be attending. Your father will be there, you know."

Jacqui sighed. "Yes, I know. Father has some land dealings with Mr. Bingham. Which means that Monique Brisset will be there as well."

"You don't like your father's . . . companion?" Dane questioned.

"They are hardly companions, and no, I don't."

Dane's shoulders shook with laughter. "I would not want to be your enemy, *mon chaton colereux.*" He tangled his hands in her thick curls.

"Sometimes I feel as though you are my enemy." The words were out before Jacqui could censor them. She felt angry and foolish—angry because it was unlike her to blurt out her feelings and foolish because it was ludicrous to refer to a man in whose arms she was clasped as an enemy.

But Dane seemed unsurprised by the bizarre statement. "No, sweet," he murmured softly, stroking the nape of her neck, "never that. We will be many things to each other, but enemies? Never." His penetrating silver gaze reached deep inside her. "I am going to know you as no other man ever has or ever will, Jacqueline." He paused, weighing his words. "In many ways I already do."

A knot of fear tightened Jacqui's stomach. Amid the pleasure of the past weeks, she had all but dismissed the idea that Dane knew who she was, knew what she was doing. Now, with his words, her doubts returned full force. Could he possibly suspect? Was this "courtship" more than it appeared? And how on earth could she find out? The uncertainty was maddening.

"Seven o'clock," he was saying, running his knuckles across her smooth cheek. "I'll come for you." He kissed her softly. "Can you be ready by then?"

Jacqui was strained from apprehension, spent from physical sensation. All she could muster was a weak nod.

Dane smiled tenderly. "Good." He scooped her into his arms and gently deposited her on the settee. "There. Now you needn't worry about falling." He winked. "Until Saturday, my love." He lifted her hand and kissed the inside of her wrist. *"Au revoir, chaton."*

Jacqui watched him go, feeling a sudden shiver run through her. She was profoundly aware that she stood on the fringes of an enveloping tempest . . . one that had the potential to destroy her. She could confront it . . . or she could walk away. The decision was hers.

It appeared she had much to think about before Saturday.

So did Dane.

Strolling toward home, he devised his plan.

Obviously, Jacqueline was not ready to consider marrying him. That presented a definite problem. Definite, but not insurmountable. Other than the totally unacceptable choice of conceding defeat, Dane was left with only one option. He would have to call upon the sole advantage he had over his brilliant, headstrong Jacqueline, use the only means he had for changing her mind.

Dane was going to shamelessly, purposefully, relentlessly seduce Jacqueline Holt. He was going to heighten her need for him until it overcame all doubt, driving her into his arms. When that happened, he would teach her the mysteries of passion, bathe her senses in pleasure, love her in every possible way a man could love a woman.

Then, when she was glowing and sated, he would ask her to marry him . . . and she would accept.

It was an infallible plan.

CHAPTER
7

"You're rather morose tonight." Dane took a deep swallow of whiskey and regarded Thomas with concern. "Is it business again?"

Thomas looked restlessly about the City Tavern's Coffee Room. "Among other things . . . yes."

"Other things," Dane repeated thoughtfully. He rolled his glass between his hands, seeming to contemplate the amber liquid. In truth, he was thinking about the deep lines around his friend's eyes, lines that had not been there before. "What happened to that large payment you said you were expecting?"

"Soon," Thomas replied, shifting in his chair. "But not soon enough. My debts are getting rather . . . extensive."

Dane's response was immediate. "Let me lend you——"

"No." The last thing Thomas wanted was to take Dane's money. He was already ridden with guilt . . . for betraying this fine man he called friend, for endangering the stability of his country, for disregarding every principle he had learned fighting beside the brilliant leader who had taught him the meaning of integrity . . . Alexander Hamilton. But there was just so much a man could take before he reached the breaking point. And Thomas had definitely reached his.

Clearing his throat roughly, he waved away Dane's offer with a definitive sweep of his hand. "Thank you, Dane, but I have to extricate myself from my financial dilemma." He tossed down his drink. "And I will . . . very shortly." He hesitated. "Actually, the waiting would not be nearly so difficult if . . ."

"If?"

"If my personal life were in better order," Thomas answered reluctantly.

"A problem with your mystery lady?"

Thomas grimaced, drumming his fingers nervously on the table. "Not a problem, precisely. Just a disagreement regarding our degrees of involvement."

Dane recognized the symptoms only too well. "You're in love with her."

Thomas gave a short, humorless laugh. "To say the very least . . . yes."

"And she?"

A pause. "She *says* she loves me. But every blasted time I make plans for our future, she becomes vague and uncooperative. I don't know what to think."

"Women have a way of keeping us off-balance," Dane concurred dryly. "But perhaps she is truly not ready to settle down. Is she very young?"

"Not *that* young."

Dane frowned at Thomas's evasiveness. "Why won't you allow me to meet her?"

Thomas brought his glass to the table with a thud and came to his feet. "Please, Dane, don't press me. I'm not up for it." He straightened his waistcoat and glanced down at his timepiece. "Besides, it's half after six. Didn't you say you were due at the Holts' at seven o'clock?"

Dane stood as well, his elegant black evening clothes perfectly molded to his tall, powerful physique. "Yes. I'm escorting Jacqueline to the Binghams' party."

"You're becoming rather involved with Jacqueline Holt, are you not?"

Dane grinned. "Rather." He placed a supportive hand on Thomas's shoulder. "Thomas . . . if you need assistance from me . . ."

". . . then I shall certainly ask for it," Thomas finished with a tired smile. "Go and fetch your lady, and enjoy yourselves."

"Are you seeing *your* lady tonight?"

"No. Not tonight." Thomas looked away.

"Thomas—"

"Good night, Dane," Thomas interrupted abruptly. "I really must be off."

Dane nodded. "Of course."

But he was worried.

"Tell me, *mon père,* do I look suitably dressed for an evening with Philadelphia's aristocracy?" Jacqui's question was asked in a bantering tone, but George Holt did not laugh. Watching his elegant daughter spin about the sitting room in her scarlet and gold satin gown, he realized, with more than a twinge of sadness, that his little girl was gone. In her place was a stunning young woman. A young woman who, if George's suspicions were correct, was falling in love.

"You look exquisite, Jacqui." He gave her an indulgent smile. "Lovely enough to dine with the President himself. Dane Westbrooke is a very lucky man."

Jacqui flushed, brushing an imaginary speck off her full skirt in order to avoid her father's knowing eyes. He'd always been able to read her thoughts far too easily.

"You're beginning to care for him." George's voice was filled with gentle understanding.

Jacqui lifted her head with a start. "He intrigues me," she qualified. "And he accepts me for who I am."

George smiled. "Who is that, my beautiful daughter?"

Jacqui gave him a pointed look. "You're teasing me, Father. You, better than anyone, know the answer to that question. I am exactly as you raised me to be . . . strong, independent, and committed to what I believe in."

It was true. Since Marie Holt had died unexpectedly ten years before, George had encouraged Jacqui to be, not only his beloved only child, but his intellectual partner and confidante as well. So, unlike the other young ladies of her age, Jacqui had been educated, not only in French, music, and the like, but in politics, literature, and business. All of which she took to like a fish to water.

She had been keeping the ledgers for Holt Trading throughout her teens, and George couldn't ask for a more thorough, painstaking accountant.

If there were times when Jacqui's bold tongue and unwavering political opinions made George wonder if perhaps he'd been too lenient in her upbringing, he did not allow himself to dwell on it. Nor did he allow himself to ponder the ramifications of her controversial undertaking this year past. Some things were better left alone.

With eyes that were suspiciously bright, George went over and took Jacqui's hands. "Yes, Jacqueline, you have turned into exactly the woman I always prayed you would be. I only wish your mother were alive to share in my joy."

Jacqui felt her throat tighten. She and her father rarely spoke of her mother. After ten years, the pain was still fresh.

Raising up on tiptoes, Jacqui placed a warm kiss on her father's smooth-shaven cheek. "You'd best be going, *papa,*" she murmured. "Monique will be waiting."

He gave her a mock scowl. "You'll forgive me if I act the part of the doting father for a bit. I plan to wait until your escort arrives before I take my leave."

"Then you needn't wait any longer, Herr Holt," Greta announced, appearing in the room. Her normally ruddy complexion looked even rosier than usual. "Herr Westbrooke has arrived." She smoothed her hands down the front of her apron and adjusted the bow in the back.

Jacqui fought back a smile. "Thank you, Greta. Please show Mr. Westbrooke in."

Greta scowled. "You should not be down here, Fräulein,"

91

she scolded. "A gentleman should be kept waiting a respectable period of time before his lady appears."

Jacqui could no longer suppress her laughter. "That is ridiculous, Greta. I *am* ready. Why would I pretend *not* to be?"

"It isn't proper for . . ."

"Don't waste your breath, Greta," George advised, seeing an oncoming argument. Checking his timepiece, he noted that he was expected at Monique's home in a quarter hour. "Show Mr. Westbrooke in."

Bristling, Greta barked, "Very well, sir." She cast an annoyed look at Jacqui and made a loud sound of disapproval. Then she hastened off.

"Thank you, Father," Jacqui said, her eyes twinkling. "We might have been here the remainder of the night."

"That is precisely what I was afraid of."

"Herr Westbrooke," Greta bellowed from the doorway.

Dane strolled in, tall and bronzed as a Greek god, dark as Lucifer himself . . . and magnificent as sin.

Jacqui felt her insides melt.

"Good evening, Dane." George extended his hand.

Dane shook it. "Good evening, George." The acknowledgment was automatic and Dane hardly knew he'd made it. His gaze was fixed on the melting vision in red and gold who stood beside her father.

"Jacqueline." Dane kissed her hand. "You look beautiful." He wanted to do much more than kiss her hand. He wanted to take her in his arms and bury his lips in hers, to run his hands through her thick, shining mahogany curls. He wanted to drag her to the floor and make slow, exquisite love to her.

"Dane." Her tone was even as she greeted him in return, but her eyes promised him a far warmer greeting when they were alone.

"We had best be going." Dane was eager to collect on that promise. He raised his head and, for the first time since he'd arrived, met George Holt's stare. The older man was watching Dane's reactions to Jacqui with a combination of keen insight and paternal protectiveness. Both of which Dane recognized. He felt a twinge of guilt for what he had planned . . . but only a twinge.

"Shall we?" He offered Jacqui his arm.

Jacqui slid her hand into the crook of his elbow, accepting his arm . . . and all that she suspected went with it. The die had been cast. "Father . . . we'll see you there?"

George gave a definitive nod. "You most certainly shall. I'm on my way now to fetch Monique and then it's off to the Binghams' home." He turned back to Dane, a trace of concern in his eyes. "Take good care of my Jacqui." The message was clear.

"I will," Dane assured him soberly. It was no lie. The method he had chosen was a bit unorthodox, but his final intent was as decent and honorable as any father could wish. "Come, Jacqueline, my coach is waiting."

Dane led Jacqui out of the house, where his liveried driver waited patiently beside a light but elegant coach. Dane instructed his man as to their destination, then assisted Jacqui into the enclosed vehicle, settling himself across from her.

"This is lovely," Jacqui murmured, gliding her hand over the fine upholstery. "I am impressed."

"Don't be." He grinned easily. "At least, not with my carriage."

"Imported directly from England, I presume?" Jacqui asked pointedly.

Dane's grin widened. "Actually, purchased from the Clark Brothers on Chestnut Street right here in Philadelphia. They readied it for me at the same time that they prepared a similar one for President Washington. Anything further you'd like to take exception to, my sweet?"

Jacqui lowered her lashes, her lips curving into a teasing smile. "The night is young, Dane. Perhaps later I shall think of something else we might debate."

Abruptly, Dane moved from his seat to Jacqui's, dragging

her onto his lap. "Fine. But for now, I don't want to argue. In fact, I don't want to talk at all." He buried his hands in her hair, lifting her mouth purposefully to his. "This ride will be far too short for my liking," he muttered against her lips. "I plan to use every minute to my advantage." He caught her bottom lip lightly between his teeth. "Every minute."

He didn't wait for her response, but took her mouth wholly, hungrily, under his. He lifted her small, resisting hands from his chest and wrapped them about his neck, pressing her so close to him that she could scarcely breathe.

Breathing was the last thing on Jacqui's mind. Crushed against the solid wall of Dane's chest, plundered by the demanding pressure of his mouth, she felt surrounded by his power, possessed by the dark, enveloping, sensual allure that drove them together. The slow rocking motion of the carriage lulled her, the illusion of being utterly isolated from the world intoxicated her, and the exhilarating feeling within her built higher and higher . . . the relentless urge to give in to the forbidden taste of what was to come.

Dane tasted his victory. "Let yourself go," he whispered against her trembling mouth. "Just this once, love. Let yourself go." His open mouth slid across her cheek to the side of her neck and up, until Jacqui could feel his hot breath against the shell of her ear. "We're finally alone, *mon chaton,*" he told her, sliding his hands up and down her quivering arms. "We have only a few precious moments. Please, Jacqueline, give in to it. You want more. I know you do . . . I can feel it. Let me give it to you." His mouth returned to hers, urgent, coaxing. "Let me . . ."

Jacqui gave a soft whimper, whether of surrender or protest, she wasn't sure. It didn't matter. She was already sinking into a hypnotic sexual spell, tightening her hold around Dane's neck even as he lowered her to the smooth seat of the carriage. She felt his weight on top of her and it was heaven . . . heaven. Giddy with newfound sensation, she arched her body upward, seeking more contact with this addictive man who held her pleasure in his hands.

Dane had thought he was in control of his passion. He was not.

Feeling Jacqui's soft beauty, even separated from him by layers of clothing, he went taut, desire crashing through his being with the force and intensity of a tidal wave. He tore his mouth from hers, blindly tugging down the sleeves of her gown, kissing her shoulders, her collarbone, the upper swell of her breasts. He said her name in an agonized whisper, slid his hands beneath her, his fingers shaking so badly that he could barely get past the first button of her gown.

He had just managed to free the last of her buttons, his hands gliding inside to touch the warm satin skin of her back, when the carriage came to an abrupt halt.

Lost to everything save the exquisite ecstasy of having Jacqueline beneath him at last, Dane was slow to respond to her urgent plea for him to stop.

"Dane!" The second time Jacqui pounded her fists on his shoulders, frantic with the knowledge that their carriage had arrived at the Binghams' grand mansion and that Dane was making no attempt to release her. "Damn it, Dane, we're here!"

This time her words penetrated his passion-drugged haze. With a low groan of pain, Dane lifted his head, his breathing harsh, his jaw clenched with the discipline of bringing his body under control. He met the startled, vulnerable look in Jacqui's eyes, and all at once nothing mattered but the self-censure, the bitter regret he knew she must be feeling.

"Sweetheart, I'm sorry." He hoisted himself back to a sitting position, appalled at his own lack of restraint or discretion. He had planned to seduce her slowly, gradually, this short coach ride merely the first step toward completion, a skimming of the surface. Instead, he had all but tossed up her skirts and taken her in a five-second frenzy of need. So much for his iron control, his reputation as the consummate lover. Dane scowled, cursing under his breath. He could hear his driver preparing to dismount, and, determined to save Jacqui further embarrassment, Dane hastily drew her up, refastened her buttons, and adjusted her gown. "I'm sorry, love," he repeated softly as he completed his task.

"I'm not."

Dane froze at Jacqui's blunt admission, uttered with absolute candor.

"You're not . . . what?" He must have misunderstood.

Jacqui reached up to rearrange her disheveled curls. She felt marvelous, on the brink of some incomparable sensual discovery; vital, alive. "I'm not sorry," she qualified, tucking the loosened pins back into her thick tresses. She lifted her head and gave Dane a dazzling smile. "It was wonderful, wasn't it?"

Dane stared at her in amazement, hopelessly captivated . . . and, yes . . . wildly aroused, by her startling, uninhibited spontaneity. "Yes, *chaton*," he managed, "it was wonderful. But I was concerned—"

"The Binghams', sir!" the driver called loudly from the other side of the carriage door.

Jacqui flushed. "I believe we have arrived at our destination."

Dane caught her hand, brought it to his mouth. "We are not finished," he told her, his voice raw, his gaze probing her haunting midnight eyes. "In fact, we have barely begun."

Jacqui met his penetrating look without shyness or hesitation, letting her fingers brush the warmth of his lips. "I know," she returned quietly. Then, without another word, she turned to alight from the coach.

Taking a deep, calming breath of the scented June night, Jacqui forced herself to focus on the splendid Bingham residence, its formal gardens running the full length of the ground from Fourth Street to Willing's Alley. Escorted by her father, she had attended but one of the Binghams' renowned balls, but their lavishly decorated home, modeled after that of the Duke of Manchester, was not easily forgotten. Tonight, it was fully lit, bidding entry to scores of powerful and affluent guests.

Not merely guests, Jacqui amended to herself. Federalist guests. It was no secret that Anne Bingham's brand of aristocracy, so close to that of the English nobility, was shunned by most of the Republican party. Even Jefferson, a close friend of the Binghams, was reluctant to attend their glittering, ostentatious gatherings.

Imagine the information one could glean within these dazzling walls tonight.

Driven by that tantalizing thought, Jacqui's composure returned full measure. Her small chin set, she was ready to begin the evening.

It took Dane longer to recover.

Upon joining the party, he felt out of sorts, still aching with unappeased, heightened arousal, wanting nothing more than to make his excuses, drag Jacqui from the room, and take her home to his bed.

Instead, here he was, in the Binghams' fashionably decorated salon, oblivious to the elaborately mirrored parlors and marble hallways that admitted Philadelphia's elite. To Dane, the evening ahead appeared endless.

He did, however, immediately approach their host and take him off to a side.

"Good evening, William." Dane's tone was intense.

"Good evening and welcome, Dane." Always charming and eloquent, William Bingham was, at this moment, highly curious as to the reason for Dane's purposeful expression and the nature of his urgent request to speak with him alone. "I'm delighted that you and Miss Holt could join us tonight."

Dane was in no mood for small talk, not even with Bingham, who was both a good friend and a respected colleague. Immensely successful, the Federalist merchant and land speculator was, in Dane's estimation, a likely candidate for the U.S. Senate.

But despite Dane's high regard for their host, he wasted no time in getting to the point. "I presume you'll soon be drawing lots?"

"Shortly . . . why do you ask?"

"Because I want my number to match Miss Holt's."

Bingham looked astonished, then amused. "I believe that must be left to chance, my friend."

"Not if you choose to intercede." Dane ignored William's knowing smile, glancing around to make sure Jacqui was not in earshot. "William, you are the presiding official of the dance assembly here tonight and are therefore the only one who can . . . make any changes in the drawing procedure."

"Make any changes? Am I to be bribed, then?"

Dane didn't bat an eyelash. "I intend to be the one who dances with Jacqueline Holt."

Now Bingham was openly grinning. Dane's avid pursuit of Jacqueline Holt these past months was no secret. The only unanswered question was, with what degree of success? "I see. And what incentive do you believe would influence me to make these 'changes' for you?" Bingham goaded good-naturedly. "Perhaps *I* will be the one to select Miss Holt's number. I would consider it a great stroke of luck. She is beautiful, intelligent, and—"

"And mine," Dane calmly finished. "Which everyone knows with the exception of Jacqueline. So you see my dilemma."

Bingham laughed. "I do."

"You could provide me with the matching lot as a simple act of friendship," Dane suggested, inclining his head thoughtfully, "or there is always the possibility of discussing my new mare, who I do recall you've admired once or twice. Have I mentioned that she is ready to race?"

Bingham's mouth fell open. "You would *give* me that magnificent horse just to ensure a night of dancing with Jacqueline Holt?" he asked incredulously.

"I prefer to think of it as a trade." Dane's expression took on that familiar predatory look. "I'll do whatever I have to in order to get what I want. And, William, I want Jacqueline Holt." He waited, his steel-gray eyes on his host's face.

The other man shook his head in amazement, then handed Dane the requested folded billet. "You astonish me, Westbrooke. But I do admire your determination." He grinned again. "Keep your mare. I have a feeling that I am about to bear witness to the most exhilarating of competitions right here tonight. I wish you luck."

"And I shall need it." Dane took the billet and gave a thoroughly entertained Bingham a mock salute. *"Merci,* my friend."

Hurrying off to find Jacqui, Dane was most annoyed to discover her being fawned over by a salivating crowd of admirers and trying, unsuccessfully, to extricate herself. With a curt nod and little else in the way of preliminaries, Dane acknowledged the group and then dragged Jacqui with him.

"Who the hell suggested that we attend this party anyway?" he muttered for her ears alone.

Jacqui looked up at him and laughed. "I believe it was you, sir. I warned you of what to expect." Her restless gaze roved the room and she inched away from Dane. "Nevertheless, I thank you most kindly for your gallant rescue. And now, if you will excuse me . . ."

He caught her arm. "Where are you going?"

She raised her chin. "To quote you, 'I am off to accumulate more ammunition for my Republican cause.'"

Dane's disgruntled mood eased a bit. "In other words, you are going to eavesdrop on any number of conversations, then choose the one you wish to interrupt, and do so."

Jacqui looked impatiently about the crowded parlor. "Exactly." She tugged her arm free. "So, if you will permit me, I will take my leave. I haven't much time to immerse myself in enlightening discourse. Before long, lots will be chosen and I will be assigned a partner with whom I must dance." She grimaced. "At which point one of these perfectly intelligent, polished gentlemen you see"—she made a wide sweep of her hand—"will be suddenly transformed into a lecherous, simpering fool, interested only in admiring my charms on the dance floor . . . and sampling them later in the bedroom. After which, all hope for a spirited political discussion will be lost."

Dane tapped his wineglass thoughtfully, his silver eyes twinkling. "A dreadful dilemma, to be sure. But don't give up, my love. Perhaps it will be someone slightly more deserving who has the honor of being paired with you this evening."

Jacqui cast a skeptical glance about the room. *"That* is highly unlikely, given the choices."

"Faith, *mon chaton colereux.* Faith." Dane waved her off with his hand. "Your unsuspecting public awaits."

Drawn by the allure of the night's potential challenge, Jacqui complied, eagerly blending into the crowd, simultaneously reminding herself to be extra cautious about the way she obtained her information.

"I would suggest eliminating that very blatant, suggestive look from your face, Dane. Especially in light of the fact that the young lady in question's father has just arrived."

Dane's gaze darted to the doorway in time to see George Holt make his entrance, a lovely and smiling Monique Brisset on his arm. Chuckling, Dane turned to address the warning voice behind him. "Thank you for your sage words of advice, Alexander. When did you arrive? I never saw you . . . or Betsey, for that matter."

Hamilton smiled, inclining his head slightly. "Indeed? Why does that not surprise me? I don't believe you would have noticed an armed battle taking place right before you . . . not when your attention was so totally consumed with the very lovely Jacqueline Holt."

Dane averted his head to view Jacqui, who had boldly

joined a group of men arguing over what John Jay should hope to accomplish in England. "Jacqueline is nothing if not consuming," he agreed, his voice laced with tenderness and humor.

Hamilton clasped his hands behind his back. "Yes, she appears to be quite a handful," he noted dryly. "Willful, forthright, and most vehement in her political opinions, which, incidentally, are the antithesis of yours. I would watch what I say if I were you, lest you hear your own thoughts spouted back at you before a crowded ballroom."

Dane laughed aloud at the vivid . . . and accurate . . . image Hamilton's words conveyed. He was not offended by his friend's admonition, for Dane understood its basis. Betsey Hamilton was as gentle and malleable a mate as any man could want . . . especially a man like Hamilton. "You are just unused to a headstrong woman, Alexander, nor would you choose to wed one. Jacqueline is quite different from your Betsey."

Giving credence to his words, Jacqui's voice rose clearly to their ears.

"Let us hope that Jay does not concede *too* much to the English. After all, they have lied to us, attacked our ships, and now expect us to compromise to suit their needs!" She paused only to take a breath.

Hamilton winced, shook his head in disbelief. "I do not envy you, Dane. Jacqueline Holt is more than a challenge; she is a brazen little hellion that I doubt even *you* can tame!"

Dane laughed even harder, watching Jacqui with unconcealed pride. He might not share her beliefs, he might question the wisdom of her blunt and forthright vocalizations, but he felt a tremendous respect for her integrity and her commitment, and he gloried in her fervent, genuine love for their country. "Perhaps I cannot tame her," he cheerfully agreed, "but I can certainly enjoy my attempts to do so."

Hamilton counted off Jacqui's vices on his fingers. "She is unconventional, unrestrained, and overly spirited."

"True. But those very traits, while agreeably irritating in politics, do have advantages." Dane's eyes twinkled. "Remember, my friend, how brightly those same passions must burn elsewhere."

Hamilton digested Dane's words carefully. "I don't doubt that is so," he said at last. "I wonder, however, if it is worth the price."

While the words themselves were teasing, something about Hamilton's tone struck Dane as pointed.

"Is that supposed to mean something?" he demanded.

Hamilton studied his friend, then shook his head. "I was merely noting that you seem to be rather taken with the lady."

"I've made that no secret, especially from you."

Hamilton nodded. "True." He cleared his throat. "I wouldn't think a party at the Binghams' home would interest Miss Holt . . . in light of her obviously contrary political beliefs, that is."

The grin returned to Dane's face. "I take credit for Jacqueline's reluctant decision to attend. I appealed to her thirst for information . . . among other things."

Hamilton stiffened. "Meaning?"

Dane shot him a puzzled look. "Meaning that Jacqueline's curiosity won out over her stubbornness. She is a very intelligent young woman who wished to be part of something more substantial than a quilting circle. Hopefully, she also wanted to spend the evening with me . . . which I intend to ensure she does. What on earth is wrong with you tonight?" he asked abruptly.

Hamilton pressed his lips together thoughtfully. "I'm not certain, Dane. But I believe it could be possible that . . ."

"Good evening, Mr. Secretary. It is a pleasure to see you." George Holt interrupted whatever it was Hamilton was going to say. "And good evening again, Dane. Where, may I ask, is Jacqui?"

Dane turned and gestured toward the speechless group of

men who were now being instructed in the *true* causes of France's revolution, Jacqui elaborating on the atrocities committed by the French monarchs. "Your lovely and fiery daughter is holding court," Dane informed him. "Feel free to join her."

George rolled his eyes. "Thank you, no. I believe I've heard this particular argument already." He gave Hamilton an apologetic look. "If you'd like me to speak to her . . ."

"No." It was Dane who answered at once, shaking his head emphatically. Seeing George's surprised look, he added, "Soon numbers will be called and the dancing will commence. After which, I can promise that your daughter will be far too busy to indulge in political debates." He took a sip of his Madeira. "Is Miss Brisset with you tonight?"

George nodded, gesturing toward the corner of the room. "Yes, Monique has joined the ladies. In fact, I did offer to bring her a glass of wine. So if you gentlemen will forgive me . . ."

"Of course," Dane said. Actually, he was not sorry to see George take his leave, for he wanted to speak with Alexander alone. His friend's conduct was most odd tonight; in fact, he'd not said a word the entire time George was present. Highly unusual behavior for a man known for his wit and charm. Not to mention the bizarre turn their own conversation had taken just before George Holt's arrival.

Anxious to resolve the matter, Dane turned to Hamilton, only to realize that he too had moved off. Very strange, Dane mused silently, scanning the salon. When he didn't immediately spot his friend, he decided to let the matter drop for now. There was plenty of time to continue their discussion tomorrow. Tonight, Dane had something else on his mind.

"Jacqueline."

Inwardly, Jacqui groaned, recognizing not only her father's voice, but his quiet, no-nonsense tone. She stepped away from the gaping group of gentlemen and turned to

103

receive her lecture. "Yes, Father?" She gave him her most winsome smile.

This time it didn't work.

George Holt was shaking his head emphatically from side to side. "Do not attempt to divert me . . . it won't help. Now that you have educated the entire Federalist party in the proper way to run a country, do you think you might control yourself a bit? If nothing else, you are calling a great deal of attention to both of us."

Jacqui studied her father's expression, which revealed nothing of what his words might imply. Was she just imagining the warning note she heard?

Countless times over the past year Jacqui had found herself wondering if her father suspected she was Jack Laffey; countless times she had actually considered broaching the subject with him. But always something had stopped her. And that something was the fear that, if she were wrong and her father were totally unaware of the truth, her telling him could do naught but cause friction between them. Because Jacqui knew, beyond the shadow of a doubt, that even if her father should forbid her from penning her column, she would not obey him. Her principles would not permit it.

She took a deep breath. "I apologize, Father. I didn't mean to cause you any embarrassment."

"There is much more than embarrassment at stake, Jacqui, and I believe you know it."

Jacqui's head came up and she met her father's pointed gaze. A current of communication ran between them. *He knows,* she thought, worried and relieved all at once. *He must know.* Keeping her features carefully schooled, she nodded. "Yes, Father," was all she said. But she sensed that her underlying meaning was not lost to George, who smiled his approval and guided her over to greet Monique.

But it also was not lost to the Secretary of the Treasury, who stood, silent and undetected, close beside them. Thoughtfully, Hamilton watched father and daughter move into the crowd as he cautiously digested the cryptic conversation he had just overheard.

He would speak to Dane on Monday, although he had no proof to uphold his suspicions. All he had was his instinct.

But his instinct was rarely wrong.

"Jacqueline, how stunning you look!" Monique Brisset's smile was sunny as she greeted George's daughter . . . a smile that didn't quite reach her eyes.

"Thank you," Jacqui acknowledged graciously. Out of respect for her father, she was always courteous to Monique, despite the Frenchwoman's subtly conveyed antipathy for Jacqui. It was as if Monique sensed Jacqui's ability to see through her loving facade and despised her for it. Time after frustrating time Jacqui was tempted to alert George to Monique's insincerity, to shake him into seeing Monique for the hypocrite she really was. But she loved her father dearly, and George loved Monique with all the intensity of a schoolboy. So Jacqui kept her silence.

"You look very lovely as well, Monique," she added politely.

"That is only because I am on the arm of the most handsome of men." Monique squeezed George's hand.

He chuckled, then gestured toward the front of the salon, where Bingham had begun calling numbers. "Your delightful praise comes at the very worst of times," he teased tenderly. "Since I must soon relinquish you to the arms of another man."

Jacqui's heart sank as she wondered which dreadful male she herself would be saddled with for the duration of the ball. Automatically, she searched the room for Dane. Her heart sank as she saw him chatting with Anne Bingham. Apparently they had been paired together and were ready to begin the first set.

The musicians were tuning their instruments, and Jacqui used that time to slip out of the salon, through the hallway, and into the warm night. She had but a minute or two before she had to return and endure the remainder of the evening, but she could at least enjoy a breath of air until the dancing commenced.

Out of the corner of his eye, Dane saw Jacqui disappear. "Forgive me, Anne, but I must go and claim my partner. Evidently, she did not hear her number called."

Anne Bingham's lovely eyes glittered. "Why do I believe that your chance pairing with Jacqueline Holt had little to do with coincidence?" she mused aloud.

Dane's look was pure innocence. "It could be nothing but fate, I assure you, madam." He gave her a slow wink and bent over to kiss her hand. "Until later, my lovely hostess."

"Of course." Anne gave him a glowing smile and gestured grandly toward the salon door. "Go and claim your lady."

Dane's expression grew intense. "Oh, I intend to, Anne. I intend to."

Jacqui was just where Dane had guessed she'd be: in the gardens, as far from the merriment as possible.

He came up behind her. "The musicians have begun, *mon chaton*. Shall we?"

Jacqui turned, startled. "Shall we . . . what?"

His eyes twinkled. "Ah, the answers I could give! But for now, all I want is to dance with you."

Jacqui sighed. "Dane, that is impossible . . . at least for tonight."

He looked mildly surprised. "And why is that?"

She made an exasperated sound. "Because your number was called with Anne Bingh . . ." She broke off as Dane extended his arm and opened his hand. On his broad palm lay a piece of paper . . . with her number on it. "You were saying?" he inquired pleasantly.

"How did you do it?" she demanded.

"Do what?"

"Damn you, Dane Westbrooke! How did you—"

"Does it matter?"

Their eyes met and she fell silent.

"No," she said at last, in a small voice.

Dane took her arm gently. "Good." He drew her to him. "Then shall we go in and dance? Or would you prefer to remain out here and finish where we left off in the coach?"

He saw the indecision in her eyes and stroked her cheek slowly with his fingertip. "We can have both," he told her quietly. "Dancing now . . . and each other later. How would that be?"

Jacqui nodded wordlessly and allowed him to lead her back into the salon.

After that, the evening passed on clouds of pleasure. Suggestive words, subtle caresses, and hushed conversation accompanied each breathless dance, deepening the sensual spell that held them in its web of enchantment. Jacqui and Dane moved together with a naturalness that neither of them could ignore and neither wanted to deny.

And each moment that passed led them closer to the dark magic they knew lay ahead.

The Holts' sitting room was cast in shadows when they entered.

"Your father?" Dane prompted softly.

"Father will spend some time with Monique before he returns home," she said as tactfully as she could.

Dane nodded, understanding her meaning. "Greta?"

". . . will be asleep." Jacqui crossed the room and lit a small lamp on the table beside the settee. She turned at the firm click of the sitting-room door as it shut.

Dane leaned back against the closed door, looking dark and predatory in the shadowy room. Their eyes met in the flickering light.

"Would you like a drink?" Jacqui felt suddenly and inexplicably nervous.

"No."

"Something to eat?"

"No."

She swallowed. "Perhaps . . ."

"No," Dane interrupted. Slowly, he walked over to her,

placed his strong hands on the gentle curve of her shoulders. "What I want . . ." he said in a husky whisper, "is you."

Jacqui tilted her head back and her eyes slid shut, anticipation coursing through her in wide rivers of sensation. Her heart pounded furiously as she felt Dane swallow her in his embrace, possess her within the circle of his arms. She had expected this, had known from the first that this whole night was leading up to it. And, with a great sigh of elation, she welcomed it.

Dane's hair felt like thick silk beneath Jacqui's questing fingers, his body a towering force of elegant fabric over steely muscle, crushed against her willing body. She heard the rustle of satin as he lifted her small frame off the floor with effortless ease, inhaled his wonderful, masculine scent as he molded her soft curves to his hardened contours. His mouth opened over hers with near punishing strength, forcing her head back to his shoulder, branding her with the plunging, primitive thrusts of his tongue, the echoing motion of his hips. Jacqui responded like a wild thing, her tongue tangling with his, her body instinctively cushioning his hardness, the action sending an answering pool of moisture to converge between her thighs.

Torrents of raw sensation pulsed through Dane's blood, a madness so stark it obliterated everything in its path. Without thought or reason, he carried Jacqui the short distance to the settee, dropping with her onto the rich purple and gold brocade.

Her buttons were dispensed with in seconds, the costly gown tugged down to her waist. The straps of her chemise followed, and at last, Dane feasted his eyes on a portion of the lush, perfect body that beckoned him with every heartbeat.

"Jacqui . . ." His voice sounded hoarse, strained with need, his silver eyes turned smoky gray, hot with passion.

Jacqui had no time to think or react. Dane's mouth was on her breasts, tugging, tasting, sending wild jolts of energy through her with each hard pull of his lips. She couldn't help it . . . she cried out, overwhelmed by the breathtaking splendor that jolted through her at a blinding pace. Dane responded to her muted cry with hushed, erotic words; love words that only served to fuel the flames higher . . . higher.

Dane buried his mouth in the fragrant hollow between Jacqui's breasts, rubbing his face slowly from side to side, inhaling the sweet floral scent of her perfume. He couldn't get enough. Never enough. "So sweet . . . so soft . . . so perfect," he murmured against her hot skin. He lowered himself beside her, wrapping one hand in her hair and using the other to draw her to him. "Kiss me," he commanded, taking her mouth at the same time.

Jacqui responded instantly, opening her mouth to accept his tongue, whimpering with pleasure when his hand slid up her back and around to cup her breast. She quivered at the contact, then cried out as his thumb glided slowly back and forth across her hardened nipple, again and again, until she thought she would die from sheer bliss. "Dane . . ." she breathed, "that feels so . . ."

"I know," he answered against her mouth. "I know, darling. Just keep feeling . . . keep responding to my touch. That's right, love, like that . . . like that." He kept kissing her, hot, drugging kisses that dragged her deeper and deeper under his sensual spell, until all she could do was cling to him and moan.

Dane felt her move against him, arching her breast more fully into his hungry palm. Of its own accord, his other hand left her hair, gliding down her arm, across the bunched material of her gown, over her slender hip and lower. He gathered handfuls of the rich satin and lifted it up and out of his way, until his fingers met the smooth silk of her stocking. Without pause, his hand slid up her leg, caressing, stroking, seeking more. All the while his mouth continued its relentless assault, breathing her name with each penetrating kiss.

They both tensed when his hand reached the warm, bare

skin of her inner thigh. Jacqui tore her mouth from his, her breath coming in short, hard pants, her eyes glazed with passion. "Dane?" she whispered in hushed uncertainty.

"Sh-h-h, let me," he answered, massaging her breast, his thumb moving against her nipple even as his other hand crept higher . . . higher. "Just let me touch you . . . let me show you." He brushed her lips softly with his. "Don't be afraid, *mon chaton.* I'd never hurt you. I just want to love you." His hand moved that last tantalizing inch to claim the warm wetness between her legs. "Jacqui . . . let me love you." His demand ended in a harsh growl, his breath forced from his chest in a rush. Nothing had prepared him for this moment, this shattering feeling that erupted in his soul. He listened to Jacqui's sharp cry of pleasure, watched her eyes widen with ungovernable sensation, and knew he was lost. He had never held a woman, never touched a woman, never loved a woman before this night. No other woman could feel this soft, this incredibly warm, this velvety wet.

Overcome with emotion, Dane drew Jacqui close, feeling her tremble against him as he gently stroked her delicate swelling flesh. He closed his eyes, all thought concentrated beneath his caressing fingertips, wondering who was more profoundly affected . . . he or she.

"Dane . . ." As if she had read his mind, Jacqui caught at his shoulders, the swamping sensations suddenly more than she could bear.

He bent to taste his name on her lips, drowning in the midnight blue of her eyes. "Feel . . ." he murmured softly, "feel me, my love. Feel your body awaken to my touch. Feel how right we are together. Just feel . . . and know that this is but the beginning." With his words, he slowly entered her with his fingers, immersed himself in the very essence of her, only to withdraw just as slowly and repeat the motion.

"Oh . . . God . . ." Jacqui arched upward instinctively, alive and afraid as she had never been. "Dane . . . stop . . . I can't . . ."

He heard her frightened protest, felt her struggling, and he shook his head, gentling her with his kiss. "No, darling, don't fight it. Don't fight me. Let yourself go." He slid his fingers deeper inside her, stroking the sensitive bud of her passion with the pad of his thumb. "I'll catch you," he promised in a forbidden whisper, feeling her nails dig into his coat. "I won't let you fall. I promise. Jacqui . . ." He could feel her inner muscles tighten, knew she was close. And he wanted this for her, wanted it desperately. "Let it happen, sweetheart. Let it happen."

He felt her peak even before she called out his name, and he silenced her cry with his mouth, cradling her close, sharing in the glory of her climax. Reveling in the hard spasms that gripped his fingers, Dane was suffused by joy and tenderness and a profound sense of pride that he was the first, the only man, who would ever share this intimacy with her. The elation of this absolute knowledge, together with the ecstasy of experiencing Jacqui's newly awakened passion, was so acute that Dane's own rampaging desire, though excruciatingly intense, became insignificant.

He waited until the final tremors had subsided, until she was limp and still in his arms, before he lifted his head, looked tenderly into her stunned, sated eyes. "I love you, Jacqueline Holt," he told her quietly. "And all I want right now is to have you under me, wrapped around me, surrounding me with your warmth, your softness." He hardened at his own words, the image they conveyed. "I want that more than you will ever know." He shook his head, pressed his forefinger to her lips when she tried to speak. Very gently, he smoothed down her skirts, rebuttoned the back of her gown, and eased away from her. "When you want that as much as I do, come to me. Come to me, *mon chaton colereux,* and I promise you . . . I'll make love to you until there's not a doubt in the world that you belong to me." He kissed her lightly, smiling a bit at the dazed expression still on her face. "You're mine, Jacqueline," he whispered. "You always will be."

CHAPTER

8

Dane strode down Chestnut Street, a besotted smile on his face.

Under normal circumstances, he would have been troubled by the unusually ominous tone of Alexander's terse message, the urgency of the Secretary's command to see Dane first thing Monday morning. Not to mention the fact that the summons had been delivered on a Sunday, a rarity indeed. Yes, this uncustomary occurrence would typically cause Dane great concern.

But today was the Monday after the Binghams' ball. And Dane had done nothing but smile since Saturday night.

The memory of Jacqui's first climax, the shimmering culmination she had found beneath his coaxing caresses, still made Dane ache with a poignant sort of tenderness he had never known existed until now. Lust . . . the urgent need for sexual satisfaction . . . *that* he had experienced time and again. But a bottomless desire for only one woman . . . a desire that wrapped itself around his heart, clawed at his soul; longing this acute was a stranger to him. And longing, coupled with a fierce swell of protectiveness and a raw vulnerability that only a promise of forever could alleviate; emotion as profound as this humbled him.

112

So this was love.

Dane tried, for the hundredth time, to imagine how Jacqui was feeling, what she was thinking. No doubt she was confused, overwhelmed, torn by what had happened between them.

On fire for more.

The latter was what Dane was counting on. Knowing his passionate Jacqui, he was willing to bet that, having had but a tiny taste of forbidden fruit, she would be addicted to its sweetness, to its intoxicating flavor. Eventually, despite the internal battles he was sure she would suffer, her driving hunger and her curiosity would compel her to take another bite.

No, Jacqui would not relinquish her freedom or herself without a valiant struggle, Dane acknowledged as he knocked at Hamilton's door.

But, fight though she would, she didn't stand a chance.

"Come in, Dane," Hamilton called out. He greeted his friend soberly, lines of worry beside his eyes. "Please sit down."

Dane shot him a curious look and eased himself into a chair. "What is it, Alexander? Does this emergency meeting concern whatever it was you began to tell me at the Binghams'?"

"It does."

Dane's sixth sense stirred, issuing a warning. "I'm listening."

Hamilton sat down heavily, clasping his hands on the desk and frowning down at his laced fingers. Whatever he had to say, he wasn't happy. "It concerns our search for Jack Laffey."

Dane leaned forward. "You've found him?"

"Possibly. I don't know. I have no proof," Hamilton said cautiously.

"Who?" It was a demand, uncluttered by tact.

Hamilton met Dane's directness with his own. "George Holt."

"George Holt?" Dane recoiled as if he'd been punched. Rapidly, his steel-trap mind recounted the events of the past months, every function he had attended at which Holt had been present, and, finally, the contents of the last few Laffey columns. Frowning, he shook his head. "It doesn't fit, Alexander. The details of Laffey's column just after your Long Room gathering, for example, included specific quotes that Holt could *not* have heard. He was nowhere near us during most of that evening."

"But his daughter was."

Dane stared. "What are you saying?"

"I'm saying that it is very possible, given Holt's political inclinations, his social opportunities . . . his daughter's sudden interest in you that—"

Dane bolted to his feet. "What the hell is that supposed to mean?"

Hamilton studied his friend quietly. He had expected Dane's anger, his denial. But the raw emotion on his face . . . the immediate leap to her defense; Dane's feelings for Jacqueline Holt had gone far deeper than even the Secretary had guessed.

"I'm saying," Hamilton answered, "that I overheard a conversation between George and Jacqueline Holt on Saturday night that leads me to believe—"

"I'm not going to listen to this." Dane was on his way to the door.

"Not even if I'm right?"

Alexander's words stopped him in his tracks. Slowly, he turned back. "What evidence do you have?"

"Very little. Only that conversation, Miss Holt's sudden and profound attachment to you, and my own suspicions."

"That's not enough."

"True. All I ask is that you hear me out."

"Fine." Dane remained at the door, his rigid stance making his feelings quite clear.

Hamilton sighed. This was going to be even more difficult

114

than he thought, but Dane had to be forewarned. For if, in fact, George Holt was Laffey, and if Jacqueline was aiding him in obtaining his information, Dane would have to be on guard.

Quietly, the Secretary repeated the exchange he had overheard between Jacqui and George on Saturday night, as well as its undertone . . . the unspoken communication between father and daughter. He then enumerated his own logical sequence of thoughts: George's subdued but intrinsic allegiance to the Republican cause, his pro-French ideas, his friendships and business dealings with both Federalists and Republicans alike, and his ability to appear at functions given by both party members. And his avidly, vocally, pro-Republican daughter, who just happened to burst into Dane's life at the same time that a fresh surge of accusatory columns, penned by Jack Laffey, had appeared in the *General Advertiser.*

"This is pure speculation on your part, Alexander." A muscle worked furiously in Dane's jaw. "I don't like your implication that I am being used."

"I like it even less. And you're quite right . . . all that I suspect could be entirely untrue. I ask only that you consider what I've said . . . and that you keep it in mind as you mull over recent events." He took a deep breath. "Dane, I have successfully eliminated every other person on our guest list as a possible suspect. So let's go on from there. Can you really deny Jacqueline's obvious political biases? From whom do you think she acquired her vehement opinions? She is young and unable to mask her impassioned beliefs. Her father is older . . . more practiced . . . and possibly more covert. He has also been present, though ofttimes unobtrusively, at every function that Laffey has managed to infiltrate. And my intuition tells me . . ." He hesitated, seeing the doubt, the pained reluctance on Dane's face. They both knew just how accurate Hamilton's instincts were.

"I'm not suggesting that you stop seeing her, Dane." Alexander tried desperately to soften his accusation. "Only that you be cautious. Guard your thoughts, your words. . . ." He paused. "Your feelings," he added gently.

Dane shot him a grim look. "I'm afraid it's far too late for that," he replied. He reached for the door, wanting nothing save solitude for himself and his thoughts. "I've heard what you had to say, Alexander. I pray, this once, that your instincts prove false."

Dane barely remembered the walk to Westbrooke Shipping. His head reeled with the impact of Alexander's words and his own uncertainty. George Holt . . . Jack Laffey. Could it be?

Yes, it definitely could. George Holt had the access, the political connections, the opportunity. But the accomplice?

A jolt of betrayal tore through Dane as he contemplated the possibility that Jacqueline's very new, yet rapidly escalating feelings for him could be anything but genuine. He forced himself to consider the idea rationally. True, Jacqueline had stayed by his side all evening the first night they'd met . . . albeit reluctantly. Their courtship had been fast and furious . . . and filled with volatile political debates. She made no secret of her loyalties, nor of her overt curiosity at attending . . . and interrupting . . . Federalist functions. All of this could well be for the exact reasons Alexander had just stated . . . to gain information for her father.

But the way she responds in my arms, Dane remembered with an involuntary wave of tenderness. It was magic, it was real, and it belonged only to them. Dane shook his head adamantly, staring at the ground as he walked, seeing her face. The midnight eyes that darkened with desire, the softly parted lips that reached for his, the flawless, flushed cheeks that burned with everything she was feeling, thinking, needing. *No.*

Jacqui could never feign the emotions so helplessly revealed to Dane by the trembling of her small, lush body when he stroked her, bared her to his hungry eyes and hands. Dane was a worldly man. He knew honest passion when he saw it, felt it, tasted it. Just as he knew when a woman was deceiving him.

But most of all, he knew Jacqueline Holt.

She was all that Alexander said she was. But a liar? Never. Perhaps George was guilty. But Jacqui was not.

Dane slammed the office door behind him and rubbed his throbbing temples. For a day that had begun with joy and promise, it had deteriorated into a bloody mess.

"My, you look positively threatening, darling. Have I come at a bad time?" The slim, raven-haired woman rose gracefully, a questioning look on her lovely face.

Dane blinked in surprise. He hadn't expected anyone to be here, for no one was permitted in his office during his absence. With one exception.

With a warm grin, he walked over and kissed the exception soundly on the cheek, then wrapped her in a hug. "No, love, you haven't come at a bad time. Actually, you're just the one I needed to see."

The sole woman who could see beyond Dane's fatal charm stepped back and gave her only son a quick, knowing appraisal. "Just the one you needed to see? Why don't I believe that?" Lenore Westbrooke teased. "From the gossip that's been reaching me way out in the country, I fear that my position as the only constant woman in your life is being threatened." Seeing Dane's scowl, she laughed. "By your reaction, I assume it's true."

"Gossip certainly travels fast, doesn't it?" Dane opened a walnut cabinet and proceeded to pour himself an unusually early drink. "Would you like one?"

"Goodness, no, it's barely ten o'clock!" She watched him carefully. "As for the gossip, there is not exactly an ocean between us, Dane. The estate is but an hour's drive from the city. It's only natural for people to tell me when my son,

Philadelphia's most handsome, most sought-after bachelor, is being seen consistently and attentively by the side of one woman."

Dane turned to face her abruptly. "I don't want to discuss Jacqueline with you, Mother. Not yet."

Lenore's brows rose. "My . . . this *does* sound serious." She held her hands up to ward off his scathing reply. "Never mind; I won't ask anything more," she quickly assured him. She had learned, long ago, never to interfere in her son's life. He made his own decisions, planned his own future. They were much alike, the two of them, and both had to walk their own paths. Sadly, however, their mutual trait of independence, while necessary to their integrity, had cost them . . . dearly.

With quiet compassion, Lenore scrutinized Dane's tired, handsome face from beneath lashes as thick and dark as her son's. "However," she gently qualified, "should you wish to talk . . . I'm here."

"I know." Dane drained his glass, then placed it on the desk. "Are you well?" he asked. "I'd planned to get out to Greenhills before now, but I've been . . . preoccupied."

"I understand. I am just fine." She dimpled. "Quite busy, in fact."

Dane groaned. He knew that look. "What are you up to, Mother?"

"I've taken over many of the household chores."

"Chores? What chores?"

Lenore gave a careless shrug. "Oh, the usual. Marketing, a bit of cooking, exercising a few of the horses . . ."

"Where the hell are the servants?" Dane exploded. His expansive pillared mansion, Greenhills, nestled in a wooded area on the banks of the Schuylkill River, had over a dozen servants to manage its upkeep, to tend to Lenore's needs, and to keep her company in her often self-imposed isolation. Dane visited as frequently as he could, but he himself preferred to dwell in his more modest city residence, with but one manservant and close proximity to Westbrooke Shipping.

"The servants?" Lenore questioned brightly. "Oh, they're all with me. They each have a specified task, for which they are handsomely paid at week's end. Did I mention to you that I have been dabbling at the household accounts? That is another of my list of tasks . . . which, I might add, I perform superbly. I can now proudly boast that the servants and I work side by side, that Greenhills is run efficiently, and, most important, without any class distinction."

"Mother . . ."

Lenore raised her chin in a gesture that, between Jacqui and his mother, Dane was beginning to despise. "How can we speak out against slavery when, with our antiquated indentured-servant structure and horridly poor level of compensation, we are doing little better than keeping slaves ourselves?"

Dane listened to her fervent tirade and began to chuckle. "Mother, I believe I've changed my mind. I think you should meet Jacqueline after all. I have a strong feeling that the two of you are going to get along famously."

Lenore's face lit up, making her look aeons younger than her forty-nine years. "I would love to meet your Jacqueline!"

Her pointedly possessive reference to Jacqui as *his* was not lost to Dane. But he chose not to address the issue. "Good. I'll make arrangements for Jacqueline and I to come to Greenhills for dinner next week." Humor danced in his eyes. "Will you be cooking?"

Lenore gave him a challenging look. "Did you think I was incapable?"

"Mother, I think you are capable of almost anything," he answered affectionately. "Including exasperating me beyond belief. With both you and Jacqueline in my life, I fear any hope for a peaceful existence is eternally lost."

"Eternally?" she questioned quickly.

"Mother." Dane's tone was firm. The subject of his feelings for Jacqui was, indeed, closed.

Lenore coughed delicately, bracing herself for Dane's reaction to the next forbidden topic. "I received a letter from your father yesterday."

Dane stiffened and abruptly turned away. "Really." A long pause. "How is he?"

"Involved with his businesses and with the running of Forsgate." A flicker of sadness crossed her face. "Getting older, somewhat lonelier . . ."

"But no less obstinate," Dane finished with icy sarcasm.

"Dane, you know I share your views and your feelings. But try to understand—"

"I can't," Dane shot back. "We've been over this and over this dozens of times in the last decade, Mother. Circumstances are no different than they were the day we left England. The man is stubborn, willful, and opinionated."

"Like his son?"

"No, damn it, not like his son. I lead a life I can be proud of."

"As he is proud of his."

"Well, I find it impossible to condone a hierarchy that gives a man superiority over others based solely upon his title. A title, I might add, that is his from birth. At least in America a man must earn his rank and the respect of others."

"I just hate to see you so bitter," Lenore said softly, placing her hand on Dane's taut arm. She had prayed, after an eleven-year separation, that the bad blood between Dane and Edwin Westbrooke would have diminished. She herself had been heartbroken by her necessary, yet painful, breach with her husband, but she had endured, and for her, the years since their parting had helped dull the hurt to a passive acceptance of differences that even time and separation could not heal. But Dane was just as angry today as he had been at twenty-one, when he stormed from Forsgate . . .

and all it symbolized . . . for a life that, to him, represented decency and honor and, to his father, represented blasphemy.

"I'm not bitter, Mother," Dane was responding. "Merely resigned."

Lenore sighed, nodding her understanding. How could she argue with Dane when her motives had been—still were—much the same as her son's? She loved Edwin, had loved him since she'd been little more than a child. But, despite her love, she was no longer the impressionable and adoring sixteen-year-old girl he had wed thirty-three years ago. Somewhere in the process of her growth and maturation she had become a very strong woman with beliefs that were the antithesis of her husband's. Lenore needed her own voice, and Edwin, unyielding in his opinions of a wife and marchioness's proper role, refused to allow it to her. Finally, she had been compelled to seize it herself. So, in 1783, she and her embittered son had sailed for America . . . alone.

"Mother?" Dane's concerned voice broke into Lenore's reverie.

She squeezed his hand. "If I were to spend the morning in the city, would you have time for lunch?"

The charming smile returned to Dane's face. "For you . . . I always have time."

Lenore smiled back. "Good. Then I shall do some shopping. And Dane," she added, "I really am looking forward to meeting Jacqueline. She must be a very unique woman."

Dane nodded, nearly laughing aloud. Unique? Yes, Jacqueline was that. And Lord knew what else. His insides knotted as he recalled what had been plaguing him earlier. He needed to see Jacqueline . . . and soon.

Jacqui hadn't slept a wink since Saturday.

Both nights she'd lain in bed, tossing and turning . . . and burning; hearing Dane's dark promises, feeling his exhilarating caresses on her most intimate flesh. Again and again she relived that staggering explosion of pleasure that erupted inside her at the last.

So this was the wondrous act that people whispered about, lived for, died for, longed for. So this was where the wanting actually led.

I love you, Jacqueline Holt. Dane's declaration drifted through Jacqui's thoughts again.

She was not fool enough to believe that the tenderly whispered words had been motivated by anything more than passion. Nor did she want them to be. But the invitation that lay beyond the words, the sensual enticement that danced like live flames in Dane's silvery-gray eyes, called to Jacqui like a siren's song, luring her to fulfill their heated vow.

Oh, how she wanted him. Over her, inside her . . . teaching her all she ached to know, all his powerful body could give.

Dane was right, damn him. What he had prophesied would indeed occur. She would go to him. She would join herself to him until the bone-melting ecstasy had played itself out. After which she would be whole, sated, wise in the answers she sought.

But Dane was wrong about one thing.

She would never belong to him.

Her mind made up, Jacqui dressed quickly in a gown of pale peach, which made her look soft and feminine and, hopefully, desirable. She then tied a bonnet beneath her chin and hastened off into the warm June day, bent on seduction.

Westbrooke Shipping was on Market Street, a healthy walk from the Holts' home. Jacqui hurried along, not pausing to catch her breath until she neared the docks. Dane's office was just beside them, a modest brick building with large, airy windows. Cautiously, Jacqui approached, uncertain, now that she was here, of how to go about announcing to Dane that she had come to take him up on his offer. From inside the open windows, laughing voices drifted out to her, and with her usual curiosity, Jacqui peered inside. And froze.

Dane was teasing and hugging an attractive dark-haired woman, who was, in turn, clutching him possessively and ruffling his hair. She appeared to be of middle years, but was nonetheless quite striking.

Jacqui felt ill.

Before she could be seen, she retraced her steps, running nearly all the way home. The delicate filaments of trust, newly formed and fragile, splintered further with each step.

Tears were unacceptable. Jacqui chose anger.

How stupid could she have been? she fumed. To actually think that what Dane wanted, needed, was *her*. When, in fact, any female body would do, had apparently *been* doing, if what she'd seen today was any example. Abstinence was, quite obviously, not even a consideration in Dane's mind. Nor was faithfulness.

She should have known better than to allow herself to care.

Jacqui spent the day in her room, alternately pacing, cursing, and planning Dane's demise. She called a halt to her internal tirade only long enough to finish Laffey's column, which had to be delivered that night, and to eat dinner, so Greta wouldn't be suspicious.

Just after dusk, Jacqui slipped into a dark gown, slid the column inside her sleeve, and headed down the stairs. It was not a pleasant night for her weekly mission, as a severe summer storm was about to strike. The winds had picked up and occasional bolts of lightning streaked across the hot, humid skies.

As Jacqui moved down the deserted hallway, she could hear Greta finishing up in the kitchen and scolding Whiskey, who had sprung onto the counter to sample the leftovers. George was working late. Jacqui wouldn't be missed.

She opened the front door and walked headlong into Dane.

"Hello, *chaton,*" he said in an odd voice. "Were you on your way out? I wouldn't suggest it . . . there is a bad storm brewing."

Jacqui blinked and hot color rose to her cheeks. How dare he come here tonight . . . after what she'd witnessed! *"You* wouldn't suggest it?" she spat. "What I do is none of your business! So get out of my way!"

Dane started. He had not known what to expect from her after Saturday night, had not even been certain of his own actions after all he had learned today. But this?

He caught her elbows as she attempted to walk past him. "Jacqueline . . . what is it?"

She threw back her head, her eyes flashing midnight fire. "I don't wish to discuss it . . . or anything else . . . with you, Dane. Now let me pass!"

She was exquisite in her rage. All the warmth and tenderness Dane had tried to suppress churned through him. It was no use.

He dragged her back against him. "You're angry at me."

"And you are a scholar."

He chuckled. "Care to tell me why?"

"No, actually I don't."

He lifted her up until their faces were level. "Is it because of Saturday . . . of what happened between us?"

Jacqui's flush deepened. "Nothing happened between us. For that you'll have to go to one of your other paramours."

"My other paramours?"

"Please don't pretend. If nothing else, be honest with me, damn you!"

Dane looked genuinely puzzled. "I have always been honest with you, love. I have no idea what you're talking about. I haven't even *seen* another woman since you and I met."

Jacqui bristled. "Not even today?"

"Today?"

"I saw you, you bastard! I saw you with her! Kissing

124

her . . . holding her!" She pounded on his shoulders with her fists. "Don't make it worse by lying to me!"

Dane made no move to still Jacqui's flailing wrists. He simply carried her back into the house, through to the sitting room, and sat down on the settee, placing her on his lap as she battled frantically to free herself.

"Now," Dane said calmly, ignoring her struggles, "what is this all about? What woman did you see me with that I was supposedly kissing?"

Jacqui paused to catch her breath. "Let me refresh your memory, *Mister* Westbrooke. A mature woman . . . lovely dark hair . . . tastefully dressed . . . in your office this morning?" She saw understanding dawn on Dane's face and continued. "I see you are beginning to remember. Good. Do you also recall kissing her?"

"I do." Dane grinned. "Several times, in fact."

Jacqui's jaw dropped. "You admit it?"

Dane's smile widened. "Certainly. What I don't understand is what *you* were doing at Westbrooke Shipping. Dare I hope that you came to see me?"

Mortified, Jacqui recalled the reason she had gone to Dane's office. "It doesn't matter."

"It does to me." He couldn't help himself; he kissed her. Her *very* real, *very* artless jealousy enthralled him . . . for several reasons.

Jacqui dragged her mouth away. "How dare you?"

"Do you want to know who she is, Jacqueline?" he asked softly, bringing her lips back to his.

Jacqui shook her head wildly. "I assume she is merely one in a long line of your *women* . . . the wife of a business associate, perhaps?"

"My mother," he murmured against her warm cheek. "And there is no long line of women . . . there is only you."

Jacqui grew very still. "Your mother?"

Dane laughed softly, gliding his thumbs up and down the silky column of her throat. "I do have one, you know."

"Your mother," she repeated again, feeling like a complete fool. "I had no idea your mother lived in Philadelphia."

"There is much about me you don't know," he whispered, pressing her into the cushions and following her down. "Let me teach you."

Jacqui took his kiss blindly, opening her mouth to his tongue and lifting her arms to wrap about his neck.

Inside her sleeve, she felt the papers rustle against her skin and reality flooded back in a great, untamed wave.

"Dane . . . not now!" She shoved him away and wriggled out from under him.

"Why? Don't you believe what I've told you?"

"Yes, I believe you." Nervously, she rose, fixing her sleeves and smoothing down her gown. "But Greta is in the kitchen and my father is due home from work any moment. This is hardly the time . . ."

He stood and took her in his arms. "Tell me you've thought about what happened Saturday. Here"—he glanced meaningfully at the settee—"in my arms. Under my body, my hands."

"I have," she admitted in a small voice.

"So have I. Constantly." He gazed down at her, his eyes dark with emotion. "Did you also think about what I said . . . about your coming to me?"

"Yes."

"And?" He lifted her hands to his shoulders and Jacqui froze, feeling the papers slide up to her elbow.

"Dane, you have to leave."

He looked stunned. "Why?"

"Because . . . you must. I have things I need to take care of, right away."

"What things?"

Jacqui thought frantically. "I need to help Greta in the kitchen."

"Haven't you eaten? It's almost eight o'clock."

"No . . . yes . . . I mean, she needs my help in straightening up."

"I see."

"So you'll have to go." She was already tugging him toward the door.

"When will I see you?"

"Soon. Tomorrow," she hastened to add when she saw the glower on his face.

"Tomorrow," he repeated. "And every day thereafter."

In that instant Jacqui would have promised him the world if he would only leave. She was already going to be dreadfully late. . . . She only prayed her young messenger would still be waiting. "Yes, Dane. And every day thereafter," she vowed.

Dane's eyes narrowed on her, like a tiger sizing up its prey. Then he nodded. "Very well. I'll go." He kissed her lightly. "But I'll be back, Jacqueline. Tomorrow. Always. Remember."

She shut the door behind him and let out her breath. That had been close . . . too close.

She waited a full five minutes and then slipped out into the night.

The rain poured down in torrents.

Jacqui caught her breath, feeling her saturated gown mold itself uncomfortably to her chilled skin.

The rain wasn't terribly cold, but the air was so hot that the water felt icy as it struck her in relentless sheets. Thunder crashed through the heavens, heralded by the jagged streaks of lightning that pierced the skies and shot precariously close to the soggy ground.

Jacqui wiped the rain from her eyes and inhaled sharply. Thank goodness the storm had held out until her papers were safely delivered and she was well on her way home. She was now but a few blocks from her house, but the area between here and Spruce Street was lined with trees, the perfect targets for wayward lightning bolts. The last thing she needed was to be assaulted by a heavy falling branch.

The alternative was to use the roadway. Jacqui had never even considered that in the past, for fear of being seen, but who would be about in this downpour to witness her flight?

Hurriedly, she moved toward Spruce Street, staying along the road's edge, but as far from the trees as possible. She was getting quite a soaking, but it was better than being hurt.

Most of the houses were dark, their occupants abed, as it was close to ten o'clock. Sidestepping a puddle, Jacqui ran on, suddenly wondering what Dane would be doing now. Would he be asleep . . . or awake . . . possibly thinking of her?

She had certainly been thinking of him . . . and the great relief she had felt upon learning that his "paramour" was, in fact, his mother. He had said there were no other women in his life, that he wanted no one but her.

Lord knew she wanted him.

Spruce Street appeared and she stopped, panting, running her fingers through her wet curls. She remembered from her father's records that Dane lived on Pine Street . . . just one block farther south. Jacqui stared through the rain, shivering, this time not with the cold but with a new and exciting thought.

It was late. Both her father and Greta would assume she was asleep by now. No one would visit her bedroom until morning. She was wildly curious . . . and absolutely unwilling to spend another restless night in solitary ignorance. Her heart began to pound furiously. Dared she?

It was scandalous; it was unheard of; it was insane.

It was perfect.

Dane stared into the fireplace. It was rare for him to light a fire in June, but the air was chilled from the storm, and besides, the darkened sitting room seemed to suit his pensive mood tonight.

He stretched, leaning back in his chair and sipping at his brandy in the hopes of shaking his intangible restlessness.

Maybe not so intangible, he thought, finishing his drink. The ache that filled his mind, his heart, and his loins had a definite name: Jacqueline.

Dane stood, running his fingers through his hair. Her totally irrational, thoroughly adorable reaction tonight had more than confirmed what his instincts had told him . . . that Jacqui's obvious, though grudgingly admitted, feelings, her delightful and heady possessiveness, were indeed genuine. Whatever else was true, Jacqueline cared.

The problem still existed, however, that if Alexander's intuition proved accurate and George Holt were, in fact, Jack Laffey, Holt could be using Jacqueline to obtain information for his columns. If that were true, was Jacqui a willing or an unknowing accomplice?

Dane knew he was too deeply involved with Jacqueline to objectively answer that question. At the same time, he was far from oblivious to the skittishness of her behavior tonight, not to mention the odd fact that she'd been going out alone at eight o'clock in the evening and was strangely unwilling to tell him her destination. Why?

Dane wasn't certain of the answer, but he *was* certain that he was going to have to keep a watchful eye on his beautiful hellion.

The clock chimed and Dane contemplated going to bed. He dreaded the prospect. All bed seemed to represent these days was endless, sleepless nights.

He wandered over to the sitting-room window, tightening the belt of his black silk robe. There was something exciting and forbidden about a thunderstorm, something that exhilarated Dane, fired his blood. A clap of thunder reverberated through the skies, and the very earth seemed to tremble with its wrath. Lightning followed in its wake, illuminating the saturated ground and drenched grass and . . .

Dane stiffened, peering into the darkness. He'd seen a

129

movement, fleeting but definite nonetheless. He waited. There it was again. Who the hell was about on a night like tonight?

He was on his way to find out when the knock sounded. He yanked open the front door and found himself staring into Jacqui's huge midnight eyes, her small frame shivering with cold.

Wrapping her arms about herself, she inclined her head slightly and gazed up at him with her customary directness. "You wanted me to come to you," she managed through chattering teeth. "Well, I am here."

For one dazed moment, Dane simply gaped at her in astonishment. Then he reached out and drew her into the house.

"You're drenched," he said softly, rubbing her wet arms with his warm hands. "And freezing." He shook his head. "What am I going to do with you? Come. I don't want you to become ill."

He took her into the sitting room, where he left her in front of the fire while he went in search of towels. When he returned, she was huddled on the rug, letting the blazing flames warm her, and looking about with open curiosity.

"Your home suits you," she said, taking in the elegant Chippendale furniture and walnut-carved easy chairs. "It's sophisticated and charming . . . and powerful."

Dane enfolded her in the towels and drew her against him. "Thank you, *chaton.*" He kissed her hair. "My wet little kitten . . . whatever possessed you to come out in this storm?"

Their eyes met.

"I ache," Jacqui admitted with breathless candor, taking the irrevocable step and never looking back. "Make love to me."

Silence reigned . . . taut, charged.

"Jacqueline . . ." Dane enveloped her in his arms, absorbing her cold, wet body with his warmth. He knew he should ask if she was certain, but the question lodged in his throat, refused to be spoken. Instead, he searched her expressive face, saw the undisguised longing written there, and, with the knowledge of how utterly right this was, he gave them what they both so desperately craved. Tenderly, totally, he took her mouth under his, telling her without words that the gnawing hunger that consumed them would, at last, be satisfied.

Jacqui pressed closer still, clutching the soft silken folds of Dane's robe, closing her mind to everything but the magnificent man who was already making love to her with the lusty strokes of his tongue, the restless movements of his hands as they roamed her body. She met his tongue with her own, feeding their passion, wanton and unafraid.

Small puddles of water pooled onto the floor beneath them and were absorbed into the plush woven carpet, but neither Jacqui nor Dane noticed. With a swift, purposeful motion, he lifted her and placed her on her back, tugging her wet clothes off even as he continued to kiss her with bone-melting thoroughness. Jacqui gave herself to the magic, wanting it as much as Dane did, trusting him to give her body the blissful relief it sought.

The fanning heat of the fire spread through Jacqui's limbs as Dane peeled her soaked chemise away and tossed it aside. Her pulse racing, she watched him kneel beside her, gaze at her nakedness with a scorching intensity that singed her blood and drove all traces of the remaining chill into burning oblivion.

"Breathtaking . . ." he said in a ragged whisper, barely able to speak past the tightness in his chest. She exceeded his every dream, put to shame his most erotic fantasy. He wanted to drink her in all at once, to forever etch upon his memory the sight of her flawless nudity as it was diffused by firelight, the elegant curves softly aglow, the sleek hollows concealed by shadows. Reverently, Dane's eyes caressed her, beginning with her heavy, mahogany tresses, over the flawless perfection of her face, down the slender column of her neck to the rounded fullness of her breasts. Her nipples responded as if they'd been touched, hardening and throbbing beneath his consuming stare. Dane drew a deep, ragged breath, trying valiantly to control the passion that threatened to beat its way outside his body. But control it he would. He'd waited an eternity for this, and now that it was finally here, he wanted it to last forever.

Slowly, his hot gaze traveled lower; lingering on Jacqui's small waist, the gentle curve of her hips, the long, tapered legs and silky thighs, and, at last, the soft, dark nest that was the haven of all he sought.

Jacqui lay absolutely still, as Dane's openly carnal scrutiny swept through her like a narcotic. She wanted nothing more than to pull him down to her, to beg him to fill the void he'd created inside her. She shifted restlessly, feeling no modesty or shame in her nakedness, but totally urgent in her need.

Dane heard her silent plea.

"I know, darling," he murmured in a raw voice, reaching down to lightly caress her breasts. "I feel it, too." He defined her softness with his fingertips, letting his hands learn the beauty that his eyes had only just uncovered: the silken weight of her breasts, her warm, smooth abdomen, the quivering wonder of her inner thighs. He watched her lips part, the rapid rise and fall of her labored breaths, the glazed, unfocused look in her dark blue eyes as she writhed beneath his touch, and he felt that he would surely go up in smoke. "Soon," he promised in a dark whisper, gliding his palm down to graze the tight curls between her legs. His hand shook, tightened possessively. "Very soon, *mon chaton.*"

"No," she countered, unable to wait another second, "now." She raised up and tugged insistently at his sleeves, greedy and impatient. Dane chuckled at her undisguised eagerness; but his laughter died in his throat as her small hand found its way into the opening of his robe, made its first contact with the hard wall of his bare chest. He sucked in his breath as, slowly, with wonder and curiosity, Jacqui discovered his body, gliding her fingers through the soft, dark chest hair, finding the steely muscles that defined his massive frame. Her other hand joined the search, and she eased more of the material away from his broad shoulders so that she could see as well as feel the powerful man that was shuddering beneath her fingertips.

Dane closed his eyes, the erotic feel of her hands lighting a brushfire to his blood, driving him so dangerously close to the ragged edge of control that each tentative caress threatened to push him over the brink. His body was painfully rigid, a heartbeat from eruption, and he knew in mere seconds it would be too late.

Tearing himself from her touch, he shrugged out of his robe in one fierce movement and dragged Jacqui off the carpet and into his arms. Swiftly, deliberately, he melded her nakedness to his, groaning harshly at the most excruciatingly euphoric contact he had ever known.

Jacqui whimpered his name, her senses flooded with the drowning pleasure of her totally unclothed body crushed to his. It felt wonderful . . . unbearable . . . and she needed more. Now.

Guided by instinct, she rubbed her breasts sensuously against Dane's chest, hearing his agonized gasp. Vitally aware of his huge, pulsing erection throbbing against her soft belly, Jacqui boldly pressed herself closer still, amazed by the heat, the enormous size and power of his arousal . . . and by her body's own immediate response. The ache that was building inside her grew until it became unendurable in its intensity, and a rush of wetness flowed through her, pooling heavily between her legs. Helplessly, she arched her lower body to Dane's, silently begging him to alleviate the torment.

Dane went wild.

He barely heard Jacqui's joyful cry of surprise as he pushed her backward onto the carpet, covering her with himself. He had wanted to wait, to take his time arousing her, to fully possess her only when she was openly pleading with him to do so. He had promised to love her slowly, to make it last forever. But she had made that impossible, pushing him beyond his limits with her innocent sensuality and the seductive motions of her lush, tantalizing body. At this point, he was so desperate for completion that he had to get inside her now, or spill himself waiting.

He pressed her thighs apart with his knee, feeling her open herself still farther to accommodate his weight. With his last shred of sanity, he slid his hand between them to find and caress the warm delicate flesh he'd claimed Saturday as his own, the satiny wetness that told him she was more than ready for their union.

With elation and triumph, he caught her face in his hands, feeling the heat of her flushed cheeks, her erratic pants, seeing his own urgent need reflected in her eyes.

"Jacqui . . ." He settled his hips in the cradle of her thighs, the tip of his rigid shaft nudging the moist, heated entrance it sought. Even that teasing contact caused pleasure to course through them both in relentless waves, and Dane pressed his forehead to hers, desperately trying to bring himself under a control that had long since evaporated.

"Dane . . . don't stop . . . not now. . . ." Jacqui lifted herself to take more of him, frantic now to feel him inside her, desperate in her drive for fulfillment.

Feeling her body's natural resistance, Dane shook his head intently, bracing his hands on either side of her and locking his arms to hold himself away. "I won't hurt you," he bit out, sweat dotting his forehead. Gradually, he eased forward, an inch at a time, determined to merge his body with hers as slowly and painlessly as possible, refusing to give in to the clamoring wildness both their bodies demanded, no matter how great the urge was to do so.

He should have known Jacqui would have other ideas.

With a soft whimper of protest, she twined her arms around Dane's neck, wrapped her legs about his waist, and arched up to meet him. Open and wet, she glided around him, stretching to take him deeper, and put an end to all his noble intentions.

A red haze exploded inside Dane's head, and with a feral growl, he gave in to the inevitable, surrendering to the flaming inferno their joining was always destined to be, burying himself inside her in one savage thrust.

He went deadly still at her cry of pain, the feel of her delicate membrane tearing as he made her his.

"Jacqui . . . love . . ."

She clutched at his sweat-drenched back with possessive hands. "Please . . . don't leave me . . . not yet."

"Not ever," he rasped. "Not . . . ever. . . ."

He began to move in deep, rhythmic thrusts, aware of nothing save the lush softness of her body beneath him, the tight clasp of her slick, hot passage all around him, caressing him, driving him out of his mind. The world spun away, and there was only Jacqueline and the exquisite reality that was theirs at last. Dane pushed deeper and deeper inside her, burying himself fully only to withdraw and press higher, farther into her honeyed wetness, intent on possessing her more totally than any woman had ever been possessed.

Jacqui was lost in pure, dazzling sensation. She cared nothing for the brief, sharp pain that had accompanied Dane's entry. . . . In fact, she'd welcomed it as a gateway to the dizzying pleasure that was escalating within her. She clung to Dane, feeling the powerful muscles of his back contract with each plunging stroke. Instinctively, she began to undulate her hips to meet him, intensifying the already painful pleasure that coiled tighter and tighter, until she felt sure she would die.

Dane kissed her face, her mouth, her neck, her breasts, finally sliding his hands beneath her to lift her into his thrusts, to impale her with his fiery hardness. Again and again their bodies merged in a mating that was savage, plummeting, frenzied, urgent. Jacqui began to cry out beneath him and Dane drank in the sound as it mingled with the hoarse rasps that were torn from his chest. And then she arched, calling out his name in a shocked, wild little cry that he would remember for the rest of his life.

They both felt the hard, gripping spasms of her body as it contracted around his, and Dane held himself perfectly still, absorbing every glorious pulsation of her climax. Jacqui dug her nails into his back, letting the ecstasy wash over her in great, untamed waves of splendor, sobbing his name over and over as the rapture spun itself out.

Abruptly, Dane went taut above her, seized by helpless shudders that wracked his broad frame and distorted his handsome features into a mask of agonized pleasure.

"Jacqueline . . . my God, Jacqui . . ." The words were torn from his chest, followed by a wild, exultant shout that made the tempest of sensation wash through Jacqui anew. Still reeling with her own aftershocks, she felt Dane lunge forward, onto her and into her, heard his husky voice begging her to take him, to hold him . . . to love him. Tenderly, she wrapped her arms around his back, closing her eyes at the unexpected feelings that claimed her in that final moment of passion. She felt the burst of wet heat within her as Dane gave himself to her, poured himself endlessly inside her, and melded their bodies so close that they were one.

Long moments passed before the maelstrom of sensation had subsided and their breathing had returned to normal. Dane buried his face in the damp satin of Jacqui's hair. "I knew it would be like this." His voice was laced with wonder. "It never was before, but with us . . . I knew we would touch heaven . . . this time, every time." He gave a deep, resigned sigh. "God help me, but I love you, Jacqueline. And I plan to have you . . . always."

His vow terrified her. For she suddenly realized, not only the enormity of her power over this commanding man . . . but the enormity of his power over her.

CHAPTER
9

Dane knew she was gone before he opened his eyes.

Jolted into wakefulness by some intangible instinct, Dane found himself alone on the carpet, the room cold and dark, the fire having died down to embers.

Cursing, he raced to the window, peering into the darkness. It was past midnight and the storm had subsided, leaving behind a clear night sky and a cool breeze . . . but no Jacqueline.

The emptiness Dane felt was so acute it was like a knife in his gut. *Damn her,* he fumed inwardly, heading for the stairs. *Damn her for being such a wretched, obstinate little coward. Damn her for running away.*

She wouldn't get far.

Dane took the steps two at a time, snatching a pair of breeches and a shirt from his drawers, determined to go after Jacqui and beat some sense into her stubborn, willful head.

It was then that he saw the traces of blood on his body. Jacqueline's blood.

Dane closed his eyes, choked by a myriad of conflicting emotions: tenderness, anguish, rage. He wondered if Jacqui had discovered the bloodstains, and if they had frightened her. He wished he could have been there . . . to hold her, to comfort her, to tell her that everything would be all right, be as it was destined.

Tugging on his clothing, he tore out into the night. He had to find her, to assure himself of her safety.

After which, he planned to kill her himself.

He circled the Holts' house quietly, knowing that knocking was out of the question at this hour. Still, he was determined to find evidence that Jacqui was safely abed.

He found the scrap of material on the tall oak beside the house. Following the height of the tree with his eyes, Dane saw a weak light coming from the second-floor bedroom; a room that could easily be reached by scaling the oak. Jacqueline's room.

Weak with relief, Dane realized that it was the middle of the night and that their altercation could not take place here and now, much as he would have wished. But tomorrow morning he planned to march into Jacqueline's sitting room and put an end to this ridiculous cat-and-mouse game. Tonight had sealed her fate. Whether she liked it or not, Jacqueline Holt was his.

"She won't see you, Herr Westbrooke."

Greta's ample frame filled the doorway while something surprisingly akin to sympathy filled her voice.

"Yes, she will see me, damn it!" Dane raked his fingers through his hair, his silver eyes ablaze. "Because I'm not leaving until she does!" He slammed his fist so hard against the door frame that the wood vibrated. "Give your mistress a message for me, Greta," he told the undaunted housekeeper, who was calmly smoothing her severe bun into place. "Tell her that I've put up with her childish nonsense for as long as I plan to. Tell her that my patience has run out. Tell her that I'll stand here all bloody night if I have to. If that doesn't work, I'll break down the blasted door! But I *am* going to see her . . . *today!*"

"Very well, Herr Westbrooke." Considering how formidable Dane was when he was angry, Greta sounded not at all intimidated by his wrath. She tucked a last stubborn strand of hair into place and took herself off to do his bidding, leaving behind a heavy trail of spicy perfume whose pungent smell made Dane's eyes water.

To escape the irritating odor, Dane waited in the garden, pacing its length until he'd worn an indelible path in the grass. For the hundredth time since the night of the storm he lambasted himself for allowing Jacqui to escape him. He should have known that she would bolt at her first given opportunity . . . especially after the hurtling intensity of their lovemaking, which had doubtless left her feeling vulnerable and afraid. But he hadn't been thinking clearly, his guard lowered, stripped away by the engulfing tenderness that had followed in the wake of their passion. With Jacqui still warm and soft in his arms, the fanning heat of the fire against his back, he had felt so peaceful, so utterly replete and sated, that he had dozed off, content in the knowledge that, at last, she was his.

What a stupid fool he'd been.

Knowing Jacqueline as he did, what had ever possessed him to believe that she would allow the giving of her body to represent anything more than a physical joining; that, despite their growing emotional involvement, she would surrender the one part of herself she guarded far more fiercely than her virtue?

Yet she *had* relinquished more than her lush innocence, Dane reflected with absolute conviction. During those dizzying minutes when they had been one, she had belonged to him. In every way. Dane knew it. And so did Jacqui. That was why she was running away.

Damn. He had to see her, to convince her that she had nothing to fear.

"He is still out there, Fräulein."

Jacqui let her bedroom curtain fall back into place,

139

turning to where her housekeeper loomed in the doorway, an accusatory look on her face. "I know he is, Greta. I can see him."

"What do you plan to *do* about it?"

Jacqui rubbed her eyes, which burned from a week of sleepless nights. "I shall deal with Mr. Westbrooke."

"When?" Greta persisted. "It is nearly dark and Herr Westbrooke hasn't strayed a step from the garden all day! Nor does he intend to. Eventually, Fräulein, you must resolve this misunderstanding. . . ."

"Enough!" Jacqui had reached her emotional breaking point. "This misunderstanding, as you put it, is between Dane and myself . . . so stay out of it, Greta!" Jacqui heard the housekeeper's shocked gasp, but was not deterred. This time Greta had definitely overstepped her bounds. "Please go and see to your duties now. I do not need a lecture on my behavior, no matter how well-meaning. Although," she added pointedly, "I ofttimes wonder who your sympathy is *truly* with, me . . . or Dane."

Greta's lips were pressed so tightly together that her mouth nearly disappeared. "You've made your point, Fräulein. If you will excuse me, I shall see to the duties you referred to." With her spine so rigid Jacqui feared it might snap, Greta marched out of the room, closing the door—a little too loudly—behind her.

Sighing, Jacqui turned back to the window and gazed out, standing to one side so she could not be seen from below. The final rays of sunlight were cloaking the city in a fiery orange glow, illuminating the garden . . . and its imposing occupant.

Dane looked no closer to departure than he had ten hours ago when he had begun his vigil. And Jacqui felt no readier to deal with her careening emotions than she had this morning . . . or last week in Dane's arms.

She closed her eyes, struggling again for the control she never lost; control, not only of her thoughts, but of her life and its components. What happened between her and Dane during the thunderstorm should have been so simple . . . learning the mysteries of passion, exploring the forbidden, exciting yearnings of her body, satisfying the relentless cravings that consumed her. Well, she had done all that.

Only it had been replaced by something even more incomprehensible and far more threatening.

So she cared for him, her logic countered. That was to be expected. After all, she wasn't a prostitute . . . it was only natural that she should have feelings for the man she chose to share her body with. But, a small voice acknowledged, it was the intensity of her feelings that terrified her. They were deep, eddying, making her breath catch and her throat constrict each time she relived those moments by the fire, creating a never-before-known longing that welled up inside her, slid easily beneath the protective wall that sheltered her from the world.

She sat down heavily upon the bed, uncertain and afraid and alone. *Mother, if only you were alive,* she mused wistfully, *you would know what I ought to do; you'd make some sense out of what I am feeling.* . . . Jacqui gave her head a hard shake . . . forced the painful reflection away. For beneath it, she knew, lay too many repressed emotions that she had never been strong enough to face, much less conquer.

Gathering Whiskey against her, she stroked her cheek against his soft fur. "Whiskey, there is only one answer. I cannot allow this relationship to continue . . . for many reasons. It is just too dangerous. I must end it . . . now."

Whiskey purred his agreement and swatted at a sheet of paper on the bed.

Idly, Jacqui watched him, feeling the emptiness of loss well up inside her at the course of action she must take, to protect herself . . . and her secret. Giving up Dane would be the hardest thing she'd ever had to do, but . . .

Suddenly, Jacqui tensed, focusing on the paper that Whiskey was now raking with his claws. "Lord . . . it's Monday!" She dumped Whiskey onto the floor and snatched up the page of writing. "I must deliver the column!"

One glance out the window told her that darkness had fallen. It also told her that Dane was still maintaining his post . . . but not without assistance. Reinforcements were in the process of being provided by Greta, who was handing Dane a tray laden with roast mutton garnished with horse radish, boiled potatoes, and cauliflower. It was obvious to Jacqui that, with her traitorous housekeeper's help, Dane was settling in for the evening.

"Damn!" she exclaimed, frustration replacing sentiment in the blink of an eye. Her thoughts raced over her choices. She could miss tonight's meeting . . . which would result in her column's absence from this week's *General Advertiser*. That possibility was ruled out before it had even been considered. One choice remained. She *had* to get to her messenger, which meant slipping by Dane without being seen. And there was but one means for that accomplishment. The back entrance.

Jacqui tucked the damp tendrils of hair behind her ears, trudging the last steps home. It was after ten and quite dark, for there was no moon at all tonight. Not that she needed the light to guide her. After making the same weekly excursion for over a year, she could find her way blindfolded.

Glancing surreptitiously about, she saw that her garden was deserted. Acute disappointment mingled with vast relief when she realized that Dane had finally gone. Following her customary ritual, she rounded the corner of Spruce Street to the side of her house. She ran the last few steps, lifting her skirts as she sped to the old oak . . . and collided with a solid wall of muscle.

Hard arms wrapped around her. She opened her mouth to scream, fighting to free herself, but a strong hand smothered the sound of her startled cry.

"Jacqueline. At last."

She knew it was Dane even before he spoke. How well she

remembered the feel of his powerful body, the heady masculine scent that made her senses throb . . . the infuriating arrogance that made her blood boil. She forced herself to go completely still.

When Dane felt Jacqui's struggles cease, he released her . . . a mistake.

She shoved herself away from him, venom in her eyes. "What the hell do you think you're doing?" she hissed.

"Waiting for you." He was livid, enraged at her continued refusals to see him, more so at her mysterious disappearances. But right now, as he came face to face with the exasperating woman he loved for the first time since the night of the storm, all Dane could feel was a rush of emotion that obliterated all else. "Are you all right?" His voice was thick with memories, his eyes a blanket of tenderness.

"I'm fine." She stared past him to the old oak. Then her speculative gaze returned to Dane, realizing that he had obviously been awaiting her arrival. "How did you know . . ." Abruptly, she broke off.

"How did I know your special 'route' to and from your house?" he finished for her. "I followed you home last week. After we'd made love." The rich timbre of his voice was a tangible caress.

Hot color flooded Jacqui's cheeks. "Why are you still waiting here?"

"Why did you leave me?" Dane responded, ignoring her ludicrous question.

Jacqui's flush deepened and she lowered her head to hide the telltale reaction. "You know why I left."

He raised her chin with his forefinger. "Yes, *I* know," he said softly. "But I wonder if you do."

She refused to look at him. "We were finished."

"We had barely begun. And if you really think that's the reason why you left, then you're lying . . . to me and to yourself."

Jacqui stepped away. "Dane, I must go in now."

"Where were you tonight?"

She swallowed. "Please . . . leave me alone."

"Jacqueline, do you really believe you can pretend nothing is changed, that your life can go on as it was?" He tugged her back into his arms, rubbing his chin, his lips against the satiny tresses of her mahogany hair. "I burn for you," he whispered, stroking his hands up and down her spine. "I lie awake and relive every moment of the night we were together. I can see you, taste you, smell your perfume. I can remember every whimper you made, every plea for me not to stop, and, at the last, the way you cried out my name . . . again and again. I can feel the velvety heat of your body tightening all around me, driving me over the edge. I can feel your harsh little pants against my skin, the rake of your nails across my back, your beautiful, silky legs wrapped around my waist."

Jacqui closed her eyes, unknowingly gripping the cool linen of his shirt in tight, trembling fists. "Stop."

"No."

"It can never happen again."

"You won't be able to prevent it."

"Damn you," she said in a tortured whisper, unable to cope with the staggering emotions storming her senses.

Dane tightened his embrace possessively. He felt her resistance . . . and her vulnerability. "Come home with me," he murmured into her hair. "Fill the void inside me that you created . . . and only you can fill."

She stiffened. "I can't. I must go inside before I am missed."

"Where is it that you are coming from at this hour of the night?" he asked again, this time more insistently. When Jacqui refused to answer, Dane frowned, renewed doubt, repressed but ever present, forcing its way to the forefront of his mind. "Why is it that you never want to discuss your comings and goings with me, *chaton*? Is it merely stubborn pride . . . or is it more?"

A wave of anxiety rushed through her. "What does that mean?"

He continued the gentle motions of his hands on her back, a gesture that was belied by the steely edge to his tone. "The hour is rather late for a stroll, sweet, is it not? Could it be that you are keeping something from me? Something that you don't wish for me to find out?"

Jacqui wrenched herself free in one frantic movement. "I don't answer to you, Dane. I never will. So stop interrogating me!"

"Interrogating you? I would hardly call my asking to know where you've gone, alone and unattended, in the dead of night interrogating you!"

"Perhaps I've been with another man!"

She flinched as he dragged her against him, the look in his blazing silver eyes lethal. "Then I shall have to kill him."

She didn't doubt that he was capable of doing just that. She licked her dry lips, a little afraid of Dane's anger, but refusing to back down. "As it happens, I was alone. As to *where* I was . . . I am not obligated to tell you that, Dane. That or anything else."

"Aren't you?" He breathed the demand against her lips, his handsome features still taut with fury. "After last week, don't you feel in any way bound to me?"

More than I can afford to be, she wanted to cry out. Instead, she shook her head. "I won't be your mistress."

"I don't recall asking you to be."

A shaft of pain cut through her. "True. You agree, then, that it is best for us to discontinue our . . . association."

"I agree to nothing of the kind." He lowered his head, closing the distance between their lips.

Jacqui tried to turn her head away, but he wouldn't allow her to retreat. He caught her chin with a gentle but insistent hand, forcing her to receive his descending mouth. Jacqui squeezed her eyes shut, as if by doing so she could deny what was happening between them. "It's over, Dane," she managed in a last frantic attempt to escape.

He kissed her, deeply, totally, refusing to stop until she

145

was weak and clinging to him. "It will never be over, Jacqueline. Not for either of us."

"I won't see you again," she whispered.

"Won't you?" He drew back slightly. "And what if you discover that you're carrying my child?" His voice was hushed, laden with emotion.

Their gazes locked.

Jacqui lowered hers quickly, but not before Dane had seen the intensity of her reaction. "Ah, Jacqueline, you lie so poorly," he taunted, stroking her cheeks with his thumbs. He raised her face again and buried his lips in hers.

This time Jacqui didn't fight it but gave in to the urgent yearning that clamored within her. She kissed him back, leaning into him, her arms wrapped around his neck. The world tilted, reality spun away.

"I want you now more than I did before," he told her huskily, his tongue fencing with hers, their breath mingling in short, heated pants. Slowly, purposefully, Dane swept his hands over the lush concealed curves of Jacqui's body in a possessive and tantalizing caress that made her knees buckle. "Now that I've had you . . . it's unbearable when we're apart." He cupped her soft bottom and lifted her against him. "I need you, Jacqueline. Under me. Hot and wet and pleading. Taking all of me into all of you. It's that simple. Nothing else matters."

"I want that too," she admitted shakily.

"I know you do." His burning gaze fixed on the revealing evidence of her hardened nipples, clearly visible through the thin material of her gown. He bent his head and closed his mouth over one straining tip, tugging lightly with his teeth, stroking the fine muslin with his tongue.

Something akin to a sob escaped from Jacqui's throat as raw desire shot through her. "Dane, I have to go." She was trembling violently and in mere seconds she was going to cast aside resolve and discretion, lay down in the scented grass, and make love with him in full view of her house and her neighbors . . . and let the world and her earlier decisions be damned.

Dane didn't answer. Nor did he release her immediately, but kissed her throat, the erratic pulse fluttering at her neck, and finally, sensing her turmoil, he scattered light kisses across her forehead and cheeks, ending with soft, repeated brushes of his lips against hers. Finally, he raised his head, silently gazing into her beautiful flushed face until her dark lashes fluttered, then lifted, revealing the dazed midnight blue of her eyes.

Still, Dane didn't speak, merely lowering Jacqui to the ground and studying her with a tender but bemused expression. He cupped her chin, gliding his thumb across the sensuous mouth that was still moist and swollen from his kisses. "Will you tell me where you've been?" he asked at last, his voice raw.

Jacqui swallowed, burning from the rhythmic stroking of his thumb. "No."

His fingers stilled. Her answer was not the one he sought . . . yet it was the one he'd expected. He plunged his hands into the thick waves of her hair, anchoring her head tightly. "Is it merely your independence you are protecting, *chaton,* or is there some sinister secret in your life?"

Dane's demanding words and hard, possessive grasp were like a temporary douse of frigid water on the fires raging inside her, and Jacqui's resolve returned in a rush. "Goodbye, Dane." She twisted out of his grasp, lifted her skirts, and marched to the oak, securing her hands on the first sturdy branch within her reach.

"Good *night,* Jacqueline," he corrected. He ambled over and raised her effortlessly to a spot midway up the trunk. "Allow me to make your task easier," he offered in a deceptively silky tone. He held her firmly about the waist, ignoring her protests and waiting until she had a solid grip on the branch before he released her. At which point he did not retreat as Jacqui had expected, but remained where he

ANDREA KANE

was, watching her from beneath hooded lids, a mixture of
hunger and accusation in his steel-gray eyes.

Jacqui felt the power of that penetrating stare down to the
soles of her feet. Desperate to escape his dangerous, magnetic presence, she willed herself to reach upward for the next
branch . . . but her body refused to obey the dictates of her
mind. All she could do was cling helplessly to where she was,
terrified . . . not of falling, but of the man she knew would
catch her.

As if reading her thoughts, Dane leaned slowly forward,
sliding his hands beneath her hindering skirts to caress the
length of her legs . . . gliding up and down, again and again,
lingering a bit longer each time, until he felt the tremors run
through her and into him. "Dream of me, *chaton*," he said
in an enigmatic whisper, more determined than ever to
reaffirm the intensity of his effect on her. "For I promise that
I shall dream of you." He met her wide-eyed stare with
triumph, purposefully easing his hands higher . . . higher,
until Jacqui let out a soft moan. "I'll dream of the next time
we're together," he continued softly, ". . . the next time you
give yourself to me." His thumbs grazed the bare skin of her
inner thighs and, with flawless skill, found the very heart of
her, opening her to his seductive exploration. He smiled
darkly at the wetness that told him of her vulnerability and
her need. "You made the choice, my love," he reminded her
huskily, lightly stroking the soft, delicate folds. "You came
to me." He was being a bastard and he knew it. But, damn it,
he wanted *all* of her . . . her body, her heart . . . and whatever it was she was withholding from him.

"Dane . . . stop . . ."

It was the defenseless sound of her plea that reached past
his primal need for possession. He saw the turmoil, the
warring emotions on her face, and he felt ashamed. The
reasons for his actions might be sound, but the method was
unfair. He, better than anyone, knew that Jacqui was a
complete innocent when it came to matters of seduction, so
using his experience to break her resolve was beneath

148

him . . . beneath what he felt for her. He wanted her fairly, willingly, and with her spirit intact.

Gently, he withdrew his hands and smoothed down her gown, watching her struggle for control, feeling a mixture of guilt and satisfaction. "Don't fight me, *chaton*," he told her, his own breathing unsteady as he backed away. "You can't change our fate. Like it or not, you are mine."

He waited, hands clasped behind his back, until she had regained her bearings, sent him a bitter, scathing look, and shot up the tree like a frightened squirrel attempting to escape from a hungry wolf, disappearing through her bedroom window.

"Mr. Westbrooke!" Stivers, Dane's manservant, flung open the door to the house, looking harried and concerned.

"What is it?" Dane asked in surprise, stepping into the front hallway. Stivers had usually gone home by this hour, since Dane required his services only during the day. Living here by himself, Dane saw no need for a live-in servant.

"You have a visitor, sir. He's been waiting for some time now. I didn't want to leave until you arrived home."

"A visitor? At this hour?" A quick look at his timepiece told Dane that it was after eleven o'clock. "Who is it, Stivers?"

"It's the Secretary of the Treasury, sir. He said that it is extremely important he see you tonight."

Dane digested this information carefully, and with a sinking heart. If Alexander were here at nearly midnight, it could mean naught but ill. "Thank you, Stivers," he said aloud. "I appreciate your waiting. Go home and get some sleep."

"Very good, sir. Good night."

"Good night, Stivers." Dane closed the door behind him, then went into the sitting room where Alexander was pacing beside the fireplace.

Hearing Dane's footsteps, he turned. "At last." He looked haggard, lines of strain about his mouth.

"What is it?" Dane minced no words.

"We've received word back from Jay."

Dane tensed. "He's met with the English?"

"He has."

"And?"

"And the negotiations will probably go on for weeks, if not months. However, the manner in which Jay was received by England's Minister of Foreign Affairs . . ." Hamilton raked his fingers through his hair. "It was as if Grenville had anticipated all our demands and was thus prepared to negotiate them in England's favor."

Dane looked stunned. "Jay said that?"

"Not in so many words. But Grenville's reaction makes it perfectly obvious. He countered us, point by point, skirting the issue of compensation for our seized ships, limiting our free trade in the West Indies, and putting forth a preliminary outline of a treaty of commerce that diverges greatly from the one our cabinet drafted in April."

Dane's head was spinning with thoughts of the consequences of the English response. "Republican sentiment is openly hostile toward England at this time and vehemently opposes these proposed terms," he said grimly.

"Exactly. Thus we must work toward a healthy compromise that will satisfy both countries and prevent a war between us. However," Hamilton went on somberly, "the immediate implications are more pressing . . . in fact, urgent."

"How is it that England anticipated Jay's proposal?" Dane supplied, his tone severe.

Hamilton began to pace again. "There is no conceivable way the English could have made their counter-demands so quickly without prior knowledge of America's bargaining position."

"But how could they possibly have known our terms? That could only have happened if someone had passed along the information you had drafted for Jay to take with him."

"Yes, that's true." Hamilton came to a dead halt, his bleak gaze meeting Dane's. He waited.

He knew precisely when the dreadful realization dawned on his friend.

"The documents that we couldn't find," Dane said slowly, the color draining from his face. "The ones we thought you misplaced in your office." Sickened by his own words, he lowered himself onto the sofa, his hands tightly gripping his knees.

Hamilton gave a terse nod. "The ones that reappeared in a different drawer than I remember placing them."

Dane swallowed convulsively. "You believe that someone took those papers and used them to inform the English before Jay's arrival."

"I do."

Dane knew there was more. "You have an idea who that might be."

"Yes."

"Who?"

Hamilton drew a deep breath and prepared himself for what was to come. "Do you recall the conversation we had last week regarding Laffey?"

Dane stiffened. "I remember."

"Have you given it any thought?"

"As a matter of fact, yes . . . but what has that to do with Jay?"

Hamilton didn't answer the question. "What was your verdict concerning my suspicions about George Holt?"

Dane frowned, wondering what the link was between Laffey and the far-more-threatening issue at hand. "It is possible that Holt is Laffey," Dane reasoned, confident that Alexander would supply him with the answer he sought. "Your reasons for believing him guilty are sound, given Holt's political inclinations. Although I do not believe Jacqueline is involved," he added quickly, ignoring Hamilton's skeptical look. "Not only because I care for her, Alexander, but because it makes no sense. Holt loves

151

Jacqueline dearly. He would never endanger his daughter by sending her out alone in the dead of night to gather information for a political column—"

"Jacqueline goes out alone at night?" Hamilton's response was immediate. "Are you certain?"

"I've seen her," Dane answered reluctantly. "But, as I said, there is not enough justification—"

"Unless the Laffey column is but a small part of what Holt is involved in," Hamilton interrupted.

Dane stared. "What . . ."

"Do you recall the day after my social gathering in April?" Hamilton pressed on, hoping to defer Dane's explosion long enough to complete his train of thought. "When you and I met in my office to discuss Laffey's identity? Your clerk interrupted us, arriving to inform you that George Holt had requested an emergency shipment be sent to the mainland." He continued, an intent look on his face. "I was puzzled . . . no, bothered, by what appeared to be an uncharacteristic action from a man you yourself described as painstakingly well organized. At the time, I dismissed my reaction as extreme and unwarranted. Now I'm not so certain. For if the shipment he was sending included something more treacherous than . . ."

"Do you know what you're accusing the man of?" Dane asked quietly.

Hamilton pressed his lips into a tight line of frustration. "I haven't proof to accuse him of anything. I'm merely conjecturing aloud. But hear me out. Holt is known to be closely aligned with the Republicans in his sympathies toward France and their revolution. What if he believed that, by jeopardizing our negotiations with the British, it would propel us into an alliance with France? He might view his actions as patriotic, not treasonous." He took a deep breath. "Which brings us to Jacqueline. You know how she feels about the English monarchy . . . and about the French Revolution. You're telling me that she goes on mysterious excursions, alone, at night. Doesn't it seem likely—"

"No!" Dane lurched to his feet, negating his friend's words with a wild shake of his head.

But Hamilton had been prepared for just this reaction, and this time he was ready for it. "One way or another, we must be certain, Dane." He pushed on, disregarding the pain in his friend's eyes. Having thoroughly considered every angle prior to Dane's arrival home, Hamilton was convinced that there was only one way to ascertain the Holts' guilt or innocence . . . that was for Dane to investigate their activities, to use his relationship with Jacqueline to arrive at the truth. Given the amount of time Dane spent in Jacqueline's company, the plan would be simple enough to execute. Simple, yes, but with one grave flaw. If Jacqueline were guilty of betraying her country, the result would be tremendous personal anguish for Dane.

In the end, there had been no choice. Hamilton had forced himself to come to terms with the guilt his decision had elicited. Dane was his friend, yes, but the truth was, neither Dane's feelings for Jacqueline nor Hamilton's friendship for Dane could take precedence over America's national security.

"I know exactly what you're thinking," Dane said in a cold, strained voice. "I won't do it."

"You have no choice, my friend." Hamilton's gaze was filled with sympathy.

Dane slammed his fist against the wall. "She would never do what you're suggesting, damn it!"

"Then where is she going at night?"

"She loves her country."

"And you love her."

Dane drew a deep, agonized breath. "Yes. I love her."

Hamilton laid an understanding hand on Dane's shoulder. "I'm sorry, Dane. I, more than anyone, hope that I'm wrong."

"But you think that you're right."

"Yes."

Silence swelled until the room was filled with it.

"You've said what you came to say," Dane managed at last. "Now I'd like to be alone."

"All right." Hamilton felt old and terribly tired. He walked away, pausing in the doorway. "I'll be in my office all day tomorrow," he said. Then he left Dane alone with his thoughts.

Jacqui stared into her bedroom mirror, seeing her own stricken expression reflected back at her. Her life had been so uncomplicated, so calm before Dane Westbrooke had stormed into it, upsetting the straightforward direction of her existence and turning her life into an emotional tempest.

She tugged her brush through the loose waves of her hair, feeling the dull throb in her body that refused to be silenced. Damn him, damn him! Why did he make her feel like a helpless leaf being blown about by a powerful wind? Why did he make it so damned impossible to forget him?

But he was right . . . she couldn't forget.

Laying the brush on her dressing table, Jacqui stared at her chemise-covered body as if seeing it for the first time. She, who had thought herself to be so worldly and independent, had been no better than a silly child. Until she had become a woman in Dane's arms.

But she was still behaving like a child.

For she had run from the tenderness she'd seen in his eyes . . . even more so from the surge of emotion he'd drawn from her.

No, she had forgotten nothing of those hours by the fire. Not the intensity of their union, nor the sweetness of lying in his arms when their passions had been spent.

Slowly, she raised her hands to touch her nipples, which had hardened at the mere memories of her night with Dane. What a complete and utter fool she'd been to think that one night in his arms would be all it took to satisfy her, that she could walk away and still remain whole.

She couldn't be whole . . . not without him.

The realization was more than terrifying . . . it was paralyzing. For it meant that Jacqui was forever changed, that nothing could ever be as it was. How could she need Dane so much and still be the same self-reliant person she was determined to be?

He had told her he accepted her as she was, that he would never try to change her. But he had no idea what he was saying, for he did not really know her.

Or did he?

No, if he knew her identity he would not have been so persistent with his questions tonight. Perhaps he suspected? It was possible, although unlikely. She could never, ever let him find out, for he would immediately tell Hamilton, who would find a way to ruin her, or, at the very least, pressure Bache into refusing her work. And that she could not bear, for the people deserved to read the truth and it was up to her to provide it.

She needed her principles.

She needed Dane.

She couldn't have both.

With a soft moan, she closed her eyes, dropping her hands to her sides. It was futile.

A soft thud sounded behind her, startling her out of her reverie. Jacqui's eyes flew open and she stared, amazed, at what her mirror's image was telling her.

"Hello, *chaton*." Dane straightened and walked toward her, a haunted look on his face.

"Dane . . . what are you doing here?" She whirled around, knowing the answer to her question even as she asked it.

He loomed over her, his eyes glittering with a reckless emotion that could have been excitement or anguish . . . or both. "I think you know the answer to that, my love." His burning gaze swept over her half-naked body. "I'm here to reaffirm what is real; what is mine. Since you were kind enough to leave your window ajar"—he traced one tanned finger across her shoulder and down her arm—" I simply used your covert method to gain access to your bedroom . . . and to you." He seized both straps of her chemise and dragged them down, bending to press his open mouth to her throat.

Even as Jacqui shivered beneath his caress, she recognized that to allow this to happen . . . under her father's roof, in her own bed . . . would be insane. Her mind also registered that Dane was acting oddly, that he was somehow different than he'd been earlier tonight.

"Dane . . ." Her voice, while breathless, demanded an explanation.

Dane didn't provide one, but instead continued to circle his lips and tongue against her skin, tasting her, lightly drawing the sensitive flesh into his mouth.

When he reached the upper slope of her breasts, she finally gasped out her protest. "Dane . . . we can't. My father . . ."

"Yes, your father." His fingers dug more firmly into the smooth skin of her arms, his grip just short of punishing. "Well, *chaton,*" he muttered thickly against her breast, "Your concerned father is in one of several places: either hard at work at Holt Trading, out for the evening with the lovely Miss Brisset, or sound asleep in his own bed." He raised his head, stared down at her with a tight, enigmatic expression on his handsome face. "Isn't that right, sweet? Those are the only places he would be at this hour, aren't they?" He searched her face for some answer he seemed not to find, then let out a low sound of masculine need. "It doesn't matter, Jacqueline . . . not tonight." His voice was thick with passion. "Tonight, nothing short of death could stop me from taking what I want. Nothing and no one." He devoured her with his hot gaze, making the ache between her thighs intensify until it became unbearable. "I've been patient with you, Jacqueline . . . too patient. I'm finished providing you with time to accept the inevitable, finished waiting for you to relinquish your bloody independence . . . and your carefully guarded secrets." He swallowed convulsively, as if fighting some difficult, internal battle. "Now it's my turn. My turn to take control, to find out everything I need to know. I want it all, *mon chaton colereux* . . . all you have to give, all that you are. And damn it, Jacqueline, you *will* give it to me. . . ."

Before she could speak, he'd raised his hand and, with one purposeful gesture, ripped her chemise down the middle, letting the torn pieces fall to the floor.

Jacqui stared down at herself as if doubting what had just taken place. Then she raised wide, midnight eyes to Dane's, her own registering shock and disbelief, his a fiery silver gray. "Have you gone mad?"

Dane gave a harsh laugh and swept her into his arms. "Indeed I have." He lowered both of them to her bed. "And do you know why?" Capturing her face, he lifted it to receive the searing brand of his kiss. "Because one night last April, I met a vision in lilac, a luscious hellion with the body of a goddess, the face of an angel . . . and the elusive secrets of the darkest seas." He kissed her, deeply, possessively, forcing the response that he so desperately needed.

Jacqui felt a prickle of fear run up her spine as the ominous meaning of his words sank in. But the fear was swept away beneath the drowning tide of desire that submerged her as Dane's tongue took hers. And suddenly, something inside her snapped, and she surrendered in a rush, giving in to the relentless inner voices that clamored, compelling her to lose herself in the fire of Dane's passion. She flung her arms about his neck, kissing him back with fierce, unrestrained longing, tangling her hands in his hair, desperate to escape the world and all its unresolvable complications.

Together, they tore at his clothes, frenzied now in their need to be one. With an impatient sound, Dane vaulted from the bed, kicking his breeches free of his painfully aroused body, growing harder still at the sight of Jacqui watching him and reveling in his nakedness with unashamed wonder.

"You are magnificent," she whispered in awe. And he was . . . all rippling muscle over bronzed skin, his erection huge and rigid and pulsing with its need for her.

Dane said her name in an agonized growl, coming down over her, parting her legs with an insistent knee.

He took her without preliminaries . . . she welcomed him without restraint, biting her lip to keep from crying out as his first fiery thrust entered her, filled her, nearly drove her over the edge. Dane withdrew and buried himself again, deeper, harder, his breath coming in ragged pants, his greedy hands lifting her legs higher around him, pushing him farther into her tight, hot wetness. Jacqui matched his wildness with her own, digging her fingers into his sweat-drenched back and arching into his battering thrusts, devoured by a mating that was savage in its demand, poignant in its significance . . . and over in a few lightning strokes.

Seconds later, the universe exploded.

Jacqui arched back, dissolving into throbbing spasms of near painful completion, lurching upward to pull Dane as deep inside her as possible. In return, Dane crushed her into him, flooding her with huge, convulsive bursts of release, covering her mouth with his to drink in her cries of pleasure and to silence his own.

The room was quiet, but for their sharp, ragged breaths. Bathed in perspiration, Dane dropped his face into the crook of Jacqui's neck, tasting the salt of their union and feeling physically drained . . . and emotionally raw. Beneath him, Jacqui shivered, and Dane became aware of how small and fragile she was, how violently he'd taken her.

All his rage drained away with the last of his seed. Softly, tenderly, he kissed the damp tendrils of hair at her temple, rolling to one side and taking her with him. "Did I hurt you, *chaton?*"

"No." The one syllable was barely audible.

Dane tensed. What the hell had he been thinking of? Of course he'd hurt her. After all, it was only the second time she'd been with a man. The first time, she'd bled. "Jacqueline . . . are you all right?"

She sighed, a whispering ripple against his chest. "I think so."

He forced her head back, cupped her face in his hands. "I'm sorry, love," he murmured with tender remorse. "After last week . . . I promised myself I'd go slowly, give you the prolonged hours of lovemaking you deserve. But it seems that every time we're together I lose all my control, become so frantic that I behave like a callow youth." He kissed her flushed cheeks. "Forgive me."

A faint smile touched Jacqui's lips and she closed her eyes, suddenly overcome by weariness. "There is nothing to forgive. It was wonderful." She stifled a yawn. "Oh Dane, I'm so very tired . . ." she said in a small voice, ". . . tired of fighting, tired of deciding what is right . . . tired of being strong." She leaned her forehead against his chest.

A wave of feeling swept over him and he wrapped his arms around her possessively. "I know, darling, I know." He stroked her tangled curls, then reached down and drew the quilt up over them, fitting her body against the hard warmth of his. "I know you're tired. Sleep." He felt her slim body tense as she wrestled against her need to sink into his strength. "Don't fight me, *chaton*. Not tonight. Let me hold you. Just for a little while. Let this night be ours; let's leave the battles for morning. I'll go before dawn, I promise. But until then, sleep in my arms. Be mine . . . totally mine . . . if only for tonight." He touched his lips to her shoulder, joy welling up inside him as she gave up the struggle, melted against him. "I love you, Jacqui," he whispered, feeling her breathing even out into slumber.

Asleep, she was all innocence, so incredibly young and beautiful that Dane couldn't accept any truth other than the one he held in his arms, the one he felt in his heart.

He cradled her gently, filled with intense emotion that refused to be quieted. She couldn't be guilty of treason . . . not even for the most honorable of causes. Despite her political convictions, she would never betray her country . . . nor would she betray him.

With drowsy tenderness, Dane wrapped Jacqui tighter in his embrace, and, secure in his faith, he drifted off, joining her in slumber.

Neither of them heard George Holt arrive home.

CHAPTER
10

Preoccupied, his step heavy, George climbed the stairs to bed. Something was troubling Monique. He had suspected as much for weeks now, but after her behavior tonight, he was certain. He'd escorted her to the elegant New Theatre on Chestnut Street, in the hopes that an evening of opulent entertainment would erase the faraway look in her eyes. Yet, throughout the splendid performance of *Richard III,* she'd fidgeted in her seat, scanning the room restlessly, her hand growing cool and limp in his.

Later, when they were alone, she'd been moody, withdrawn. Filled with an intangible sense of unease, George had taken her to bed, desperate to solidify what was between them through the joining of their bodies.

Even that was an abysmal failure. Oh, she'd whispered the same words of love as always, given herself to him with the same generous abandon that he'd become addicted to . . . but all the while she seemed detached, leaving him cold and empty, as if he'd possessed her body, but not her soul.

Could it be another man? he asked himself for the thousandth time. His heart protested, crying out that it was not possible.

But his mind continued its nagging doubt.

A faint scratching and a soft cry jolted him from his morose reflection. Puzzled, he followed the sound to its source, locating it just outside Jacqui's bedroom.

Crouched on the floor, looking totally flabbergasted and thoroughly annoyed, sat Whiskey, raking his claws against the tightly shut door. Hearing George approach, he redoubled his efforts and emitted a plaintive wail.

George smiled indulgently. "What seems to be the problem, Whiskey? Has Jacqui forgotten you tonight?" He strolled over to the kitten, bending to scratch his ears. George was familiar with Jacqui's standing ritual: to open her door a crack just before retiring so that Whiskey could slip in whenever he was ready for sleep. Obviously tonight she had neglected to perform this customary procedure. Well, that was easily remedied.

Straightening, George pressed the door handle, noiselessly admitting the impatient cat. Along with Whiskey, a shaft of light from the hallway penetrated the dark, silent room, illuminating the bed and its two occupants.

Two occupants?

For a split second George couldn't breathe. And when he did, his breath exploded from his chest in a roar of anger.

"What is the meaning of this?" he shouted, storming into the room.

Dane awakened instantly, automatically shielding Jacqui with his body. "George . . ." he began, wondering what the hell he was going to say. Denial was certainly not an option . . . not with their clothes strewn all over the floor and their bodies intimately entangled under the bedcovers.

"Damn it, Westbrooke . . . what the hell were you thinking of?"

Jacqui blinked sleepily and sat up, trying to focus on what was happening. "Father?"

Dane yanked the quilt up to her shoulders, and all at once, Jacqui came fully awake. "Hell and damnation," she muttered, clutching the bedding to her. Even the bronzed width of Dane's massive shoulders could not shelter her from the pained, accusing look on her father's face. "Oh, Lord," she breathed, struck by the total impact of what was occurring.

"It's a bit late for prayers, Jacqueline." Angry and brimming with paternal protectiveness, George stared from his naked daughter to the powerful, disheveled man beside her.

Dane tensed, instinctively defending the woman he loved. "Don't blame Jacqueline, Holt. Blame me. She is a total innocent. It was *I* who seduced *her*. So if you'll allow me to dress"—he reached to the floor for his breeches—"you can vent your rage at me full force."

"That's very noble of you, Dane," Jacqui interrupted, her dismay rapidly transforming to annoyance, indignation overshadowing discretion. "But your recounting is most inaccurate. You hardly dragged me into bed. Or have you so quickly forgotten that it was *I* who offered myself to *you*, *I* who pleaded with you not to stop, *I* who—"

"Spare me the details!" George exclaimed. He turned to Dane. "Get dressed and join me in my study at once."

Jacqui winced, wondering if she would ever learn to control her impulsive tongue and volcanic temper. "I've never seen him like that," she murmured, staring after her father. "God, Dane, what have I done to him?"

Dane had been struggling to contain the shout of laughter elicited by Jacqui's shear audacity. But the ache in her voice obliterated his smile, tore at his heart. Abruptly, he dropped his clothes and turned to her, took her shoulders in his hands. "Don't you dare choose this moment to become conventional, Jacqueline. First of all, *you* have done nothing. *We* have. Second, there is no reason for us to be ashamed. We both know how right this is between us . . . how real." He paused, drawing a slow inward breath, alerting Jacqui to the magnitude of his next words. "Jacqueline . . . marry me," he said quietly.

Seeing her stupefied expression, the intent look on his face softened and he caressed the satiny skin of her shoulders with strong, tender fingers. "I did not expect that I would propose in this manner either, *chaton*. I would have preferred a more romantic setting, such as strolling in a fragrant garden at sunset or"—his teeth gleamed wickedly—"lying together before a roaring fire." He ran his fingers through the thick waves of her hair, lifting her face to meet the warm humor in his gaze. "But, given the fact that your father is readying his pistol in preparation for my demise, I believe that to wait would be a bit imprudent."

When she still didn't reply but continued to gape at him, the tenderness faded from his eyes and he scowled. "Surely you are not *totally* dumbfounded by my proposal, Jacqueline. Lord knows, there was never anything casual about our relationship. The simple truth is that we are hopelessly unable to stay away from each other. We also cannot go on as we are." He glanced pointedly down at their naked bodies, barely concealed by the thin layer of rumpled bedcovers. "Which leads us to but one solution . . . marriage." He stroked his thumbs across her cheeks, attempting to allay her fears. "I know the way you feel . . . *felt* . . ." he corrected, "about marriage. But surely by now you know that I have no intention of changing you, or trying to usurp your independence." He paused meaningfully. "All I ask is for your respect . . . and your honesty. Both of which we already have between us, do we not?"

His words struck home, penetrating Jacqui's dazed, cluttered mind. She swallowed convulsively.

"Jacqueline?" His hands tightened on her face.

She stared up at him, dizzied by her conflicting thoughts. She was shocked by his unexpected proposal, appalled by her own pleasurable reaction to receiving it . . . and sickened by the implication of his last words.

Honesty. With that sole utterance, reality descended upon Jacqui, seized her, extinguished all else that had occurred tonight. For she knew that, in truth, there could never be total honesty between them. So there could be nothing at all.

Dane saw the myriad emotions flash in her eyes: confusion, pain, conflict . . . and guilt.

It was the guilt that tore at him. "Jacqueline . . . what is

164

it?" He wished he could climb into her stubborn head and drag out the answers he sought. "Once and for all, tell me what you're keeping from me! I have a right to know, damn it!" He shook her, exasperation and fury converging into an onslaught of emotion.

She looked away from him, unwilling to see his blazing rage, unable to escape the accuracy of his words. Yes, as her husband he *would* have a right to know . . . everything. And the point was a moot one, for, even if she chose to defy him, to keep her activities shrouded in secrecy, how long would it take an astute man like Dane to guess the truth? In either case, it would mean the death of Jack Laffey. As her husband, Dane would have every right to forbid her to continue writing her column and would make certain, whatever the cost, that his orders were obeyed.

No, she could never wed Dane, nor, after being discovered with him in her own bed, could they continue as lovers. Which left no recourse but to bring whatever was between them to an end.

Slowly but firmly, Jacqui locked her fingers around Dane's wrists and pulled his hands away. "You are right, Dane," she said with quiet determination. "We cannot go on as we have. In truth, we cannot go on at all." She moved away from him, wrapping the sheet around her in a dignified and symbolic gesture of separation. "Tonight was an illusion," she told him, carefully keeping her tone matter-of-fact. "The reality is what follows—the morning . . . and all the mornings thereafter. I realize you are acting honorably as a result of my father's outrage, but I assure you, your concern is not necessary. Father loves me very much and, despite his current state of mind, he will eventually forgive me. As far as marriage, it would be absurd for you and I to wed simply out of a misplaced sense of duty. I've told you in the past that I plan never to marry—that, as you just pointed out, my opinion on the state of matrimony is, to say the least, skeptical." Jacqui pushed the final words past the lump in her throat. "In short, I must reiterate what I said to you last week. . . ." She raised her chin in apparently unwavering decision. "What happened between us tonight can never happen again. Ever."

Dane fought the impulse to strike her, so great was his frustration at her oh-so-eloquent rejection. He didn't believe her glib words for a moment. Then what, he was forced to ask himself, was the true motivation behind her refusal? The mere preservation of her autonomy seemed a weak excuse for the intensity of her reaction. What drove Jacqueline more powerfully than her longing for him? Compelled her to forfeit all that had grown between them? *You know how she feels about the English monarchy . . . and about the French Revolution.* Alexander's implication reared its ugly head. *Now you're telling me that she goes on mysterious excursions, alone, at night. Doesn't it seem likely . . .* Dane closed his eyes, seeing the thought through to its heinous conclusion. Yes, it did seem likely; more and more so each minute. All the pieces fit: Jacqui's political beliefs, her unexplained midnight strolls, her refusal to commit herself to him when he knew damned well that she wanted him as much as he wanted her.

Dane clenched his fists until his palms tingled their protest, attempting to control his rampaging emotions. Jacqueline Holt was either a terrified, proud little girl holding fast to her unraveling independence or . . . Dane's blood ran cold as the alternative cruelly asserted itself in his mind . . . or she was no more than a prevaricating schemer and . . . God help him . . . a traitor.

There was only one way to find out.

His decision made, Dane came to his feet and pulled on his breeches with quick, violent movements. He was livid, despising himself for his well-founded doubts, despising Jacqueline for her possible deceit, despising the whole damned situation and what was necessary to resolve it.

With an outward calm that was far more chilling than his anger, Dane turned to face Jacqui, moving toward the bed with slow, pantherlike strides until he towered over where she sat watching him apprehensively from amidst the disheveled bedding. Wordlessly, he sank down beside her, every corded muscle of his commanding physique taut with leashed restraint. After an endless moment, he raised his hand, just brushing the pulse at her throat with his thumb, gliding his fingers down over the delicate edge of her collarbone, running the back of his hand over the swell of her breast. Jacqui quivered, helpless to control her potent response to his touch.

Dane's course of action instantly took shape.

"Never again, Jacqueline?" he murmured, leaning over to nibble at her lips. "Was that not what you just said?" He felt the inadvertent shiver that ran through her body like a pinpoint of fire and rewarded her with a deeper, more thorough kiss that took her breath away . . . and gave it back. "Are you certain . . . never?" he whispered. With tantalizing skill, he cupped her breast through the sheet she still clutched like a lifeline, teasing her hardened nipple with a caress so feather light that Jacqui moaned and leaned closer, seeking more.

In one fluid motion Dane tore the sheet from her unresisting hands, arching Jacqui back against his arm and bending his head to answer her silent plea. Without prelude, he drew the entire pleading crest of her nipple deep into his mouth, simultaneously tugging with his lips and lashing with his tongue until Jacqui emitted a strangled cry, pulling him closer with trembling fingers.

Dane lifted his head, triumph glittering in his eyes.

"As I said earlier, you are the very worst of liars, Jacqueline," he taunted softly, ignoring the bewildered look on her face and the heavy ache in his loins. "I defy you to tell me now . . . with your nipples hard and wet from my mouth and your seductive little whimpers begging me for more . . . tell me that this is not what you want, that I couldn't take you right here, right now, even with your father waiting in his study and the sheets still drenched from our earlier passion. Tell me!"

Shocked by the vehemence of his tone, Jacqui lifted an instinctive hand to slap him, but Dane caught it, holding her wrist in a viselike grip, his silver gaze boring through her like steel. "All right, sweet, let us discuss the truth . . . something you are very adept at distorting. The truth is that you have as little desire to end the wildness that is between us as I do. Isn't that right, *chaton?*" He stopped her other hand in midflight, lacing his fingers tightly through hers and holding her captive. "You believe you have won, Jacqueline, but I assure you that the battle has only just begun. You say that what happened tonight was an illusion. I say it is the only reality that exists between us. But there will soon be another. Would you like to hear what that reality will be?" He dragged her against him until her naked breasts burned into the hot skin of his bare chest. He felt her breath, her body quicken, and his lips curved into a dark smile. "You *will* marry me, *mon chaton colereux*. That is not only a reality, but a promise. And as you know, I always keep my promises, don't I?"

Jacqui responded with another unsuccessful attempt to break away from his iron hold.

Dane pressed her closer still. "No answer? Then let me refresh your memory. Do you recall my promise that one day it would be *you* who asked *me* to make love to you? *You* who came to *me?* And you did, didn't you, my sweet? You came to me, asked me . . . no, *begged* me"—his cold silver gaze swept her exquisite nudity in insolent appraisal—"to love you. Repeatedly, as I recall." He ignored her furious gasp, the blazing flames in her dark blue eyes. "Hear this promise and hear it well. You *will* wed me, Jacqueline, if I have to drag you down the aisle to ensure that you do. And once you belong to me I am going to strip away all your secrets, one by one, until your mind and your heart lie as naked before me as your body does now." He took her lips in a punishing kiss that sealed his vow, dared her to contest it, branded her as his.

Jacqui tore her mouth away. "How dare you, you bastard!" she hissed, enraged . . . and exhilarated by the challenge he issued.

Dane chuckled, seeing through her protests to the kindled fire beneath. "You will soon find that there is little I wouldn't dare, *chaton.*" He gave her a long, knowing look. "That is one of the things that most excites you about me. That . . . and the way I make you feel when I'm deep inside you. Isn't that right, Jacqueline?" He bent to taste her other breast as he had the first.

Jacqui licked her dry lips, determined to combat the spell he was purposefully weaving about her. "No . . . that's not right," she said in a soft pant, shards of pleasure piercing through her as his teeth and tongue worked their magic. "I . . . only . . . want . . . you . . . to . . . release . . . me. . . ."

Dane savored the flavor of her, reveling in the passion she couldn't disguise. He lifted his mouth for a scant second, watching the telltale signs of her desire: her dark lashes sweeping the fine bones of her cheeks, the soft flush that stained her satiny skin. He wanted to pull her beneath him and love her until his doubts and her protests had disintegrated into dust. Valiantly, he fought the impulse.

"Your hands have been free for some time now," he drawled instead in a dry, mocking tone.

Jacqui's eyes flew open, her face flooding with furious color. "Damn you!" She fairly flew from the bed, storming over to her wardrobe and snatching a silk dressing gown from within it. It took three attempts and six oaths to don it, so badly were her hands shaking. All the while Dane lounged on the bed, watching her with an intense, brooding expression on his handsome face.

"Get out!" Jacqui yanked the door open and waited, all regal stance and maidenly outrage. "Father expects you in his study."

Dane came to his feet and scooped up the rest of his strewn clothing, taking his time dressing. Jacqui's response was more than enough to convince him that his battle was as good as won. He forced his conscience to remain still, silently assuring himself that this crucial a war left no room for sentiment or guilt. Buttoning his shirt, he joined Jacqui at the door.

She was an enchanting, barefoot vision of smoldering anger, her mahogany curls a tousled waterfall about her shoulders, her small chin raised in mutinous demand. Dane felt emotion claw at his gut, despite his best intentions to remain unmoved. He saw past the flames that burned in her eyes, saw through to the fear and vulnerability that lay beneath.

"It needn't be this way, *chaton,*" he murmured, trying one last time to shatter her misguided veil of secrecy. He nuzzled her sweet-scented hair, allowing his heart to speak past his judgment. "The type of marriage we will share is entirely up to you."

"We are not going to share *any* marriage," Jacqui snapped, jerking her head away from his seeking lips.

Dane ignored her fervent denial. "I'll repeat what I said earlier . . . give me your respect and your honesty, full measure, and I shall stand beside you for the rest of our lives." He raised her stubborn chin a notch higher, regarding her soberly. "Let us stop pretending, my beautiful, exasperating love. We both know you are hiding something from me. Know this as well. You have my word that whatever truth you tell me, no matter how grim, I'll give you my strength, if not my blessing, and I'll protect you from whatever repercussions I can." He looked like he wanted to say more, then thought better of it. "I do not want to keep your father waiting any longer. The particulars I shall leave to you . . . for our wedding as well as our marriage."

Jacqui bristled, throwing back her shoulders and clenching her fists at her sides. "For the last time, I am *not* going to marry you, Dane."

Dane gave her his slow, charming . . . infuriating . . . grin. "And for the last time . . . I promise that you *are,* Jacqueline." He walked past her, pausing only to raise her tightly closed fist to his lips. "Good night, *chaton.*" He stepped away, appraising her with possessive deliberation. "You will look magnificent in white."

She slammed the door in his face.

George Holt abruptly ceased his pacing as Dane entered the study looking as unruffled as if he'd just come from a business meeting rather than a condemnable liaison with George's virgin daughter. The two men eyed each other warily, George's gaze accusing, Dane's direct.

"I'm not even certain how to begin," George stated flatly, lines of pain etched on his face. "Years of fatherhood have not prepared me for this." He shook his head, as if searching for an answer that was not to be found. "How could you do it?"

Dane felt a wave of sympathy for Holt. Regardless of what else he might be, he was obviously devoted to his only child. The shock of finding his young and precious daughter in Dane's arms must have been devastating. In his mind, Jacqui was ruined.

"Before I begin," Dane replied with gentle understanding, "I want to reiterate that none of this was Jacqueline's fault. It was I who—"

"I heard your chivalrous confession the first time you offered it," George cut in, scowling, "and the fact that you admit to having seduced Jacqueline offers me no solace whatsoever. First, it matters not whose initiative it was, for the end result is still the same. Second," and he shot Dane an astute look, "I know my daughter very well, Westbrooke. *very* well. And I can assure you that, experienced at seduction though you might be, she would not have succumbed to your charms had she chosen to remain immune. To be blunt, if Jacqueline didn't want you, not only could you not have seduced her, you couldn't even have taken her by force. She would have unmanned you first. So, apparently, my daughter possesses strong feelings for you."

Dane's lips twitched. "You're absolutely right, Holt." He

folded his arms across his chest in a decisive gesture, proceeding as he had planned. "Very well, I am going to be equally as honest with you as you were with me. The fact is, I've wanted Jacqueline from the first night we met. I have done everything in my power to charm her into my bed . . . and am elated that I finally succeeded in getting her there." He ignored Holt's outraged gasp, pressing onward, determined to achieve his end. "There is but one piece of the puzzle with which you are unfamiliar. And that is the piece that is my gravest disappointment."

"What the hell is that?" George was now beyond anger and into disbelief. No man would speak thus about another man's daughter and expect to live. Pouring himself a much-needed drink, George prayed for strength. "It seems to me that you have taken all you could possibly want from my Jacqueline. What is there left over which to feel disappointment?" His hands were shaking so violently that he sloshed two-thirds of the glass's contents onto the carpet.

"To the contrary, Holt, I want much more than your beautiful daughter is prepared to give. What I *want* is Jacqueline, not as my mistress, but as my wife."

George turned, stunned. "Your wife? But I don't understand . . . if you wish to marry Jacqui, then why . . ."

"You provided the answer yourself not two minutes past," Dane remarked dryly. "If Jacqueline does not want to do something, then there exists no earthly force that can coerce her to do it. I'm sorry to say that your daughter has turned down my marriage proposal in a most emphatic manner."

"I see." George downed his drink, then studied the empty glass as if assessing the situation.

Dane waited, tense with the awareness that Holt's next reaction might provide some important answers. If the older man were half as close to his daughter as he professed, he would be privy to the true motivation behind Jacqueline's refusal, be it staunch independence . . . or something far more menacing.

George cleared his throat roughly. "What, may I ask, are your feelings for Jacqueline?"

That was one question Dane could answer without deceit or hesitation. "I am in love with Jacqueline and have been from the instant I set eyes on her."

George's jaw sagged with relief. "I rather thought as much." He paused briefly. "I suspect Jacqueline is also falling in love with you."

Dane broke into a broad smile, inordinately pleased at hearing that possibility vocalized. "Despite her struggles to the contrary, I suspect you are right." A startling realization struck him as he spoke, exploding in his skull with all the force of an avalanche and causing the triumphant smile on his face to vanish instantly.

Though he was relentlessly bent on discovering the truth about Jacqueline, the outcome of his findings would not change the fact that he wanted her as his. If Jacqueline were implicated, if she were, indeed, a traitor to America, it would wreak havoc on his soul, drive an unbreachable wedge between them . . . yet the reality of his love for her would not alter. Loathe her he might, but love her he would. Always.

Somewhat shaken by the overwhelming magnitude of his feelings, Dane went over and helped himself to an unoffered drink, tossing it off in one quick gulp. The irony of the situation was uncanny. He, who for two and thirty years had walked his own path, controlled his own destiny, earned the respect and ofttimes fear of those who knew him, was now reduced to putty in the hands of one small, compelling woman. It was downright laughable.

He refilled his glass.

George was watching Dane's bleak expression and odd behavior with a frown. "You find the fact that Jacqueline loves you displeasing?"

Dane gave a hollow laugh. "No, Holt, I find the fact that Jacqueline loves me too bloody pleasing for my own good." He bit off his own damning words. "However, the point is

173

moot, for it changes nothing. She still refuses to marry me."
He glanced at George, gauging his position. "So you see my
dilemma."

George nodded. "I do." He refilled his own glass. "As I
said, Westbrooke, I know my daughter." He stared down
into his whiskey, lost in thought, apparently searching for
the right words. He cleared his throat once, twice, shifting
his weight from one foot to the other. "Am I to assume . . .
could Jacqueline be . . . with child?" he blurted out awkwardly after a long interval.

"She could. I did nothing to prevent it."

Blotches of angry color stained George's cheeks and his
jaw tightened imperceptibly. "Then it is up to us to change
her mind from refusal to acceptance, is it not?"

"It is indeed." Dane inclined his head. "Then I can expect
your support?"

"My support? I believe that it has gone far beyond the
point of my offering my blessing, Westbrooke. After what
took place here tonight, I haven't any alternative *but* to
sanction a marriage between you and my impulsive, headstrong Jacqueline. The two of you have taken matters into
your own hands and, as far as I'm concerned, sealed your
fate. In every capacity but the lawful one, Jacqui belongs to
you."

"Yes she does, doesn't she?" Dane knew he sounded smug
rather than remorseful, but he just couldn't feign regret. Not
when victory loomed closer with each passing second.
"Jacqueline, however, doesn't agree. So you see, Holt, my
only remaining problem is our charming, but reluctant,
bride-to-be."

George placed his glass firmly on the table. "I'll talk to
her."

"We'll both talk to her."

"No." George shook his head emphatically. "Give me
some time alone with my daughter, Dane. There are . . .
things about Jacqueline you don't understand, things only I
can approach."

174

Dane's head came up. "Your daughter is soon to be my wife, Holt. Shouldn't I be privy to all that concerns her?"

"You will . . . in time. But for tonight, let me speak with her alone."

It took all of Dane's self-control not to press the issue, but his common sense told him that no further headway would be made tonight; not when Holt was totally preoccupied with Jacqueline's lost innocence.

"Very well, George." His decision made, Dane headed toward the door. "I'll give you until midday tomorrow to make Jacqueline see reason." He paused, his jaw set. "Then I am returning to claim her . . . be it willingly or kicking and fighting . . . as my betrothed."

"For the last time, Father, I am not going to marry Dane Westbrooke!" Jacqui flung herself onto her bed with such force that Whiskey flew into the air, then landed amid the rumpled bedding with a soft plop. He sniffed the pillow where Dane's head had been, turned his nose up with haughty distaste, and returned to nap on the warm indentation where Jacqui had lain.

George leaned back against the closed door, his expression one of anguish. "Your behavior is totally irrational, Jacqueline, and completely unlike you."

"Perhaps that is because what you are asking of me is insane," she returned stubbornly. "I am truly sorry that you discovered Dane in my bed. I did not intend for that to happen. I did not intend for *any* of tonight's events to happen," she added pointedly. "But they did. I refuse to sacrifice my entire life for a mere indiscretion."

Crossing the room, George sat down beside her. "We are not speaking of a mere indiscretion, and you know it, Jacqui," he said softly. "Just as you know that I would forgive you anything . . . even this . . . and never punish you by forcing you to, as you put it, sacrifice your life. What happened tonight, *ma petite,* involves much more than your virtue. It involves your heart."

Jacqui looked away. "I can't marry him, Father."

"Ah, now we arrive at the true problem: *can't,* not *won't.* So you do love him?"

Jacqui made a choked sound. "I care for him."

"Quite a lot, I should say." George's tone was filled with gentle wisdom. "Enough to take the risk of conceiving his child." He saw her narrow shoulders tense.

"I doubt there could be a child this quickly."

George put a supportive arm around her, drawing her close. "And if you are wrong? Would you want to deny your daughter the right to share with her father what you and I have shared all these years?"

"That's unfair," she whispered.

"Perhaps, but it is true nonetheless." He stroked Jacqui's hair tenderly. "You've been a blessing to me from the beginning. I could wish no less for any grandchild of mine than to be wanted and welcomed by her parents"—he smiled in fond remembrance—"as you were by your mother and me. Do you know that, when you were but a newborn babe, Marie would stare down at you for hours as you slept, telling me time and again that you were a rare and special child, destined to be someone of great importance, not just to us but to the world?" He chuckled. "She spoke with such conviction that I had no choice but to believe her.

"Time proved her right. By the time you were three years of age, you were already challenging things that others accepted without question . . . why night became day and why people needed to sleep when it wasted time better spent exploring." He stared off, a faraway look in his eyes, as he became lost in memories. "At five years of age you discovered my library, and life was never the same after that. You struggled through all that you could on your own, and when a book was beyond your abilities, you demanded that I read it aloud. As you grew, so did your interests . . . and your questions."

"I was quite a rebel," Jacqui interrupted softly. "I often wondered why you and Mother encouraged it. Especially

Mother. She was so very traditional, so loving, so . . . content."

"Marie's very sun rose and set on you." George returned to the present with his daughter's words. "She recognized that you were different than she, but she rejoiced in that difference. Ah, Jacqui, if she were only alive today, she would be so immensely proud of you."

Jacqui closed her eyes against George's shoulder. "I hope so," she said in an unsteady voice.

George pressed his cheek against the silk of Jacqui's hair. "I know so. She loved you more than anything else on earth."

"I loved her too. . . ." Jacqui was besieged by the insurmountable wave of remorse that enveloped her every time she allowed herself to think of her mother. Years had not dimmed the pain, nor the sense of isolation. "I miss her so much." Jacqui's words were choked, uttered in a small, strangled voice that was barely audible. But George heard. And he knew better than anyone how Marie's sudden death of an inexplicable fever had affected their bright and inquisitive ten-year-old, who had never understood . . . or accepted . . . why her beautiful mother, who was the very center of her universe, had been taken from her so abruptly and without cause.

Jacqui hadn't shed a tear since that day, nor had she ever been quite the same.

Withdrawing, she kept her pain and her remorse locked tightly within her, months passing before she could reach out for anyone, even her beloved father. When she finally emerged, it was slowly, warily, offering her love to but a few and never with the same joyful openness as she had in the past.

But George, brokenhearted by the loss of his adored Marie, understood. He wept for himself, for his precious child, and for all that had been taken from them.

"I miss her also, *ma petite*," he murmured now. He paused, weighing his next all-important words. "Having

177

ANDREA KANE

shared the great love we did, Marie would want nothing
more than for you to find the same . . . to fall in love with a
man as unique as you; a man who not only loves you with all
his heart, but who is capable of being a partner who will
share your life rather than dominate it. Dane Westbrooke is
that man, Jacqueline. You and I both know it. Just as we
know that your mother would want you to marry him . . . to
be happy."

Jacqui sat up abruptly, torn between emotion and reason.
"There is more at stake than just my happiness."

"Ah," George said thoughtfully. "You speak of the infamous Jack Laffey."

Stunned, Jacqui turned to face her father. "So you *do*
know."

George chuckled. "I would be incredibly stupid not to
have spotted the supreme coincidence of my forthright,
ofttimes disappearing daughter having the identical views as
those of the infamous *Jacques la fille,* would I not?" George
pronounced the farcical pen name as Jacqui had devised it,
using the French translation of Jacqueline: Jacques the girl.
"Let's enumerate the evidence," he continued, counting off
on his fingers. "You eavesdrop at the Subscription Room
rather than join the ladies who are dancing in the Long
Room. You read every newspaper from front to back . . .
most especially the *General Advertiser* . . . while other
young women indulge in romantic novels. You attend gala
balls and stand amidst a circle of senators who are discussing America's plight, never noticing the eager, doting gentlemen who lie panting at your feet." He paused, his eyes
twinkling. "Need I go on?"

An admiring smile tugged at Jacqui's lips. "How do you
feel about my successful facade?" she asked with caution
and curiosity.

"Proud. Worried. Protective." He smiled back, his lined,
handsome face filled with paternal pride. "Can you blame
me for any of those feelings?"

Jacqui shook her head, still absorbing her father's revela-

178

tion. He *knew* . . . had known . . . all along. Despite her speculations to that effect, she was shocked.

George stood slowly and sighed, turning to gaze down at his remarkable daughter. "I read your words each week and I'm amazed by your insight, more so by your accomplishment. No other woman would dare speak out as you have."

"Bache would have my job if he knew I was Laffey," Jacqui shot back, her delicate brows drawing into a frown. "He believes me to be a Republican politician . . . a *man* with strong connections and constant access to our government's innermost circles. 'Tis the only reason he gives credence to my work."

"I know," George agreed solemnly. "Which is why I've refrained from discouraging you . . . despite my worry for your safety."

"My safety?"

George cupped her chin. "Jacqueline . . . I've watched you, time and again, leave the house late at night. Several times I followed you to ensure that you were unharmed while meeting that young lad who delivers your column. But I cannot be with you constantly. So I worry."

Jacqui gave George a wry grin. "I thought I was being so discreet. You knew all along."

"Yes, and I've struggled with my decision since then."

Jacqui went white. "You wouldn't attempt to stop me. . . . Please, Father, it means so much. . . ."

"I know how much your cause means to you, Jacqui. But these are volatile times . . . considering America's strained ties with England and the blood that is still being shed in France. . . . I fear you are taking a great risk."

"I'm certain of all my facts and my opinions are printed as just that . . . my own beliefs."

George shook his head. "I am not questioning your integrity, *ma petite*. What concerns me is how your articles affect public opinion. . . . Are they inciting people and thereby creating a further division within our own country, not to mention more hatred toward the English? Or are they merely enlightening, and therefore necessary during times when there is already too much secrecy? I just don't know."

"You sound like Dane," Jacqui muttered without thinking. "Those are his concerns as well."

"Dane *knows* your identity . . . that you are Laffey?" George was astounded.

"No . . . of course not," she denied, coming to her feet in an agitated rush. "Although"—she gave voice to the nagging fear that plagued her—"I've often wondered if he suspects." Even as the words left her mouth, she shook her head, refuting her own speculation. "But I must be wrong, for if Dane suspected I was Laffey, he would refuse to see me again." She grew quiet, uncomfortably fingering the folds of her dressing gown. "Dane despises Laffey and everything he represents."

"I would imagine he does. Dane and Secretary Hamilton are very close friends. And staunch Federalists, I needn't add."

Jacqui nodded mutely, and George saw the anguish she tried so hard to hide. "So how can I marry him, Father?" she asked in a strangled voice. "We are so very different. Dane would strip me of everything I believe in."

"Would he? It seems to me that he would allow you far more freedom than any husband I've ever known would allow his wife."

Jacqui's cynical look told George she was not cheered by his words. "That doesn't say very much, does it? Except that perhaps Dane is not as tyrannical as most men."

"I believe it says quite a lot," George countered, trying to make Jacqui see the truth. "Don't fool yourself into thinking that Dane's indulgence where you are concerned implies that he is weak, Jacqueline. I can assure you he is *not;* not in business or personal matters."

Jacqui's expression changed. "Dane has known a great many women, hasn't he, Father?" Her meaning was clear.

George cleared his throat roughly. "I'm not privy to

Dane's social life, Jacqueline. Let's suffice it to say that, between the ladies I've seen draped on his arm and the stories I've heard told . . ." He cleared his throat again. "Yes, there have been quite a few women over the years." George's tone was reproving, but his heart welcomed the telltale spark of jealousy that glimmered, for one unguarded moment, in Jacqui's eyes.

"I thought as much," Jacqui retorted, lowering her lashes to hide the unexpected pain her father's words elicited. Erotic memories of Dane's accomplished lovemaking shivered through her, coaxing her pulse to race and her blood to kindle. The realization that he had shared even a fraction of his exhilarating passion and heartstopping masculinity with other, more experienced women, made Jacqui's insides clench with possessive rage. She could cheerfully, and without guilt, line his previous paramours against the wall and shoot them, one by one.

"To the contrary, my dear." Jacqui's seething was interrupted by George's continued discourse on Dane's exceptional personality. "Dane is one of the strongest and most respected men I know . . . and a far more formidable enemy than most. No, Jacqui, I can assure you that, in business as well as pleasure, Dane Westbrooke is a force to be reckoned with, a man who displays no visible weakness . . . save one. You."

"Me?" Jacqui gave a hollow laugh. "Father, I believe you are exaggerating my influence where Dane is concerned. Generally, all he and I do is argue." She flushed as George cocked a dubious brow, rushing on in an abrupt, defensive tone. "Passion might be a compulsion but it is no basis for a marriage."

"True. But love is."

Jacqui pressed her lips tightly together, her heart pounding frantically.

"Dane Westbrooke is in love with you, *ma petite*," George went on gently. "He told me so himself."

Jacqui turned away, recalling how Dane had murmured those same words to her . . . and when. "If he is, he'll just have to get over it. Because—"

"And you're in love with him."

Jacqui flinched, her entire body going taut. "That is impossible, Father," she denied in a fierce whisper. "I cannot be in love with Dane. . . . I won't permit it."

Reacting to the distress in his daughter's voice, George went to her at once, turning her around to face him. Jacqui's dark blue eyes were wide and terror-stricken. George took her hands in his. "We don't always have control . . . at least not over our feelings, darling." He hesitated. "I of all people know that."

"You're speaking of Monique." Jacqui was surprised. George rarely discussed Monique with her.

George nodded.

"You *do* love her, don't you, Father?" she pressed.

"Yes, Jacqueline, I do. Very much." *Even if at times I wish I didn't,* he added to himself, recalling Monique's odd and unsettling behavior of late.

Jacqui hesitated. "Is it the same as what you felt for Mother?"

"No," he answered immediately. "The love I had for Marie is something that comes but once in a lifetime. No one could ever replace her in my heart. My feelings for Monique are . . . complicated . . . different." He frowned, trying to explain. "She is a very important part of my life, filling a void that has been empty for too long. But it is not the all-consuming love I had with your mother . . . and what I believe you are destined to share with Dane."

Silence reigned as George's final words sank in. Then Jacqui gave a bleak sigh. "I don't think life's complications would agree with you, Father. Fate seems determined to prevent any kind of future for Dane and me."

George squeezed her fingers. "Is Laffey truly the only avenue through which you can speak your views?" he asked carefully.

Jacqui met his gaze. "No, I could speak my views through many avenues, but, given that I am a woman, would those convictions be seriously received? I think not." She regarded him with a sad, defeated look. "You want me to give it up."

"I want you to be safe and happy."

"I'm not certain that it's possible for me to be both, Father. I *cannot* give up Laffey. However"—she dropped her head—"I seem not to be able to give up Dane, either." The last words were uttered in a pained whisper, and George knew how much they cost Jacqui to say.

Softly, he stroked her cheek. "Think about your choices, *ma petite.* I won't force you to marry Dane against your will. But think long and hard before you throw away this rare chance at happiness. Consider your feelings, your future, and"—he glanced at the rumpled bed meaningfully—"the future of your children. But, most important, trust your heart, my pragmatic daughter. In this case, it will serve you well." He kissed her forehead lightly. "Dane will return midday tomorrow for your decision."

Midday tomorrow. Jacqui's throat constricted as she bid her father good night, closing the door after him and leaning her aching head against the solid wooden frame.

A mere twelve hours to decide her fate.

CHAPTER
11

Weak sunlight trickled through the bedroom window, alerting Jacqui to the fact that morning had arrived.

No reminder was necessary.

The night had passed in endless indecision, trapping her in a puzzle of darkness from which there was no relief.

With a deep sigh, Jacqui stared at the ceiling, no more certain of her future than she had been when her father left her, long hours before.

The facts could not be altered.

Dane knew she was guarding a secret . . . he had vowed last night to uncover it. If they were wed, he would be ruthless in his attempts to do so . . . something Jacqui could not allow. No, the importance of her cause outweighed all else. Thus her personal situation was futile. She could never marry Dane Westbrooke.

Unable to surmount that unhappy reality, Jacqui rolled onto her stomach and buried her face in the pillow. Dane's scent, clean and starkly masculine, rose up immediately to tantalize her, filling her senses with a tingling reminder of their passion, the magic that occurred when they were one. Unconsciously, she dug her nails into the cool sheets, despair assaulting her in great waves. Damn him, the conniving scoundrel, she fumed . . . he had been certain to leave his mark on her body and her soul, rendering her helpless to forget him and unable to own herself again.

She inhaled again, submerged in the raw, virile essence that was Dane combined with the wildly exciting smells of their midnight lovemaking. Her nipples tightened at the memory, sending jolts of pure carnal sensation through the pit of her stomach to the yearning emptiness between her legs.

The thought of never again feeling Dane's powerful body possess hers, never hearing the dark promises he whispered as he took her closer and closer to heaven . . . Jacqui wasn't certain she could bear the loss. And she dared not allow herself to consider the remote chance that she was carrying his child, for that possibility wreaked havoc on her emotions.

You will wed me, Jacqueline . . . Dane's vow drifted through the turmoil of her mind . . . *if I have to drag you down the aisle to ensure that you do. And once you belong to me I am going to strip away all your secrets, one by one, until your mind and your heart lie as naked before me as your body does now.*

Jacqui vaulted to a sitting position, her eyes wide with sudden realization. How very stupid she had been . . . how blind! The answer had been there all along, needing only that she see it.

Dane had known from the first what her decision would be. It was there . . . in the very words he had spoken, in the manner in which he had delivered them. She should have immediately understood his intent, but she'd been so caught up in her own emotions that she'd been unable to think clearly.

But now, like a bolt from the blue, Jacqui vividly recognized the dare Dane had issued . . . a dare he knew would be impossible for her to resist.

With a triumphant laugh, Jacqui stood, scooping Whiskey off the bed and into her arms. What had minutes ago been a noose about her neck had now become the greatest challenge of her life.

"Oh, Whiskey, this is going to be my grandest adventure to date," she informed the sleepy kitten, who gave a huge yawn and meowed his discontent at being awakened. Unperturbed, Jacqui hugged him to her. "You and I will be making some changes in the near future, my little friend," she informed him, her eyes dancing with excitement. "I shall acquire a new surname and you shall acquire a new home." She tossed Whiskey onto the quilt and grinned at herself in the mirror, seeing far beyond her own tousle-haired reflection. "Yes, Dane, I am going to accept your tempting offer. I'll become your wife . . . and your mistress." She slid her dressing gown from her shoulders and let it fall into a silken pool at her feet. "I'll marry you and enjoy your splendid charms most thoroughly," she continued, glancing back at the bed, her lips curving into a sensual smile.

"But you'd best think again if you plan to delve into my secrets, Mr. Westbrooke. For, wife or not, they shall remain my own." She slipped a clean chemise over her head and watched it slide along the slender contours of her body. "You believe I cannot have it all, Dane?" She raised her chin in spirited defiance. "Well, I intend to prove you wrong. Your challenge has been issued. At midday I shall accept. And our contest of wills can begin."

Still smiling, Jacqui finished dressing and ran a brush through her tangled curls. "We'd be wise to prepare ourselves, little friend," she informed Whiskey, "for we have a formidable battle ahead of us." Jacqui's gaze fell on the quill pen she kept on her nightstand and she walked over to touch it, a surge of excitement rushing through her. "In perhaps a month, Whiskey, we'll begin our new life," she declared. "You, I . . .

"And Jack Laffey."

* * *

George folded his morning paper and tossed it onto the table beside his uneaten breakfast, rubbing his eyes wearily. He'd spent the long predawn hours mulling over what had transpired. Being a pragmatic man, George understood that to belabor the mourning of Jacqui's lost innocence would be a total waste of time. His unique daughter had never been bound by convention; why should he expect her to behave otherwise when it came to her virtue?

No, anger and regret were not what kept George awake until daybreak. What kept him awake was worry.

Jacqui was so damned headstrong that, had he pushed her too hard, she would have staunchly refused to even consider marriage to Dane. But, under the circumstances, had he been too lenient? She was in love with Dane, despite her protests to the contrary. And although she herself didn't recognize it, she needed Dane, badly, to exorcise the ghosts of the past and teach her how to love again.

She could be with child.

George tensed in his chair. No, he concluded with total conviction, there could be no refusal.

"Good morning, Father." Jacqui sailed into the room, looking a bit peaked, but fresh and lovely in a lemon-yellow gown . . . and determined as hell, a decisive gleam in her eye that George found tremendously unsettling.

"Jacqueline," he began quickly, even as she seated herself at the dining-room table, "I have had much time to think, as I know you have." Jacqui's chin came up and George braced himself for a battle he intended to win. "I understand how much your independence means to you, how upset you are over the prospect of relinquishing it and"—he glanced rapidly about to make sure Greta was not within hearing distance—"possibly abandoning Laffey's column," he finished, seeing they were alone. "Therefore, I also understand your reluctance to wed Dane. However, given the circumstances, I feel *strongly* compelled, as your father, to insist that you do." He paused, waiting for the explosion.

"Agreed." Jacqui helped herself to a freshly baked strawberry tart and a cup of coffee.

George blinked. "Pardon me?"

Jacqui swallowed her first bite. "I said, fine." She dabbed at her mouth with a delicate linen napkin.

"I just announced that you will marry Dane," George repeated, thinking that per chance she had misunderstood him.

"I know. And I concurred." Jacqui calmly sipped her coffee. "I have every intention of wedding Dane."

"You do?"

Jacqui gave him a brilliant smile. "Yes, Father, I do. So stop worrying and eat some breakfast. I don't want you to become ill. . . . After all, I need a strong arm to lead me down the aisle."

George leaned forward, a dubious look on his face. "What are you up to, Jacqueline?"

"I?" She was all innocence as she continued to nibble on her tart. "Why, nothing, Father. I'm simply doing what you . . . and my soon-to-be betrothed *requested* that I do." She squeezed George's arm lovingly. "So cease this unnecessary fretting. All will be well." She finished her coffee, then rose. "Please ask Greta to fetch me when Dane arrives."

Mystified by her uncharacteristic behavior, George watched Jacqui hurry off. A slow smile tugged at his lips. Whatever was behind his daughter's surprising decision, he knew one thing for certain: Dane Westbrooke was about to meet the challenge of his life.

Dane would have been the first to agree.

Since leaving the Holts' home, he had alternately paced, cursed, and drunk half a bottle of his own whiskey. Now, sleepless and troubled, he trekked the last few blocks to Hamilton's office, hating what he was about to do, knowing that it had to be done.

He knocked briefly, entering at Hamilton's summons.

188

Once inside, he stopped short, surprised to see Thomas seated across the desk from Alexander.

"Good morning." Hamilton leaned back in his chair, his keen gaze taking in Dane's stiff stance, noting the lines of tension that surrounded his chiseled mouth.

"Alexander. Thomas." Dane acknowledged both men with an inquisitive tilt of his head. "Forgive me, I didn't know you had planned a meeting for this morning. Have I come at a bad time?"

Thomas cleared his throat awkwardly, coming to his feet. "No, of course not. Actually, I simply ran into Secretary Hamilton on my way to work and took the opportunity to speak with him. . . . It's been a long while since we've seen each other."

"Of course." Dane accepted the explanation without question, knowing how deep Thomas's respect for his ex-commander went. "Indeed, it is fitting that I found you together." Dane strolled across the office, his tone hollow, his expression bleak. "After all, my two closest friends should be the first to hear my news."

Hamilton followed Dane's movements with shrewd blue eyes. "What's happened?" he asked quietly.

"Yes . . . you look dreadful," Thomas added, frowning at his friend's somber mood.

"Dreadful? Why, this is an auspicious occasion," Dane returned, pouring three early morning drinks. "One that requires a toast." He handed each man a glass of whiskey, keeping the most generous portion for himself. "Gentlemen, you are looking at a soon-to-be married man. With a modicum of success, my betrothal will be a *fait accompli* by nightfall."

"Your betrothal?" Thomas repeated, his eyes widening. "To Jacqueline Holt?"

"The very same." Dane raised his glass in mock tribute.

"Dane, what do you think you are doing?" Hamilton stood slowly, placing his untouched drink on the desk.

"Doing?" Dane took a gulp of whiskey, feeling it burn a

189

path to his empty stomach. "Why, solving all our problems, Alexander."

Blinking in confusion, Thomas looked from Hamilton's stony expression to Dane's haunted one. "What are the two of you talking about?"

Dane hesitated, noting Alexander's almost imperceptible shake of the head. "Alexander is worried about me, Thomas," he answered in half-truth. "I suppose he never expected that I would become so utterly smitten with one woman. Especially *this* woman."

Thomas absorbed that information with a crooked grin. "From what you've told me, Jacqueline is completely different from all your previous entanglements."

The rigid lines of Dane's face softened momentarily. "Thankfully, yes. Jacqueline is refreshingly direct and spirited."

"And honest?" Hamilton added softly.

Thunderclouds seemed to darken the room in silent threat.

"That has become my job to find out, has it not?" Dane replied bitterly.

Thomas pressed his lips together, aware of the veiled aura that surrounded the conversation. "Is Jacqueline displeased about your impending marriage?" he tried.

Dane drained his drink in one gulp. "I could safely wager that Jacqueline would prefer wedding Satan himself."

"You've argued?"

"Constantly."

"Then why in the hell are you marrying her?" Thomas burst out.

Dane regarded his empty glass with a smirk, as if enjoying some private joke. "Let's just say that Jacqueline and I share a mutual . . . passion. For each other and for our country." A look of pain cut across his face, revealing the naked emotion he hid beneath his scornful veneer. "Or so I pray."

Understanding slowly dawned in Thomas's eyes. Obviously, something about Jacqueline Holt rendered Hamilton suspicious and Dane uneasy and vulnerable. Knowing Dane as long and as well as he did, Thomas sincerely doubted that Jacqueline's emotional involvement was at issue. By nature, women adored Dane, were drawn to him like moths to a flame. It was unlikely that Jacqueline would be the first to remain immune to his charm. So if her passion for *Dane* were not the question, that left but one thing ... her commitment to her country.

Thomas's heart gave a leap of hope. "You care very deeply for Jacqueline." He knew he had to tread carefully.

Dane nodded. "Very deeply."

"And she for you?"

A dark smile tugged at Dane's lips. "To her chagrin ... yes."

"You are troubled that her political views are so different from yours ... rather, from ours?" Thomas quickly amended.

Apparently he was nearing his mark, for Dane and Hamilton exchanged brief glances.

"That in itself is not a problem," was Dane's guarded answer. "Unless Jacqueline carries the difference in our convictions to an unforgivable extreme."

The underlying agony in Dane's qualifying statement, together with the pointed, charged look he leveled at Hamilton, confirmed Thomas's suspicions.

He had his answer.

"Let me be the first to congratulate you, Dane," he said abruptly, suddenly eager to be gone. He shook Dane's hand, his heart lighter than it had been in weeks. "The best of luck to you ... and Jacqueline. I look forward to meeting your bride-to-be in the very near future."

Dane nodded. "Thank you, Thomas. As for meeting Jacqueline, I plan to make this wedding happen as soon as possible ... for many reasons." He paused briefly. "I'd be pleased if you would act as my groomsman."

"I'd be privileged to stand up for you." Thomas clapped Dane on the shoulder, then extended his hand to Hamilton.

"Thank you for seeing me, Mr. Secretary. It's been an honor, as always." He headed for the door. "I'd best be off. I cannot afford to neglect my business. . . . It's not exactly thriving." He forced a smile. "Good day, gentlemen."

Dane waited until the door had closed behind Thomas before he addressed Hamilton, no longer disguising the intensity of his feelings. "In light of your misgivings, Alexander, I find myself relieved that your married state prevents you from serving as my groomsman. There is already too much hypocrisy surrounding this marriage."

Hamilton leaned forward, assessing his friend with understanding and concern. "Are you sure this is what you want, Dane?" His voice was gentle.

"Yes. Very sure."

"Have you considered—"

"Damn it, Alexander!" Dane slammed his fist onto the desk, his control splitting in two, the cords of his neck taut and straining. "I'm doing what you asked of me . . . investigating the Holts. Let that be enough!" He strode to the door, turning back with blazing silver eyes. "But remember this. Regardless of what I uncover, no matter what the outcome of my search, Jacqueline Holt will be my wife. God help anyone who forgets it."

Thomas was breathless with anticipation as he hastened up the steps of Monique's modest home on Walnut Street. He knocked impatiently, pacing on the narrow walkway until Monique opened the door.

"Thomas?" She looked stunned, holding the sides of her dressing gown together, glancing uncomfortably up and down the street. "Why are you here? It's daylight!"

Thomas eased past her and into the hallway. "Then you'd best let me in at once!" he teased. Seeing her distress, he kissed her hand softly. "Stop worrying, love, it's barely morning. No one is about to witness my arrival."

Monique shut the door quickly and turned to face him. "What is it?" she demanded.

"It's important, *chérie,*" he answered gently, stroking her cheek. "Or I wouldn't have come. Now, may I have a more enthusiastic welcome?"

A reluctant smile tugged at Monique's lips. "I can never resist you, Thomas," she murmured, stepping into his arms and raising her face for his kiss.

"Good. Keep it that way." He took her mouth in lingering possession, pressing her pliant body against his. But, when he would have deepened the kiss, made it last, Monique pulled away, purposefully shaking her head.

"Soon, *chéri.*" She stroked his lips with her fingertips. "But first, tell me what prompted this unexpected visit." Despite her smile, there was no mistaking the reprimand in her tone. "It would ruin all that we've worked for if the wrong people were to see us together."

"I have a feeling that the 'wrong people' are searching in the 'wrong places,'" Thomas returned cheerfully, unperturbed by her admonishment.

"What have you learned?"

Thomas grinned. "Far more and with far greater ease than I ever expected and, ironically, not from my meeting with Secretary Hamilton . . . but from Dane."

"Dane? Dane Westbrooke?" Monique pursed her lips in annoyance. "I thought you were attempting to discover Hamilton's reaction to Jay's lack of success with Grenville."

"I was. I did."

"And? Hamilton knew the American conditions intimately, Thomas; he drew them up himself." Monique dug her fingers into his forearms, exasperation lining her lovely face. "He is aware that the English smoothly countered every point. Certainly he *must* suspect something!"

"He does. And I have a strong inclination as to *who* he suspects."

"Who?"

"Jacqueline Holt."

Monique's face drained of color. "Jacqueline Holt? You think Hamilton and Dane Westbrooke suspect Jacqueline

Holt of supplying the British with their information? But she's just a young girl. . . ."

Thomas shrugged. "I doubt they believe she's doing this unaided. Who knows? Maybe they think her father is involved as well."

"Dieu . . ." Monique thought she might faint. Desperately, she tried to hide the intensity of her reaction, clutching the folds of her dressing gown in order to still the trembling of her hands. "Are you certain of this, Thomas?"

"I'm not certain of anything these days, Monique." He sighed, feeling relieved, yet so weary. "But my instincts tell me I'm right." He looked at her oddly, wondering why she was not pleased that guilt had been cast elsewhere rather than concerned with insignificant details. "Dane is obviously convinced that Jacqueline is somehow involved, convinced enough to marry her in order to gain the information he needs." He frowned at Monique's inadvertent gasp. "Why does this upset you so?"

"Marry her!" Monique heard nothing past those words. Her eyes widened in fear. "Did you say that Dane Westbrooke is marrying Jacqueline Holt?"

"Yes, that's what I said." Now Thomas was becoming impatient. "What difference could that possibly make to you? You don't even *know* Jacqueline Holt!"

Monique turned away from him, burying her face in her hands. Her carefully constructed web of deceit was collapsing all around her, threatening to destroy all she sought to accomplish. Thus far she'd managed to keep Thomas believing that their sole purpose was to steal secrets for England in exchange for money. He knew nothing of her communications with France, nor of the way she achieved them . . . enamoring George Holt, stringing him along for his shipping contacts with her country.

Until today, Thomas and George had been kept deliberately apart. But now the impending marriage of Dane Westbrooke and Jacqueline Holt would force those concentric rings to cross, with potentially disastrous results.

Monique's mind raced ahead, trying to find a solution.

"Monique?" Thomas came up behind her, wrapping his arms about her waist. "What is it?"

"I do know Jacqueline Holt . . . and her father . . . very well." Monique turned in Thomas's arms, her fine-boned features once again composed, serene. Ignoring his surprised expression, she supplied a calculated skeleton of the truth. "The Holts and I are old friends. I was introduced to George at a ball several years ago, and Jacqueline shortly thereafter. George and I travel in much the same social circles, which is no surprise given the fact that we share a common view of the importance of an American alliance with France."

Thomas ingested her admission carefully. "You never mentioned knowing the Holts prior to this."

"There was no reason to. Now there is. If Jacqueline Holt is getting married, I will be expected to attend. Therefore you must not."

Thomas gave her an incredulous look. "Monique, Dane is my closest friend. Despite what I've done to him," he added bitterly, guilt twisting his gut once again. "I've agreed to act as his groomsman. Of course I must attend. . . . I have no choice."

Blue fire raged in Monique's eyes. "We cannot be seen together."

"Why the hell not?" Thomas exploded, seizing her shoulders. "We've kept our personal relationship a secret for months now . . . and I'm tiring of it. Why can't anyone know about us?"

"Listen to me, Thomas, and listen well!" Monique pressed her fists against his chest. "We cannot take the risk of anyone thinking of us as a twosome . . . in any capacity. We are too close to achieving our goal. Nothing can stop us, do you understand!" She was shaking.

"Oh, I understand," he shot back, loathing himself for his weakness. "My money and your cause . . . what could be more important than those?" He tangled his hands in her hair. "Tell me, Monique, where do *we* fit into all this? What will become of us *after* we've accomplished our task?"

Forcibly, Monique calmed her raw emotions. She relaxed her hands and slid them up Thomas's chest and around his neck. "Ah, Thomas"—she stepped closer—"once we have completed our work, the world will be ours. We can leave America and start our life together." She pressed her lips to his neck, smiling at the involuntary shudder that ran through him. "No more talk," she murmured against his skin. "We must take advantage of this unexpected time together, *oui?*"

Thomas's arms tightened and he dragged her to him, closing his eyes, helpless to prevent the need that swamped him, body and soul. Giving himself over to it, he smothered his misgivings and his guilt, lifted her into his arms, and carried her up to bed.

"Greta, please tell Jacqueline I'm here to see her."

Dane loomed in the open doorway, his jaw set in grim determination.

Greta nodded complacently, smoothing her newly styled hair, and gave Dane what he would have instantly recognized as a smile had he not been so preoccupied. "Certainly, Herr Westbrooke. Won't you come in?"

"Thank you." Dane almost knocked her over as he took the hallway in four determined strides, pausing before the open sitting room. "I'll wait in here."

"Of course." Greta headed toward the stairs. "I saved some fresh strawberry tarts for you. I'll bring them to the sitting room after I inform Fräulein Holt that you have arrived."

Dane nodded, barely hearing her words. He paced the length of the sitting room several times before halting beside the settee where he'd first held Jacqueline in his arms. His fists clenched at his sides, fury and possessiveness accompanying memory. He forced the anger away, refusing to allow himself to feel anything that might complicate this moment.

All the repercussions of the next months would have to wait. For now, all his energies would be channeled into one unshakable resolution.

He was going to make Jacqueline Holt his wife.

"Good morning, Dane. You've arrived early."

Dane turned abruptly, taking in the woman he both loved and distrusted, arming himself for battle.

"I saw no point in waiting, Jacqueline. Another hour would have changed nothing."

"True," Jacqui conceded, glancing up as Greta sailed into the room, carrying a tray laden with strawberry tarts and an enormous pot of coffee. Placing it on the table, she hovered beside it, reluctant to leave.

"That will be all, Greta," Jacqui instructed firmly. "Mr. Westbrooke and I would like to talk . . . alone."

Greta's lips thinned. "Very well, Fräulein." She gave Dane a sidelong glance. "If you need anything further, let me know."

"Goodbye, Greta." Jacqui gestured toward the door.

Stiffly, the housekeeper marched out.

"Would you like some coffee?" Jacqui inquired pleasantly, seating herself in the large armchair beside the settee.

"No." Dane took her elbows and dragged her from the chair. "Nor do I want to play games. What I want is an answer to my question."

Jacqui gave him a beatific smile. "Which question was that?"

"Damn it, Jacqueline . . ."

"Is that any way to speak to your betrothed?" she queried sweetly.

Dane tensed. "What?"

"You did ask me to marry you, did you not?" Jacqui inclined her head.

"Several times. Are you consenting?"

"You issue quite a challenge, Mr. Westbrooke. But you already know that, do you not?"

Despite his black humor, Dane felt his lips curve. "I do."

"And I have never been one to refuse a challenge . . . but you know that as well, correct?"

"Absolutely."

Jacqui placed her hand on the fine linen of his shirtfront, acutely aware of his power, his dizzying presence. "And there's no denying what happens when we're together, is there?" she asked, wonder in her voice.

"No, there isn't." He was smiling now, the smell of victory tantalizing his senses.

Jacqui gazed up at him. "If we wed, will there be many nights like last night?" Her eyes were alight with mischief, her cheeks flushed.

"Ah, Miss Holt," he drawled back, gliding his fingers through the silken strands of her hair, *"when* we wed, I can promise you endless nights that blaze so hot, they will melt last night's passion beneath their embers." He brushed his lips against hers, teasing her mouth with his tongue. "I'll make love to you in ways you've never even dreamed of," he promised softly, arousing her . . . and himself . . . with his words, the images they conveyed. "I'll take you again and again . . . until you can't breathe, can't move, until you plead with me to stop." He murmured the last into her parted lips.

"And if I never do that?" she whispered back, her heart skipping a beat.

"Then we'll love until we die." He took her mouth in a scalding kiss, enveloping her in a bottomless emotion that defied all the ugliness hovering between them. "Say yes, Jacqueline," he urged, his plea caressing her fevered skin. "Say that you'll marry me."

Unblinking, Jacqui stared into Dane's glowing silver eyes, feeling reckless but certain, accepting his proposal, his possession, and his challenge with all the spirit and fire they demanded.

"Yes."

CHAPTER

12

There is no reason to be nervous, *chaton*. I have not the slightest doubt that my mother will love you." Dane leaned back and stretched his arms nonchalantly across the back of the elegant coach seat, regarding Jacqui with tender amusement.

From the opposite seat, Jacqui settled herself into a position of exaggerated ease. "I am *not* nervous," she countered, smoothing her skirts for the sixth time.

"I'm glad to hear that, love." Dane swung over and slid alongside her, tugging her tense body against him. "Because I don't want to waste this rare hour alone together on nonsense." He nuzzled her hair. "I have a far more delightful diversion in mind."

"Have you gone utterly mad?" Jacqui jerked away as if his touch burned. "We're on our way to see your mother, for heaven's sake!"

"True. However, the trip to Greenhills will take the better part of an hour, at best. So," and he moved closer again, drawing her to him and kissing the side of her neck, "I plan to take full advantage of these wonderful moments we have to ourselves." He leaned past Jacqui to draw the curtains of the carriage. "We've hardly seen each other, much less been alone together, in nearly a fortnight . . . since we announced our betrothal." He kissed the curve of her shoulder. "I ache for you, *chaton.*" Before Jacqui could speak, he'd covered her mouth with his.

"Dane . . . we can't." Jacqui pressed the heels of her hands against Dane's chest in a firm show of protest. She'd missed him too . . . dreadfully. But she needed a clear mind for the evening ahead, and she knew only too well where their kisses would lead.

Dane gave her a look of tender understanding. "We won't." He caressed her cheek with his knuckles while he slipped his other hand into his coat pocket. "I only want to hold you. And to give you this." He took out a small box and snapped it open.

Cushioned on its velvet bed was an enormous glittering emerald, its shimmering fire intensified by the halo of tiny diamonds encircling it in a shower of twinkling stars.

Dane took the ring from its nest and slid it onto Jacqui's finger. "A fiery jewel for my fiery kitten," he murmured, lifting her fingers to his lips.

"Dane . . . it's lovely." The surge of emotion that assailed Jacqui, though still unwelcome, was becoming a more frequent and persistent visitor. She stared at the ring in silence, watching Dane's lips caress her hand. "It's far too extravagant."

Dane smiled. "No common betrothal ring would do for you, my unconventional love. This one suits you perfectly. It has your flame, your spirit." He kissed her palm. "I was beginning to think I would never have you to myself long enough so that I might give it to you."

"I'm sorry, Dane." Jacqui sighed. "I know I've been constantly surrounded by seamstresses and well-meaning shopkeepers. Not to mention Greta, who is always barking out advice, and my father, who is too nervous and over-wrought to offer me much assistance. Truthfully, I never realized how much preparation went into a wedding." Her gaze grew wistful. "If only . . ." She broke off abruptly, withdrawing her hand and lacing her fingers tightly together in her lap. "Anyway, I am not *totally* to blame for our lack of time together. Westbrooke Shipping seems to be very demanding these days."

Dane didn't answer. He felt certain that Jacqui had been about to reveal something, something that could, perhaps, provide Dane with the insight he needed to better understand his complex betrothed. He studied her in brooding silence, wondering if he'd ever get inside Jacqueline's beautiful, complicated head.

He pondered her last words, and a twist of guilt wrenched him. No, Westbrooke Shipping hadn't claimed nearly as much of his time as he'd pretended. Much of his evening hours had been spent watching the Holts' house, waiting to see if either Jacqui or George did anything suspicious.

Nothing had occurred.

And Dane was beginning to feel like a bastard.

For the hundredth time, he found himself praying that Alexander was wrong, that all their concerns had been for naught. After all, there had been no further news from Jay, other than the fact that he was vigorously negotiating with the British. Perhaps there was another explanation for . . . for what? For the fact that each and every American condition had been anticipated verbatim? No, that was impossible. The reality was that someone close to their government was a traitor.

But Dane still could not accept that it was Jacqui.

He looked down at her now as she nervously shifted in her seat, the typical picture of a beautiful young woman about to meet her future husband's mother. A wash of feeling swamped him and he wrapped his arm about her shoulders, pressed her head to his chest.

"All will be well, *chaton*," he told her softly. "Just learn to trust me."

Jacqui closed her eyes, allowing herself . . . just for an

instant . . . to believe Dane's words. It felt glorious to lean on him, to be absorbed in his strength. She nestled closer, feeling relaxed and content and . . . home.

"Dane . . . tell me about your mother."

Dane smiled against Jacqui's silky hair. "My mother is a most unusual woman. Quite the rebel, actually. She is spirited and so full of life that I often forget she is no longer a young girl. The two of you will get along famously."

Jacqui looked up at him curiously. "Was she stunned by your news of our betrothal?"

"Stunned? No." Dane chuckled, remembering his mother's relieved *At last! I thought for certain you'd never recognize your feelings for this young woman, much less act on them!* "Not stunned, Jacqueline, but very pleased."

"Have you told her much about me?" Jacqui continued cautiously.

Dane's smile faded. There was too much he couldn't tell his mother, too much he himself had yet to learn. His stomach clenched.

"My mother and I haven't seen each other these past weeks," he answered curtly. "I rode out to Greenhills long enough to tell her of our plans and to receive her invitation to dinner. You can speak with her yourself tonight."

"I see." Jacqui fingered the folds of her rose-colored gown. "She must miss your father dreadfully."

"I've told you in the past, I don't wish to speak of my father. I haven't the slightest idea whether my mother thinks of him or not. I only know that I don't."

Dane's tone was glacial, as it had been the first time Jacqui had mentioned his father. Only this time she wasn't fooled into thinking his vehemence signified coldness or detachment. This time, with months of growing to know Dane behind her, Jacqui was startled to find that, rather than becoming miffed by Dane's curtness, she was besieged by a wave of sympathy and remorse, an innate understanding of the internal pain that prompted his bitterness. To her amazement, she wanted to help him.

202

"What did he do to make you so angry?" she asked quietly.

Dane's head jerked around, and his eyes narrowed at the question. "Leave it, Jacqueline!" he ordered.

Jacqui reached up to touch his face. "I only want to help."

Something inside Dane snapped at the never-before-seen tenderness on Jacqui's face. He fought the tide of feeling that reminded him how bloody much he loved her, how ill-fated that love seemed destined to be. When that attempt to stem his emotions failed, he channeled them the only way he could handle, the only way she would accept, dragging her onto his lap, burying his vulnerability beneath his passion. "Help me by giving me this," he muttered thickly, burying his lips in hers. "Only this."

By the time the coach bounced into the curving drive of Greenhills, they were wrapped in each other's arms, lost in the deep, consuming kisses that manifested all that was left unsaid between them. Feeling the carriage slow, they broke apart, Jacqui hastily smoothing her skirts and fixing her hair and Dane readjusting his shirt and coat.

"What is your mother going to think?" Jacqui demanded, her breath still coming in uneven little pants.

Dane studied Jacqui's softly flushed cheeks and moist, sensual mouth, knowing his love for her would be his undoing. Aloud he said, "My mother will think that I have the most exquisite taste in women and that I cannot keep my hands off my beautiful wife-to-be." He raised Jacqui's chin and ran his thumb over her kiss-swollen lips. "She'll be right."

What Lenore Westbrooke thought was that Jacqueline Holt represented the challenge of a lifetime . . . the ideal mate for her strong, commanding son.

"Jacqueline . . . I am delighted to meet you at last." Lenore met them as they walked up the path leading through the gardens. She kissed Dane's cheek, then took Jacqui's hands in hers and squeezed them, her expression open and welcoming.

Taken aback by the unexpected show of affection, Jacqui returned Lenore's smile a trifle uncertainly, thinking that Dane's tall, raven-haired mother was the perfect feminine counterpart of her son . . . right down to his breathtaking smile. The only exception was their eyes, not only the color, but the intensity. Rather than the piercing silver-gray of Dane's, Lenore's eyes were a keen, warm shade of hazel, as gently insightful as Dane's were penetrating and capable of delving into one's very soul.

Jacqui took a deep breath. "I'm pleased to meet you as well, Mrs. Westbrooke." She hesitated, then plunged on with her customary directness. "I'm sorry, but I'm not certain how to address you. Would you prefer 'my lady'?"

Lenore laughed, not only at the absurdity of the thought, but at the undisguised look of distaste on Jacqui's face. Definitely a woman after her own heart. "Absolutely *not!* I haven't used my title in over a decade, Jacqueline, not since Dane and I came to America." Her eyes danced. "However, 'Mrs. Westbrooke' poses a bit of a problem as well, does it not? After all, in but a few short weeks you too shall be 'Mrs. Westbrooke'!" She made a wide sweep with her hand, carefully planting the first tentative seeds of friendship, intuitively discerning that Jacqueline's friendship was not easily won. "Why don't we settle on 'Lenore'?"

Jacqui looked startled before a genuine smile curved her lips. "Very well . . . Lenore."

"Good." Lenore released only one of Jacqui's hands, using the other to lead her toward the house. "Now that we've settled the formalities, we can discuss the important issues. I'll take you through the house and you can decide which room would be best for a reception."

"Pardon me?" Jacqui was totally at sea. She glanced over at Dane, who was walking beside her, but he only shrugged, as lost as she.

"Oh dear, I haven't asked, have I?" Lenore came to a screeching halt and bestowed upon Dane and Jacqui another of her melting smiles. "I would be honored if you would consider holding the wedding at Greenhills. We have so much room here. The gardens are exquisite; we could hold the ceremony amid them, if you'd like. Afterwards there are a half dozen parlors large enough to hold hundreds of guests . . . and another half dozen small enough, should you prefer a more intimate reception." She paused, studying Jacqui's surprised expression. "Forgive me, Jacqueline, it is not my intention to coerce you or make you feel obligated. I am certain you've begun making plans, and I have no idea if Greenhills would fit into them. Alter nothing on my account; this wedding is yours and it should be exactly as you wish it to be."

A hint of sadness touched Jacqui's face, then was gone. "Actually, I am having a very difficult time with the staggering number of details that must be attended to," she replied evenly. "As I've never before planned a wedding, I find the whole thing quite overwhelming."

Lenore heard the same wistfulness in Jacqui's tone that Dane had heard earlier. But, being a woman and a mother, she understood its cause . . . and, hopefully, its cure. "Jacqueline," she said softly, "I have but one child . . . Dane. I will never have the joy of planning my own daughter's wedding. Please, won't you give me the supreme pleasure of helping you with yours?"

A rush of relief swept through Jacqui, and she met the older woman's warm gaze gratefully. "Thank you . . . Lenore," she said, her heart suddenly lighter than it had been in ages. "I would very much appreciate your help." She looked around at the manicured gardens, alive with pink, red, and white peonies, and suddenly she could visualize herself becoming Dane's wife here, among flowers as lush and vibrant as the union they'd herald. "And I agree," she said, smiling up at Dane's mother. "A wedding at Greenhills would be perfect."

Lenore's whole face lit up. "Wonderful! We'll begin

planning at once!" She tilted her head quizzically at Dane. "Can you amuse yourself for an hour or so, dear? Jacqueline and I have a lot to discuss."

Dane shot his mother a quick, appreciative look, fully aware of what she hoped to accomplish. And, watching Jacqueline thaw beneath Lenore's sincere yet carefully measured doses of affection, Dane knew that his mother was on her way to success.

"An hour, Mother? I think I can manage to take care of myself for that brief a time. In fact," Dane glanced in the direction of the stables, "I believe I shall have Shadow saddled for a ride. No doubt he misses our wild jaunts together, racing with the wind, galloping across Greenhills at a breakneck pace."

"Worry not," Lenore fired back instantly, hands on hips. "Shadow is well exercised, and as I am equally adept on horseback as you, yet much lighter in the saddle, Shadow has missed you not at all."

Dane chuckled, his amused gaze sliding to Jacqui, who was watching the exchange between mother and son with great interest. He couldn't help but notice how her eyes sparkled victoriously at Lenore's response. "You see, *chaton?*" He sighed with mock regret. "As I said, you and my mother have much in common. Enjoy getting acquainted." He gave Jacqui a slow, tender wink before strolling off.

Lenore took in the play of emotions on Jacqui's face as she stared after him.

"You're in love with my son." The words were out before Lenore could censor them and she cursed herself for the blunder. The mistake cost her, as she knew it would. Jacqui's eyes grew shuttered and Lenore could feel the coldness of her withdrawal.

"Jacqueline, forgive me," she said hastily, before the breach could widen further. "Every once in a while the mother in me rears her head. I want Dane to be happy." She smiled. "I think you will do an excellent job of making him so. Actually, I believe the two of you will make each other very happy."

The shutters lifted, Jacqui's wintry stare supplanted by a flicker of doubt. "I hope you're right," she replied, knowing, even as she spoke, that Lenore's wish was a virtual impossibility. She and Dane could never be truly happy . . . not with the wall of deception that towered between them. They could wed, stoke the flames of their passion . . . and destroy each other in the process.

"Come," Lenore was continuing, "let's have some tea and discuss your ideas for the wedding."

The olive branch had been extended.

Jacqui took it.

"That sounds wonderful, Lenore." Somehow the name was getting easier to utter.

Greenhills was every bit the lavish English country house, Jacqui noted, strolling through its pillared halls. Lenore had not been exaggerating about the number or size of its rooms, each one decorated with a warmth and flair that Jacqui suspected belonged to its mistress. The whole first level was marble with delicate oval windows and a magnificent winding staircase that rose to a breathtaking skylight at its peak. Grand and thoroughly modern in design, Greenhills still managed to retain its classic lines, and Jacqui couldn't help but fall in love with its gracious splendor. The house was much like Lenore herself, Jacqui mused, smiling as she seated herself on the lime settee in the manor's sitting room: uniquely beautiful, yet tasteful and elegant.

"Tell me," Lenore began, settling herself beside Jacqui, "have you planned a large wedding? Do you have much family in Philadelphia?"

"No, unfortunately not. It is only my father and myself. And, of course, Greta, our housekeeper, who is like family. She has been with me most of my life, a combination governess, cook, and disciplinarian."

"I see." Indeed, Lenore *did* see, noting that Jacqui avoided referring to Greta in any type of parental role . . .

such as mother. "Well, then, have you, your father, and Greta made traditional plans for your wedding?"

Jacqui's eyes sparkled. "You will soon find, I'm afraid, that there is very little that is traditional about me."

Rather than appearing nonplussed, Lenore gave Jacqui an approving smile. "In other words, you are a woman of both depth and dimension who is not afraid to speak her mind and who is very much her own person! Excellent!"

Jacqui couldn't help but grin at Lenore's enthusiastic definition. "You might not feel that way when you hear some of my opinions on things," she felt compelled to warn.

"Really? Such as?"

Why did Lenore's words, her daring expression, make Jacqui feel challenged in a suspiciously similar manner to the way she felt whenever Dane engaged her in one of their frequent battles of the wits?

Lenore was about to be shocked right off her velvet cushion.

"Planning her own wedding is every woman's dream," Jacqui began.

"But not yours?"

Jacqui chewed her lip pensively, determined to answer Lenore's question with total candor. "I am but one person in a very complex world. Even as we speak, hundreds are dying in France, struggling to establish a government that is sympathetic toward *all* its people, not only the wealthy and titled. Our own country is torn between honor and pragmatism, hovering on the brink of war with England, unable to look away from the English atrocities." Jacqui stared down at her folded hands. "Given these volatile conditions, the ugliness and the bloodshed, how can I concentrate solely on my own wedding day?"

"I can now add compassion to your list of attributes," Lenore declared. "But sympathy for others and devotion for your country does not preclude joy at a milestone such as your forthcoming marriage."

A stout servant with a plump, red-apple face chose that

minute to scurry into the room, bringing a pot of tea and a plate of warm scones and honey. She placed them on the table, then wiped her hands on her apron. "Will there be anything else, ma'am?" she asked Lenore.

"No, thank you, Dora. This is lovely."

The maid beamed her thanks and scurried out as quickly as she had come.

"Continue with your shocking opinions, Jacqueline." Lenore gracefully poured two cups of tea. "Surely you will reveal qualities that are far more scandalous than intelligence and patriotism?"

Caught up in the fervor of the conversation, Jacqui rose to Lenore's challenge. "Apparently you employ quite a few servants at Greenhills," she blurted out. She waited for Lenore's affirmative nod, then went on. "Well, I do not believe in a class structure. As far as I am concerned, servants should not be treated as chattel, any more than wives should. Wives are partners and servants are workers, hired to do a reasonable job for a reasonable wage."

"Wives?" Lenore inquired politely, handing Jacqui a cup of tea. "Or only servants?"

"Pardon me?"

"I was wondering if your beliefs about payment were restricted to servants or if you felt wives should be paid wages as well."

Jacqui's mouth fell open. "No, of course not. What I meant was—"

"Why not?" Lenore continued calmly, sipping her own tea. "If you consider all a wife does . . . running a home, hiring, firing, and training a staff, bearing and rearing children, sharing her husband's bed . . ." Lenore broke off, pursing her lips thoughtfully. "Let me see, that's a steward, an overseer, a housekeeper, a hostess, a governess, a companion, and a mistress. Seven positions—therefore, by your theory, seven times the wages." She frowned. "Well, perhaps not seven. I really don't believe a woman should be paid for making love with her husband. First, it cheapens her to the role of a mere prostitute, and second, as lovemaking is a mutually enjoyable task, it cannot be considered a job. So," she brightened, "six times the wages one would pay to a trusted servant would suffice." She gave an approving nod, placing her cup delicately back in its saucer. "I rather like that concept, Jacqueline. We'll have to share it with Dane."

After a stunned silence, Jacqui began to laugh. "For once, Lenore, I believe that Dane is right: You and I are going to get on famously." She leaned forward with mock concern. "I shudder to think how our staunchly traditional leaders would react to the views we've just expressed."

Lenore gave a casual shrug. "Our leaders are merely men and must, therefore, be excused for their inferior thinking."

"I believe I have just been cruelly maligned."

Both women started as Dane strolled into the sitting room, his tone rich with disbelieving humor. He cast a speculative look at Jacqui and Lenore. "I am delighted to learn that, in the opinion of both my betrothed and my mother, women are superior to men in their ability to think." Bypassing the tea, Dane helped himself to a glass of brandy.

"Not in ability, dear, but in extent," Lenore qualified. "Women devote more time to perceiving things as a whole, whereas men simply skim the surface." Lenore gave Jacqui a conspiratorial wink. "It is a plight we women must learn to endure."

Dane put his glass down with a thud. "I am ready for dinner." He strode over and seized Jacqui's hand, tugging her to her feet. "And a change in subject as well. Shall we?"

Both Jacqui and Lenore laughed at Dane's response, and, taking his less-than-subtle hint, rose to accompany him. Yet each of the women was aware that, through the respect and understanding that had been forged between the two of them this day, a new and fragile relationship had begun.

Hours later, it was a much more relaxed, happier Jacqui who bid Lenore goodbye on the front steps of Greenhills.

"We are going to be great friends, Jacqueline." Lenore took Jacqui's hand in hers, speaking the words that Jacqui could not yet verbalize.

Dane studied Jacqui's radiant face as she descended to the walkway. Then he turned and kissed his mother's smooth cheek. "Thank you, Mother," he said simply.

Lenore didn't pretend to misunderstand his message. "Thank *you.*"

"For what?"

"For giving me a daughter."

Dane squeezed her shoulders affectionately and walked after Jacqui.

"I'll come into town at the end of the week," Lenore called after them. She gazed warmly at Jacqui. "That way I can be there for the final fittings of your gown and, at the same time, we can send out the invitations."

"Wonderful," Jacqui agreed.

"The wedding is but several weeks away . . ." Lenore broke off as a sudden thought occurred to her. "Will you be going on a wedding trip?" she asked.

Jacqui looked at Dane questioningly. "I don't know. We haven't discussed it."

Lenore hesitated briefly, then plunged on, giving voice to the hope that refused to be quieted. "England has a great deal to offer at this time of year," she said quietly.

Dane stiffened. "This is not a good time for me to be away . . . for many reasons." He stared straight ahead, his face averted, his expression hidden. "There is growing unrest in western Pennsylvania," he said at last. "Many of the distillers are blatantly refusing to pay the excise tax on their whiskey. The fervor is spreading, making the whole situation highly volatile. I might be needed."

"You fear violence?" Despite Dane's casual delivery, Jacqui was instantly alert.

A warning bell sounded in Dane's head, a reminder of the distrust that existed between Jacqueline and himself. "I don't know," he replied tersely. "But any traveling on our part will have to be delayed for a time. And Mother," he added pointedly, his back still toward her, "when Jacqueline and I do make our plans, *we* shall decide where our wedding trip will best be spent."

Lenore nodded, saying nothing. But Jacqui saw the determined light in her eyes and knew that Lenore's suggestion that they visit England had little to do with that country's climate or scenic views.

Jacqui's curious gaze returned to Dane, who suddenly appeared most eager to be gone, and found herself wondering what had caused his abrupt foul humor. Was it Lenore's subtle reference to the past or was it Jacqui's interest in the rebel farmers?

"Come, Jacqueline, I want to get you home before dark." Dane clamped his hand around Jacqui's arm, dragging her forward, his brows drawn together in a black scowl.

With a quick, puzzled glance at Lenore, Jacqui followed Dane's lead.

"We'll see you at week's end, Mother?" Dane called over his shoulder, without turning.

Lenore smiled, unbothered by her son's brooding tone. "Yes, Dane. I'll see both you and Jacqueline then."

She returned to the house light of heart. Unhindered by Dane's anger or Jacqueline's youth, Lenore could foresee far more than either of them was able. What she saw convinced her, now more than ever, that all would be well.

CHAPTER
13

Eleven o'clock. The wedding was but a quarter hour away.

In Greenhills' pale pink bedchamber, the bride donned her gown, readying herself for the ceremony. Behind the manor, amid the sun-drenched gardens, the groom paced back and forth, willing away the minutes that separated him from his bride. In the parlor, Lenore surveyed her handiwork and, content with what she saw, hastened toward the stairway with the intent of assisting the bride in dressing. Instead, she nearly tripped over George Holt, who stood, still as a statue, at the foot of the stairs, anxiously awaiting the entrance of his precious child. Stomping by them both, Greta bellowed out orders to passing servants and, adjusting her own dark muslin gown, trod up to her anxious mistress.

"The guests are all here," she announced, flinging open the bedroom door, trumpeting her words as if there were more than just the two of them in the room. "We are ready to begin."

Jacqui fought her smile, wrapping her arms about herself and reveling in the rich satin of her gown and the warm glow of the sunlight streaming through the window.

She had known the sun would shine. While her father and Greta had fretted needlessly about the prospects of a

213

waterlogged ceremony in the gardens of Greenhills, Jacqui and Lenore had disregarded that possibility, counting on July's more promising extreme: sunshine and bright skies.

What Jacqui had not counted on was this unexpected feeling of avid anticipation.

"I said it is time, Fräulein!" Greta barked again.

Jacqui nodded, unbothered by her housekeeper's fierce tone. Greta was terribly uncomfortable with emotional displays of any kind, but Jacqui suspected that, in her own way, the older woman was feeling sentimental about her charge's forthcoming marriage. It was the sole explanation for her strange behavior this past week. Why, just yesterday afternoon Jacqui had searched the entire Holt house for Greta, only to find the elusive housekeeper locked in her third-story quarters, where she had purposefully ignored Jacqui's insistent knocking.

Recalling this odd behavior, Jacqui fingered the folds of her wedding gown and studied Greta curiously, finally blurting out, "What in heaven's name were you doing in your bedroom yesterday?"

Greta gave an indignant sniff. "What would you expect me to be doing, Fräulein Holt? I was readying myself for our move."

"*Our* move." Jacqui was stunned.

Greta leveled a cool, assessing stare at Jacqui. "Certainly *our* move. You didn't for a moment believe that I was not going to accompany you to your new home, did you?"

In truth, Jacqui hadn't given any thought at all to Greta's position once the marriage took place. Greta had been a part of the Holts' household forever, and Jacqui had just assumed it would continue that way.

"After all, I can hardly remain living there, alone with your father, Fräulein," Greta continued decisively. "Besides, you need me to take care of you. As does Herr Westbrooke. It was he who made all the arrangements," She smoothed her bodice. "Why, I am the only one who can prepare the strawberry tarts he enjoys. So, it is settled."

With that reverent declaration, she folded her arms across her ample bosom.

Jacqui bit back a laugh. So *that* was it. She should have guessed. Greta did have one weak spot. And that spot happened to be Dane.

"Of course, Greta," she agreed solemnly. "I wouldn't have it any other way."

Greta sniffed disdainfully, appalled that her new status had ever been questioned.

A sudden thought occurred to Jacqui. "What about my father, Greta?" she asked. "Who will look after him?" The most likely choice made Jacqui feel ill.

"That has been taken care of as well," Greta returned. "Herr Westbrooke consulted with his manservant and it appears Herr Stivers has a friend who boasts both references and experience. Herr Redding will assume his new position immediately."

"I see." Jacqui shook her head in amazement. Efficiently and without her knowledge, Dane had seen to everything.

"My belongings are being delivered to Herr Westbrooke's home early this morning, where I will go directly after the ceremony," Greta stated. "I'll make a brief stop at Herr Holt's house to pick up your impudent pet, who I assume will be joining us at our new residence as well."

Jacqui grinned, thinking of the antipathy that existed between that impudent pet and her soon-to-be husband. "Of course. Whiskey goes wherever I do."

"Fine. Then we shall both be waiting when you arrive with your new husband." Greta cleared her throat roughly, staring at some invisible spot on the carpet. "I hope you will be very happy, Fräulein." She shifted her large frame from foot to foot, periodically glancing at Jacqui. "You look very lovely," she barked.

"Thank you, Greta." Jacqui was actually grateful for Greta's unease, as she herself disliked overly sentimental scenes. She drew herself up to her full, diminutive height. "I am ready."

The door opened again and Lenore glided into the room, looking extremely elegant in her light blue watered silk gown. Her eyes lit up when she saw Jacqui. "Oh my!" She came closer, appraising Jacqui's heartstopping beauty. The shimmering satin wedding dress, intricately trimmed with lace, and the delicate headdress, adorned with small white roses and baby's breath, made Jacqui look ethereal, like an enchanting angel on the threshold of a new life. Although Lenore had been darting in and out of the bedchamber all morning, assisting Jacqui as she dressed, nothing had prepared her for the dazzling effect of Dane's bride in full array.

"You are positively exquisite," Lenore declared with a gentle smile. "My son is a very lucky man."

Jacqui raised her brows in dubious amusement. "I'm not certain Dane would agree with you."

"Why don't we let him be the judge of that?" Lenore returned, brushing an imaginary speck off Jacqui's modestly scooped bodice. She took Jacqui's hands in hers. "I wish you every happiness, Jacqueline. If ever you need me, I shall always be here." She dabbed at her eyes. "Now I'll go and prepare your father. The poor man is nearly beside himself."

When Jacqui came down a few moments later, George stopped pacing, simply staring at his daughter as if she were a stranger.

"Jacqui? My God, you are beautiful." He swallowed, his throat clogged with emotion. "Jacqueline . . . there is so much I want to say, so much I am feeling . . ." He broke off, anxiously raising her chin with his forefinger. "This marriage . . . it is what you want, is it not, *ma petite*? Because, no matter what has occurred, if you do not wish to wed Dane Westbrooke . . ."

"Father," Jacqui interrupted softly, placing her fingers over his lips. "This *is* what I want . . . very much. The choice was mine and I have made it. I have no regrets."

He kissed her palm gently. "Then be happy. And know

that your mother is with us now, if not in body, then in spirit."

Jacqui's lips trembled. "I know." She took George's arm. "Shall we begin?"

A hushed silence settled throughout the gardens as the bride and her father made their entrance. Over a hundred necks craned and a hundred pairs of eyes strained to gape at the exquisite young woman who had reputedly captured Dane Westbrooke's elusive heart. An audible murmur of approval began, along with Jacqui's ceremonial walk down the aisle between the double rows of benches that led to where her groom stood, quietly awaiting his bride.

Jacqui raised sparkling eyes to Dane's and her heart quickened at the profound expression on his face. She drank in his masculine beauty, thinking how resplendent he looked in his formal black attire, the crisp white shirt emphasizing the tanned column of his throat and heightening the impact of his bold, handsome features. His consuming magnetism seemed to reach out and claim her with the promise that every step she took brought her closer to the blazing challenge that was their future.

Dane watched the vision in white draw closer.

He could never have explained the powerful flood of feeling that swamped him when Jacqueline appeared in the garden. It was an emotion so deeply rooted, so painfully acute that it was nearly unbearable. There was admiration, yes, together with an explosive sense of pride. But most of all, there was love . . . a love so profound Dane thought he would burst with it, a drive for possession so total that he nearly leapt forward and dragged Jacqui the final distance to his side. But he waited, waited until the moment she stood before him, smiling up at him without shyness or regret, meeting him on his own terms, ready to share his life.

They stood, side by side, speaking aloud their vows, committing themselves to each other. Dane slid the ring onto Jacqui's left hand, his eyes glowing with pleasure and triumph as the ring reached its final destination on her finger and the clergyman pronounced them man and wife.

Silence reigned as the finality of their words echoed through the skies.

Slowly, Dane drew Jacqui to him, murmuring, "You're mine now, Mrs. Westbrooke." He brushed her lips with his.

Jacqui smiled against his mouth. "Am I?" she whispered back, giddy with excitement, channeling the unexpected emotion into teasing banter. "Yet your kisses were far more impressive beforehand, Mr. Westbrooke."

Dane straightened slightly, ignoring the throng of curious onlookers, one brow cocked in amused challenge. "Really?" He smiled in a way Jacqui knew only too well. "We certainly cannot allow that, not when I promised you our marriage would be enveloped in fire."

Before she could protest, he had wrapped his arm about her waist, pulling her closer and covering her mouth in a kiss of very deliberate . . . and very public . . . possession.

Jacqui clutched his coat for support, too stunned to react.

The kiss was over in an instant, amid chortles of good-natured laughter. Jacqui barely had time to recover. She opened her eyes and blinked.

"Better, my demanding wife?" Dane questioned, laughter lurking in his eyes.

"It will do . . . for now," Jacqui responded, refusing to give in to embarrassment.

Dane extended his arm to her. "I believe it is traditional for me to escort you back. Not to mention the fact that holding on to my arm will prevent you from succumbing to your customary reaction to my kisses. You wouldn't want to collapse in front of all our guests, now would you?"

She shot him a scathing look and he chuckled, leading her back into the house.

Once inside, he grew serious, catching Jacqui's elbows and drawing her close.

"In less than one minute, we are going to be surrounded by hundreds of well-wishers." He cupped her face. "It will be hours before we're alone. I need something to sustain me."

He parted her lips hungrily, wanting Jacqui to feel what he was feeling, to need what he needed. Jacqui required no urging. She glided her hands up the front of Dane's coat and clung to his broad shoulders, willingly opening to the kiss, touching her tongue to his until a tremor ran through Dane's powerful body.

When he released her, his breathing was ragged. *"Your* kisses, on the other hand, have grown infinitely *more* impressive since we wed, Mrs. Westbrooke." He inhaled sharply, striving for control.

"True. And that applies to more than just my kisses." Jacqui tossed him a suggestive look, letting her pointed gaze linger on the revealing bulge in his breeches.

Scorching flames leaped to life in Dane's eyes, and only the sound of approaching guests kept him from carrying his new wife off to a bedroom . . . any bedroom.

"Don't tempt me," he warned, his expression dark with passion.

"Oh, I *plan* to tempt you . . . later," Jacqui promised with a seductive smile. "Tonight." She stepped away.

"All night," he whispered fiercely, just before Greenhills became a hub of reveling guests eager to congratulate the newly married couple.

"May I be the first to congratulate you and your lovely bride?" Thomas shook Dane's hand with enthusiastic warmth. But his voice was unusually loud and his eyes suspiciously bright.

"Thank you, Thomas. And thank you for standing up for me today." Dane returned the handshake, wondering uneasily why Thomas was drunk at half after eleven in the morning.

Thomas kissed Jacqui's hand. "Dane did not exaggerate when he spoke of your beauty."

219

"Nor when he spoke of anything else concerning me, I'm certain." The look Jacqui gave Thomas was pure innocence.

Thomas blinked, as if he weren't quite sure he had heard right, then moved on to fetch himself a glass of champagne.

"Behave yourself," Dane chuckled quietly in Jacqui's ear, wrapping his arm about her waist and squeezing gently. "We cannot have you intimidating the guests."

"Dane, may I offer my good wishes as well?"

Dane's smile faded, and he turned to meet Hamilton's cool blue gaze. "Thank you, Alexander." His tone was stiff, and his hand tightened protectively on Jacqui's waist.

"Mrs. Westbrooke . . ." Hamilton stumbled on the name for but an instant, "my congratulations to you." He bowed, brushing Jacqui's hand with his lips.

Jacqui lowered her dark lashes, then surprised Dane by giving Hamilton a practiced smile. "Thank you, Mr. Secretary." Her smile became genuine as her gaze found Betsey Hamilton's. "Mrs. Hamilton," she greeted her. "I'm delighted that you could come."

Betsey took her hands. "As am I. May I wish you and Mr. Westbrooke a wonderful life together," she grinned impishly, *"Mrs.* Westbrooke."

While Betsey and Jacqui chatted, Hamilton discreetly scrutinized Dane's bride. Outwardly, nothing seemed amiss. She was, as he had surmised on the previous occasions when their paths had crossed, a highly intelligent, strikingly beautiful young woman with an unusually sharp tongue. Equally obvious was the fact that Dane was hopelessly besotted with her. Hamilton frowned. He only prayed that Dane's personal feelings would in no way cloud his ability to uncover his wife's secrets . . . and to act on them.

"Good evening, Mr. Secretary, Mrs. Hamilton. May I interrupt long enough to kiss the bride?" George Holt, accompanied by a smiling Monique, interrupted both Hamilton's thoughts and Betsey's conversation.

"Of course, Mr. Holt," Betsey said, moving aside for him.

"Yes," Hamilton agreed, taking Betsey's arm. "We should

be moving on and giving others a chance to offer their good wishes." He met Dane's gaze briefly. "We'll speak later." Then he led Betsey into the gaily decorated parlor.

Stepping forward, George's smile faded and he gripped Jacqui's shoulders tightly, suddenly overcome by the need to have his little girl back, small, belonging only to him . . . knowing at the same time that those days were gone forever. Swallowing, he pressed a kiss to her smooth forehead. "Be happy, *ma petite,*" he said softly. "I love you very much."

"Thank you, Father." Jacqui lay her hand against his smooth-shaven cheek. "I shall."

"Yes, Jacqueline, may you know only happiness." Monique swept forward, pressing her face to Jacqui's. "And you also, Mr. Westbrooke."

Dane saw Jacqui visibly flinch at Monique's touch, and he found himself wondering at the intensity of his wife's dislike for the Frenchwoman. Jacqui had never actually given him a reason for her feelings, and Dane made a mental note to discuss it with her later. *Much* later, he added to himself with a grin. Conversation would not be high on his list of priorities when he finally had his bride to himself.

"Thank you, Miss Brisset," he said aloud. "I have no doubts that Jacqueline and I shall be very happy." He met George's gaze, saw the raw emotion reflected there, and once again Dane was moved by the obvious love Holt felt for his daughter. "Jacqueline shall never want for anything." Dane's words were publicly stated, but the vow was meant for Jacqui's father.

George knew it. He nodded, his eyes damp, and took Monique's arm. "Come, *cherie.* Let us join the others in the parlor." He led Monique into the brightly lit room, pausing to admire Lenore's handiwork.

Sprays of flowers, fresh from the garden, were everywhere, the highly polished floors gleaming as servants wove their way about, trays held high above their heads, some with fresh fruits and confections of every kind, others with crystal glasses filled with champagne. In the doorway nearest the kitchen, Greta stood, barking out orders like a military commander leading her troops. The bewildered maids and footmen obeyed her without question, casting curious glances in her direction, as if wondering why the formidable stranger dressed as a guest was acting the part of an overseer. In one corner of the room, a trio of strings played with all the solemn dignity that befit the occasion, filling the air with soft strains of music. All the while the guests filed in, laughing and chatting, enjoying this rare party at Greenhills.

"The marchioness did a lovely job," Monique commented, her eyes darting quickly about the room. She could feel Thomas's stare boring into her and she knew she must tread very carefully. She could not afford to alienate him, not until the Jay negotiations failed and America was at war with England. Nor could she allow George to become suspicious. Success was too close at hand.

Monique wet her lips with the tip of her tongue.

The turmoil in France had grown to a frenzy; Robespierre's reign was on the verge of crumbling. And then Monique's country would need rebuilding, a task that would be far more painless if America were to stand beside France, united against their common enemy . . . the English. Yes, France could emerge from her revolution solid, formidable . . . with a strong and powerful leader.

With a start, Monique realized that George was addressing her. "From what Jacqui tells me, I don't believe you ought to refer to Lenore Westbrooke by her title," he suggested. "She evidently does not use it." He smiled tenderly down at Monique, covering her hand with his. "Have I told you how beautiful you look today?"

"Yes . . . several times, *cheri.*" Monique laughed uneasily. "I am unused to so much flattery in one day." Gently, but purposefully, she relinquished her hand, a gesture that was not unnoticed by her escort.

George frowned. "Monique?"

Monique cursed her own carelessness. "Yes, darling?" She

slid her hand through the crook of his arm, caressing the soft material of his coat.

Across the room, Thomas gulped down another glass of champagne, his glazed stare fixed on Monique and George. Whatever Monique was doing might be necessary, but it made his guts twist. Family friends? Hardly. Thomas reached for another glass as a tray passed by. Monique might be acting out of duty, but the man with her most definitely was not. George Holt was in love with Monique.

At that moment, Thomas's bitter gaze met Monique's innocent one. She blinked, then, without a flicker of recognition, she turned back to the man at her side.

Thomas turned back to his drink.

Hamilton also was studying Monique and George. Sipping his champagne thoughtfully, he took note of the tension that seemed to spring up between them, then subside. Patiently, he waited to see who else Holt might speak to, what else he might inadvertently disclose.

But, whether it was out of deference to his daughter's wedding day or because there was no one present he needed to approach, Holt's actions appeared completely innocent. Hours later, the Secretary had learned nothing.

"The two of you need only stay a short while longer," Lenore said quietly, coming up beside Dane and trying desperately not to laugh. Her son had been staring at the parlor clock for the past thirty minutes.

Hearing his mother's voice, Dane turned and gave Lenore a wry grin. "Am I *that* obvious?"

"Truthfully? Yes."

Dane chuckled. "Honest enough. Accurate as well." His hungry gaze found Jacqui, who was across the room, deep in conversation with Greta. "How long is a 'short while'?" He muttered the moot question aloud.

Lenore squeezed his arm. "I'll rescue your bride from her maid's evil clutches." She raised her skirts and made her way to where Jacqui was, Greta scowling by her side.

"Jacqueline? Pardon me, but may I have a word with you?" Lenore asked politely.

Jacqui was more than ready to be interrupted. She had just finished arguing with Greta, who was terribly offended over Jacqui's *firm* request that the housekeeper make herself . . . and Whiskey . . . scarce once the reception ended. Greta was adamant that Jacqui required assistance in preparing for her wedding night. Jacqui was equally adamant that she did not, specifically because she had no intention of waiting for nightfall to begin enjoying her role as Dane's wife.

Gratefully, Jacqui responded to Lenore's request. "Of course, Lenore." She shot Greta a warning look. "Greta and I have completed our discussion, have we not, Greta?" There was no mistaking the command in her voice.

With an indignant sniff, Greta rose to her full height and folded her arms across her ample bosom. "We have, Fräulein Holt," she managed through tight lips. Then she blinked, realizing her error. "Forgive me . . . Frau Westbrooke."

Jacqui giggled, undaunted by Greta's obvious annoyance. "*That* particular form of address is going to take some time to accustom myself to." She patted Greta's arm. "Have a glass of champagne and try to relax, Greta."

"I prefer to keep busy." The housekeeper wasn't going to give in graciously.

Assessing the situation, Lenore interceded. "If you wouldn't object, Greta, I would be terribly relieved if you could oversee my staff in straightening up after the reception." She gave Greta a winsome smile. "You are far more experienced than many of Greenhills' servants."

A slight softening of the housekeeper's features told Jacqui that Lenore had won. "It would be a pleasure, madam."

"Wonderful! Then, after I've spoken with Jacqueline, I'll return to you and we shall discuss what needs to be done."

Lenore took Jacqui's arm and led her off. "Cleaning up should take, oh, perhaps ten or twelve hours, shall we say?" Lenore murmured for Jacqui's ears alone.

Jacqui's lips twitched. "Thank you, Lenore."

"You are quite welcome." Lenore was moving purposefully toward the doorway. "Have you said goodbye to your father?"

Jacqui looked across the room and met her father's loving wink. "Yes," she answered past the lump in her throat. "I have."

"Fine." Lenore paused, pulling Jacqui away to one side. "Jacqueline, I know how close you and your father are, but I'm not certain how comfortable he is discussing things of a personal nature with you." She watched Jacqui's face carefully. "I will not patronize you with silly euphemisms, but will simply ask you in a forthright manner . . . has anyone prepared you for what to expect tonight?"

Jacqui bit back her laughter. "Yes, Lenore. I am quite prepared."

"I see. Why do I suspect that your 'preparation' has been provided firsthand and certainly not by your father?"

"Perhaps because you know your son."

A hint of mischief danced in Lenore's warm hazel eyes. "Not, apparently, as well as you do." She glanced over Jacqui's head to where Dane had begun pacing near the doorway. "Oh, dear, I believe your bridegroom's patience is wearing thin." She took Jacqui's arm. "We'd best not keep him waiting any longer."

Dane looked up as his mother made her way through the crowd, Jacqui in tow.

"As promised." Lenore grinned, easing Jacqui forward. "Your bride."

Dane was engulfed by a sense of reckless euphoria as the reality of the situation stormed his senses. His bride. *His.* At last.

Without thought, he reached out and slid his hands down

the curve of Jacqui's neck to her shoulders, stroking his thumbs over the cool satin of her gown. "Shall we go, Mrs. Westbrooke?"

His touch, the rich timbre of his voice, blazed through Jacqui like a brushfire, igniting a need too long silenced. "Yes."

Dane dragged his burning gaze from Jacqui's. "Mother, you'll make our excuses?"

Lenore nodded, moved by the tangible emotion that hovered between her son and his new wife. "With pleasure."

"Good." Dane was already heading for the entranceway, tugging Jacqui with him.

On the front steps, Lenore kissed them both, a wealth of emotion on her lovely face. "May your future be paved only with joy . . . and contentment," she said, striving to control the silly tears that threatened to erupt. She took a deep breath, wanting to offer Jacqui and Dane the wisdom granted her by age and experience.

"Always look to each other for solace and for strength," she said at last, speaking from her heart. "Share your thoughts and your feelings. Respect one another and be honest . . . with each other and with yourselves. These are the elements that keep a marriage whole." A sad, faraway look came into her eyes and was gone. "Be off." She blinked quickly and ushered them toward the waiting coach. "I shan't expect to hear from you anytime soon," she continued in a teasing tone. "Oh . . . and I hope you won't be requiring Greta's services today. I believe I shall need her until quite late this evening." She gave Jacqui an innocent look. "Is that all right?"

Jacqui bit her lip to keep from laughing. "Quite all right, Lenore." She leaned forward impulsively and hugged her. "Thank you," she whispered, just before she swept up her full skirts and climbed into the carriage with her new husband.

The footman closed the door behind them and the horses sped off for the return trip to Philadelphia.

Dane drank in Jacqui's pink-cheeked excitement with a wicked grin. "Your gown is lovely, but a bit uncomfortable for traveling, is it not?"

Jacqui smoothed the elegant satin layers that draped across the carriage seat and onto the floor. "A bit." She shrugged. "But changing would have taken time."

"I would have waited."

Jacqui raised midnight blue eyes, showering Dane with sparks of fire. "No, you wouldn't have. Neither would I."

Her words burned through Dane's body and his smile faded instantly. "You're right. I wouldn't have." He leaned forward to take her into his arms, then abruptly checked himself. "God, I want you," he breathed, his fists clenched at his sides. "But once I touch you, I won't be able to stop." He exhaled sharply and leaned back in his seat. "This ride is going to be endless."

It was, aeons passing before the horses came to a halt in front of Dane's house on Pine Street. Neither Jacqui nor Dane spoke, silently waiting for the footman to assist them from the coach, the air between them charged with anticipation.

The house was deserted, Stivers having been given strict instructions *not* to report to work today. Dane guided Jacqui up the stairs, pausing before the bedroom that they would now share.

"Would you like some time alone?" he asked hoarsely.

Jacqui stepped into the room, slowly appraising her new domain. Her personal things had been delivered this morning, at the same time as Greta's, and now waited patiently to be unpacked and hung away . . . something Jacqui planned to do . . . later.

"Jacqueline? Shall I leave you to get settled?"

Jacqui turned to her husband, making no attempt to hide her open eagerness. "No."

In two strides Dane was beside her, kicking the door shut behind him and dragging Jacqui into his arms. By the time his mouth took hers in ravenous possession, Dane had dispensed with Jacqui's buttons and was urgently tugging the elegant gown down to her waist. Jacqui helped, shedding her layers of clothing as quickly as she could without freeing herself from Dane's enveloping grasp. Their kisses deepened, grew hotter, wilder, broken only by the sound of their sharp, rasping breaths, the soft rustle of fabric as it struck the floor.

Dane scooped Jacqui into his arms, carrying her the short distance to the bed, dropping heavily onto it with her. He lifted her lacy chemise over her head, tossing it down to join the rest of her discarded attire. He slid his shaking hands into her tumbled curls, pulling out the pins and letting the dark tresses cascade down over her naked body.

Raising up, Jacqui unbuttoned his shirt, gliding it off his massive shoulders. She ran her fingers down his powerful biceps, through the dark hair that curled on his chest, over the flat planes of his abdomen, down to the buttons of his breeches. Dane made a wordless sound, pulling away only long enough to shed the remainder of his clothing before he pressed her into the bed, cupping her face in his hands and capturing her mouth for another endlessly eloquent kiss.

"I don't want to wait," Jacqui breathed, struggling to open her legs, unable to free herself beneath the weight of his lower body.

"I do," he surprised her by answering.

Jacqui blinked up at him, her face flushed, her eyes widening with surprise. "Why?"

Dane nibbled lightly at her lower lip, repressing the force that commanded him to take her . . . now. "Because for once, for this first time as my wife, I am going to love you the way you were meant to be loved. Slowly." He kissed her parted lips. "Totally." He trailed kisses down the side of her neck. "An inch of you at a time." He licked a lazy circle around the hollow at the base of her throat, glorying in the shivers of pleasure that ran through her in dizzying currents. "Until you think you'll die of it," he whispered, breathing in the scent of her perfume, "die without it . . . die for it." He raised her arms above her head, intertwining their fingers, raking her with his melting silver gaze.

Jacqui could barely speak. "No," she managed, shaking her head from side to side.

"Yes." He buried his lips in hers, demanding that she meet him on his terms.

"Dane . . . please," she whispered into his open mouth.

"Soon . . . not yet," he answered, battling her desire and his own.

She tried again, unsuccessfully, to open her body to his. "Why are you doing this?"

The naiveté of her question, the bewilderment on her beautiful, glowing features, reminded Dane once again that, despite their two passionate encounters, despite Jacqui's naturalness in his arms, his new wife was a total innocent when it came to the savored joys of lovemaking. He kissed her cheeks softly, tenderly, feeling something warm and wonderful unfurl within his chest. Silently, he vowed that this time would be everything a bride could ever dream of.

"Dane?" she whispered again, her palms warm against his. "Do you want me to beg?"

"Never." He fondled her earlobe lightly with his tongue. Jacqui shivered. "Then why must we wait?"

"To enhance your pleasure, my darling." He kissed the furrow between her brows. "I want you to experience the sun and the stars . . . every touch, every taste, every shimmering sensation. . . ." He closed his eyes, undone by his own words.

"I'm no longer an innocent virgin, Dane," she protested, her fingers tightening within his. "I know what to expect."

Her only answer was a dark smile and a murmured, "Do you?" And then he silenced her objections with his mouth, kissing her until she was limp and weak beneath him, lost in the words of love he breathed into her mouth, her hair, her scented skin.

Nothing they had shared previously had prepared Jacqui for the relentless, tormenting pleasure of the next hour. As long moments melded into one, Dane slowly, expertly awakened every nerve ending in her body with prolonged, lazy caresses, light, nibbling kisses and hot, explicit promises of what would follow, until Jacqui was melting into the bed, drowning in a bottomless well of desire. Her breath was coming in short, hard pants, her body covered with a fine sheen of perspiration.

Still Dane continued the exquisite torture he inflicted on them both, refusing to give in to their bodies' demand to be one. He held both Jacqui's hands tightly in one of his, letting his other hand explore her perfect curves and hollows, following the same path with his lips and tongue. "You're so beautiful." He stared down at her swollen breasts, the nipples he had drawn into hard, damp points of need. Jacqui arched her back, moaning softly, and Dane answered her body's plea, bending his head to her breast, drawing the tip into his mouth with an erotic suction that made Jacqui cry out.

"No more," she gasped, shaking her head frantically. "Dane . . . I can't bear it."

To her relief, he eased her legs apart, gliding his hand up the softness of her inner thigh. "Can't you?" he murmured against her other breast. Without hesitating, he opened her to his touch, entering her with his fingers, immersing himself in the hot, melting wetness that told him how much she wanted him. "Jacqui . . ." He pressed his face into the satiny skin of her abdomen, wanting her with a ferocity that stripped away everything save the primitive drive for possession.

"Now . . . now . . ." She repeated the word mindlessly, opening herself more fully to his touch, her hips lifting in lush, silent invitation, grateful that, at last, he would fill her, put an end to the fire he'd ignited inside her.

He fueled it instead.

With a ragged groan, Dane released her hands, wedging himself totally between her parted thighs. But, rather than moving up and entering her as Jacqui had expected, he slid lower down, cupping her soft bottom and lifting her to his seeking mouth.

"Dane?" Her confused whisper ended on a sharp cry of pleasure as Dane found and tasted the flowing sweetness he'd created. Shocked and exhilarated, Jacqui tangled her fingers in his hair, white-hot sensation shooting through her in great, unchecked currents. She threw back her head in helpless abandon, chanting his name over and over in a litany of stark, utter madness.

Dane was lost to everything but the very essence of his wife. Her intoxicating flavor, the utterly feminine taste and scent of her permeated his senses, while her wild little cries echoed inside his head, pounded through his blood like a hammer. Never had he imagined desire this intense, hunger so acute that he actually shook with it.

He could take no more.

In one fluid motion, he was over her, meeting her astonished gaze with eyes that glowed molten silver. Urgently, he lifted her legs around his waist, burying himself deep within her in one hard, primitive thrust. He felt her body's natural resistance, heard her sharp inhalation of breath, and he forced himself to still.

"Am I hurting you?" he managed, his eyes closed with the agony of holding back.

Jacqui couldn't speak. She was floating on the brink of a sensation so acute, so magnificent, that every fiber of her being was focused on achieving it. When Dane paused, broke her ecstatic fall, she knew she was going to die. Helpless to stem the tide of pleasure that hovered just out of reach, she arched her back, dug her nails into his shoulder blades, silently begging him not to leave her a mere heartbeat from completion.

Dane understood her plea, felt the tightening of her body around his, and, with a guttural cry, he released all the wildness that had been building up inside him, plunging into her once, twice . . . catapulting them both over the edge together. He met Jacqui's rhythmic contractions with an endless, explosive release, shouting her name again and again with each scalding burst of heat, filling her body with all the love that filled his heart.

A long time passed before either of them moved. Finally, Dane raised up enough to see Jacqui's face, brushing damp tendrils of hair off her forehead. "Ah, Mrs. Westbrooke." He kissed her closed eyelids. "You are a fantasy come true."

Jacqui's lids fluttered open and she gave him a weak, sated smile. "And you, evidently, have had a great deal of prior practice from which to judge."

He chuckled, rolling to one side and cradling her against him. "Do you still think there are no surprises that await you in our marriage bed, *chaton?*" With a thrill of surprise, he felt her curl more closely against him.

"I shall have to alter my opinion, I suppose," she replied, exploring the muscled planes of his back with her palms.

"I'm glad to hear that." He breathed in the sweetness of her hair, already contemplating the delightful possibilities offered by the long hours still ahead.

"Dane?" Her voice was muffled, her face buried against his chest.

"Hm-m-m?"

"How long do we have to wait?"

He looked down at her and blinked. "For what?"

She gave him an exasperated look and dropped her pointed gaze to their still-joined bodies. "For this!" She wrapped one slender leg intimately about the powerful length of his thigh, gliding the sole of her foot along its hair-roughened surface.

Dane shook his head in amazement, renewed desire crashing through him like a tidal wave. "You stun me." He tangled his fingers in her hair, lifting her face for his kiss.

"Why?" She wound her arms about his neck, the look she gave him pure seduction. "Don't all brides ravish their new husbands repeatedly while the sun is still high in the sky and but a few hours have passed since the vows have been exchanged?"

Dane rolled onto his back, pulling Jacqui up to straddle him. "I don't care about all brides," he said huskily, gripping her hips and teaching her the motion, "only the impossibly outrageous one who belongs to me."

Jacqui shook her head, breathless with passion. "I don't belong—"

"Yes, *chaton,* you do." Dane dragged her mouth down to meet his, negating her protest with the erotic circling of his hips, catching Jacqui's whimper as sunbursts of sensation shimmered through them. "You belong to me," he said in a ragged whisper, moving deeply within her. "Legally. Physically. Totally." He melded their bodies together, watching her expressive features glaze over with passion. "You're mine, Jacqueline," he breathed, repeating the words he had spoken the first time they loved. "Mine."

All was silenced but their need to be one.

CHAPTER

14

"I beg your pardon, madam, but I have worked for Mr. Westbrooke for five years and I happen to know he despises sweets of any kind first thing in the morning!"

Stivers's voice, always modulated and respectful, bellowed through the halls and echoed through the house. In the study, Dane rolled his eyes to the heavens, wondering if he would *ever* catch up on the Westbrooke Shipping contracts.

"And *I* happen to know you are wrong, Herr Stivers!" Greta snapped. "Herr Westbrooke *adores* my tarts . . . at *any* time of day! Now, stand aside while I take some to his study. The man works far too hard; he needs to keep up his strength!"

The sound of the kitchen door slamming made Dane wince. Resignedly, he put down his quill pen and massaged his temples. His once-peaceful home hadn't been the same all week long. But then, he was married to Jacqueline now. So had he really expected anything short of utter turmoil?

"Come in, Greta," he called, grinning as the very walls shook with the force of her knock. He rose, bracing himself against the side of the desk as Greta marched in and deposited a tray full of strawberry tarts on top of Dane's towering pile of paperwork.

"You must be hungry, Herr Westbrooke," Greta declared, hands on ample hips.

"Actually, I am, Greta," he replied, surprised to realize it was true. "What time is it?"

"It is half after ten," she scolded, tucking a wisp of hair demurely into her bonnet. "I am off to the market. But I couldn't leave knowing you hadn't eaten since last night."

Not even then, Dane thought, wondering what Greta would say if she knew he had skipped the late-night dinner she'd kept warm for him . . . and why. Greta's cooking was superb . . . but his new wife's enticements were far more alluring. "Is Jacqueline awake?"

"Yes, sir. Frau Westbrooke is dressing."

"Good." Dane headed for the door. "Then I'll wait and join her for breakfast." He gave Greta a melting smile. "Could you possibly bring the tarts into the dining room so I might share them with my wife, Greta? They smell wonderful!"

Taking up the tray, Greta flushed with pride. "Of course, Herr Westbrooke. Right away."

"Thank you, Greta. You are indispensable," he praised, following her into the hall.

"Among other things." Jacqui muttered the words under her breath. She paused at the foot of the stairs, shaking her head as Greta fairly flew past, humming on her way to the dining room.

Dane walked over to greet his wife. "Good morning." He traced the small pucker between Jacqui's brows with his forefinger. "You seem perturbed, sweet."

"My damned housekeeper fancies herself in love with you," she retorted with dry exasperation. "It's positively sickening the way she fawns and fusses over you."

"Jealous, love?" Dane rubbed his thumb across her soft lower lip, chuckling at the poisonous look that was his response. "You needn't worry about my becoming conceited, *chaton*. You keep me humble with expressions such as the one you're wearing now." He kissed her lightly, his voice growing husky. "After last night, this is hardly the manner in which I expected to be greeted."

Jacqui met his tender, heated gaze, and a small smile played about her lips. "Why not? I have been allowed a scant three hours' sleep and every muscle in my body aches."

"Come back to bed with me and I'll make the ache go away."

Jacqui stopped the progress of his arms as they reached for her. "Dane . . . it's nearly eleven o'clock. Shouldn't you be at Westbrooke Shipping?" Concealing her annoyance was nearly impossible, for if Dane remained at home her own plans would be ruined.

Jacqui pressed her fingers tightly into her palms, as if the action itself could control her need to resume what she had begun late last night. Long after Dane's steady breathing had assured her he was in a deep slumber, Jacqui had crept from their bed and, by the light of a single candle, begun Laffey's column on the plight of Pennsylvania's destitute farmers and the unnecessary taxes being levied on their whiskey. She desperately wanted to complete the essay and deliver it to Bache. But she couldn't very well do that with her very astute husband lurking about.

"I was working in my study," Dane said, as if reading her thoughts. He frowned, thinking about the untouched contracts on his desk. "Unfortunately, there is more work to do than the hours can hold."

"Perhaps you need to hire a larger staff," Jacqui suggested, deciding to bide her time. She took his proffered arm and strolled toward the dining room with him.

Dane shrugged. "It's difficult to find men who possess both the intelligence and the integrity necessary to run my business."

"What about women?"

Dane halted in his tracks. "Pardon me?"

Jacqui's eyes sparkled. "What about women who possess both intelligence and integrity?" She clutched his arms in excitement. "Dane, let me work for Westbrooke Shipping! I can keep the ledgers better than *any* man you could hire." She saw his jaw tighten, saw the indecision race across his face, and her temper flared. "I see," she said, turning away. "You profess to support my independent nature . . . but it is all a sham when it comes to acting upon the words."

Dane stared at Jacqui's stiff back in silence. She was right about his reluctance . . . but wrong about his reasons. He did not doubt her capabilities, nor was his vacillation caused by anything so foolish as concern over her gender. But it would be idiotic to entrust his wife with Westbrooke Shipping when he remained so unsure of her motives. For she still guarded a secret . . . a secret Dane knew he must learn.

Unbidden, memories of the past few nights' passion flitted through Dane's mind . . . the total, natural way Jacqui gave herself to him, the uninhibited honesty of her response to their lovemaking . . . and his resolve melted. How could he doubt her when, time after time and in all ways but words, she told him she loved him? Further, despite his own carefully repressed declaration, he loved her with every fiber of his being. So how could he deny her anything?

"Jacqueline." He glided his palms over her shoulders, pulling her back against him. "Why do you want to keep my ledgers? You already keep those of Holt Trading."

Jacqui turned in his arms. "But for how long?" she said bitterly. "If there is a way to ease me out of that responsibility, Monique will find it."

Dane tipped her chin up, asking one of the questions that had nagged him since their wedding day. "Why do you dislike Monique Brisset so much? I should think you would be grateful for your father's happiness."

Jacqui's expression hardened. "And I would be . . . *if* I thought Monique was worthy of his love. But I don't trust her, Dane. I just *know* she is using my father . . . and that she will hurt him terribly."

"Why? How?"

"It is simply a feeling I have. Pure instinct." She lowered her lashes. "I realize how absurd that must sound."

"No, it doesn't sound absurd," Dane surprised her by answering. "I believe wholeheartedly in listening to one's instincts." It struck him that his words applied to a great deal more than Jacqui's dislike for Monique. They applied to his faith in Jacqui as well.

Dane drew Jacqui to him, pressing her face to his chest and praying that he was not playing the part of a blind, lovesick fool. "Very well, *chaton,*" he murmured. "If you wish to help me with my business, it would be an honor to have you work for Westbrooke Shipping."

Jacqui's head came up instantly, her face aglow. "Do you mean that?"

Dane chuckled. "You know I never say anything I don't mean. What wages will you require?"

"Oh, I think we can come to an agreement that is amenable to us both . . . with regard to wages . . . as well as other forms of payment."

Hearing the suggestiveness in her tone, Dane's arms tightened about her. "Now," he commanded.

Jacqui shook her head, her eyes dancing, and extricated herself from his hold. "Oh no, sir, I couldn't accept any payment until I've proven my worth. Besides," she began to back up toward the dining room, "I cannot work on an empty stomach. So our discussion of payment will have to wait until lat . . ." She broke off, laughing helplessly, as Dane lunged at her, then raced through the doorway with her husband in close pursuit.

Both Greta and Stivers stared in openmouthed shock as the master and mistress of the house exploded into the dining room, circled the table twice, and finally collided into each other near the sideboard, breathless with laughter. Stivers stood, not five feet away, totally unsure of how to react when Mr. Westbrooke took his wife in his arms and began to passionately kiss her . . . and she him . . . in broad daylight and in plain view of any onlookers.

Greta, however, harbored no such reservations. "My tarts are getting cold," she barked in their ears.

Dane made no move to release his wife. "Thank you, Greta." His eyes remained on Jacqui's beautiful, flushed face. He stroked her cheek with his knuckles. "Didn't you mention being hungry, *chaton?*" he questioned softly.

"I did."

Dane guided her to her chair and eased her into it. "Never let it be said that I allowed my wife . . . and the keeper of my ledgers . . . to starve," he said with mock seriousness. He sank into his own chair, only to leap up just as quickly, a spitting black flash of fur beside him. "Damn it!" Dane erupted, spinning about to confront the hated offender.

Whiskey landed gracefully on the carpet, then arched his back, hissing furiously, green eyes ablaze.

"That is it!" Dane roared. "I've withstood all I plan to from you, you vicious little viper . . . this time I'm going to wring your blasted neck!"

"Dane, don't!" Jacqui was on her feet in an instant, stepping between her raging husband and spitting kitten. "He didn't mean anything!"

"The hell he didn't! He *meant* to rake off a layer of my skin!"

"You nearly squashed him," Jacqui reasoned calmly, pointing at the chair. "Else he never would have—"

"Oh no? Then what was his excuse last night when he pounced on my face, claws extended, and attempted to maul me off the bed?"

Jacqui chewed her lip to keep from laughing. "He is not accustomed to sharing a bed with anyone other than me."

"Then he'd bloody well better *get* used to it, and quickly, if he wants to live!"

"He will." Jacqui shot Whiskey a pointed look. "Won't you, Whiskey?"

Whiskey hissed louder.

"Whiskey!"

This time the kitten relented, skulking out of the room with a haughty air that told Dane their war was far from over.

Jacqui placed a restraining hand on Dane's arm. "I'm famished," she tried. "Greta's tarts smell heavenly."

Dane's body, drawn taut as a bowstring, gradually relaxed. "Very well. *This* time." He helped Jacqui into her seat. "But I don't know why the hell you're so attached to that reprehensible cat. He has the foulest of tempers . . . save those times when he's managed to sneak into my whiskey. He's very docile when he is inebriated." Dane glared down at the chair cushion as if to assure himself that the distasteful kitten was indeed gone, then settled himself for breakfast.

"At least Whiskey appreciates fine liquor," Jacqui put in brightly.

"True. Hence I shall make certain to purchase additional spirits in order to accommodate your cat's unusual preferences."

"If you do that, the farmers will have additional taxes to pay, based on the system devised by your friend Secretary Hamilton."

Dane slammed his untouched cup of coffee back into its saucer, splashing dark splotches of liquid onto the snow-white tablecloth. "Jacqueline, don't start!"

Jacqui bit into her strawberry tart. "Treading where I oughtn't, am I?"

Dane tossed his unused napkin onto the table. "I spent the greater part of the morning listening to your maid browbeat my poor, unsuspecting manservant. Following that, I was subject to your misplaced theories on my opinions of women and their abilities, not to mention being questioned for choosing to work in my own home today. I was then nearly maimed by your alcoholic feline and now you are preparing to begin a tirade spouting your bloody unrealistic, radical views." He stormed to his feet. "Perhaps you were right after all. Perhaps I *should* do the remainder of my work at the office. At least there I can have some peace. If not of mind, then of spirit."

"Good idea," Jacqui returned eagerly . . . and a bit too quickly.

Dane's eyes narrowed. "And what have you planned for the afternoon, my complacent wife?"

Jacqui gave a careless shrug. "Oh, I thought perhaps I'd pay Father a visit. I haven't seen him since the wedding."

"An excellent notion." Dane straightened his waistcoat. "I'll escort you to your father's office on my way to Westbrooke Shipping."

Jacqui paled. "No! That is . . . I'm not finished dressing."

"You look lovely to me. But I'll wait while you ready yourself." Dane leaned nonchalantly against the wall, regarding his wife with noncommittal ease. "I'll take you to your father, leave you to have a lovely visit while I finish off my contracts, then fetch you on my way home. It all works out rather nicely, don't you think?" He flashed her a disarming smile.

Unable to extricate herself, Jacqui rose. "Very well, Dane. I'll be down in a few moments." Placidly, she left the room, climbed the flight of stairs, and then, as soon as she was out of Dane's line of vision, tore off to her bedroom at a breakneck pace. She scooped up Laffey's article, dashed off a few quick sentences, then hastily reread it, scowling as she did. There was so much she'd wanted to elaborate on, so much that needed to be said. But, given the circumstances, she hadn't much choice. It was now or not at all.

Jacqui carefully folded the article and tucked it inside her bodice. The next challenge lay just ahead . . . convincing her father that he *must* help to keep Jack Laffey alive.

"Jacqueline, are you mad?" George Holt shut his office door with a firm click, determined to keep this particular conversation private. Having just shared a delightful two-hour visit with his beloved daughter, he was totally unprepared for the shock that accompanied her outrageous request.

He spun on his heel to face her, purposefully ignoring the sparks of anger that glinted in her eyes. "What you are suggesting is absurd . . . out of the question!"

"Why, Father? Why is it out of the question?" Jacqui fired back, raising her chin defiantly. "Did you expect Jack Laffey to quietly expire with the advent of my marriage?"

"You won't *have* a marriage if Dane discovers what you are planning!"

"I have no intentions of allowing him to discover what I am planning. That is why I am asking *you* to do what I cannot."

George rubbed his palms together, totally at a loss.

"Father." Jacqui went to him, took his hands in hers. "You were the one who encouraged me to pursue both my marriage and my beliefs."

"But I never meant for you to deceive your husband!"

Jacqui's delicate features hardened. "I have no other choice."

"You most certainly have. You could tell him the truth."

"And he would demand that I cease writing my columns."

"Yes, indeed he would."

"I cannot accept that. Not now . . . with all that is happening, not only in Europe, but right here in our country, in our own state." She shook her head in adamant decision. "No, Laffey must continue." So saying, she extracted the folded sheet of paper from her bodice. "Here is this week's column for Bache."

Reluctantly, George took the paper, scanning its contents. "Many important people will be incensed by this essay," he stated flatly.

"It would not be the first time. But I cannot remain silent when Pennsylvania's farmers, already in dire straits, are being forced to pay taxes they simply cannot afford. Taxes levied by statesmen whose concerns are only for the rich and never the needy." She reached up, touched George's cheek. "Please, *mon père.* All I ask is that you deliver the column. The responsibility is entirely mine and I will suffer any repercussions that occur." She gave him a beseeching half-smile. "Once the farmers are victorious, the need for me to air my views will not be nearly as pressing."

"Another equally urgent cause will require your attention, I assure you," George said skeptically.

"I will consider telling Dane the truth."

"Will you?"

Praying for some divine act that would restrict her from fulfilling this vow without forcing her to lie to her father, Jacqui nodded. "Yes . . . but in the interim, will you help me?"

George released his breath on a defeated sigh. "When have I ever been able to refuse you anything, *ma petite?*"

Jacqui squeezed his fingers gratefully. "Thank you, Father." She rushed on, before he could change his mind. "Since you've unobtrusively accompanied me on my past excursions, I assume you know the time and place of the meetings?"

Recalling the deserted location where he had, several times, followed his intrepid daughter as she staunchly delivered her column, George frowned. "In the alley behind the courthouse and burial grounds, just past Market Street. Tonight. At eight o'clock." He slipped the paper into his coat pocket. "And don't thank me, Jacqueline. I shudder to think what Dane's reaction would be to our arrangement."

"I assure you, he shan't learn of it from me." Jacqui's nerves tensed immediately. "Father?"

"Nor shall he learn anything from me. I trust you to handle the situation with your husband."

Dane froze, his hand poised to knock. The final words of the conversation taking place on the other side of the door cut through him like a knife, piercing his gut, his faith, his heart.

243

Tonight's meeting? The situation with your husband? Our arrangement?

Slowly, Dane lowered his arm, his fist clenched so tightly his knuckles were white. He had suspected this ugly truth, though he'd fought to deny its lethal existence. Lord knew, Alexander had tried to prepare him, warned him time and again. Then why did he feel so damned betrayed?

He had to hear more, to be certain . . . to know the extent of his wife's treachery. Pressing his ear to the door, Dane strained to listen, but the voices had dropped down to a murmur and the occasional phrases he could make out were innocent in content.

Composing his features, he knocked.

There was a brief silence, then George's tentative "Yes?"

Dane stepped into the office. "I've come to collect my wife." Despite his best attempts, his tone was curt.

George wet his lips nervously, an odd look on his face. Guilt? "Certainly, Dane. Jacqui and I have had a lovely visit."

Jacqui, on the other hand, was all sweetness and smiles. She stood on tiptoe and kissed her father's cheek. "It was wonderful to see you, Father. You'll have to come for dinner sometime soon. Oh, and Monique too, of course," she added quickly.

Dane was silent during their walk home and Jacqui glanced up from time to time, studying his rigid profile, gauging the significance and extent of her husband's odd, brooding humor.

"Did you accomplish your work?" she tried at last.

"More or less."

"Problems?"

"None."

"Then what is wrong?" she blurted out, pausing on their front walkway.

Dane came to a dead stop, staring down into her face with a predatory look that chilled her. "You tell me."

Jacqui swallowed. "I don't know what you mean."

Storm clouds erupted in Dane's eyes. "Don't you?"

Slowly, apprehensively, Jacqui shook her head from side to side. "No."

The pounding in Dane's chest expanded into an explosion of pure fury. He wanted to shout out his agony and his betrayal, to shake the lies from Jacqui's traitorous mouth, to hurt her as profoundly as she'd hurt him.

And yet . . . he wanted her to deny her guilt, to explain away the truth, to eradicate the past.

To love him as he loved her.

With a muffled curse, Dane seized Jacqui's hand, dragging her into the house. "Go home, Stivers," he ordered the surprised manservant, who stood, blinking, in the empty hallway. "I won't be needing you until tomorrow."

"Very good, sir. Have a pleasant evening."

Dane didn't answer. He had reached the top of the stairway, tugging a thoroughly stunned Jacqui in his wake.

"Dane, where are we going?" She struggled to free her wrist, a bit frightened by the demons that seemed to be driving her husband.

Dane shoved her into their room and slammed the door behind them. "We are going to the one place where you cannot lie to me . . . or to yourself. Our bed." He ignored her protests, nearly tearing both their clothing in his haste to affirm what was real between them, what her deceit could not erase.

"Dane, stop it!" She pushed at his massive shoulders as he lowered them both to the soft mattress. "Tell me why you are so angry!"

He lifted her face roughly, forcing her to meet blazing gray eyes that scorched her with heated accusation. "You don't *really* want the answer to that question, now do you, my love?" he asked, his voice a lethal whisper. When Jacqui fell silent, he gave a bitter laugh. "I thought not. So instead, *you* tell *me*. Tell me how much you want me, how much you crave my touch, my hands, my mouth." He glided his fingers up her back, along her spine, smiling darkly at her inadvertent tremor of pleasure. "Give me this truth, Jacqueline . . . the only truth we share. Tell me what you feel when I'm deep inside you, when nothing in the world exists but my body taking yours, possessing yours, giving you pleasure so unbearable that you cry out my name, beg me not to stop. Tell me, my beautiful wife. Tell me." He parted her lips, his own mouth violent, hungry. "Melt for me, *chaton*. Give me your passion, your fire. Show me that sole shimmering reality that is ours." He swallowed her helpless whimper, digging his hands in her hair and rubbing his body slowly over hers. "Tell me, Jacqueline. Show me."

Jacqui wasn't sure if the words were an order or a plea. Nor did she care. Driven by the innate realization that whatever information Dane had gleaned would forever change the bond that had grown between them, she responded without hesitation, craving the reaffirmation of their passion as much as Dane did. And despite the rage that drove her husband, despite all that was wrong with this mating, she wanted him . . . desperately.

Jacqui opened her body to his and arched her back in silent invitation. She saw the flicker of surprise in Dane's eyes, but it vanished instantly beneath the urgency pounding inside him. With a primitive growl, he wedged himself between Jacqui's thighs and plunged deep, hard, shuddering as he felt her warm wetness close around him.

"Jacqueline . . ." He said her name once . . . in a raw, tortured voice . . . and then there were no more words. Governed by emotions too sharp to withstand, but too profound to express, Dane gave Jacqui the unendurable pain of his love and betrayal and Jacqui responded with all the fear and conflict warring within her.

Their climax was unbearable, endless in its intensity, speaking far more eloquently than words ever could.

A long moment ticked by, neither of them willing to relinquish the tenuous wonder of their joined bodies. Dane clutched Jacqui to him, savoring her softness, his own breathing ragged, unsteady. Then abruptly, he released her, rolling away and coming to his feet in one purposeful motion. Angrily, he yanked on his breeches and walked over to the open window, gazing moodily out into the late afternoon sky, brutally aware that their passion, no matter how staggering, could no longer annihilate all the lies looming between them.

Jacqui opened her eyes, feeling limp and sated, yet strangely void, bereft without her husband beside her. Silently, she watched Dane's taut, bare back, bathed in the molten orange light cast by the setting sun as it filtered through the room. She shivered, frightened by the fragile tenderness that was suddenly and unexpectedly born inside her, urging her to go to Dane, to give him the truth he sought and to suffer whatever consequences might result.

More frightening was the possibility that he was already in possession of that truth.

Confused, Jacqui turned onto her side, wishing she could fathom Dane's state of mind. Always after they made love, he'd held her, whispered words of passion and praise, taken her again before she'd even caught her breath . . . made her feel cherished and wanted. But this time he'd withdrawn into himself, where he clearly wished to remain.

Studying his rigid stance, Jacqui made her decision, gathering up the quilt and wrapping it about her shoulders. Now was not the time to approach him . . . not yet. She would wait until later, when he came back to bed. Then they would talk.

She yawned, snuggling into the bedcovers, suddenly and dreadfully weary. Her last thought before drifting off to sleep was that soon her father would be delivering Laffey's column.

For a long time Dane listened to Jacqui's even breathing, knowing without turning around that, deep in slumber, she was curled on her side, her hair a rich mahogany waterfall over her bare shoulders and back, her face innocent and exquisite, buried in the softness of the pillows. He gritted his teeth, trying again to separate truth from deception, to make the agonizing decision he could no longer put off. His love for his wife, consuming though it might be, could not allow him to jeopardize his integrity and his country. He had to act . . . immediately.

Forcing himself from the window, Dane slowly approached the bed, gazing down at the beautiful woman who held his heart. Inadvertently, he reached out, wrapped one long, silky curl around his forefinger, and, for a brief moment, considered waking her, confronting her with his suspicions. But he dismissed that idea as quickly as it had come, knowing she'd only deny the accusation, adding to the enormity of the lie underlying their marriage, making him despise her . . . and himself . . . even more. Soon enough she would learn that her father's plan . . . and hers . . . had been uncovered, that the betrayal was at an end . . . that she would have to suffer the painful ramifications of her guilt.

Dane's grip tightened around Jacqui's lock of hair until his finger tingled its protest. Why, he asked himself, after all his wife was guilty of, did a part of him still want so desperately to shield her?

Sighing heavily, he moved quietly from the bed, dressing quickly and efficiently. With a final glance behind him, he left the bedroom and the house, pausing but once to slip his knife into the waistband of his breeches . . . should it be needed.

All the while, the words he'd heard George utter earlier that day reverberated in his head.

Tonight. At eight o'clock. In the alley behind the courthouse and burial grounds, just past Market Street.

In an hour, George Holt would be meeting someone, delivering covert information into that person's hands. Wouldn't Holt and his contact be more than a little surprised to find Dane waiting there too . . . bearing witness to Holt's treason firsthand?

Dane quickened his pace, knowing full well that, within

the hour, he would have his answers . . . and his headstrong, passionate wife would feel nothing for him but hatred.

Jacqui came awake with a start, unable to give a name to the knot of apprehension in her stomach. Swiftly, her gaze swept the room, beginning with the now-abandoned window where Dane had stood when she'd drifted off. It was deserted. Her husband was nowhere in sight.

Scrambling out of bed, Jacqui's knees nearly buckled and she clutched the nightstand for support. Her limbs felt weak as water, a reminder of the wild, desperate mating she'd shared with Dane . . . a wrenching combination of hunger and passion and torment.

And, for Dane, inexplicable fury . . . fury that surpassed any he'd ever displayed, any that could be caused by mere suspicions, any that could be based on anything but concrete fact.

Jacqui's head came up, her heart beating frantically as a sudden, implausible possibility struck her. Could Dane have overheard her conversation at Holt Trading? Could he perchance *know* of tonight's meeting?

With escalating fear, her eyes fell on the clock: seven forty-five.

Ignoring the ache that pervaded her body, Jacqui raced to the wardrobe and snatched the first dark gown she could find, tugging it on with shaking hands. Each button took forever to slip into its casing, her stockings aeons to cover her legs. Letting the gown's muslin folds fall to her ankles, Jacqui simultaneously stepped into her slippers, tied back her hair from her face, and headed for the door, willing time to stand still, cursing herself for taking an eternity to dress.

It was seven forty-nine.

Dane shifted position, eager for Holt to appear . . . praying he would not. It was a futile prayer, for just then footsteps sounded, approaching the alleyway . . . hesitating . . . then entering, growing surer, nearer. Dane pressed deeper into the shadows, waiting for the dim moonlight to reveal his arrival's identity. Seconds later, he could make out the smooth, fresh features of a young lad . . . apparently, the contact George was going to meet.

With clenched fists, Dane waited, knowing it would all be over in a matter of minutes.

The second set of footsteps followed immediately, echoing in the deserted alley, resounding hollowly in Dane's heart.

"Miss Holt?" The boy stepped forward, halting in his tracks, white-faced, as he encountered not Jacqui, but George.

"Wait!" Anticipating the boy's reaction, George grabbed at his sleeve, staying the youth's flight. "I work with Miss Holt. I'm her . . ." He hesitated. "I'm here at her request. I have the document you need."

The boy stopped struggling when he saw the paper George offered, recognized, in the faint shaft of moonglow, the familiar strokes of Jacqui's pen. "Miss Holt sent you?" he repeated quizzically, scrutinizing George as he took the single sheet.

George nodded tersely. "Yes. I presume you know how to proceed from here?"

It was the boy's turn to nod. "Yes, sir. I should . . . I've been doin' it for over a year now."

"Not after tonight, you aren't." Dane's scathing words cut through the night. He emerged from the shadows, ignoring George's shocked gasp, extending his hand to the startled youth. "Give me that paper. Now."

The boy backed away, terrified by the furious spark in this dark stranger's silver eyes. "W-w-ho are you?" he stammered.

"Give it to me!"

"Don't!" George shook his head violently. No matter what Dane suspected, this was not the way for him to learn the truth about Jacqui. "Run, lad! Take the paper and run!"

The boy needed no further urging. Turning on his heel, he shot off like a bullet, swallowed up by the blackness of night.

For a moment Dane considered going after him, then decided against it. Much as he wanted that document, he could not take the risk that George would bolt. The only conceivable option was to drag the information out of Holt. As for the lad, he was no more than an innocent accomplice and could easily be traced, and the paper recovered . . . later. The true culprit remained before Dane, silent and waiting.

Dane swung around, his expression murderous. "We reach the truth at last, Holt." He inhaled sharply, battling for control. "I'm not sure who I want to choke more at this instant. You . . . or my *wife.*"

George tensed. "Jacqui has nothing to do with this."

"Really?" Dane's tone was lethal. "Funny, I was certain I heard the boy mention her name. Unless there is another Miss Holt I have yet to meet?"

George sucked in his breath, ready to protect Jacqui at all costs. "She is nothing more than my messenger, Dane. Your argument is with me."

"My *argument?*" Dane stared at him, incredulous and sickened. "My God, Holt, you've betrayed your country, made a mockery of everything it stands for, and you refer to this revelation as an *argument?*"

"Betrayed my country?" It was George's turn to look shocked. He had been prepared to plead his case, to shield Jacqui from her husband's certain outrage. Outrage, yes . . . but this? "I thought you, of all men, would show more understanding, Westbrooke," he bit out. "Since when has freedom of speech signified treason?"

"Don't bait me, Holt," Dane shot back. "Your provoking column is but a small portion of your crime."

"My *crime?*" George sputtered. "Penning honest, informative political statements?"

"Honest? Informative? Don't you mean reckless and instigating?"

ANDREA KANE

"The American people have a right to know what propels their government. I merely provide them with that information."

Dane swooped down on George's words. "So you admit you are Jack Laffey?"

Silence reigned as George absorbed the severity of Dane's ire.

Then: "Yes . . . I'm Laffey."

Dane took a menacing step toward him. "Do you also admit that you and Jacqueline furnished the British with enough details to undermine John Jay's negotiations?"

"What?" George's voice shook.

"Oh, come now, Holt. You've gone this far. Finish what you've begun." Dane's fists closed around George's lapels. "Tell me how you and Jacqueline managed to convey stolen documents to the British, and how you used your column . . . and me . . . to further your misguided cause." He shook him. "Then tell me what was in that paper you just passed on. Was it more information for Grenville?"

"You're insane," George choked, struggling to free himself. "I'm no more a traitor than you are!"

Dane's grip tightened. "It is not *I* who is Jack Laffey!"

"Nor is it he!"

Jacqui's voice rang out, sure and clear, silencing both men with a start. Neither had heard her arrive, too caught up in their growing anger and escalating shouts to notice her presence.

"Jacqueline . . . this doesn't concern you!" George wasn't sure how much his daughter had overheard or if she knew the harshness of Dane's accusation. Nor was he waiting to ask. "Let me handle this," he ordered, praying that, for once, she would obey. "Go home to bed."

Jacqui shook her head fiercely, marching up to her husband, fire brimming in her eyes. "Release my father, you miserable, arrogant bastard!"

Dane stared down at her, his jaw tightening until it

252

threatened to snap. "Listen to your father, Jacqueline . . . go home. Now. Before I do something I'll regret."

"Go ahead and do it, damn you!" she fired back, clamping her fingers around the rigid muscles of his arm. "But to *me*, not my father! *I'm* the one you're livid with! I'm the one you loathe! So vent your rage at me, not him!"

"Jacqueline!" George's hoarse shout was a warning and a plea.

Valiantly, Dane fought the urge to beat Jacqui senseless. "I'm warning you, *wife*," he ground out. "You don't know what I'm capable of right now."

"And you, apparently, don't know what *I'm* capable of!"

That did it. Dane released George in a rush, dragging Jacqui against him with an anger that was as palpable as it was savage. "To the contrary, sweet, I applaud your grand deception!" he taunted. "You and . . ." He cast a scathing look at George. "Jack Laffey."

"My father is *not* Jack Laffey!" Jacqui's nails dug into Dane's coat.

"He's admitted it, you little fool."

"Only to keep you from the truth!"

"Jacqueline!" George made one final attempt to quiet her. "Now is *not* the time!"

"The truth?" Dane ignored George's protest, his smoldering gray eyes burning through his wife. "*What* truth?"

Jacqui raised her head proudly, her chin set in stubborn defiance, and met Dane's accusing stare. "*I* am Jack Laffey."

CHAPTER
15

Whatever Dane had been about to say lodged in his throat. Slowly, deliberately, he released his breath, an audible hiss in the suffocating silence. His immediate thought, on the heels of his wife's bold declaration, was that, while he was stunned by the impact of hearing the truth spoken aloud, he was not shocked by its reality. He should have known Jacqueline would never be content with the passive role of an accomplice. She had to be right at the heart of the explosion.

With cold assessment, he surveyed the proud, upturned face that stared back at him, awaiting his response.

"So . . . you are Jack Laffey," he repeated, an affirmation uttered for his own ears as well as for Jacqui's.

"Pronounced correctly, it is *Jacques la fille*," she corrected with a smug grin. "Translated, that means—"

"Jacques the girl," Dane finished, a spark of unwilling admiration flickering in his eyes. "How clever. And how stupid of me not to guess."

"I thought maybe you had. Or at least that you suspected. But it appears you had a far more sinister explanation for my actions."

254

He jumped on her words. "Are you telling me that my accusations are false?"

"I'm telling you nothing," she spat, wrenching her arms free of his hold. "Believe what you like."

"Jacqui, for God's sake!" George burst in. "Tell the man the truth! He believes—"

"I *heard* what he believes, Father. I have no intention of justifying my actions . . . now or ever."

"Jacqueline . . ." George tried again.

"Leave us, Holt," Dane commanded quietly, never taking his eyes off Jacqui. "This is between my wife and myself."

George made a sharp sound of protest. "I refuse to leave my daughter alone with you in your present state of mind, Westbrooke."

"If I haven't struck her yet, I don't suppose I shall," Dane muttered between clenched teeth.

Jacqui's furious gaze locked with his.

"Do as Dane says, Father," she said at last. "I can take care of myself."

George shook his head. "I don't think . . ."

"Please, *mon père*," she interrupted softly, giving her father a gentle, reassuring nod. "Let me handle this my own way."

George cleared his throat roughly. "If you need me—"

"I won't."

He hesitated. "Very well." He shot Dane a scathing look. "If my daughter is hurt in any way, you will answer to me."

"You've made your point." Dane's reply was a terse dismissal. "Oh . . . and Holt," he added in swift warning, "I would suggest you remain . . . accessible."

George blanched. "I'll be at my home, Westbrooke." He cast a final defeated glance from his daughter to the enraged man who was her husband, then reluctantly headed for home.

Dane waited until the echoing sound of Holt's footsteps had faded into the night. Then he lunged forward and caught Jacqui's shoulders in his strong hands.

"I want the truth. Are you responsible for urging us toward war with England?"

"You don't deserve the truth," she fired back, fighting the gnawing hurt that began deep inside her. "You've already decided my father and I are guilty."

Dane's grip tightened. "Do you have any idea how often . . . how badly I've wanted to be proven wrong?" His voice was hoarse, his expression taut with pain.

An appalling thought struck Jacqui. "Is *this* why you were so anxious to marry me?" she demanded, crashing her fists against the hard wall of Dane's chest. "To determine whether or not I was a traitor to our country?"

"No, you damned, impetuous little fool! I married you in spite of it!"

"I don't believe you!" She shoved him away, mortified by the welling emotion clogging her throat, the aching loss that was an unwelcome reminder of times long past but never forgotten. "You're nothing more than a lying hypocrite!" She lashed out, her only defense against the anguish.

"*I'm* a hypocrite?" The cords in Dane's neck bulged, his fists clenched in tight balls of rage and frustration. "*You're* the one who has lied to *me* . . . time and again . . . since the moment we met."

"And if I'd told you the truth?" she countered, her midnight eyes suspiciously bright. "Would you have embraced the idea? Welcomed the prospect of marriage to Jack Laffey? Or would you have *demanded* . . . no, *ordered* me to cease writing my columns?"

Dane wanted to choke her and comfort her all at once. "You *still* don't understand, do you, Jacqueline? You still believe, despite all that has transpired between us, that I want to *take* everything *from* you, strip you of your identity . . . or walk away from who you are." His voice dropped, grew raw, vulnerable. "No matter what we have become together, you still aren't willing to trust me."

"As you trust me?" Jacqui returned in a thin voice.

"It was not I who kept something from you."

"Except your suspicion that I was a traitor."

Dane had an uncontrollable urge to crush her to him, to eradicate the past hour together with that look of naked pain on her face. "Come here, Jacqui." He held out his hand.

She shook her head wildly, backing away. "Not this time, Dane. We can't close this gap with our bodies." To her horror, she actually felt tears burn behind her eyes. "I won't explain myself to you," she vowed in a small, shaken voice. "I won't ask for your understanding, your approval." Her eyes grew wide, frightened. "I won't need you," she whispered fiercely, turning away.

Before Dane could respond, she fled, away from her husband . . . away from the feelings that could no longer be silenced.

Alighting from the carriage, Jacqui peered through the darkness to the faint outline that was Greenhills, wondering why, of all places, she'd chosen to run here. Absently, she dismissed her driver, moving through the tree-lined path leading to the manor.

She couldn't go to her father . . . not after she'd confidently informed him she could manage on her own. Her concern for his worry wouldn't allow it, nor would her pride.

She certainly couldn't face Dane. So that left only Greenhills and its enchanting mistress.

But Lenore was Dane's mother.

Jacqui paused on the steps, hanging back at the intrusive thought. Yes, Lenore *was* Dane's mother . . . but she was also Jacqui's friend. Instinct told Jacqui she would be welcome.

Lenore herself answered the door.

"Jacqueline?" Her lovely face registered surprise, genuine concern . . . but not displeasure. "What's happened?"

Jacqui swallowed, lifting her chin determinedly. "Nothing's happened."

"Dane?"

"Dane is fine . . . that is . . . I just needed to talk and I thought . . ." Her voice trailed off in embarrassment. This proud young woman who had never asked anything of anyone in her life.

With one quick, insightful glance, Lenore took in Jacqui's distress, seeing instantly that it had no physical cause, and visibly relaxed, drawing her into the house. "Of course, dear. I'm glad you came." Wisely, she made no mention of the lateness of the hour or of Dane's conspicuous absence. When Jacqui was ready, she would explain.

Jacqui hung back. "Your pleasure might dim considerably when I tell you the circumstances that brought me here," she warned.

Lenore gave a faint smile, urging Jacqui along and closing the door firmly behind her. "I doubt that very much. When you've achieved my level of maturity, there is little left that can shock you." She led Jacqui to the kitchen. "Come. We'll have tea and chat."

Jacqui sat on a stool and watched Lenore heat water for tea. "I'm so confused."

Lenore didn't even look up. "Most of us are, at one time or another." She smoothed her hands down the front of her gown. "I assume this has to do with Dane?"

Jacqui stared at the tips of her shoes. "I've made quite a mess of things, Lenore. I don't understand your son . . . I don't even understand myself anymore."

Lenore poured two steaming cups and guided Jacqui into the sitting room. "*I* understand Dane very well," she put in, seating herself beside Jacqui on the sofa. "I've never seen him happier than he's been since the two of you met."

"I don't think you'd say that if you'd seen him several hours ago when he was accusing me of treason."

Lenore's cup and saucer descended to the tea table with a clink. "Treason?"

"Dane believes my father and I are supplying the British with information that will lead to a war with America."

Lenore gaped silently, then folded her hands in her lap. "I

retract my earlier statement, Jacqueline. Apparently I am still capable of being shocked."

Jacqui nodded. "I thought you might be."

"Where in the name of heaven did Dane get such an inconceivable idea?"

Jacqui felt a pang of conscience. "I suppose my rather . . . irregular behavior might have contributed to his suspicions."

Returning to her tea, Lenore held her remaining questions for later. "I think you'd better tell me the whole story, Jacqueline."

Jacqui did, leaving nothing out, concluding with the revelation that she and the infamous Jack Laffey were one and the same.

Lenore's cup paused but for a moment, then continued its graceful journey to her lips. "No one can accuse you of being idle, my dear," she commented, having finished the last of her tea.

"You're not appalled?"

"Did you expect I would be?"

"Frankly, yes."

Lenore smiled, a gesture that registered more sadness than amusement. "You are speaking to a woman who performed the most scandalous, unthinkable act imaginable . . . abandoning her husband and her former life in order to begin anew in a strange country with nothing but her principles . . . and her wonderful, devoted son . . . to accompany her."

Focusing on the reality and the severity of Lenore's actions, Jacqui carefully replied, "I know very little of your . . . or Dane's . . . life in England. Dane refuses to speak of it, or of his father."

Reflexively, Lenore smoothed the soft brocade of the camelback sofa. "I think it is time you and I discussed it."

Jacqui nodded, sensing that this unexpected turn to the conversation might finally answer many of her unasked questions. She leaned forward, a rapt expression on her face.

"Dane's father is a fine man . . . a good man," Lenore began. "But what the English define as proper behavior differs considerably from what you are accustomed to; it is a good deal more rigid, especially among the nobility."

"Dane's father is a marquis," Jacqui voiced aloud.

"Yes . . . he is. The Marquis of Forsgate. And Forsgate, together with all it represents, is his life." Lenore spoke simply and without anger. "I married Edwin because I adored him. My parents, both born of noble blood, heartily approved of the match. I was sixteen when we wed, and a year later Dane was born. I thought my life complete . . . I had an adoring husband and a magnificent son. What more could a woman require?"

Jacqui thought she knew the answer to that, but, wisely, she remained silent.

Lenore met Jacqui's gaze candidly. "For many years, my life as it existed was enough . . . I *made* it enough. Oh, I always found Edwin's rules with regard to my conduct antiquated. I wanted to be free to express my beliefs, to make my own choices. But the circles in which we traveled demonstrated that my husband was far from unique in his demands and that it was I who was at fault for my unconventional ideas. So I remained a dutiful wife, remembering my role as his marchioness at all times, agreeing with everything Edwin said and did, concentrating on being a proper hostess and relinquishing my only child into the care of others."

Lenore's face creased with pain. "Of all Edwin's rules, I despised that one the most. *I* wanted to raise Dane, to nurse him at birth, to share his childhood, to be the one he turned to when he was ill or afraid. Instead he was nourished by a wet nurse, reared by a governess, then sent away to school when his father deemed him ready." She sighed. "I know Edwin meant well, but I loathed his decision just the same."

Instinctively, Jacqui leaned forward and squeezed Lenore's hand.

Lenore smiled her gratitude. "The situation worsened as

Dane grew to manhood. Dane had always been a strong-willed, independent child, but as he matured, he discovered that his personal convictions were directly opposed to those of his father. Edwin believed in his land and his possessions, and he expected Dane to carry on in the same vein. Dane despised the idea of relying upon his title to earn people's respect, hated the hierarchy that existed at Forsgate, the blatant difference between our mode of living and that of our servants and tenants . . . in short, he totally rejected his father's ambitions that he commit himself to Forsgate and to the businesses that would one day be his. The more adamant Dane grew, the more furiously rigid Edwin became. The hostility between them intensified until neither could tolerate the other's presence.

"The terrifying part was that I found myself sympathizing with Dane, defending him and his beliefs until Edwin and I did nothing but argue. The more I spoke my mind, the more enraged Edwin became, squelching every independent thought I expressed. And slowly, all the love, the respect, the trust were overshadowed by a chasm that grew wider every day, colder every night, until I could no longer bear it."

Lenore closed her fingers around Jacqui's. "It was at this time that Dane graduated from Oxford and announced his decision to leave for America. He asked me to go with him. I considered my life as it was, my goals as I saw them . . . and I made my choice. It was the hardest decision I've ever had to make, for I knew that Edwin would never forgive me or allow me to return home once I'd gone. But I could no longer exist in the empty prison we called a marriage. So I went." Her eyes grew damp with emotion. "I miss Edwin to this day. No other man could ever take his place in my heart."

"You still love him," Jacqui said softly, amazed at the depth of Lenore's feelings.

"Yes. I always shall."

"Have you forgiven him?"

Lenore nodded. "I have. Dane, however, has not." A tear

slid down her cheek, unnoticed. "And, without that forgiveness, my son will never know peace. You see, Jacqueline, despite his stubborn refusal to admit it, Dane loves his father and regrets the rift between them. The irony is that what Dane and Edwin fought over was freedom; but unless they reconcile their differences, neither of them can truly be free." Pain flickered in Lenore's eyes, but she pushed on, anxious for her own experience to benefit Dane and Jacqueline. "Edwin is a product of the world in which he was raised, and I cannot fault him for his beliefs, though I choose not to share them. So, in answer to your question, yes, Jacqueline, I forgave my husband . . . long ago. But love and forgiveness are not enough. For a marriage to flourish, not merely survive, there must be trust, respect, and understanding underlying love and passion. I'm not certain Edwin is capable of all those qualities . . ." She paused. "But I *am* certain Dane is."

Jacqui swallowed. "You think I should have told Dane the truth about Laffey and hoped for his understanding?"

"What I think is that you should give Dane . . . and yourself . . . a chance before you condemn your marriage to failure." She gave Jacqui an astute look. "Or is that the very thing you fear? That your marriage might succeed?"

"What do you mean?" Jacqui's throat constricted.

"Do you want the truth?"

"Yes," Jacqui replied, her heart screaming, *No!*

"Very well." Lenore braced herself and plunged forward. "Obviously, you take great pride in fostering your independence. The idea of caring for Dane . . . or for any man . . . would directly conflict with that and is, therefore, unwelcome. In all candor, don't you feel somewhat relieved by tonight's confrontation with Dane? Almost as if you've been waiting for him to doubt you and thereby prove true all your dismal convictions about what this marriage would effect?" Lenore caught herself up short, although she longed to say more. From various things Dane had told her, she was almost certain that Jacqui's reluctance to love was rooted in something far deeper than a need for sovereignty. Somewhere inside Jacqueline was a young girl whose memories of love were firmly tied to her memories of loss and loneliness. But, until Jacqui was ready to reach out for help, Lenore had no right to tread on forbidden territory.

Choosing her words carefully, Lenore gripped Jacqui's other hand. "Don't do this, Jacqueline. Don't push Dane away with your determination *not* to care for him, your vehement denial that he cares for you. Is protecting yourself really worth sacrificing your happiness?"

Jacqui lowered her lashes, trying to swallow past the frightened lump in her throat.

"You don't have to answer me, Jacqueline . . . I have no right to pry. But please, answer yourself. You deserve to be happy. So does Dane."

Dane. Jacqui's mind began to race, replaying snatches of the past months, hearing Dane's fierce loyalties and fervent declarations, made all the more significant in light of what she'd just learned.

I'm an American, Jacqueline . . . as much an American as you. Who and what my father may be is irrelevant. . . .

I have no intention of changing you, chaton, or trying to usurp your independence. All I ask is for your respect and your honesty . . . and we already have that between us, do we not? . . .

I love you, Jacqueline Holt. . . . You're mine and you always will be.

She closed her eyes, visualizing the pain on her husband's face earlier that night when he'd learned how little honesty she'd given him, how little trust she'd offered . . . how she'd inadvertently led him to believe she could be guilty of a far greater crime.

The memory of that accusation twisted a knife in Jacqui's heart.

"But what he suspects me of . . . treason . . . to my own country . . ." She whispered the protest aloud.

"Dane doesn't believe you're a traitor, Jacqueline,"

Lenore said gently. "He may have known moments of doubt, but haven't you done your part to encourage those?"

Jacqui stared at her, a bewildered look in her eyes. "I suppose I did. I don't know what to think."

"Then don't think any more tonight." Lenore rose. "It's late and you're exhausted. You need to rest." She frowned, as a sudden thought occurred to her. "Does Dane know you're here?"

Wordlessly, Jacqui shook her head.

"Then he must be out of his mind with worry!"

"I won't go back . . . not tonight," Jacqui returned instantly, a spark of defiance reasserting itself.

"I'm not asking you to. I'm merely asking if I may send Dane a message advising him of your whereabouts and telling him you're safe. I will make certain he understands you do not wish to have your privacy disturbed . . . not until you are ready. At the same time, I'll have a similar message delivered to your father, who is most assuredly worried as well. Would that be satisfactory?"

Jacqui nodded, beyond protest. All she wanted was to sleep, to put her turbulent emotions to bed, to regain her strength.

She would need all of it when she faced Dane.

Dane paced the length of his sitting room, debating whether or not to notify the authorities of Jacqui's disappearance. He had already stormed over to George Holt's house, demanding that Jacqui return home, only to be met by Holt's white-faced denial that Jacqui had come to him. Between the worry in Holt's eyes and the stunned expression on his face, Dane had no doubt the man was sincere. Nor could Dane dismiss Holt's repeated, heartfelt assurances that he and Jacqui were innocent of treason.

Because in his heart Dane knew it was true. Just as he accepted that his proud and stubborn wife was, indeed, Jack Laffey, he was equally certain she was guilty of nothing more.

Why in the name of heaven couldn't she have trusted him?

More important, if she wasn't with her father, where the hell was she?

A sharp pain twisted in Dane's gut. Slamming his fist against the wall until the furniture rattled, he headed for the door, fear overshadowing anger and confusion in his heart. *She is fine,* he assured himself over and over again. *Jacqueline is nothing if not resourceful. She is accustomed to avoiding danger. She can take care of herself.*

But if anything had happened to her . . .

Dane collided with the messenger in his doorway.

"Pardon me, sir." The wiry little man righted himself, nervously adjusting his coat.

"Yes . . . what is it?" Dane was in no mood for idle chatter. It was the middle of the night, Jacqui was missing, and this stranger would have to get his directions . . . or whatever it was he needed . . . elsewhere.

"Mr. Westbrooke?" the rattled messenger asked uncertainly. "I have a message for you, sir."

That got Dane's attention. "Let me see it." Dane nearly snatched the paper from the startled man's hands. The fellow blinked, then backed away.

By the time Dane looked up to thank him, the messenger and his carriage had disappeared.

Retreating to the hallway, Dane reread his mother's cryptic note: *Jacqueline is well and with me. If you come to Greenhills and drag her home, you will undo everything I have done. Let your wife come to you. Trust me. Mother.*

Cursing under his breath, Dane crumpled the note and flung it across the room. He was relieved as hell that Jacqui was unharmed, but totally at sea with regard to her intentions. She was at Greenhills . . . but for how long? What had she told his mother? What was her state of mind?

He rubbed his eyes wearily and went back to the sitting room, where he poured himself a highly potent glass of whiskey. With any luck, he would drink himself into oblivion.

Daylight splashed into the sitting room, drenching the sofa with sunshine and crashing through Dane's throbbing skull. He groaned, clutching his head and squeezing his eyes shut.

"Good morning, Herr Westbrooke!" Greta stood beside the curtain she had flung wide, her voice thundering through Dane's brain and making him grit his teeth in pain.

"What time is it, Greta?"

"It is half after nine." She sniffed loudly. "Apparently Frau Westbrooke has already gone out."

Hearing the mention of Jacqui's name, Dane shot to his feet, simultaneously groping for the arm of the sofa and attempting to steady himself. The previous night came back to him in a rush, and he forced his burning eyes open a crack.

"Coffee," he managed between clenched teeth. "I need coffee, Greta. Now."

"Coffee is ready . . . in the dining room," she retorted pointedly, studying Dane's disheveled appearance. "Together with a large breakfast to begin your day. I've made a fluffy soufflé, smoked bacon, fresh bread with a tub of sweet butter—"

"Stop!" Dane's stomach lurched in protest. Catching a glimpse of the disapproving expression on Greta's face, he had the distinct impression she knew just how her description was affecting him.

"Will Frau Westbrooke be joining you for breakfast?"

So, Greta's ultimate loyalties were with Jacqueline, after all. Jacqui would be pleased.

"No, Greta." Dane straightened to meet her gaze. "Frau Westbrooke will *not* be joining me for breakfast. She is visiting at Greenhills for several days." He glared at Greta through slitted, bloodshot eyes.

"I see."

"Will that be all?" Dane snapped, anxious to bathe and change his clothes.

"No," Greta barked back. "A message arrived for you from Secretary Hamilton." She produced the note from her apron pocket. "Here."

Dane rubbed his forehead wearily, unfolding the slip of paper and scanning its contents. Alexander wanted to see him as soon as possible. Dane's jaw set. Well, he wanted to see Alexander, too . . . to tell him where his suspicions had led . . . and to impress upon him that, Laffey or not, Jacqui was innocent. Hamilton would just have to find his traitor elsewhere.

"This column becomes more provoking by the week!" Hamilton slapped down the *General Advertiser,* his mouth drawn in frustration and worry.

Dane scooped up the newspaper, skimmed Laffey's column with objective efficiency, then tossed it back onto the desk. "I agree," he said calmly. "In light of the violence occurring in western Pennsylvania, it is ill-timed at best." He leaned against the wall, arms folded across his chest. "Was that why you wished to see me?"

"Indirectly . . . yes," Hamilton replied, puzzled by Dane's bland response. "Laffey's articles, together with Bache's whole damned newspaper, have fed the growing unrest in Pittsburgh. Tempers are at a fever pitch. The farmers are convinced they are justified in refusing to pay excise taxes on their whiskey. They are being drawn into the violent outbursts and assaults of the radical Republicans who are determined to oust all federal authority from their midst."

Hamilton paused, drew a slow breath. "Excise officers have been beaten, while those distillers who *do* comply with the law have watched their property destroyed. Then, just last week, a group of armed men attacked the post rider and seized the mails." He made a wide sweep with his arm. "We cannot allow this madness to continue. It has reached the

267

point where a large display of military action could be our only alternative."

"A display?" Dane echoed.

Hamilton turned his quill pen thoughtfully in his hand, then leveled his cool blue gaze on Dane. "If an overwhelming number of troops are assembled, that in itself might be sufficient to subdue the rebels and deter further bloodshed. To that end, President Washington has issued a proclamation ordering the insurgents to cease their violence. Should they refuse, they can expect our troops to convene and, in mid-September, move to ensure that our laws are enforced." He sighed. "As fate would have it, Henry Knox, our Secretary of War, has just been granted a leave of absence. Therefore, until his return I shall be the acting Secretary of War."

Dane muttered an oath under his breath. He was neither surprised nor distressed by the news of Hamilton's additional cabinet post. President Washington's choice was sound; no one was more qualified for the position than Hamilton. Dane also concurred with Alexander's assessment of the government's unavoidable course of action. Still, internal strife was the last complication America needed right now.

"We are in grave danger of civil war, Dane." Hamilton verbalized the very fears that were plaguing Dane's mind. "And at the worst of times, given our precarious international position with the British. We *must* expose Laffey . . . *and* our informant . . . before American hostilities escalate too far. Which brings me to George Holt . . . and your wife."

"Stop right there, Alexander." Dane's tone was lethal.

For the first time, Hamilton suspended his train of thought long enough to focus on Dane. He noted his friend's rigid stance and realized that Dane's odd behavior had been present long before Hamilton had given him the disturbing political news.

"Dane, what is it?"

268

"It's Jacqueline. She's gone."

It was Hamilton's turn to tense. "Gone?"

"Fear not, my friend," Dane said bitterly. "She hasn't fled with any national secrets. She's at Greenhills with my mother."

"Why?"

"Because I accused her of being a traitor and a British informant. She found that a bit difficult to endure coming from her husband."

"You confronted her?" Hamilton was astounded.

"I did. And she is innocent . . . at least of treason." Dane ignored the skeptical look on Hamilton's face. "Believe what you will, Alexander. My wife has done nothing to betray our country. She has, however, managed to mislead us in a most thorough manner." His mouth curved a bit as he recalled the pride in Jacqui's eyes when she'd announced her identity.

"How do you know she is innocent?"

"The same way you believed her guilty. Instinct. In this case, mine is correct . . . yours is not."

"I see." Hamilton was taken aback by Dane's definitive statement. He had seen his friend's intuition prevail too often to blithely disregard Dane's belief in Jacqueline's innocence . . . despite the impediment of his feelings for her. Still . . . "Then how do you explain Jacqueline's bizarre behavior?" Hamilton persisted, brimming with unanswered questions. "And what do you mean she has misled us?"

Dane's jaw set. He had known this conversation wouldn't be easy. "I can answer both those questions as one. Jacqueline's bizarre behavior is simply a way for her to accomplish her work while, at the same time, keeping us from discovering what that work really is. My wife is clever, impulsive, rash . . . and, unfortunately, completely devoid of trust in her husband." Dane's expression darkened. "And she is one thing more."

"Which is?"

269

"Jack Laffey."

Hamilton just stared, stupefied. "Jack Laffey . . . Jacqueline?"

"Yes. Jacqueline. My own *Jacques la fille.* You and I were so dogged in our belief that George Holt was the notorious reporter we sought that we overlooked the obvious . . . although *she* was right under our very noses."

"Jacques la fille," Hamilton repeated, the lightning bolt of realization accompanied by an equal dose of self-disgust. How could he have overlooked so exact a translation? Jack the girl. But Laffey . . . a woman? Hamilton absorbed this bit of information with great difficulty. "Jacqueline told you this herself?"

"She did."

The Secretary's mind was racing. "You believe Laffey's columns are her only crime?"

"I *know* they are." Dane looked tormented. "You should have seen the expression on her face . . . and on George's . . . when I accused them of treason. It was as if they'd been struck. Such extreme shock and bewilderment cannot be feigned, Alexander. Neither Jacqueline nor her father had a clue as to what I was talking about. Yes . . . I am quite certain that my wife's secret identity is her only transgression." He shifted restlessly, glancing out the window in the direction of the Schuylkill . . . and Greenhills. "I only wish she'd allowed herself to confide in me."

Alexander shook his head in amazement. "So we are no closer to discovering our traitor than we were a month ago." He frowned. "That is distressing news indeed. However, we have, at least, solved one part of our dilemma. We can finally stop Laffey's unfounded instigation."

Dane's brows rose. "Can we?"

Hamilton blanched. "Good Lord, Dane . . . she's your *wife!*"

"Yes," Dane agreed, seeing Jacqui's face when she'd defended her actions. "She is."

"Then you will simply forbid her to continue writing and put an end to Jack Laffey!"

"Will I?" Dane murmured, half to himself. He stared off into space, deep in thought.

Terminate Jacqui's writing. Yes, that would silence Laffey, temper the agitation of the populace, and end Jacqui's unorthodox nighttime excursions. It was the only logical course of action; the one any proper husband would command. The one Jacqui expected him to take.

Dane had no intention of taking it.

CHAPTER

16

The whiskey burned a path straight to his stomach.

Dane grimaced, pushing the drink away, and ordered a cup of black coffee. He'd had enough spirits last night. Today he needed a clear head to plan his approach to the problem at hand: his wife.

Leaning back in the cushioned chair, Dane closed his eyes. The City Tavern was quiet, as it was not yet noon, and the Coffee Room was deserted, save Dane and the sleepy-eyed waiter who ambled over to clear away the whiskey and leave the coffee in its stead.

Dane barely noticed the waiter or the coffee. He was weighing his options, deciding the best way to handle the quandary in which he'd found himself. He knew what Alexander expected him to do. The Secretary had made it quite clear that he was unconditionally opposed to any option other than strictly forbidding Jacqueline to continue her columns.

Dane vehemently disagreed. The day he'd asked Jacqueline to become his wife he'd vowed to respect her individuality, to accept the unconventional traits that were so much a part of her. By commanding the cessation of her columns, he was breaking that promise, using his role as her husband to mold her against her will. And, while assuring her obedience, he would be crushing her spirit and fulfilling every negative accusation she'd ever hurled at him.

On the other hand, she'd lied to him, purposefully led a double life, made a mockery of their marriage. She was stubbornly determined to believe the worst of him, because she was an unyielding, self-protective little rebel. . . .

Who was falling in love with her husband.

Dane smiled to himself. He'd suspected Jacqueline's feelings for months now. But last night, he'd seen the naked truth in her eyes. She loved him, and, for her own reasons, she was terrified by that love. Dane could only suspect what those reasons were, but he did understand that Jacqui's feelings for him were very new and very fragile. He had no intention of allowing them to shatter.

"Dane?"

Dane's eyes flew open. "Thomas."

"I thought it was you." Thomas lowered himself into the chair beside his friend. "Why are you away from Westbrooke Shipping in the middle of the morning? Is anything amiss?"

Even as he began to shake his head, Dane abruptly stopped himself. He badly needed an objective ear . . . and a friend. Thomas was both. "Yes, Thomas. Something is amiss. But it has nothing to do with Westbrooke Shipping."

Thomas signaled for coffee, then turned his attention to his friend. "Is it Jacqueline, then?"

"In a word, yes."

"Not surprising." Thomas grinned. "Your bride is quite a handful. I'd be happy to listen and to help in any way I can."

"I'm afraid it's more serious than a mere marital dispute." Dane hesitated. "Thomas, I want your word that this conversation will go no farther than this table."

"Of course." Thomas took his coffee and nodded his thanks to the waiter. "Now, what mischief has Jacqueline gotten herself into?"

"The *General Advertiser*."

"What about the *General Advertiser?*"

"That's what my *bride* has gotten herself into."

"She's written something for Bache's newspaper?"

"Many things." Dane's lips twisted in a sardonic smile. "Brace yourself, Thomas." He inhaled sharply. "Jacqueline is Jack Laffey."

Thomas nearly toppled from his chair. *"What?"*

"You heard me. My wife is none other than Jack Laffey— or, rather, *Jacques la fille.* She writes his weekly column, sneaks out every Monday night in order to deliver it to a young messenger who in turn brings it to Bache. So you see my dilemma."

Thomas still hadn't recovered. "Jacqueline . . . Laffey?"

"Your reaction is similar to Alexander's."

"The Secretary knows?" Thomas asked quickly.

"I told him. Let's just say he has an avid interest in my wife and her actions."

I'll just bet he does, Thomas thought, remembering the conversation he'd been privy to between Dane and Hamilton prior to Dane's marriage. Thomas's impression that Hamilton suspected the Holts of betraying their country had, apparently, been correct. And while he was startled by Dane's surprising revelation, Thomas was, nonetheless, lighter of heart than he'd been in months. Everything was falling into place. The fact that Jacqueline was Laffey would give Hamilton all the more reason to doubt her loyalties . . . and divert him from the truth.

Thomas swallowed his euphoria with great difficulty. "How do you plan to deal with Jacqueline?"

"I'm torn between giving her the world and choking her to death."

"That bad, is it?"

"That bad," Dane agreed, scowling.

Unbidden, Thomas felt a twinge of pity. The invincible Dane Westbrooke had certainly picked one hell of a time to fall in love. Thomas, better than anyone, knew how painful love could be.

"She married you, Dane," he said quietly. "She wouldn't have done that if she didn't care for you . . . would she?" He paused, casting aside his allegiance to Dane in lieu of his commitment to the future . . . *his* future. The end was so close. Any day, Jay's deadlocked negotiations with the English would completely disintegrate. Then America would be thrown into war, forced to align with the French. Thomas's job would be done. He would have his money, his new life . . . and Monique. Above all, he couldn't risk losing her.

"I don't know Jacqueline's motives," he continued, hating himself for the pained look on Dane's face. "But I *do* know women. And so do you . . . too well to allow your wife to own your heart. Lord knows what else she's kept from you . . . and why." Thomas stood. "Were I you, Dane, I would keep a close eye on Jacqueline." For a long moment he grappled with guilt, feeling as low as a snake. Unable to look Dane in the eye, he glanced down at his timepiece, reminding himself of what would soon be his.

"Unfortunately, I must be off. . . . I'm late for an appointment." He placed an unsteady hand on Dane's shoulder, wishing there were some other way to have all that he so desperately craved.

"Thank you, Thomas. I appreciate your concern." Oblivious to Thomas's internal torment, Dane finished the last of his coffee and set the empty cup on the table. "I must be going as well. I plan to have a long talk with my wife . . . *today.*"

Monique received Thomas's message with a great show of impatience. She waved the messenger away, wondering what juvenile nonsense was on Thomas's mind now. She had no time for his romantic drivel . . . not while she was contemplating the next step in her rapidly progressing plan. Between Thomas's adolescent adoration and George's smothering tenderness and declarations of love, it was a wonder she had enough time to accomplish her work.

Her life in America was growing more suffocating by the day.

She tore open the envelope and read the note, her blue eyes widening with increasing interest. So . . . George's headstrong little hellion of a daughter was that radical reporter for the *General Advertiser*. That altered things considerably.

Monique crossed the sitting room and dropped down on the settee, absently massaging her temples. She had to think this through. Carefully. Lifting her head, she reread the note once, then again. Thomas was correct that Jacqueline's involvement with the Republican newspaper would cause Hamilton to believe, more than ever, that she was the traitor who was passing information to the English. That would, of course, remove Thomas and Monique from suspicion and leave them free to finish their work and send their missive off to England. It was the perfect diversion.

That settled, Monique considered the more serious problem generated by Jacqueline's supposed guilt: that being communication with France. Monique desperately needed to transmit messages to her mother country, as she pushed America and England closer to war. For, once America aligned herself with France, a long-deserved supremacy would be realized, not only by France, but by the brilliant man who would soon lead it . . . the man Monique loved.

And how could her messages reach Bonaparte if not on George Holt's shipments to the mainland?

Monique frowned, lines of concentration furrowing her brow. There was no doubt that, with Jacqueline suspected of treason, George's activities would be carefully monitored as well. So how could Monique continue to send information to France via George's transports?

On the other hand, how else could she contact her homeland if not through George's shipments? She certainly could not approach Thomas for any of his contacts. She dared not breathe a word of the situation to Thomas, lest he learn of her relationship with George. No, she would have to solve this dilemma alone. For, should either George or Thomas learn of her involvement with the other, everything could blow up in her face.

There had to be a way. . . .

"Are you sure you're ready to face Dane?" Lenore inquired, strolling beside Jacqui to the waiting carriage.

Jacqui nodded. "Yes. I'm very grateful for all you've done, Lenore, but I cannot hide at Greenhills forever." She grimaced. "Although I'm uncertain as to the reception I'll receive when I get home."

Lenore halted beside the attentive coachman, taking Jacqui's hands in hers. "Remember our discussion last night, Jacqueline. Dane is a strong, principled man. He might not agree with your convictions. But he cares for you . . . very much. And he respects you. Do not treat those emotions lightly, for they will carry you through many a storm. By all means, stand up for who you are . . . but accept Dane for who he is as well. Most important, do not be afraid to feel," she added softly, giving voice to her greater concern. "Loving and being loved are two of life's most wonderful blessings."

"Which can be snatched away at any time . . . and without warning," Jacqui replied with sad resignation.

"Perhaps. But the alternative is bleaker still." Lenore was thankful to be given the chance to penetrate Jacqui's carefully erected walls. "For without love, Jacqueline, life would be hollow and barren, creating a void far worse than any pain our hearts might endure."

Jacqui considered Lenore's words in pensive silence.

"Remember, Jacqui," Lenore proffered, giving Jacqui a tender smile, "should you need it, you shall always have a place at Greenhills."

Jacqui swallowed past the lump in her throat. These emotions were new, and she wasn't quite sure how to express them. "Thank you, Lenore," she said, a trifle unsteadily, wishing there was a way to better convey her gratitude.

Lenore hesitated, then took the final plunge. "Dane told me you lost your mother when you were quite young," she began, praying the risk *she* was taking would not be too costly. "I know that no one can ever replace her in your heart. Still, I hope someday you'll be able to think of me, never as the precious mother you recall from childhood, but as the loving friend and mother you've acquired in adulthood."

Jacqui's expression grew haunted with long-repressed memories. Then she met Lenore's sensitive, uncertain gaze, and a current of warmth seeped through her. "I hope so." As she spoke the words, Jacqui was startled to find they were true. She wanted to care for Lenore . . . desperately.

And, all at once, Jacqui knew just how to reciprocate Lenore's kindness, to bring joy to her life . . . and to Dane's life as well.

She could hardly wait.

Impulsively, Jacqui gave Lenore a quick hug, then gathered up her skirts and climbed into the carriage.

"Give Dane my love," Lenore called.

"If we're on speaking terms." Jacqui's retort was dry.

Lenore chuckled. "Good luck!"

"I shall need it." As the carriage moved off, Jacqui waved to Lenore and settled herself on the cushioned seat. She had an hour's ride to the city . . . an hour to prepare herself for her confrontation with Dane.

An hour to pen the missive she was itching to send.

"I've had enough . . . I'm going after her!" Dane muttered the words to nobody in particular, as no one was about to see him wearing out the sitting-room carpet with his pacing.

Stivers, ever diligent, was hard at work on the second level of the house, while Greta, who had done no work at all, was five minutes away from her next quarter of an hour ritual. Every fifteen minutes she would stomp into the sitting room, gaze accusingly out the window, violently fluff sofa cushions that Dane suspected were a substitute for his head, and mumble something about Fräulein under her breath. Then she would throw Dane a withering, vicious look and storm out, only to repeat the process a quarter hour later.

Dane had withstood the wait for as long as he could; it was time to reclaim his wife.

He stalked into the hallway and promptly came to a screeching halt. Several yards away, the front door opened, admitting the very object of his quest.

When she saw him, Jacqui paused, running her tongue over dry lips. "Hello, Dane," she said at last.

Dane drew a slow, inward breath. "Are you all right?"

Jacqui inclined her head. "Didn't you receive the message from Greenhills?"

"Yes . . . it arrived last night."

"Then you know I was with your mother." Jacqui managed a small smile. "Lenore took excellent care of me."

"We have to talk." Dane wasn't wasting another minute.

"Yes, we do."

He gestured toward the sitting room and Jacqui moved past him, avoiding his eyes as she sank down into the sofa.

She frowned, attempting to extricate herself from the seemingly endless cushions. "I don't recall this sofa being quite so . . . full."

Dane closed the door behind him, crossing the room and seating himself in the chair beside her. "It wasn't. . . . Your housekeeper has been pounding on it all day, presumably because she was restraining herself from bashing in my head."

"Oh . . . I see." The picture Dane painted would have been comical had the prevailing mood been less somber. As things were, neither of them laughed.

"Jacqueline," Dane began, "I have two questions for you. The first is, Are all your secrets now in the open? And the second is, Why did you keep your column from me?" He pushed on, seeing that she meant to interrupt. "I know my first question angers you, but if you examine your actions, I believe you will agree that it is justified."

Jacqui folded her hands in her lap. "Since last night, I've thought about little else *but* my actions. I intend to address both your questions. But first, I want you to answer one of mine."

"Anything."

For the first time since she'd arrived, Jacqui met Dane's gaze directly. "Do you believe I am guilty of treason?"

There was no trace of hesitation. "No."

Her face softened considerably. "Thank you for that," was all she said. "As to your questions . . . yes and isn't that obvious?"

"You thought I would forbid you to continue your work."

"Wouldn't you? Is Laffey not why you're so furious at me?"

"No, it isn't." Dane leaned forward, his expression intense. "I'm furious because you refuse to have faith in me, refuse to believe I mean what I say. How can our marriage succeed if you are so damned unwilling to trust me?"

Jacqui stared down at her laced fingers. "Trust does not come easily to me, Dane." She glanced curiously at him from beneath her lashes. "You wouldn't have forced me to stop writing?"

"I would have argued with you, just as I intend to now. But not for the reasons you think. I'm proud as hell of your capabilities . . . and your integrity in stating your views."

"But . . ."

"But I'm also worried . . . about our country's stability *and* about you. Your columns infuriate many people. Should anyone learn your identity, you could get hurt." He scowled, rubbing his chin thoughtfully. "Now that I know I can protect you."

Jacqui started. "You plan to *support* me in my writing?"

"That surprises you?"

"It staggers me." She shook her head in total bewilderment.

"I don't know why. I believe I made it very clear that I would not attempt to squelch your column."

"Tolerating my work differs greatly from giving it your blessing . . . especially in light of our conflicting views. I just never imagined—"

"Well, you were wrong, weren't you?"

Jacqui's mind was in a whirlwind. "Dane, what if Secretary Hamilton and all your Federalist associates find out?"

"I've already told Alexander."

"You *what?"* she gasped. "What did he say?"

"He instructed me to order you to cease writing Laffey's columns."

"You would blatantly disregard his demand?"

Dane's eyes twinkled. "Did you think yourself the only person with independent convictions?" he inquired mildly.

"Of course not. I simply thought . . ."

"That I would stand beside my friend rather than my wife."

Jacqui rose, turning away from Dane. "You're confusing me," she muttered, fingering the folds of her gown.

Dane stood as well, wrapping his arms about her waist and resting his chin atop her bright head. "You've been telling me that for months now," he teased huskily. "But, actually, I'm quite easy to understand . . . a most simple man."

Smiling in spite of herself, Jacqui turned in his arms. "There is nothing simple about you, Dane Westbrooke. Nothing at all."

He cupped her face tenderly. "Give us a chance, *chaton.* Trust me."

Jacqui swallowed. "I'll try."

He bent his head to her mouth, but she stopped his progress, pressing her hands against the powerful wall of his chest. "Dane, I know you don't want to hear this, but your friend, Secretary Hamilton, is *not* one to accept defeat. If he wants to prevent me from writing my column, he'll stop at nothing until he has succeeded."

"I agree." Dane's breath was warm against her lips.

"What if he should inform Bache of Laffey's identity?"

"Then I imagine you would lose your job." Dane brushed his lips softly against hers.

Jacqui recoiled. "Dane! You said—"

He smiled, drawing her closer to him, soothing the tense muscles of her back with knowing hands. *"I'll* deal with Bache. . . . And if that doesn't work, I'll buy his newspaper."

Her eyes widened in shock. "You couldn't!"

"Couldn't I?"

"But he would never—"

"He wouldn't know." He nibbled at her mouth. "I have many friends, darling, Republicans as well as Federalists. Rest assured, your job is safe." He threaded his fingers through her hair. "And so are you, now that I know what we're up against." His silver eyes darkened with an emotion Jacqui knew only too well. "I do believe we've answered each other's questions most satisfactorily, sweet. Now I'd like to resume our frank communication upstairs in our bedchamber . . . if that is agreeable to you, my contrary wife?"

Jacqui felt Dane's magnetic pull fragment her thoughts into a tumble of confusion. "We still have much to discuss," she protested halfheartedly.

"Oh, I agree." Dane leaned over and scooped Jacqui up, carrying her purposefully to the stairs. "We shall cover every conceivable topic . . . later." His grip tightened. "Last night without you was endless." He nuzzled her hair.

Jacqui inhaled his wonderful masculine scent, heard his husky, arousing words, and her determination slipped a notch farther. "We can't solve our differences in bed, Dane," she tried feebly.

"True." Dane never broke his stride. "But we *can* make

slow, magnificent love to each other in bed. And at this moment, all I want—"

"Fräulein! . . . Excuse me . . . Frau Westbrooke!"

Dane's hungry declaration was interrupted by a loud exclamation from the hallway.

"At last . . . you are home!" Greta planted herself at the foot of the stairs, unperturbed by the intimate scene she'd obviously just interrupted.

"Yes, Greta, Frau Westbrooke is home," Dane answered with deliberate emphasis on Jacqui's proper form of address. He wedged himself determinedly around Greta's imposing figure, taking the stairs two at a time. "Why don't you and Stivers take the rest of the day off?" he suggested in a voice loud enough to bring Stivers rushing to the second-floor landing. "Mrs. Westbrooke and I will not require anything until tomorrow," Dane informed the startled manservant as they passed him. Never slowing his pace, Dane chuckled wickedly when he felt Jacqui bury her flaming cheeks against his chest.

He paused when he reached their open bedchamber. "Have a pleasant day, Stivers," he called back cheerily. "Oh, and lock the door behind you, will you please?"

"Yes, Mr. Westbrooke." Stivers was still staring when Dane shut the door in his face and carried Jacqui across the room, gently depositing her on the bed.

"Dane . . ." Jacqui scrambled to her knees. "What will Stivers and Greta think?"

Dane was efficiently shedding his clothes. "The truth." He cast aside his breeches and shirt, baring his powerful, thoroughly aroused body to Jacqui's gaze. "I want you, *chaton*," he said quietly, lowering himself beside her. "I'll do whatever I must to have you. Now. Always."

He glided his hands over the smooth curve of her shoulders, watching Jacqui's breath quicken, tugging the sleeves of her gown down until he had access to the delicate skin of her throat and breasts. "Forget last night," he ordered softly,

slipping her buttons free one by one until Jacqui could feel
the cool air on her naked back, a dizzying contrast to the
scorching touch of Dane's lips on her flesh, the heat of the
seductive words he breathed against her skin. "Forget your
work, our argument, the world." He closed his mouth over
hers, tugging the remainder of her clothing from her trembling body and easing her onto the thick quilt. "Forget
everything . . . everything but this." He covered her body
with his. "Only this." He tangled his hands in her hair. "Ah,
Jacqueline . . . only this . . ."

Jacqui did.

Afterward, she lay curled beside him, worried by the
magnitude of her feelings. Physically, nothing had changed:
their lovemaking was as stormy and fulfilling as ever. But for
Jacqui, it was no longer enough. She wanted to remain in
her husband's arms, to prolong the peace she knew there . . .
to hear him say he loved her.

"What is it, *chaton?*" Dane rubbed his chin across the top
of her head, conscious of the sudden tension in her body.

Desperate to run away, more desperate to stay here
forever, Jacqui closed her eyes. "I hated when you left me
last time," she blurted out.

Dane understood . . . perhaps more than she wished him
to. He tipped her chin up, kissed her beautiful, flushed
cheeks. "I hated it as well," he replied with sober intensity.
"I won't leave you again." He held her gaze as poignantly as
he held her soft, damp body. "I missed you, *chaton.*" His
voice was like deep velvet. "Very much."

Jacqui lowered her eyes.

Dane studied her bent head silently for long moments,
wrestling with his options. At last, he gave a resigned sigh. "I
should have known your mind would not be so easily
conquered as your body, my unwavering wife," he said,
feigning ignorance in order to spare Jacqui the distress of
examining what was in her heart. "Have you resumed
pondering the affairs of the world?"

The new subject was infinitely safer than the one Jacqui

had actually been grappling with. "I'm concerned about America's future . . . yes," she answered, relieved to be on sure ground.

"As am I." Once again, Dane considered pursuing Jacqui's *true* worry, then thought better of it. That particular conversation was one Jacqui would have to initiate herself, and evidently she just wasn't ready to deal with her feelings for him. So be it . . . for now.

Dane pressed a kiss to her forehead, then settled her against him. "All right, my lovely scholar. Let's continue our discussion."

"Beginning with Laffey." Jacqui propped herself on one elbow, crisply efficient as she looked into her husband's face.

Dane grinned at the delicious contrast between Jacqui's businesslike demeanor and her exquisite, intimate state of undress. "All right. Beginning with Laffey." He folded his arms behind his head.

"I plan to continue writing my columns."

"Agreed . . . with one condition." Dane ignored Jacqui's belligerent scowl. "I want you to show me your articles *before* you turn them over to Bache."

"Why?"

"So I can be prepared for the ramifications." Dane's reply was equally as curt. He reached out, threaded his fingers through her hair, cupping her head tenderly. "Jacqueline, I will never deny you your independence . . . don't deny me the right to protect you. You're my wife . . . and I care about you . . . deeply."

Jacqui's throat constricted, autonomy warring with sentiment. "You won't attempt to influence what I write?"

"No."

She nodded. "I believe you. And I accept your condition."

Dane felt a surge of elation, not at the minor victory he'd won over Laffey, but at the three little words Jacqui had just uttered. *I believe you,* she'd said. Belief was the first step toward trust.

"I understand your concern over my columns, especially

the controversial ones dealing with the whiskey tax," Jacqui was continuing. "However, I *don't* understand what information you believed I had in my possession that could possibly interest the English."

Dane continued to absently caress her nape. "I trust you, Jacqueline," he said with slow deliberation, his gaze fixed on hers, "so I will tell you what has occurred, and why I believe there is a traitor in our midst."

Quietly and without embellishment, Dane told Jacqui about the documents that had mysteriously disappeared, then reappeared in Hamilton's office just prior to John Jay's departure for England; about the faltering negotiations still taking place between Jay and Grenville; and about Grenville's prior knowledge of each of America's preset conditions.

"Your weekly nocturnal excursions and blatant pro-French philosophy made Alexander suspicious," Dane admitted. "He assumed you were acting on behalf of your father. We already suspected George was Jack Laffey, since he had the most uncanny ability to appear at events attended by important politicians who, later that week, would be quoted in Laffey's column. Then, the day after the papers were stolen from Alexander's office, your father made a most uncharacteristic request." Dane went on to explain George's unusual and urgent need to send a shipment to the mainland. "So you see," Dane concluded candidly, "the evidence, though circumstantial, seemed pretty damning. Your father appeared to be not only Jack Laffey but an American traitor. And you, it seemed likely, were his accomplice."

"I see." Jacqui considered Dane's explanation carefully and objectively. Hamilton's suspicions had certainly been founded . . . founded but flawed. It was up to her to identify the defects and clear her family name by discovering the true felon. "Obviously, Secretary Hamilton's theory is correct," she acknowledged, her fine brows drawn contemplatively. "Information is being supplied to the

English. I presume you believe this is being done in order to draw us into war with them?"

"Exactly."

"Then the remaining question is, Why? Is our traitor propelled by a desire for English supremacy or is he concerned with forging America's ties with France? The latter goal is no longer a certainty, since we've determined that my father and I are not the guilty parties."

Dane's hand stilled. "Your brilliance never ceases to amaze me, *chaton*," he murmured, his voice laced with pride. "I salute your keen perception . . . you are quite right."

Laying her hand on Dane's chest, Jacqui propped her chin upon it. "Give me some time to think," she said matter-of-factly. "After which, I'll determine the most effective way to unearth the culprit and his motive."

Dane nearly catapulted them both off the bed. "You'll do *what?*" he bellowed.

Jacqui blinked up at him in astonishment. "I said that I'll—"

"I heard what you said." Dane seized her shoulders, glaring at her with blazing silver eyes. "And the answer is *no!* No, you will not determine the plan we will enact to catch the offender, and no, you will not take part in that plan once we determine it!" He shook her gently. "Don't even consider it, Jacqueline . . . not for a minute. I want you to stay the hell out of this. Do you understand?"

Jacqui raised her chin defiantly.

"Jacqueline . . . I'm warning you," Dane said in a chilling tone that brought to Jacqui's mind her father's words about Dane's overwhelming, carefully leashed power. "I'll tie you up if I must, keep you under lock and key, but I will *not* allow you to endanger yourself. Is that clear?"

She didn't answer.

"*Jacqueline!*" There was no arguing with *that*.

"All right . . . yes," Jacqui replied reluctantly.

"Damn . . . you drive me crazy." He jerked the quilt out

287

from under them, yanking it over their naked bodies. "Enough talking. I don't know about you, but I'm exhausted. . . . The only sleep I got last night was when I passed out in a drunken stupor." He settled himself in the bed, then pulled her to him, tucking her head beneath his chin.

"Dane, it's the middle of the day. We have to—"

"Go to sleep, Jacqueline." He tightened his grip around her waist, muttering, "You bloody impossible, unyielding woman." He closed his eyes, his final words muffled by her fragrant cloud of hair, slurred by his fatigue. "Lord only knows why I love you."

Jacqui was certain she'd never been so arrogantly chastised.

Nor so arrogantly pleased.

CHAPTER
17

I cannot believe I'm hearing this!"

Rarely was the Secretary of the Treasury at a loss for words. He was now. Pacing the length of his office, he came to an abrupt halt before his desk, slamming his hands on the walnut surface until it vibrated from the impact. "Dane, have you taken complete leave of your senses?"

Dane stood stiffly. "My senses are quite intact, Alexander. I simply will not forbid my wife from writing her columns. . . . They mean far too much to her."

"What about what they mean to America?"

"I made Jacqueline aware of the inflammatory nature of certain political issues. I trust her to temper her articles accordingly . . . but without compromising her standards."

Hamilton exhaled sharply. "You trust her? After all her deception, you can still use that word?"

"I can."

Their gazes locked.

"I could make certain of Laffey's demise by revealing his identity," Hamilton said quietly.

"You could. But you won't. And if you tried, I would do everything in my power to thwart you." Dane's reply was equally quiet.

"You believe in her that much?"

"I love her that much."

Hamilton shook his head slowly. "I don't understand a love that makes a man weak."

"Not weak, Alexander. Whole. And not blind either. I know my wife's flaws; Lord knows I've been subjected to them often enough. But I also know her virtues. She is forthright, principled, and unquestionably loyal to her country."

"And to you?"

Dane's lips curved into a smile. "And to me. Fight it though she will."

Hamilton fell into a thoughtful silence. Finally he said, "We've known each other a long time now, Dane."

"More than seven years," Dane agreed.

"When I first met you I had only just arrived from New York to attend the Continental Congress. I had grown disheartened, for it seemed I stood alone in my convictions. Many called me monarchical, when in truth I was merely being practical." He smiled faintly, remembering. "You approached me at the City Tavern to offer your support."

"I was impressed by your candid and vocal advocation of a strong national government. I concurred completely . . . then and now."

"There were many who did not trust my judgment. Many who still don't."

"You should know by now that I am not influenced by 'many.' I am very much my own person."

"As am I." Hamilton raised his head, his keen blue eyes clear, decisive. "If you believe so strongly in your Jacqueline, then so be it. I will not interfere . . . unless," he quickly amended, "she gives me reason to."

Dane approached the desk, extended his hand. "You have my thanks."

Hamilton shook it. "And you have my sympathy." His lips twitched. "Your bride's redeeming qualities must be splendid indeed."

Dane grinned broadly. "They are. And with your permission, I'm off to Westbrooke Shipping so I can return home quickly to sample those redeeming qualities."

Hamilton watched Dane go, wondering at the powerful emotion that drove his friend. He did not envy Dane's predicament, nor could he imagine marriage to so hot-headed and rebellious a woman.

Still, Alexander trusted Dane's instincts. Therefore, he accepted Dane's unequivocal conviction that Jacqueline was innocent of treason and that her motives for writing Laffey's column were honorable. Yet it worried Hamilton for Dane's wife to possess so much power. Her column had a significant impact on the masses. 'Twas a pity that the column couldn't be directed toward a more . . .

An idea exploded in Hamilton's mind with all the brilliance of a lightning bolt. Why hadn't he thought of it earlier?

Fairly crackling with energy, the Secretary eased into his chair, took up his quill, and began to pen a message.

"You wished to see me, Mr. Secretary?"

Jacqui stood in the open doorway, awaiting permission to enter. For long hours after receiving Hamilton's note, she had debated whether or not to comply with his urgent but mysterious request to see her. In the end, her curiosity had won out.

Hamilton pushed back his chair and rose. "Mrs. Westbrooke." He walked toward her with polished grace. "How kind of you to answer my summons so quickly." His tone was smooth, but his blue eyes danced with knowing humor. It had been four hours since his messenger had left with the note.

"I didn't intend to come," Jacqui asserted, her small jaw set.

"Really?" He took her hand, pressed a brief, chaste kiss to her knuckles. "Then I'm delighted you reconsidered."

"What is this all about, Mr. Secretary?" Jacqui withdrew

her hand, fingering the folds of her lime muslin gown impatiently, her gaze fixed on Hamilton's. "Your note said it concerned national security. Since I know you and Dane have spoken, I assume my being here pertains to that conversation."

Hamilton rubbed his chin thoughtfully, studying Dane's beautiful, spirited wife. Forthright, Dane had said. Well, she was certainly that. "Yes, Mrs. Westbrooke, I have spoken with Dane. And yes, that is why I've asked to see you."

"Then things stand as such: you know I am Laffey and I know you despise Laffey." She paused, her hands knotting in the soft fabric. "In all due respect, sir, if you've summoned me to demand that I cease writing my column, you are wasting your time."

With a faint smile Hamilton gestured toward the chair. "Won't you have a seat?"

Jacqui gave him a wary look, then complied. Hamilton walked behind his desk and did the same. Steepling his fingers, he rested his chin upon them and leveled his gaze at Jacqui.

"You have been quite frank with me. I shall be the same. True, I know you are Jack Laffey, although I must admit I had trouble believing it at first. However, speaking with you now, I find my skepticism rapidly fading. But no, I did not summon you here to command you to stop writing Laffey's column. Quite the contrary, in fact. I want you to write the most controversial, jarring column you've ever composed in your life . . . or Laffey's."

Jacqui blinked. "I don't understand."

Hamilton leaned forward. "Mrs. Westbrooke . . . Jacqueline . . . may I call you Jacqueline?" When Jacqui nodded, he continued, "I don't know how much Dane has told you of our suspicions."

"You believe there is an American traitor furnishing the English with information," Jacqui supplied for him. "From the evidence Dane mentioned, I agree with your assessment.

However, neither my father nor myself is the criminal you seek."

Hamilton held up his hand. "I'm not accusing you, my dear."

"Really? What changed your mind?"

Jacqui's sarcasm elicited a dry chuckle. "Dane did." Hamilton couldn't help but admire Jacqueline's spunk. "Your husband and I have been friends for a long time, Jacqueline. He possesses the finest instincts I've ever seen."

"I agree."

"Dane is convinced, beyond any doubt, that you are innocent."

"His word is enough for you?"

Again, a hint of a smile. "Not entirely. I do trust one person's instincts more than I do Dane's."

"Whose are those?"

"My own." His lips curved into a full grin. "And after this brief meeting of ours, I must admit that my instincts are in complete accord with Dane's."

Jacqui's mouth dropped open. "Oh . . . I see."

"Have I rendered you speechless?"

It was Jacqui's turn to smile. "No, Mr. Secretary. Even Dane has yet to do that." Seeing the knowing lift of Hamilton's brows, she blushed, lowering her gaze for the first time.

Curiously touched by the unexpected show of modesty, Alexander had a sudden glimpse of why Dane was so smitten with his young bride. Jacqueline was an intriguing combination of brazenness and innocence, of fire and femininity . . . an irresistible challenge to any man . . . especially a compelling man like Dane.

Calling upon his own gift of charm, Hamilton went on, determined to put Jacqueline at ease. "To continue with my reasons for requesting this visit," he said, coming to his feet and walking around his desk. "I shall be direct. I need your assistance, Jacqueline."

"*My* assistance?"

"Or, to be more accurate, Jack Laffey's assistance."

Jacqui's eyes widened with interest. "What manner of assistance do you require?"

Conspiratorially, Hamilton leaned forward. "I want you to help expose our traitor."

"I? How?"

"If Dane and I are correct, our culprit stole certain documents from my office . . . documents containing America's position for Jay's negotiations with the English. If Grenville saw those papers prior to Jay's arrival, America's position has been severely compromised."

"I understand."

Hamilton cleared his throat. "But what if our traitor were to learn we are now drafting an entirely *new* set of negotiating points, drawing up a wholly revised document which, in a matter of a fortnight, will be covertly sent to Jay in England?"

Jacqui frowned. "But if such were the case, you would keep that information secret."

"Yes, we would. But isn't it uncanny the way Jack Laffey seems to uncover even the most closely guarded secrets in our government?"

Jacqui absorbed this statement silently. "I'm beginning to understand," she said slowly. "There is no new document being prepared, is there?"

"No, there isn't."

Jacqui inhaled sharply. "So what you want is for me to write a column comprised of false information in the hopes it will trigger some kind of action by the guilty person?"

"Exactly. You can suggest that I am penning crucial papers for Jay and that no one, other than myself, knows their contents."

"A statement such as that would put you in grave danger," Jacqui pointed out.

"Perhaps." Hamilton shrugged. "But if it meant apprehending the traitor, it would be well worth the risk."

"I would be lying to my readers," Jacqui murmured aloud.

"But to what end? To protect your country, Jacqueline. Is that not worth the price?"

She met his eyes, saw the patriotic fire burning there, a mirror reflection of Dane's . . . and of her own. Maybe they were not so very different from each other after all, she mused. Maybe, although their means were different, their goals were much the same.

"Jacqueline? Your answer?"

"Yes." She committed herself without hesitation or regret. "Yes, Mr. Secretary, I'll do it."

"No!" Dane stormed back and forth across the bedchamber, shaking his head vehemently. "No, you will *not* do it!"

Jacqui gave him an exasperated look and dipped her quill in the inkstand. "I most definitely *will* do it." She returned to her writing.

"Jacqueline . . ." He crossed over to her in three strides and yanked her to her feet. "Do you have any idea how dangerous this could be? What if the traitor you seek should learn you are Jack Laffey and assume you are in possession of the information you allude to in your column . . . then what?" Dane shook her, his mind racing with sinister possibilities. "What the hell could Alexander have been thinking of?"

"Our country." Jacqui disengaged herself from Dane's grasp and attempted to reason with him. "Dane, I must do this . . . don't you understand? Not only for America, but for my father. Until we've learned the identity of the real traitor, there will always be a shadow cast on my family name."

"That's preposterous!" Dane shot back. *"I know you're innocent . . . and that's all that matters! You have to prove nothing, Jacqueline . . . nothing!"*

"Thank you," she said quietly, tenderness softening her

features. "Your faith in me means . . . a great deal. But I also have to do this for me."

"Bloody hell!" Dane clenched his jaw, plagued by apprehension that refused to let go. All he knew was that he *had* to keep Jacqui safe, to protect her from whatever ills could befall her.

Jacqui leaned into her husband, firmly gripping his biceps. "Dane, don't you see? I finally have the chance to do something meaningful: to make a difference, to take on a challenge that is unheard of for a woman." She caught her breath, knowing by the indecision in Dane's eyes that she had reached him. "I will be safe," she pledged in an attempt to allay his fears. "The only person who might be in danger is the Secretary, not I."

"I still don't like it."

"I know you don't. But I must do it anyway." She inclined her head slightly. "You did promise not to interfere with what I write in my column, remember?"

His scowl deepened. "I remember."

She gave him a questioning look. "And?"

Dane cursed under his breath. If he allowed Jacqui to follow through with this foolish plan, she could be exposing herself to grave danger. But if he refused, if he revoked his original vow to her, it would eradicate all the trust he had worked so hard to earn. Either way he was damned.

He cursed again.

Jacqui smiled, the smile of a woman who knew she had won. "Thank you, Dane." She stood on tiptoe and kissed his taut mouth, searching for a way to convey how deeply his show of support had moved her. "I know I am not what one would call an exemplary wife," she confessed. "But in the future . . . I shall try."

Despite his worry, Dane chuckled. "Will you? How?"

She slid her arms around his neck. "Once this ordeal is behind us, I shall master the wifely duty you so constantly crave."

His strong hands encircled her waist. "I'm intrigued. What is it you have planned?"

"Why, to learn to bake Greta's strawberry tarts, of course."

Dane stared down into her beautiful, teasing face and abruptly sobered, drawing her tightly into his arms.

Her own amusement vanished, and Jacqui regarded her husband with searching gravity. "I'll be fine, Dane. I promise."

But even Jacqui's vow and the warmth of her body did little to ease Dane's worry. Nor, in the days that followed, could they silence the warning bells that continued to clamor in his head.

The lone figure of a woman slipped through the night and entered the deserted alley, unseen. She paused, glanced furtively behind her, and, spotting no one, hastened along, her breath coming in short, shallow pants. Then she stopped, waited.

The man stepped out of the shadows, moving to her side. "Monique?" It was a whisper.

Monique threw the dark hood from her head and faced Thomas with blazing eyes. "Of course it is I," she snapped. "Why did you summon me here so urgently in the middle of the night?"

Thomas frowned, but did not comment on her cold, brusque manner. Instead, he thrust a newspaper at her, then struck a match so she could make out the words on the page. "Read."

Impatiently, Monique snatched the paper from his hands and did as he bid her. Within minutes, the furious spark in her eyes was transformed into stark disbelief. "What does this mean?" she demanded.

"Exactly what it says," Thomas returned in a tight voice. "Obviously Hamilton is making another attempt to negotiate with the English."

"But what new points could he raise that his original documents did not already address?"

"How the hell should I know?" Thomas bit out. He jabbed a finger at Laffey's words. "You've read the column. The only one who knows what's in those papers is Hamilton himself." He raked his fingers through his hair. "The question is, How do we divest the Secretary of this information?"

Monique frowned, tapping her foot nervously. She had already prepared the missive to Paris describing America's internal strife as escalating and their negotiations with England as futile. Nothing was going to stand in Monique's way now . . . nothing. "We must take action." She pursed her lips. "However, we cannot break into Hamilton's office again. . . . It is too risky."

"Then what do you suggest we do? We *need* those papers! And no one else—"

"Ah, but there is someone else," Monique interrupted, a smile curving her lips.

"Who?"

"The very person who has kindly provided us with this news . . . Jack Laffey."

Thomas blinked, staring at Monique's triumphant expression. "You plan to question Jacqueline?"

"No. *I* don't plan to question her . . . *you* do!"

"I? But how can I . . ."

Monique waved his protests away. "I know Jacqueline far too well to get involved, Thomas. She would recognize me. You, on the other hand, have met her but once . . . at her wedding. With the proper disguise"—Monique fingered the edge of her hood—"Jacqueline would never know your identity."

"Disguise?" Thomas was beginning to feel ill.

"Yes." Monique took his hand, brought it to her mouth. "You cannot desert me now, *cheri.*" She rubbed his fingers against her lips. "Not when we are so close to having it all."

Thomas swallowed. "She's Dane's wife. I won't hurt her."

"I'm not asking you to hurt her . . . only to persuade her." Sensing Thomas's reluctance, Monique decided drastic measures were in order. Glancing about quickly to make certain they were undetected, she tugged at Thomas's hand. "Come, *mon amour*. We'll go to my house and . . . talk. Surely we can come to an understanding that will please us both?" She gave him a brilliant smile.

For a moment, Thomas hesitated, fighting for some element of self-control, some degree of self-respect. It was no use. When it came to Monique, he was a spineless weakling. And he knew it.

With a quick nod, he seized her hand and led her from the alley.

"I know you are hungry, Whiskey. Greta should be returning from the market any time now."

Jacqui leaned back against the sofa, moved the curtain aside, and peered out the sitting-room window for the third time that morning. It was unlike Greta to be gone so long and so close to mealtime . . . unless the weather had detained her. Jacqui squinted, trying to see through the light mist still drizzling to the ground and rendering the sky a dismal shade of gray.

"At least the rain has eased up some," she observed. "After the continuous storms of the past week, I thought never to see the sky again!" Unappeased, Whiskey meowed his annoyance, sitting with stiff displeasure at Jacqui's feet and licking his whiskers in blatant reminder of the time. Eleven o'clock was well past his feeding hour.

Jacqui rolled her eyes in exasperation. "You have become quite spoiled, you know. Not long ago you were a beggar on the streets and now you live like a king! Yet you complain at the slightest inconvenience." Jacqui shook her head as she recalled the hilarious way she and Whiskey had met. "I could have abandoned you, you know," she reminded him. "Left you to suffer Dane's wrath. You were far too deep in your cups to properly defend yourself. Heaven only knows

299

what Dane intended for your fate . . . but I can assure you, it wasn't an offer of more whiskey! Then where would you be?"

Whiskey's response was to calmly begin licking his paws.

"Not only spoiled but ungrateful," Jacqui muttered.

Her critical assessment was interrupted by a knock.

Puzzled, Jacqui came to her feet. "Greta's arms must be laden," she determined. "And Stivers has the morning off. I'd best let her in." Jacqui stepped around Whiskey and hurried to the door. "I'm glad you're back, Greta," she said, flinging it wide. "I was beginning to worry—" Jacqui's words lodged in her throat as the hooded man pushed into the hallway and slammed the door behind him, pointing a pistol at her head.

"Who are you?" Jacqui demanded. "What do you want?" Her tone was forceful, but her heart slammed against her ribs and she took several reflexive steps backward.

The man made no response, stalking forward until he loomed over Jacqui, his dark, brooding eyes the only part of him that was visible from beneath the broadcloth hood.

All the color drained from Jacqui's face. "If it's money you seek, take anything you wish. Then go."

"I don't want money," the intruder rasped. "I want you."

A soft gasp escaped her throat and her hand flew instinctively to her bodice. "You want . . . me?" Why, oh why, couldn't Dane have chosen to work at home today? Why didn't Greta return from the market?

The intruder raised the pistol a notch higher. "I want you," he repeated.

Jacqui swallowed, fighting her rising hysteria. In a matter of minutes Greta would return. If it were only possible to stave this man off until then . . .

As if reading her mind, the stranger shook his head emphatically. "Not here. I want you to come with me. Now."

Jacqui's knees threatened to buckle. "Come with you . . . where?"

His finger tightened on the trigger. "Now!"

The sound of low hissing startled the intruder. He glanced beyond Jacqui to see the small, spitting kitten crouched behind her. A heartbeat later Whiskey sprang, claws extended, sinking himself into a leg of the intruder's breeches.

With a furious curse, the man shook Whiskey loose.

"Don't hurt him!" Jacqui burst out, snatching up her dazed kitten.

"Then get rid of him," her captor ordered in a spine-chilling rasp.

Jacqui licked her dry lips, forcing herself to think. On wooden legs, she carried Whiskey across the sitting room, keeping her back to the intruder. "Hush, Whiskey," she said aloud, stroking his smooth fur with one hand. "All is well." As she crooned to him, she scanned the room hastily, seeing nothing within reach that could serve as a weapon. Besides, it would be foolhardy to physically retaliate against a man who was twice her size and armed to kill. No, she would have to devise another plan.

Jacqui's eyes fell to her gown. Slowly, so as not to be noticed, she eased her hand down, pausing to tug a piece of ribbon from the opposite sleeve. Quickly, she tied the narrow strip about Whiskey's neck, knowing it was far too thin for the stranger to spot, praying it was not so indiscernible that Dane would miss it as well.

She could feel the intruder come up behind her. Swiftly, she dropped Whiskey to the floor and shooed him toward the kitchen. With a surprised and injured look, the kitten slinked off.

Jacqui turned to face her captor, her mind still racing. "My cat will cause you no further trouble."

"Let's go." The man gestured toward the door.

Where the hell was Greta? Jacqui slumped forward, praying her swoon looked believable. Having never fainted in her life, she was none too certain how it was done.

Apparently her act was convincing, because the man caught her arm roughly. "What's wrong?"

"I . . ." Jacqui rubbed her forehead weakly. "I'm frightened. I think I'm going to . . ." Her knees buckled.

Cursing under his breath, the man dragged her over to the sideboard, hastily searching for some liquor. Seizing a bottle of whiskey, he anchored Jacqui against him while he clumsily sloshed some into a glass. "Drink this," he commanded.

Jacqui took the glass in trembling hands and gulped, coughing violently from the powerful liquid.

The man looked about furtively as if he suddenly realized Jacqui's intent. Tensing, he seized her elbow and raised his weapon. "Now."

Panic swelled in Jacqui's heart. She had run out of time, and there was still no sign of Greta. What was she going to do?

From the corner of her eye, she spotted Whiskey sitting sphinxlike in the hallway, licking his lips and, in typical fashion, eyeing his mistress's liquor hungrily. An idea flashed through Jacqui's head . . . a last resort, but she was desperate.

Turning to comply with her captor's command, Jacqui allowed the glass to slip from her fingers and crash to the floor, where it shattered into bits, splattering whiskey everywhere . . . the sofa, the sideboard . . . and Jacqui's gown.

The last thing she saw before the intruder hauled her off was Whiskey, creeping cautiously back into the sitting room and staring intently at the pool of liquor at his feet . . . then raising his head to follow Jacqui's unwilling departure with keen green eyes.

"Good evening, Herr Westbrooke," Greta greeted Dane at the door, taking his coat and handing him a brandy in return. "I see the rain has finally subsided."

"Yes, it has," Dane agreed, accepting the proffered glass. "Though the streets are drenched, making travel unpleasant, if not impossible."

Greta shook out Dane's wet coat. "Why, your clothing is soaked through. . . . Without the proper care, you'll take ill. Let me get you another brandy." She turned on her heel.

"Thank you, no, Greta." Dane stopped her. "One drink is more than sufficient." He stifled a smile, amused that, since Jacqui's return from Greenhills a fortnight ago, their arrogant housekeeper had resumed her previous and uncharacteristic fussing over him.

Carrying his drink through the hallway, Dane asked, "Will dinner be ready soon?"

"As soon as you and Frau Westbrooke wish it."

Dane glanced about the deserted first floor, then turned toward the stairs. "Is Jacqueline resting?"

"No, sir. Frau Westbrooke has not returned."

"Returned?" Dane's smile froze. "Returned from where?"

"Why, I don't know, sir."

"What do you mean you don't know?" Dane heard the warning bells ring loud and clear in his head. Since Laffey's article had appeared in print, Jacqui had promised him she would not go out alone.

Greta frowned, her apple-dumpling cheeks creasing. "I was at the market when your wife took her leave, Herr Westbrooke."

"Damn!" Dane slammed his fist against the wall, making Greta flinch. "Where would she go in this weather?"

"Excuse my boldness, Herr Westbrooke," Greta admonished, bristling, "but I think you are being overly protective and worrying needlessly. I have known Frau Westbrooke since childhood and she has never advised me . . . or *anyone* . . . of her intended whereabouts."

Dane was barely listening. Something was wrong. He knew it. He felt it.

"What time did you return from the market?" he demanded.

Greta pursed her lips. "I believe it was a little after eleven. The rain delayed me."

303

"Eleven?" Dane looked at the clock and blanched. It was almost five. Jacqui had been gone nearly six hours.

"She left no note?"

"No, sir."

"Where is my carriage?" he fired out.

"In the carriage house. It hasn't been used all day."

That eliminated Greenhills. Dane shoved his drink in Greta's hand.

"Where are you going, Herr Westbrooke?" Greta asked, hurrying after him.

"I'm going to see George Holt," Dane called back, already halfway down the walk. "If Jacqueline should return while I'm out, lock her in this house!"

CHAPTER
18

Redding, George Holt's portly new manservant, darted into the dining room, flushed and breathless. "Mr. Holt!"

Blinking in surprise, George lowered his cup. During the past weeks since Jacqui's marriage, there was rarely a commotion to disturb his evening meal. "What is the trouble, Redding?"

"Pardon me, sir, but Mr. Westbrooke is here, insisting to—"

"George, is Jacqueline here?" Dane pushed past Redding and into the room, mincing no words.

George came to his feet. "Here? No . . ."

"Was she here earlier?"

"No, I haven't seen her all day."

"Damn!" Dane drove his fist into the palm of his hand.

"Redding, that will be all." George dismissed the servant at once, assessing the forthcoming conversation as one to be held in private. When Redding had withdrawn, George turned back to Dane, a knot of apprehension forming in his gut. "What's this all about, Dane?"

Dane began to pace. "She's been gone all day. *You* haven't seen her, *Greta* hasn't seen her. . . ."

George's tension subsided. "That's hardly unlike Jacqui, you know. She's probably off somewhere."

"In the rain?"

"Ofttimes, yes. Rain has never deterred Jacqui."

"Did you read Laffey's column this week?" Dane interrupted, halting in his tracks.

"Of course I did." George's worry peaked once more. "What have Jacqueline's whereabouts got to do with her column?"

"It was a ruse."

"What was?"

"The column. All of it." Dane gave an impatient sweep of his hand. "The document Alexander is allegedly drafting. The new negotiating points for Jay. Everything."

"Are you suggesting Jacqui would fabricate information that is so vital to America?"

"It's not a suggestion. It's a fact."

George shook his head emphatically, his eyes ablaze. "I won't stand here and listen to you accuse my daughter of—"

"George!" Dane gripped the back of the dining-room chair so tightly his knuckles turned white. "You're missing the point! What Jacqueline did was *not* done for illegal or immoral purposes! In fact, it was the most damned patriotic thing imaginable . . . she put herself in danger to protect her country!"

That silenced George. "I don't understand."

"Laffey's column was written at Alexander's request and in complete secrecy. Jacqueline was to provide false information in the *General Advertiser,* hopefully to trap the *real* traitor into revealing himself. Alexander asked Jacqui not to divulge their plan to anyone, which is why you were kept uninformed."

George paled as the impact of the situation struck him. "What if this . . . traitor should become desperate to acquire the new document?"

"Logically, he would go to the only people he is certain

knows of its existence . . . Alexander or Laffey. Hopefully, Alexander," Dane added quickly, fervently.

"Secretary Hamilton, yes." George grabbed hold of that probability but was unable to dismiss the more implausible, frightening alternative. "We are not alone in our knowledge of Laffey's identity, Dane. There is the lad who delivers Jacqui's column and anyone he has told."

"Exactly." Dane began to prowl the floor again, hands clasped behind his back. "If by some remote possibility the real culprit knows Jacqui is Laffey . . ." He broke off, his muscles tightening at the unfinished thought.

"Couldn't you have convinced her *not* to agree to the Secretary's request?" Even as he said the words, George realized how ludicrous they were.

Dane gave a harsh laugh, never breaking stride. "Nobody convinces your daughter of anything, George. She heeds no one, trusts no one, relies upon no one . . . but herself. And it matters not how hard I try, there is no breaking through that damned autonomous shell of hers."

The agony in Dane's voice struck a chord in George's heart. "You love her a great deal."

"With my whole being . . . for all the good it does me," Dane answered, his expression bleak. "I've shown her time and again she can trust me; I know she *wants* to trust me. And yet she cannot allow herself to do so. . . . It's almost as if she's afraid."

George studied him in pensive silence, remembering the first night Dane had stood in this house speaking of his love for Jacqui. Confronting George with honor and candor, Dane had sought even then to understand his betrothed, asking questions George chose to defer in the hope that Jacqui would herself provide the answers. She hadn't. So it was up to him, as her father, to do it for her. "Has Jacqui ever spoken to you of her mother?" George asked quietly.

Something made Dane stop, swerve about to look George in the eye. "No. Never."

"I thought not. She rarely speaks of Marie, even to me."

"I know your wife died when Jacqui was a child."

George inclined his head slightly. "She was ten. Part child, part young girl. Old enough to perceive the value of her mother's love, young enough to revere her with childhood adoration."

"Were they very close?"

"Inseparable. Marie was a rare jewel . . . filled with love and vitality, traditional . . . but wise enough to discern how *un*traditional Jacqui was. And gifted with the foresight to understand how Jacqui's uniqueness destined her to make great contributions to the world."

Dane swallowed. "How did your wife die?"

A flash of pain crossed George's face. "It was sudden. Marie was very frail. When the fever developed . . . nothing helped. Within two days, she was gone."

"Jacqui . . ." All that came to Dane's mind was the anguish his wife must have endured.

George answered the unspoken question. "You didn't know Jacqui before Marie's death. She was a different girl: open, affectionate, trusting. She expressed her feelings easily and often. Then . . . everything changed."

"She must have been badly hurt."

"She was devastated. When I told her Marie was gone, she didn't say a word, nor did she shed a tear." George inhaled shakily. "She shut herself in her room and scarcely emerged for days on end. When she finally resumed her meals and her studies, she barely went through the motions, a mere shell of the exuberant girl she had been. It took me . . . and Greta . . . months to ease Jacqui back into living life again." He shook his head sadly. "Unfortunately, some of her scars penetrated too deep even for me to reach."

"That's not true," Dane negated hoarsely. "You were with her . . . to love her, to share her grief, to hold her while she cried."

"No, Dane. That's the worst part. Jacqui didn't cry. Not

then, not after. Since the day Marie died, she hasn't shed a single tear . . . for any reason."

Dane flinched, struck by the truth of George's revelation. Since the day they'd met, Dane had never seen Jacqui weep. No matter how angry, passionate, or upset she became, she never cried . . . not even when accused of treason.

"She loves you, Dane," George was saying softly. "To Jacqui, love is a terrifying weakness. She has spent years disciplining herself to deem no one indispensable. That way, if she is abandoned, she can withstand the pain. It's her only protection against deep, personal loss."

"She'll never lose me," Dane replied vehemently.

"I know she won't. What's more, I believe Jacqui knows it too."

Dane's expression turned grim. "George, I've got to find her. If anything has happened . . ."

George shook his head, denying Dane's fears. "We must remain calm and keep a level head. Knowing Jacqui as I do, it is more than likely she found her confinement intolerable and, once the rain subsided a bit, she went out for a stroll. Why, she's probably arriving home even as we speak." He frowned. "But, just to be certain, I'll begin a discreet search. Have you tried your mother's estate?" When Dane shook his head, George continued, "Fine. I'll contact Lenore. You go see Secretary Hamilton. The fact that he is the likeliest target and no one has accosted him makes me believe Jacqui is probably just out and about somewhere." George's smile was stiff, forced. "I'll check back with you later today."

Dane nodded, no less appeased than he'd been when he arrived. No matter how hard he tried he couldn't shake the fear that Jacqui was in trouble . . . and that, despite her bloody independence, she needed him.

"Did you find Frau Westbrooke with her father?" Greta asked, coming into the hallway.

Dane's heart sank, Greta's question extinguishing his last

hope. Obviously, Jacqui had not returned home during his absence. "No, Greta, Jacqueline's father hasn't seen her all day. Did I receive any messages while I was gone? From Secretary Hamilton, perhaps?"

"No . . . none." Even Greta was beginning to look distressed. "Is there a reason to believe Frau Westbrooke is in danger?"

"I don't know. But I intend to find out."

Dane's vow was interrupted by a flying streak of black fur that exploded into the house and collided into Dane's legs.

"I'm in no mood for you." Dane glared down at Whiskey with angry impatience.

Uncharacteristically, Whiskey responded, not with his customary hissing and spitting, but by rubbing up against Dane's legs, meowing plaintively.

"I have no liquor and no time to elude your claws. So I would suggest you . . ." A tinge of color, vivid against the stark blackness of Whiskey's fur, caught Dane's eye. "What is this?" Dane squatted, plucking the pale green ribbon from around the kitten's neck. "My God . . ." Dane breathed, renewed panic erupting inside him. "This is a ribbon from the gown Jacqueline was wearing this morning."

Greta peered over his shoulder. "Yes . . . it is." She paled. "Now that I think about it, this is the first I've seen of Frau Westbrooke's cat since morning. He hasn't been in my kitchen once . . . not even for his meal."

Dane turned the ribbon over in his hands, remembering how he'd lain in bed and watched Jacqui dress, eventually taking over the task of doing her buttons . . . *his* way. He remembered how long it had taken him to finish acting the part of lady's maid . . . and why.

He closed his hand around the ribbon, irrationally feeling closer to his wife through the action.

Whiskey meowed again, rubbing up against Dane's bent knees.

Dane lowered his face to the kitten. "Were you with

Jacqueline?" he demanded quietly. "Is that what you're trying to tell me?"

Whiskey blinked his huge green eyes, sitting still as a statue.

Dane inhaled sharply and coughed. "You reek of whiskey."

"Apparently, he sampled some earlier today," Greta put in. "When I returned from the market I found a shattered glass in the sitting room and whiskey all over the sideboard and floor."

Dane rose. "A shattered glass? Belonging to whom?"

Greta looked puzzled. "I assumed to you."

"No." Dane shook his head adamantly. "I've had nothing to drink today. And it certainly wasn't Jacqueline's . . . she doesn't drink whiskey." Dane stalked into the sitting room to investigate. "So that means someone else was here today." He searched the area around the sideboard. "The question remains, who? And does that someone know Jacqueline's whereabouts?"

From the front hallway, Greta and Dane heard loud, persistent meowing. They rushed out to see Whiskey sitting pointedly by the front door, his head thrown back as he emitted noisy catcalls.

Dane narrowed his eyes. "If I didn't know better"—he walked over to where Whiskey sat—"I'd swear this damned viper knew where Jacqui was."

"Herr Westbrooke, it is possible." Greta nodded emphatically. "Cats are extremely intelligent animals. If Frau Westbrooke's pet was with her when she went out, he probably knows where she is. If that's the case, he can lead you to her."

Dane grunted in disbelief. "It sounds most unlikely." He inclined his head thoughtfully as Whiskey emitted another plaintive, reproachful meow. "On the other hand, we're running out of options. If you are right, Greta . . ." Dane strode into his study, removed a pistol from the desk drawer, and hurried back into the hallway. Flinging open the front door, he ordered, "Cat, if you know where Jacqui is, lead me to her."

In a flash, Whiskey sprung down the stairs and to the walk, pausing only to see that Dane was behind him, then disappearing around the bend.

"Bring her home safely, Herr Westbrooke," Greta called after him, clutching the folds of her apron.

Dane looked back, his jaw set. "I shall, Greta," he assured her, steely determination in his eyes. "At all costs, I shall."

Jacqui tugged savagely at her bonds, twisting her hands with all her strength. It was futile . . . the ties would not give.

She sagged in the hard wooden chair with a muffled cry of frustration. She'd been in this dingy, deserted country cabin for hours. Her fingers tingled from lack of circulation and her wrists and ankles throbbed from the biting pressure of the ropes.

Her initial paralyzing fear had diminished significantly. Her puzzlement over her captor's odd behavior had not.

For a man presumably skilled in abduction, Jacqui's assailant had turned out to be as jittery as she. Oh, he'd purposefully hauled her from her house, his pistol jabbed in her ribs lest she think of bolting. Then he'd dragged her roughly along the deserted, rain-soaked streets, through an endless length of dank woods until they reached this abandoned cabin. Once inside, he'd shoved her into a chair and tied her arms and legs.

But, that done, his whole demeanor had changed. Sweating profusely, he'd retreated to the far corner of the cabin, pacing like a nervous animal and keeping as far from Jacqui as possible. Ravaging his captive was, clearly, the last thing on his mind.

Then what did he want? she'd asked herself.

When he finally stopped prowling the floor long enough to speak, Jacqui got her answer.

What her captor wanted was not Jacqueline Westbrooke but Jack Laffey.

"I want facts and I want them now, *Laffey*," he'd hissed, wiping perspiration from his nape.

Jacqui had regarded him without flinching, digesting the fact that this man, who evidently knew her identity, was the traitor Hamilton sought. How he'd connected her with Laffey was too vast a question to consider. Logically, Jacqui had always known that the longer she penned her column, the greater the risk of discovery became. Evidently, her day of reckoning had arrived in the form of this culprit, who had brought her here to learn the details of Hamilton's alleged revisions to the Jay negotiations.

"You're privy to some new information being sent to John Jay in England." Her kidnapper confirmed her suspicions with his next words, raising his pistol menacingly. "Tell me what you know."

Perhaps it was his obvious discomfort that gave Jacqui courage, or perhaps it was her own patriotism. Whichever the case, she raised her chin, gazing innocently at his masked face. "I have no idea what you're talking about or why you've dragged me here. Who on earth is Laffey? My name is Jacqueline Westbrooke and I demand you release me at once."

A flash of something . . . was it surprise or admiration? . . . registered in her assailant's eyes.

"I have no time for evasions, Laffey," he returned in a growl.

"Why are you so stubbornly convinced I am this Laffey person?" Jacqui stalled for time, praying her clues had not been overlooked. She could have sworn she'd spied Whiskey following behind her as she stumbled through the woods. But she hadn't dared turn around for fear of giving herself away. Now she prayed her peripheral vision had not lied to her and that, having followed his nose for liquor, Whiskey had come upon the cabin and, when he couldn't get in, scampered home to alert Dane.

313

She prayed also that Dane hadn't missed the telltale clues: the shattered whiskey glass on the sitting-room floor and the ribbon around Whiskey's neck.

Jacqui's captor swore under his breath and tightened his fingers on the pistol. "I *know* who you are and I'm not playing any more games!" he rasped, sounding more exasperated than murderous.

Jacqui inclined her head. "Do you plan to shoot me?" she inquired.

"If I must."

"What is it you wish to know?"

"I told you . . . the plans Secretary Hamilton is preparing for Jay."

Jacqui's brow furrowed. "I thought John Jay was already in England."

"You know damned well he is!"

"Then I don't understand. Didn't he plan his tactics before leaving?"

The man swallowed, and Jacqui could see the bewildered look in his eyes.

"Why have you chosen this place to interrogate me?" she persisted, pressing her advantage. "How long do you plan to keep me prisoner here?"

"As long as it takes."

"Surely you could get your information elsewhere?"

He shook his head emphatically. "You are the one who has our answers, Laffey."

Our answers? Jacqui picked up on the plural instantly. So her captor was not acting alone. Well, then, she must learn the identities of his accomplices. "Where are your colleagues?"

He spun about. "Who said anything about my having colleagues?"

"You did. Just a moment ago you said, 'You are the one who has our answers.' I naturally assumed—"

"I'm asking the questions here, Laffey, not you!" he ground out.

314

"Very well." She gave him a measured look, then abandoned the notion of acquiring his cohorts' names and eyed the pistol speculatively. "Forgive my boldness, sir, but if you do use that pistol, how will you gain these vital facts you seek? Once I am dead, that is."

He looked positively flabbergasted. "I don't believe this." He shook his cloaked head.

Jacqui was thoroughly relieved by her assailant's incredulity, for it confirmed her suspicion that he'd never considered the possibility of firing his weapon. Her life, therefore, was in no immediate jeopardy. Unless, of course, one of her captor's less squeamish accomplices should arrive to take over. But that was a risk Jacqui would simply have to take. The key now was to stall for time . . . and to pray that Dane's instincts wouldn't pick this particular time to fail her.

It was over an hour later when her assailant pounded his fist against the wall. "I'm finished with our verbal sparring, Laffey! My patience has worn out." He took a threatening step toward Jacqui. "No more deception . . . only the truth."

Jacqui shifted a bit, wincing at the sharp pain in her arms. "I've told you the truth. I don't know who Laffey is, nor do I possess the answers you seek. My arms and legs are nearly numb and the ropes are cutting into my flesh. Please let me go."

He hesitated, then moved behind her and loosened the bonds. "I cannot release you," he returned.

It was time for another approach. "But I'm so hungry . . . and thirsty," Jacqui murmured, her voice breaking.

His dark eyes swept the back of her head. "I'll bring you some food. Perhaps that will jar your memory." He walked off, keeping his hooded face averted, and left the cabin.

Jacqui exhaled sharply, grateful for the opportunity to assess the situation. She had no idea how far her captor was traveling or how long he would be gone. She only knew that every second that ticked by brought her closer to safety.

Or to death.

She pushed that ugly possibility from her mind. Dane would find her. She knew he would. Hadn't he promised to always be there for her?

She blinked at the implausibility of her own thought. When on earth had she become such a romantic fool? How had she allowed herself to place any faith in her husband's unlikely guarantees? Didn't she, of all people, know that no one could be relied upon but oneself?

She swallowed past the lump in her throat. *Please find me, Dane,* her heart called out, ignoring the dictates of her mind. *Please. I need you.*

The minutes dragged by . . . and her bonds refused to give.

Several hours passed before Jacqui heard her captor's approaching footsteps. She lifted her chin, watching him reenter the cabin. Exhausted, numb, and frustrated by her inability to free herself, Jacqui studied her assailant warily, wondering what he had planned.

He'd come prepared, bringing bread, cheese, port . . . and another round of questions Jacqui had no intention of answering.

"I thought this time alone might loosen your tongue," he muttered, unpacking the food.

Jacqui wet her lips. "I'm so hungry I can barely think."

He gave a terse nod. "Very well." He seemed to consider untying her and then decided against it. Instead he walked over, stood beside her, and broke off pieces of bread and cheese, holding them to her mouth.

Jacqui ate gratefully, realizing it would be foolish to refuse the sustenance. She had eaten nothing since early morning and knew she'd need all her strength for the hours that lay ahead. "May I have a drink?" she asked.

Wordlessly he held the bottle to her mouth. Jacqui hesitated for the briefest of seconds, then took a greedy gulp of port.

"Thank you." Reluctantly, she licked the drops from her lips. Her throat was still parched, but she dared not risk drinking too much wine and thus becoming lightheaded. She had to keep a clear mind to determine her best course of action.

"More?" he asked gruffly.

She shook her head. "No . . . thank you."

He straightened and began to pace, fists clenched tightly at his sides, his movements becoming progressively more agitated.

Suddenly, he spun around to face her. "You've eaten. You've drunk. Tell me what I need to know, damn you!"

Jacqui's heart thudded loudly. "I cannot give you information I don't possess."

She flinched as her captor slapped his palm furiously across the back of her chair. Apprehensively, she waited to see if he would strike her next. But instead he stalked across the room, his back turned toward her, and gulped down a half-bottle of port.

Jacqui sagged with relief. What she really wanted was to ask him what time it was, but she bit back the urge. To do so might arouse his suspicions and alert him to the fact that she was hoping to be rescued. She glanced quickly over her shoulder. Judging from the gray daylight filtering in from the small window at the rear of the cabin, she would guess it to be late afternoon.

Had she been missed? How much longer could she hold this man at arm's length?

Dane . . . Jacqui's thoughts turned to her husband, and a surge of renewed faith flowed through her. All would be well.

"I'm right behind you, Whiskey."

Dane wound his way through the trees, grateful that the rain had finally stopped and that, since it was August, darkness would not fall for some time. He had been following Whiskey for nearly an hour now and never once had the kitten paused in his trek. Dane doubted not that

317

Jacqui's pet had gone this route earlier today; the rain had made the wooded ground soft and Whiskey's pawprints were clearly evident in the mud.

But where would the trail lead, and where was Jacqui?

The heinous possibilities made the hair on the back of Dane's neck stand up. He refused to dwell on his fear, for every fiber of his being cried out that Jacqui was still unharmed and that Whiskey would take him to her.

So Dane followed the pawprints and Whiskey followed his nose.

Suddenly, the kitten stilled, his body taut, his back arched in warning. Crouching low to the ground, he slinked forward, rumbling deep in his throat. Dane crept cautiously behind, groping for his pistol, progressing but a short distance before he came to an abrupt halt.

It was a cabin . . . nestled in a clump of trees, blending so completely with its natural setting that it was nearly invisible.

Dane's blood began to pound. He'd never known any structure had been erected in this remote section of woods, isolated from the rest of the city. One that appeared, at a cursory glance, to be totally deserted.

Quickly, he worked his way closer, until he reached Whiskey's side, a mere stone's throw from the cabin door. "Is Jacqui in there?" he demanded through clenched teeth. But he knew his answer. He could feel her presence as clearly as if she'd called out to him.

Then, from within, he heard the man's voice . . . rough, gravelly, indistinct, but a man's voice nonetheless . . . followed by a woman's.

Jacqui.

Something inside Dane snapped.

He reached the door in three strides and slammed his weight against it. "Jacqueline!"

Jacqui's heart gave a convulsive leap. "Dane . . . I'm in here!" she called out, heedless of the consequence.

Her assailant instantly froze, every muscle in his body going rigid. Then he jerked around to stare fearfully at the door, which had begun to give from the constant pounding of Dane's weight. The next moment, the masked man backed away and bolted. Sprinting to the rear of the cabin, he smashed the window with his elbow, worked his way through the narrow opening, and disappeared into the woods.

"Dane . . . he's getting away!" Jacqui screamed over the sound of splintering wood.

Apparently her husband either couldn't hear or didn't care, because the furious banging at the door continued.

With a loud crash, the wood gave way and Dane exploded into the cabin, pistol raised. His eyes instantly found Jacqui and, seeing that she was alone, he raced over to her.

"Are you all right?" He was already untying the ropes.

"Yes . . . I'm fine. He didn't harm me." She winced at the stinging sensation in her wrists as the bonds came loose, leaving her skin raw and her fingers painfully numb. "But Dane, he's escaped." She gestured toward the shattered window.

Dane stalked over and peered outside, seeing naught but an empty expanse of woods. To search so vast an area now, with darkness soon to fall, would be futile. "We'll find him," he assured Jacqui, returning to her side. "Right now all I care about is you." Tenderly, he massaged the feeling back into her fingers, bringing each palm to his lips and scowling at the ugly red welts on Jacqui's wrists. Then, wordlessly he untied her ankles, simultaneously colliding with a black fur ball who was rubbing against Jacqui's legs and purring.

"Whiskey." Jacqui smiled down at her pet. "I knew your namesake would provide you with the incentive to follow me."

Dane heard her puzzling comment but was too busy soothing the cramps from her ankles to pursue it. The time for talking would come . . . later. "I want you to try to stand up, *chaton*," he instructed. "I'll help you."

Slowly, shakily, Jacqui rose, holding on to Dane for support.

"Good," he praised. "Let's walk."

He wrapped his arm around her, led her back and forth until her limbs began to work properly on their own.

"Dane . . . thank you." She paused midway across the room, her fingers curling into the soft material of Dane's coat. Tightening her grip, she gazed up at her husband's strained, worried face. "I'm unscathed, truly I am." She gave him a reassuring smile. "My captor even fed me."

Dane ruffled her curls lightly. "*I* plan to murder you," he told her softly. "But not just yet." His hand slid down her neck in a butterfly caress, verifying through his touch that she was here and that no real harm had befallen her. "I'm so damned relieved, so grateful, so . . ." He broke off.

Tenderness clogged Jacqui's throat, and impulsively she stepped into Dane's arms, wrapping her own around his broad back. "I knew you would find me," she confided in a tired whisper, resting her cheek against his shirtfront.

Her unexpected, first-time admission of trust made Dane's heart expand with joy and a love so vast it hurt. He crushed her fiercely to him, overcome by profound emotions he no longer wished to suppress. "I'm never going to let you out of my sight again, you infuriating, stubborn little rebel." He kissed the tangled waves of her hair.

Right then Jacqui thought his threat sounded like heaven. "Can we go home now?" she asked wearily.

Dane nodded, temporarily stemming his acute surge of feeling. Clearing his throat roughly, he leaned down and swung Jacqui into his arms.

"What are you doing?" she asked, startled.

Dane crossed the room, stepped through the space where the door had been, and walked out into the woods, Whiskey at his heels. "I'm carrying you home, sweet," he informed her, making his way through the trees. "Predominately because you're in no condition to walk that great a distance."

"And . . ." Jacqui prompted, suspecting another motive.

"And this way I can be sure you don't take any hazardous detours en route to our house."

She sighed, resting her head against Dane's broad shoulder and closing her eyes. Despite her show of bravado, the day's episode had been harrowing, and Jacqui felt shaky and depleted. Drawing upon Dane's strength seemed very right and absolutely wonderful.

Common sense be damned.

"Come quickly! They're home!"

Greta's joyous shriek echoed through the Westbrooke house.

An instant later, a sea of faces appeared in the hallway, mouths agape as a triumphant Whiskey led his master and mistress into the house.

George reacted first, literally shoving Greta aside in order to reach his daughter. "Jacqui . . . *ma petite* . . . are you all right?"

Jacqui eased herself down from Dane's arms until her feet touched the floor. Then she went into her father's waiting embrace. "I'm fine, *mon père*, truly I am."

"Thank God." He hugged her, meeting Dane's gaze over Jacqui's head, his own eyes damp. "Dane . . . I'm deeply grateful to you."

Dane had no time to respond before Greta, having assessed Jacqueline's condition as good and the hour as late, began issuing orders to Stivers and Redding. The two men hurriedly accompanied her to the kitchen to assist in the preparation of a hot meal for Herr and Frau Westbrooke.

Alone with the family, Lenore moved forward to gently stroke Jacqui's hair. "I'm so relieved you're home. When I received your father's message . . ." She shot an intuitive glance at her son. "This incident goes far deeper than a mere disappearance, doesn't it, Dane?"

Dane frowned. "I'm not free to divulge anything more at this time, Mother," he replied truthfully. "Suffice it to say

321

ANDREA KANE

that Jacqueline's life was in danger and I intend to make certain it never again is."

Jacqui smiled at Lenore, squeezing her arm. "Your son was very heroic in his rescue. You would be proud, had you seen him."

"I don't doubt it." She kissed Jacqui's forehead. "I'm proud of you both." She took in Jacqui's pale face, the lines of exhaustion around her eyes, and turned to George. "It's been a long evening and I, for one, am spent. If I have my carriage brought around, would you be kind enough to see me back to Greenhills, George?"

"Now?" George blinked. "Forgive me, Lenore, but I want to remain with Jacqui until I feel assured . . ." He broke off, grasping Lenore's reasons belatedly. "Oh . . . I see." He hesitated.

"Father, I *am* well . . . truly," Jacqui assured him. "But I'm dreadfully tired." She rubbed her throbbing temples. "Would you mind very much if we were to talk tomorrow? I really need to lie down for a while." She cast a glance toward the kitchen. "In fact, I'd appreciate it if you would deal with Greta; explain to her that I promise to eat huge portions of her meal . . . tomorrow." She yawned. "After I've rested."

George relented. "Of course. You go off to bed. I'll see Dane's mother to Greenhills and then go home myself. This has been a harrowing day for all of us."

"Thank you," Jacqui said gratefully.

Dane wrapped his arm around her waist. "Come, *chaton,*" he murmured. "I'll take you up." He led her toward the stairs, calling to his mother and George, "We'll expect you both tomorrow."

"Not until around noon," Lenore said firmly to their retreating backs.

George turned to her with a frown. "Do you believe Jacqui is so badly afflicted as to sleep all night and half the following day?" he demanded, once Jacqui and Dane were out of hearing range.

"On the contrary, I believe Jacqueline will be much

herself in a matter of hours," Lenore said, patting his arm. "And while 'tis true I do not know the full circumstances of today's upsetting disappearance . . . in fact, I suspect you know far more than I"—she coughed discreetly— "Jacqueline appears to be merely worn out, nothing more."

"Then why are we delaying our visits?"

Lenore's smile was filled with joy and wisdom. "Because, sir, I believe our children need some time alone together. My instincts tell me that Jacqui and Dane are on the verge of a glorious discovery, one I've been praying they would make." She looked up toward the second-floor landing and nodded decisively. "Yes, I do believe that noon tomorrow would be an excellent hour to arrive."

George followed her gaze, then broke into a broad grin. "I begin to suspect from whom Dane inherited his fine instincts."

A commotion from the kitchen interrupted them.

"I *refuse* to argue over my tarts again, Herr Stivers!" Greta was roaring.

Lenore winced and George laughed aloud.

"I am more accustomed than you to Greta's . . . rather forward ways," George said gallantly. "So, while you send for your carriage, *I* shall break the news to her that the ten-course meal she has by now prepared must wait until morning."

Upstairs in their room, Dane lay Jacqui gently on the bed and carefully undressed her down to her chemise. By the time he'd drawn the quilt up to cover her, she was almost asleep.

"Dane . . . we have to find him . . . he's the traitor," she murmured, her eyes closed.

"Hush, love." He stroked the hair from her face. "We'll talk about it all later. Now I want you to sleep." He kissed her forehead and she sighed, giving in to the relentless need of her body to rest.

Dane sat beside her, watching her drift off, thanking the

323

heavens that she was home unharmed. Sometime later, Whiskey slipped into the room and jumped on the bed. Seeing that Jacqui was asleep, he curled up alongside her, blinking his huge green eyes at Dane.

"No argument from me, my friend," Dane assured him. "You've more than earned the right to sleep here tonight."

In reply, Whiskey licked his whiskers, then closed his eyes.

Dane remained where he was, wide awake, lost in thought. During their walk home, Jacqui had filled him in on the details of her capture, and Dane could gain no clue of the assailant's identity from Jacqui's sketchy description. All she'd felt certain of was that he was a man, not too old, somewhat nervous, tall, with dark eyes and a raspy voice, and that he was probably not acting alone. The sum of which told them nothing.

At the same time, Dane's heart swelled with pride when Jacqui explained her ingenious management of the situation: not only the successful way she'd stalled her captor, but the clever manner in which she'd arranged the clues that had ultimately led Dane to her. The shattered liquor glass, the resulting stench that had captured Whiskey's keen sense of smell, and the ribbon she'd placed around the kitten's neck . . . all those things had been instrumental in her rescue. Without them . . . Dane shuddered to think.

He stood and began to pace, wondering if there was an answer to this dark puzzle, one they could all live with.

"Dane?" Jacqui's voice was a sleepy whisper.

"Are you awake already, sweet?" His eyes fell on the clock, surprised to find that two hours had passed since Jacqui had nodded off.

She sat up, stretching. "I feel much better."

He smiled. "I'm glad."

Their eyes met in the dim, shadowed room.

"You saved my life," she whispered.

His smile faded. "You *are* my life," was his fervent reply.

She swallowed, then reached her arms out to him. "Dane . . ."

It was all she needed to say.

He went to her, gathered her against him, and covered her mouth with his. Nudging her head to his shoulder, he urged her lips apart, penetrating her with one plunging stroke of his tongue.

Clutching Dane's shoulders, Jacqui melted. Matching her husband's urgency, she opened to him at once, giving herself in a physical and emotional reaffirmation as old as time itself. Slowly, sensually, their tongues melded in a blatantly erotic caress. Dane made a husky sound, and Jacqui could actually feel him tremble as he devoured her mouth, tasted her again and again, drugging her with eloquent, consuming kisses.

She slid her hands between them and tugged his waistcoat and shirt free, spreading the material apart so she could press herself against his naked flesh. Through the thin gauze of her chemise, her nipples hardened and Dane tore his mouth away to stare down at the miracle of her response.

"My God, you're so beautiful," he breathed, bending his head and running his warm, open lips across the upper slope of her breasts. He eased away from her, kneeling beside the bed and intertwining her fingers with his. "I was never so frightened in all my life as when I realized you were missing," he told her. "No threat, not even to my own life, could be so terrifying as the fear of losing you." He gazed up at her, his burning eyes holding her still. "I never knew what it meant to be wholly vulnerable to another person. Nor would I have guessed that vulnerability could make you strong, not weak."

He kissed each of her fingers, her palms, her bruised wrists. Then he released her hands, bending to lift her feet, to kiss the red marks at her ankles where the ropes had marred her tender skin. "You have no idea how much I need you, *chaton*," he whispered, pressing soft, nipping kisses along her calves, her knees. He felt a tremor run through her as he caressed her inner thighs with his parted lips, his warm breath. "Jacqui . . ." He tugged her to the edge of the bed, urging her thighs apart with insistent hands, bending to bury his mouth in her hot sweetness.

Jacqui fell back on the bed with a cry of pleasure while the world went up in flames, glorying in the reality of Dane's fervid, absolute possession. She capitulated in a rush, knotting the sheet in her fists, giving Dane the total access he was wordlessly demanding and the erotic, abandoned response he was intent on evoking.

She arched in seconds, calling out to him, rising and falling with the spasms that seemed to go on forever before she collapsed, spent and panting, on the bed. For long minutes she floated on clouds of fulfillment, unable to move or think or even breathe.

When she finally managed to open her eyes, Dane was looming over her, his gaze riveted on her face, his expression galvanizing.

With quick, purposeful movements, he undressed, never tearing his eyes from Jacqui's, until he was magnificently naked and ready for her, his arousal rampant and throbbing.

He eased down beside her, tugged off her chemise, and glided his hands deliberately over the exquisite curves and hollows of her body. "Beyond beautiful," he murmured, his thumbs lightly stroking her nipples. "Beyond description. Beyond anything."

To her amazement, Jacqui felt the pulsing ache between her thighs begin anew and she reached for Dane, pulling him down to her.

He needed no coercion, but wrapped himself around her and began to make love to her slowly, possessing her with his mouth and hands, muttering dark, forbidden promises against her skin. With tormenting patience, he claimed the warm, silky weight of her breasts, the tight, hard buds of her nipples, the trembling wetness between her thighs.

"I love you, Jacqui," he said, looking directly into her passion-glazed eyes. "So much . . . *too* much. It astounds me how little control I have when we're together." He cupped her face with shaking palms. "See? Can you feel how badly I want you, need you?" He caught her hand in his, bringing it down to close around his throbbing erection. "Can you, my breathtaking wife?"

Jacqui whimpered, all sensation concentrated beneath her discovering hand. She took over the motion herself, curled her fingers around him, caressing gently, feeling the enormous power beneath her touch.

Dane groaned deep in his throat, throwing back his head, his breath coming in harsh pants. He withstood the exquisite torture as long as he could. When it became unendurable, he caught Jacqui's wrist. "I can't . . . no more." He shook his head wildly, silver lightning ablaze in his eyes.

But when he would have moved to take her, Jacqui slid down the length of him, exploring the taut planes of his abdomen, the flat male nipples that stiffened beneath her touch, the pulsing hardness that quivered in her hand. She bent to taste him, to bring him the same excruciating pleasure he had brought her. Surrounding him with her mouth, she learned him as she never before had, until Dane made a hoarse, anguished sound of primal male need, dragging her away mere seconds before it was too late.

Mindless with arousal, he rolled her beneath him and buried himself inside her, grinding their hips together until he could go no deeper. Hungrily, he repeated the motion, clenching his fists in the pillow beside her head, forcing her to meet the ravenous heat of his gaze.

"Love me," he commanded, a harsh, guttural sound. "Don't ever leave me, or frighten me, like that again."

Drawn by the desperate tone of his voice, the naked longing in his eyes, Jacqui whispered, "I won't. . . ." She clutched the bunched muscles of his shoulders, lifting her hips to meet the erotic motion of his.

"Love me," he repeated, this time a gentle ripple, a reverent prayer breathed into her open mouth.

Jacqui wound herself around him, arms and legs drawing him close, inner muscles clasping him tightly within her. "I do."

The long-awaited declaration pushed him over the edge.

Control having evaporated, Dane plunged deep inside his wife, joining their bodies in a poignant confirmation of her words, withdrawing only to immerse himself again.

The bed groaned with each staggering thrust, the vortex of sensation coiling tighter, tighter still. Jacqui clung to him, ascended to dizzying heights, and teetered there ... waiting, absorbing the frenzied pounding of Dane's body over hers, in hers.

Then ... time stopped, the world tilted askew.

Release came as a stunning explosion, tearing through them both simultaneously, coursing through their bodies in crashing waves, making them both lunge forward and cry out.

When the waves receded, they lay dazed and drenched, in the wake of something more powerful than either of them had ever fathomed.

"Say it again." Dane raised his head and looked solemnly down at Jacqui, brushing damp strands of hair from her flushed face and lowered lashes. "I want to hear it, not in passion, but in truth. Say it, Jacqui. Lord knows I've waited an eternity to hear it."

Jacqui's lids fluttered and Dane caught his breath at the look of intense emotion he saw glowing in the midnight of her eyes. She hesitated, a flash of fear and vulnerability flickering there but for a moment. Then she lay her hand against his strong jaw. "I love you," she whispered, astounded that she had the courage to say aloud what she'd known in her heart for months. "It terrifies me, but it's true nonetheless. I love you, Dane."

Dane turned his face to kiss her palm, his expression humble. "Don't be terrified, *mon chaton colereux*. I'll never leave you. What we have is forever." He brushed her lips softly with his. "Now listen to *me* say the words: I love you, Jacqui. Always. And, just as you belong to me, I belong to you."

CHAPTER
19

"Will it always be so wondrous?" Jacqui murmured, awed and sated in the glorious aftermath of their long night of lovemaking.

"Always, *chaton*. Forever." Dane brought a handful of her hair to his lips, marveling at the way the first golden rays of dawn shimmered on the satiny tresses.

Jacqui fell silent.

"Jacqueline." Dane looked down at her. "I know how afraid you are to believe in forever. I even know why." He answered her startled, questioning look with the truth. "Your father and I talked . . . about your childhood, and your mother."

Jacqui lowered her lashes, but Dane refused to let her retreat from him. Catching her chin with his forefinger, he gently forced her to meet his gaze. "I know how devastating her death must have been for you. I wish I'd been there to hold you in my arms and tell you the pain would pass, to promise you I'd never leave you, that you'd never have to endure so staggering a loss again. But I wasn't. So I'm telling you now. I love you, Jacqueline. My love is something you can count on, for it is yours, unconditionally and always.

329

I'm strong, I'm healthy . . . and I'm very sure of my feelings."

He caressed her cheek with his thumb, determined to erase the lingering filaments of doubt from her mind. "Did I lie when I told you I'd always accept you as you are and never try to change you?"

"No." Her voice was small.

"Nor am I lying to you now." He interlaced her fingers with his, placed their joined hands over his heart. "Fate created us for each other, darling, and nothing is going to separate us or alter my feelings. You have my word."

Jacqui smiled faintly. "Your word as a gentleman?"

He chuckled, tracing her kiss-swollen lips. "No. My word as your husband; which is guaranteed to be infinitely more reliable than my word as a gentleman."

"I'm glad," Jacqui returned, her voice breaking as she battled to regain her self-control. "Since the past months have not shown you to be much in the way of a gentleman."

"That is because you, *chaton,* make me forget all my good intentions. You're a constant challenge, in *and* out of bed." His eyes twinkled.

"Speaking of which, you did vow to murder me," she reminded him.

Dane nodded thoughtfully. "Yes, I did, didn't I?" He scowled, recalling the events that led up to that threat. "You scared the bloody hell out of me yesterday."

Jacqui propped her chin on his chest. "I know. And I'm truly sorry. Next time I promise to be more careful."

Dane shot up like a bullet, nearly knocking Jacqui to the floor. *"Next time?"*

Baffled, Jacqui gathered up the bedcovers and wrapped them around her. "Well, of course, next time," she returned, totally exasperated. "I told you, my captor is obviously one of the traitors for whom Secretary Hamilton is searching. Unfortunately, he escaped into the woods before you could apprehend him. Therefore, we must think of a plan that will expose not only him, but his accomplices as well. And since Laffey seems to be the likely target—"

"Over my dead body!" Dane exploded, silencing her words. He bounded from the bed and began pacing back and forth, oblivious to his nakedness. "After what occurred yesterday," he berated Jacqui, angry and incredulous, "how can you even suggest using Laffey's column again as bait for our trap?"

"But, Dane, I wouldn't—"

"*No!*" Dane halted at the foot of the bed, grim-faced, shaking his head vehemently. "The idea is unthinkable!"

"It's a splendid idea."

The Secretary of the Treasury nodded decisively as he spoke.

"Are you as insane as my wife, Alexander?" Dane demanded.

"I thought you might agree," Jacqui was saying, ignoring her husband's remark. "It is our only logical alternative, given the circumstances."

Dane slammed his fists on Hamilton's desk. "If you permit another column such as the last, you are inviting a repeat of Jacqueline's abduction." His eyes blazed silver fire. "And that I *will* not allow. Friendship be damned. Patriotism be damned." He jerked around to glare at Jacqui. "Promises be damned. This time the answer is no, Jacqueline. You will *not* write that column."

Jacqui marched up to him and raised her chin mutinously. "Are you *forbidding* me to write my column?"

"I bloody well am."

"And I'm refusing to accept your husbandly dictate."

"May I intercede?" Hamilton put in mildly, trying to hide his amusement at watching this tiny slip of a girl brazenly confront the invincible Dane Westbrooke. "What I was going to suggest, prior to your marital dispute, was a different approach for Laffey to take. One that would compel our traitors to act, yet not endanger Jacqueline in any way. Would you care to hear the details?" A flash of humor crossed his face. "Or would you both prefer to remain as you are, stubbornly glowering at each other?"

Dane's rigid expression did not change, nor did he tear his unyielding gaze from Jacqui's. "I'm listening."

Jacqui's chin came up another notch. "So am I."

"I can see that you are." Alexander chuckled, sitting on the edge of his desk and folding his arms. "In her last column Jacqueline alluded to the new set of conditions I was drafting for Grenville."

"That's right. It nearly got her killed," Dane challenged.

"Agreed. But suppose Laffey's next column were to inform his readers that the new Jay document had been completed and was awaiting immediate transport to England. Further, suppose Laffey openly stated that neither he nor anyone else had knowledge of the specific terms of the new proposal. Anyone else, that is, except the one person who drafted it."

"You." Jacqui turned to Alexander, interest and admiration flickering in her eyes.

"Precisely." Hamilton inclined his head perceptively. "Interrogating you, Jacqueline, would no longer benefit our culprits: first, because this new Laffey column will convince them that, despite your dual identity, you were being truthful when you feigned ignorance of the Jay negotiations to your captor; and second, because another abduction would be too risky for them, especially since Dane's appearance at the cabin means they would have him to contend with as well as you."

"Where does that leave you, Alexander?"

For the first time, Dane also turned to face his friend.

"Quite safe, actually." Hamilton smiled faintly. "Since Laffey's column will cleverly reveal that the document in question is well hidden in my office, I will be spending a greater portion of my workday at home. Dane, you and I can alternate keeping a discreet watch outside my office."

"But will the traitors believe the information I provide?" Jacqui asked.

"They will if you make it convincing yet subtle," the Secretary replied, a sparkle in his eyes. "You did boast that you were the finest of writers, did you not?"

"I did, sir," Jacqui agreed at once. Then she frowned. "But if your plan succeeds, the felons will break into your office searching for the papers."

"I'm counting on it."

"But Mr. Secretary"—Jacqui looked perplexed—"there *are* no papers."

"Ah, but there will be." Hamilton strolled around to the back of his desk and waved an intricately penned page in the air. "By the time your column has been written and printed, the narrow drawer in my side table will discreetly hold a letter whose tone bears no resemblance to the one Jay is currently using in his negotiations with Grenville."

Jacqui approached Hamilton's desk, her confrontation with Dane eclipsed by her interest in the Secretary's plan. "You intend to instruct Jay to change his negotiating tactics?"

"No. I plan to mislead the traitors into *believing* I am instructing Jay to change his tactics," Hamilton corrected. "Remember, Jacqueline, if this letter does not differ drastically from its predecessor, we cannot be assured the culprits will take immediate action. We want to apprehend them, yes, but we also want to learn for whom they are working, England or France." He stroked his chin thoughtfully. "In my original document, I urged Jay to demand indemnification for the British-seized American ships and to ensure protection for American vessels as well as improved commercial terms with Britain. In the letter I am drafting, I will advise Jay to maintain peace with the British at all costs, to concede on any point necessary in order to avoid war."

"If the traitors are British, they will be elated," Dane responded. "They'll smuggle a copy of the letter on board the first ship leaving Philadelphia for England. Once Grenville has read the document, he will assume America is prepared to yield her position. He will, therefore, be unbending in his demands."

"And if the traitors are French," Jacqui jumped in, "they will act just as swiftly, hastening the letter off to France and advising their government to initiate an immediate plan to subvert the alliance between America and England." Jacqui's heart sank as she contemplated the ease with which this feat could be accomplished. For a respectable sum, any number of English privateers could be hired to seize American ships, severing the fine thread of peace still bridging America and England and drawing the two nations into war.

"Precisely," Hamilton agreed. "Therefore, whether our traitors are pro-English or pro-French, we will disclose not only their identities but their mission as well." He gave Jacqui and Dane a questioning look. "So, shall we attempt it?"

Jacqui turned around to meet Dane's piercing gaze. "Yes." She waited.

"Yes." Dane surprised her by concurring. *"With* certain conditions," he added quickly.

Jacqui sighed. "There always are."

Dane held up his hand, counting off on his fingers. "The first condition is that I write this column with you, Jacqueline. I don't doubt your capabilities; however, not only am I more thoroughly versed in the Jay matter, I am also a good deal warier than you. So I want equal input. Second"—he didn't wait for her response—"until the culprits are safely apprehended, I want your word that you will not leave the house alone, nor open the door to anyone you don't know." He gave her a meaningful look. "And third," he concluded, "I want it understood that only Alexander and I will be responsible for keeping vigil at his office; he during the hours he is at work, and I when he is away. *No one else.*" Dane's pause was poignant. "Now, my obstinate Mr. Laffey, is your answer still yes?"

Jacqui's mind warred between autonomy and reason. Dane's points were well taken, his motives noble. But still . . . could she allow him a voice in her work?

"Compromise, *chaton*," Dane reminded her softly, reading her thoughts. With solemn tenderness, he extended his open palm. "I want to care . . . not to control." He waited, holding his breath, wondering if his wife was ready to take this all-important step.

Jacqui's mouth curved slowly upward as she placed her fingers in his. "Yes, Dane, the answer is still yes."

Dane massaged his neck vigorously, flexing his shoulders forward and back. For the fifth time that night he shifted his weight, trying to find a way to remain squatting yet comfortable in a damp cluster of trees on a humid August night. He peered across the semidarkened street to Hamilton's office, which remained peacefully deserted.

With a stifled sigh, Dane rubbed his bleary eyes. Since Laffey's article had appeared in print three days past, sleep had become nonexistent and worry rampant. Every waking hour Dane spent either glued to the corner of Third and Chestnut Street scrutinizing Alexander's empty office or, when relieved at his post by the Secretary's arrival, glued to Jacqui's side, assuring himself of his wife's safety.

Hamilton's plan was rapidly losing its appeal.

A warning instinct brought Dane up short. He tensed, eyes narrowed on the empty street. Someone was approaching.

Ready to spring ahead, Dane was completely unprepared for the muffled sound and rustle of movement from behind him. He recovered rapidly. With lightning speed, he whipped around and lunged at the shadowy figure, snapping his arm about the intruder's throat and dragging the pliant body against the rock-hard wall of his own chest. "Who are you?" he demanded, knocking the concealing hat from the now-struggling stranger's head.

Masses of mahogany curls tumbled down over Dane's elbow, while slender fingers tugged at his forearm. "Dane . . . you're choking me!"

"Jacqui?" Dane released her and, in one sharp motion, yanked her to the grass beside him, forcing her head down so their presence would remain undetected. "Damn you, Jacqueline!" Dane's clenched teeth muted the roar erupting deep within his chest to a loud hiss. "What the hell are you doing here?"

Jacqui rubbed her throat gingerly and settled herself on the damp ground. "You haven't slept in three days. I merely came to offer my assistance. I heeded all your stipulations exactly."

"Jacqueline . . ." Unconvinced, he crouched over her, reminding her of an enraged panther ready to strike.

"I didn't leave the house alone," Jacqui plunged on. "Greta accompanied me. We didn't even walk," she added as thunder erupted in Dane's eyes. "We took the carriage. I instructed our driver to drop me at the corner of Walnut Street, one block from here. He was then to escort Greta back home." Jacqui took a breath, dejectedly noting the clenching and unclenching of Dane's jaw. "I know, I know," she said with a resigned sigh. "I violated condition three: only you and Secretary Hamilton are to keep vigil at his office." She flashed Dane a small, hopeful smile. "Complying with two of your three stipulations isn't bad, is it?"

Dane's fingers dug into her shoulders. "I'm taking you home. Now."

She purposefully ignored his decree. "You hurt me, you know."

Dane frowned, stroking gentle fingertips over the red chafe marks on Jacqui's neck. "Had I acted on impulse, it would have been my pistol, not my arm, at your throat." He cursed, angry and exasperated. "Hell, Jacqueline . . . do you know how I could have killed you?"

"Never. Your instincts are too good. You would have realized it was me before it was too late."

Her praise warmed him, and Dane eased back on his haunches, wondering how his beautiful, reckless wife always managed to diffuse his anger and invade his heart. "Your faith in me is staggering," he muttered. Leaning forward, he pulled her to him and tucked her head tenderly beneath his chin. "Tell me, if my instincts are so infallible, then why did I not listen to them and murder you months ago?"

Smiling, Jacqui nuzzled his throat. "Because your superb judgment surpasses even your impeccable instincts. Not to mention your extraordinary appreciation of rare, unending talents, such as mine." She stroked his jaw. "All of them."

A chuckle vibrated through Dane's chest. "True, *chaton*. You'll get no argument from me on that subject."

Jacqui looked up, tipping her head questioningly toward Hamilton's office. "Has there been no sign of anyone?"

"No. All has been still." Dane studied her earnest face. "I presume you intend to remain here with me?"

"If you insist, I'll take my leave. But only if you insist," she rushed on.

Dane smiled faintly, brushing her lips with his. "Will you vow to remain beside me at all times?"

"At all times," Jacqui agreed fervently.

"I mean it, Jacqueline."

"So do I."

Lightly, he kissed the tip of her nose. "Very well. Besides, your point was well taken . . . for you to heed two of my three conditions is a remarkable feat indeed."

"I love you, Dane."

Jacqui's words clung to the night, sank into Dane's soul. Silently, he framed her face between his palms, stroking his thumbs over her cheekbones, caressing her with his melting silver gaze. "I know you do," he breathed reverently. "And armed with our love, *mon chaton colereux,* there is nothing we cannot do."

Easing back, Dane settled Jacqui beside him, wrapped a possessive arm about her shoulders, and turned to watch the empty street.

Hours passed.

It was the deepest part of night when Dane felt it again . . . that acute sense of imminent danger. He tensed, squeezing Jacqui's arm in warning.

Jacqui blinked, instantly snapping out of her light doze. Peering into the darkness, she wondered what sound Dane had heard, what movement he had spied. To her the night remained as it was, peaceful and undisturbed. Still, she did not stir, trusting in the uncanny accuracy of Dane's sixth sense.

Minutes later, the sound of a set of footsteps . . . tentative, barely audible . . . reached Jacqui's ears. They paused, then continued, slowing only as they rounded the corner of Third Street. Jacqui could scarcely breathe. All she could do was watch as the dim moonlight outlined the shadowy figure of a hooded man . . . a man who was quietly but insistently fumbling at the door of Hamilton's office.

Jacqui and Dane remained still as the intruder bent over the lock, working feverishly. Finally, he straightened, triumphantly easing the door ajar. He paced back to the sidewalk, peering quickly to the right and left, ascertaining that he was indeed unobserved.

Jacqui stared, studying the man. His height . . . his build . . . his carriage . . . the way he moved. She clapped a hand over her mouth to stifle a gasp.

"What is it?" Dane asked, his voice nearly inaudible.

"That's the man who kidnapped me," Jacqui hissed.

Dane's grip tightened. "Are you sure?"

Jacqui nodded vehemently. "I'm sure." She swallowed. "What do we do now?"

With predatory purpose, Dane scrutinized the enemy, half tempted to rush up and thrash the man who had endangered Jacqueline's life . . . yet restraining himself from doing anything so rash.

The intruder slipped into Hamilton's office.

"We wait," Dane replied in a lethal whisper. "For however long it takes . . . we wait."

For what seemed like aeons but was, in fact, a mere half hour, Jacqui and Dane knelt, cramped and alert, behind the trees. Their eyes followed the pale flicker of light signifying the intruder's whereabouts in Hamilton's office. To and fro it moved, again and again, until at last it remained fixed in the far corner of the Secretary's office where his sideboard was situated.

"I think our traitor has found his prize," Dane murmured.

Sure enough, on the heels of Dane's words the light was extinguished and the door was eased open. The dark figure made his exit.

Impulsively, Jacqui started forward.

"Wait," Dane commanded quietly, his fingers closing like steel manacles around her wrist.

Jacqui subsided, sinking back down beside her husband. She would not question his actions; there was too much at stake.

The intruder was halfway down the street when Dane released Jacqui's arm. "Now," he ordered softly, "I want you to stay behind me and follow my lead. Understood?"

She nodded.

"Good." Cautiously he rose, helping Jacqui to her feet. "Let's go."

Slowly, soundlessly, Dane followed his quarry at a guarded distance. Simultaneously, he stayed but several steps ahead of Jacqui, making continually certain of her presence, close behind him . . . and safe.

They didn't have far to go.

Halfway down Walnut Street, the intruder halted, veered sharply toward a small frame house, and hastened up the steps. The home's occupant had apparently expected a guest, for the front door opened at once, admitted the intruder, then shut firmly behind him.

"Good Lord," Jacqui breathed, peering past her husband.

Dane's head snapped around. "What is it?"

"That house . . . Monique lives there."

"Monique?" Dane repeated, stunned.

"Yes." Jacqui gazed up at Dane, her face pale. "Could Monique actually be involved in this? . . . An accomplice to the traitor?"

"It certainly seems likely," Dane agreed bitterly. "Why else would your captor be going to her home? Evidently, your lack of trust for Miss Brisset was well founded, *chaton.*"

"Poor Father . . ." Jacqui's mind immediately projected to the pain her father would suffer at Monique's hands. "He loves her so much."

"I know he does." Dane stroked Jacqui's cheek with gentle fingers. "He'll recover, love. We'll help him. But tonight . . ." Dane touched his pistol, tucked snugly in the pocket of his coat.

Instantly, Jacqui understood. They'd reached the culmination of their mystery . . . and sentiment would have to wait. "Do we confront them now?"

Dane shook his head. "Let's allow them time to read and copy the letter. When they emerge, we'll act." He took in Jacqui's strained expression and drew her over to the side of the house. "Sit, love," he whispered. "You're exhausted. My guess is that they'll do nothing before dawn, which is"—he checked his timepiece—"two hours away." He eased them both to the ground, curling his long, strong fingers around her small, cold ones. "We're nearing the end, *chaton.* Hold out a little longer."

Jacqui raised her chin and met Dane's tender gaze. With a decisive nod, she set her delicate jaw. "Fear not, husband. I intend to."

Sometime near dawn, Jacqui drifted off. Shivering a bit, she pressed closer to Dane, seeking his warmth. The August night, devoid of the heat generated by the summer sun, had grown chilly, the ground they sat on damp.

The waiting, endless.

Feeling her slight weight sag against his shoulder, Dane

looked down at his wife and smiled. Shrugging out of his coat, he draped it about her shoulders, wrapping her in his arms, her head against his chest. With a murmur of contentment, Jacqui settled against him . . . and slept.

Dane stared off into the gradually lightening sky, his ears strained for the sound of activity, his brain trying to fit together all the pieces of the puzzle. Monique Brisset's involvement made a pro-French cause seem more likely. Was her accomplice also of French descent? According to Jacqui, the man who kidnapped her had not spoken with an accent. However, he'd also never spoken in a normal tone . . . always in a rasp. So he could have been disguising his voice. And whether he was of French descent or not told them nothing, for many supporters of France's politics were not born on French soil.

Dane leaned his head back wearily. He had exhausted the questions . . . it was time for some answers.

As if on cue, the front door opened, accompanied by the sound of muffled voices.

Dane came alert at once, gently shaking his wife. "Jacqui," he said in an urgent whisper. "It's time."

Jacqui blinked in the first rays of morning. "What . . ." She fell silent as Dane placed a warning finger over her lips. Reality came back to her in a rush. She nodded, silently telling her husband she was fully awake and aware of the situation.

Slowly, Dane rose to his feet, tugging Jacqui up with him. Then, clasping Jacqui's hand, he crept alongside the house, stopping only when he'd reached the corner. Peering around front, Dane gestured Jacqui forward, satisfied that they were unobserved, yet possessing an unobstructed view of the walkway . . . and a clear earshot of the voices approaching it.

". . . on the next ship," the man was saying.

"That is precisely what I intend to do." The lilting French accent belonged to Monique.

"I'll return the letter," the man replied, simultaneously stepping into Dane's line of vision.

Dane recoiled physically as if he'd been punched, biting back a shout of denial as his mind refuted what his eyes and ears were telling him. Vaguely, he heard Jacqui's soft, shocked gasp as she too saw the face of the man with Monique. Her fingers curled into Dane's in a gesture of comfort and support.

"Just hurry," Monique was urging, clutching Thomas's lapels. "It is past dawn. Secretary Hamilton could return to his office at any time." She glanced around quickly. "I must go inside, Thomas . . . someone could see us."

"When *can* we be together?" He caught her arm, his tone desperate.

Monique shook herself free. "I don't know," she snapped. "First, I have a mission to accomplish. And so do you."

"I'm aware of that." Thomas's response was bitter. "But after that's completed, I want to discuss our future."

"Should we fail, we will have no future!" Monique waved him off. "Now go!" Lifting the hem of her dressing gown, she hurried back into the house.

Thomas stared after her, his face twisted with anguish. Slowly, his gaze lowered to the broadcloth hood clasped in his hand, and he turned it over and over, studying its rough texture. Then, with a muffled oath, he crumpled it into a ball and flung it to the ground. From his pocket he withdrew a folded sheet of paper, glaring at Hamilton's letter with utter contempt.

With one last tortured look at Monique's house, Thomas spun on his heels and strode off.

"My God . . ." Dane leaned against the house, his face white.

"Shall we go after him?" Jacqui asked quietly.

"No." Dane shook his head emphatically. "And not because he is . . . was . . . my friend," he clarified, seeing Jacqui's dubious expression. "But because it would serve no purpose. Clearly, Thomas is on his way back with the letter. He doesn't know anyone saw him take it, so he has no reason to bolt. Now that the paper's been copied, Thomas will merely replace it in Alexander's sideboard and go about his business." Dane swallowed hard, a muscle working in his jaw. "More important, at this time, is to find out where Monique is sending the copy and who is transporting it for her."

"Dane," Jacqui said gently, stroking his hands, "I'm sorry."

His expression was tight with strain. "So am I." He shook his head in bewilderment. "How could I not have known?"

"He was your friend."

Dane gave a short, derisive laugh. "And you thought so highly of my instincts."

"I still do." She brought his hand to her lips. "Dane, you're not the only one who was fooled. Obviously, Secretary Hamilton never suspected Thomas either."

Dane's mouth thinned into a grim line. "Thomas idolized Alexander. He served under him, fought beside him in the war. How the hell could he . . ."

"For money, perhaps?"

"Money . . . his business *was* failing." Dane was willing to grasp at straws.

"Or a woman," Jacqui ventured.

"A woman." Dane looked toward the house, hatred blazing in his silver eyes as he recalled the adoration he'd seen on Thomas's face whenever he'd spoken of his mystery lady. There wasn't any doubt that Thomas's love was strong enough to propel him to commit this heinous act. The money alone wouldn't be sufficient . . . Thomas was doing it for *her*.

"A woman who is capable of betraying not only her country but a man . . . *two* men," Jacqui corrected herself, "who love her: poor, pathetic Thomas and my devoted, unsuspecting father." Jacqui winced, wondering how she

343

was going to break the news to George that his beloved Monique was guilty not only of infidelity but of treason. "I'd like to choke her with my bare hands."

"You shall have your chance," Dane assured her, stationing himself at the corner of the house. "It is only a matter of time before Miss Brisset leaves her house, bound for the ship she mentioned to Thomas. When she does, you and I will be waiting for her."

"Now I know why my captor seemed so apprehensive," Jacqui realized, joining her husband at his concealed post.

"Yes." Dane's tone was grim. "Thomas must have been terrified you would recognize him—" Cutting himself short, Dane made a harsh, pained sound deep in his throat. "I'm the one who told him who you were," he said in hoarse incredulity. "I'm the damned fool who *confided* to him you were Laffey." Dane cursed explicitly, clenching his fists in anger. "Here I was, cautioning you to be more careful, when it was I who delivered you right into your abductor's hands."

"That's absurd," Jacqui refuted. "If poor judgment were to render one guilty, then I would be the quintessential felon. I've stood by idly while my father made an utter fool of himself over a woman who is a fraud and a criminal. I didn't suspect a thing."

"You were always skeptical of Monique," Dane reminded her.

Jacqui shrugged. "I believed her to be possessive and greedy. But this? Never."

Dane withdrew the pistol from his pocket and stared coldly at it, his handsome features taut with angry determination. "Miss Brisset's plan will never come to fruition," he vowed. "And in a short time, she will know it."

Monique shut the door carefully behind her and scrutinized the empty street. It was barely seven o'clock and no one was about . . . just as she had hoped.

Tightly clutching the small package in her hands, she descended the steps, silently rehearsing what she would say to George. She had to sound convincing, or it would arouse his suspicions and destroy her best and swiftest chance to reach Bonaparte.

Thomas, of course, thought she was dispatching the letter to England, posthaste. But as far as Monique was concerned, England could learn of the American concessions in good time. Her worry was for France.

If only there were another way of hastening the message to Bonaparte. Sending Hamilton's letter with one of George's shipments was risky, since Jacqueline and her family were no doubt being closely watched after Thomas's blunder of a kidnapping.

But there was no other way. Last night, while Thomas had searched Hamilton's office, Monique had gone to the shipping docks to check the departure schedule. The only ship leaving for France this week was departing today. It belonged to Westbrooke Shipping, its cargo to Holt Trading.

Which meant convincing George to take her package.

Monique frowned, hurrying down the walkway. She had to appeal to George's tender heart, to convince him that her dear sister was once again deeply depressed and in need of immediate comfort.

Abruptly, the crease vanished from between Monique's fine brows. A parcel of letters . . . that was it. She would tell George that dozens of letters she'd penned to Brigitte had just been returned to her, never having reached their destination. And, at the same time, she had received a desperate letter from Brigitte, telling Monique how forsaken she felt.

A satisfied smile touched Monique's lips. The way George loved her . . . the idea was infallible.

"Not yet." Dane shook his head emphatically, keeping Jacqui beside him.

"But she'll escape!" Jacqui protested, itching to capture their nemesis.

"Oh no she won't. But if she sees us, she'll abandon her plan and all our waiting will have been for naught." Dane watched Monique's progress through narrowed eyes. "Patience, *chaton.*"

He stalled until Monique was nearly out of sight. Then he nodded. "Let's go."

The streets were quiet, with few people and no carriages about at this early hour. Dane led Jacqui along silently, both of them wondering where they were headed.

Neither of them was prepared for the answer.

The building Monique approached was that of Holt Trading.

Jacqui stopped dead, clutching Dane's arm as Monique slipped inside. "Why is she stopping here? Who could she be seeing?"

Dane rubbed his chin thoughtfully. "It's barely past dawn. Try to think, love. Who in your father's company arrives for work this early?"

"I don't need to think." Jacqui shook her head vehemently. "We must be wrong about the reason for Monique's visit. At this hour, the only person she would find here is . . ." All the color drained from Jacqui's cheeks.

"Jacqui." Dane cupped her ashen face between his hands. "We have to discover the truth."

"Don't ask me to believe she's bringing that letter to my father," Jacqui denied fiercely. "He would *never* become involved in this ugly scheme."

Dane stroked his thumb over Jacqui's stubborn chin, ignoring her defiance, perceiving her fear. "You're a reporter, *chaton,*" he reminded her softly. "Haven't you learned not to make assumptions without verifying your facts first?"

Jacqui licked her dry lips and nodded, calmed by Dane's words and the realization that he intended to remain impartial. "Yes."

"Good. Now come." Dane strode up to the door and paused, pressing his ear to it. Hearing nothing, he gestured for Jacqui to follow, guiding them both inside. The front room was deserted, but soft voices emanated from behind George Holt's closed office door.

Dane burst in.

George looked up, startled. He was leaning against his desk, his arms folded, obviously in deep conversation with Monique. She, in turn, was perched beside him, her package in her lap, her lovely face tilted appealingly toward George. Seeing Dane, her eyes widened with shock . . . and fear.

"Dane? What is the meaning of this?" George was on his feet.

"I could ask you the same," Dane replied. "But I believe I'll ask Miss Brisset instead."

Monique kept her expression carefully blank. "I don't think I understand, Mr. Westbrooke."

"I believe you understand very well, Miss Brisset," Jacqui accused, stalking around Dane to confront the woman who had disrupted all their lives.

"Jacqui?" George looked stunned.

"Father, what is she doing here?" Jacqui demanded.

"Why, I came to see your father, of course." Monique smoothed a pale strand of hair from her face.

"At seven o'clock in the morning?" Dane challenged.

"I don't believe I need to justify my actions to you."

"But you do need to justify your actions to the American people," Jacqui shot back.

Monique blanched. "I've done nothing . . ."

"Nothing?" Jacqui returned, marching up until she could look Monique directly in the eye. "Is stealing papers from the Secretary of the Treasury's office considered nothing?"

George gave a sharp, agonized gasp. "What are you saying, Jacqueline? Monique merely came to ask if I would transport her package along with my shipment to France."

"Did she now?" Dane walked menacingly toward

Monique, his eyes glittering. "Just what is in this package of yours, Miss Brisset?"

"That is none of your business, Mr. Westbrooke!" Defensive color rose to Monique's cheeks. "But, if you must know, I am sending letters to my sister—what are you doing?" she cried out in rage, as Dane seized the package from her hands. "How dare you! I'll call the authorities!"

Dane gave a sardonic laugh. "I doubt that very much." He tore open the parcel, ignoring Monique's shrieks and George's angry demands that he cease.

"Give it to me!" All pretense abandoned, Monique lunged at Dane, desperately clawing to regain her condemning bundle.

Dane held her off with effortless ease. "Well, what do we have here?" he muttered, removing the copy of Hamilton's letter. "Letters to your sister, Miss Brisset?" he taunted. "Hardly."

"Give it to me, you bastard!" Monique hissed. "I've worked for this for months . . . and you and this brazen little hellion are not going to take this victory from me now!"

"It's over, Monique." Dane caught her flailing wrists. "We know everything . . . what you and Thomas were planning, the money you were being paid . . ."

"Money?" Monique flung Dane's arms away. "You believe I did it for money? No, *monsieur,* only your pathetic friend Thomas was driven by a desire for wealth, not I." Her eyes glittered with rage and hatred. "I did it for *him* . . . and for my country. He is destined to lead France to greatness . . . with America beside us, as our ally."

"He?" Jacqui cut in. "Who is he?"

Monique threw back her head, taking perverse pride and pleasure in her disclosure. "Certainly not a weak fool such as Thomas," she sneered. "Or did you think I meant your lovesick father, Jacqueline?" She raked George's ashen face with venomous ice-blue eyes. "Never. Both of them were my pawns, so blinded by love that they would do anything . . . *anything* I asked of them. No, Jacqueline, the 'he' I refer to is General Bonaparte . . . a man, not a sniveling boy."

"You bitch!" Jacqui lost control, and only Dane's restraining hand kept her from smacking the evil smirk off Monique's face.

"Don't, *chaton*. She's not worth it. Besides"—he gave Monique a look of utter disdain—"she's just provided us with the final pieces of the puzzle. We now know where Alexander's letter was going . . . and to whom. We also know why."

"I shall find a way!" Monique cried out hysterically, snatching the letter from Dane's hands and fleeing for the door.

"Not from prison, you won't," Dane countered, cocking his pistol and aiming it directly at her.

Hearing the pistol's telltale click, Monique halted in her tracks, silently debating whether to take the risk of bolting.

"Don't bother," Dane advised her, guessing her intent. "Even if you did succeed in getting the letter to General Bonaparte, it would do him no good. You see, all the information written there is false, penned by Secretary Hamilton in the hopes that you would fall into his trap, steal the letter, and thus reveal your identity to us . . . which is exactly what you did."

The color drained from Monique's face. "Are you telling me that everything on that paper is fabricated?"

"Every word."

"Then no new conditions have been drafted for John Jay, and Secretary Hamilton . . ."

"Has just put an end to your treacherous plan." Dane inclined his head in Jacqui's direction. "With the help of Jack Laffey, of course."

Monique sagged with defeat, and Dane walked over, pistol raised, clamping his hand roughly on her arm. *"Now* we can go to the authorities, Miss Brisset," he informed her.

He turned to Jacqui. "Do you wish to stay here, *chaton?*" he asked softly, gesturing toward George, who had not moved nor spoken since Monique's tirade had begun.

"Yes." Jacqui cast a worried glance in her father's direction. "I won't be long."

Dane nodded. "I'll deliver Miss Brisset to Alexander. Then I have one last unpleasant hurdle to surmount before this ordeal can be put to rest."

Jacqui understood at once: Dane had to confront Thomas. "Will you be all right?"

Dane met her concerned look, and a current of communication ran between them. "Of course," he replied in a voice filled with poignant tenderness. "Always."

The door closed behind him.

Jacqui swallowed hard and turned to George, who was crumpled against the desk, staring after Monique's retreating figure. "Father?" She touched his cheek. "What can I do?"

George relinquished the turmoil of his thoughts to respond to Jacqui's question with his own. "How long have you known?"

"Several hours longer than you. Dane and I saw my kidnapper steal the letter from Secretary Hamilton's office and we followed him. He went directly to Monique."

"He was masked?"

"Last night . . . yes. But this morning, when he emerged from Monique's house . . . no. It was Thomas Mills."

"How could he do such a thing to Dane?" George asked, still dazed. "All for money?"

"No, *mon père,*" Jacqui replied gently. "Not all for money. Thomas was in love with Monique."

"So I heard."

Jacqui took a deep breath. "Father, their . . . relationship was not restricted to business."

"I gathered that as well." George's expression twisted with grief . . . but not the shock Jacqui had expected.

"You knew?"

George shrugged. "As you are learning, Jacqui, love is not always a pleasant emotion."

"Monique didn't love you, Father."

"I know that." He sighed. "And, to answer your question, I've suspected for some time now that Monique was involved with another man. But treason? At my expense?" He gestured helplessly. "I've been such a fool. I never imagined . . ." He lowered his head dejectedly.

"I'm so sorry, *mon père*," Jacqui whispered. "I would have done anything to spare you this pain."

George looked up and lay his hand tenderly against his daughter's smooth cheek. "I know you would." He studied her lovely, worried face, a new light dawning in his eyes. "You've grown so much these past months, *ma petite*. The loving, open girl I thought was forever lost to me has returned. Only now she is a warm-hearted, sensitive woman." He smiled, cupping her chin. "You've finally let Dane into your heart, haven't you?"

Jacqui answered without pause. "I love him, *mon père*."

"And he loves you." Despite the agony of the past hour's discovery, George felt a great surge of joy . . . the kind of joy reserved for a parent who knows his child has found happiness. "Stop worrying about me," George said softly, tugging a lock of Jacqui's hair. "Like my daughter, I'm resilient. Given a little time, I promise to recover fully." He stood, drawing Jacqui to him. "Welcome back, *ma petite*."

Jacqui hugged him back. "Father . . ."

"No more." He pressed his lips to her hair. "The past is behind us. It is time for me to take you home to your future."

"Dane . . . what are you doing here?"

Thomas looked up from his desk to see Dane standing in the open doorway.

"I went to your office. They told me you were working at home today." Dane strolled into Thomas's study. "Your front door was unlocked . . . so I let myself in."

Thomas felt a curious sense of fear tingle up his spine. Resolutely, he ignored it, attributing it to a bad case of nerves and total exhaustion. He hadn't slept in two days; it was barely ten o'clock and he felt as if it were midnight.

"Did you need to see me?"

Dane paused, fingering the quill pen on Thomas's desk. "We can make this easy or we can make this difficult," he said in a wooden voice. "The choice, friend, is yours."

Thomas rose slowly, sweat breaking out on his forehead. He had seen Dane's predatory method at work too often not to recognize it. "What are you talking about?"

Dane raised cold, steel-gray eyes to Thomas's face. "If it were for money alone, I would break every bone in your body," he said quietly. "You know damned well I would have given you anything you needed . . . as would Alexander. But the money was only a small part of it, wasn't it, Thomas? The real reason was the woman. Well, that I can understand, even if I cannot forgive it. I know what it's like to love a woman so much that you'd kill for her, die for her, live for her." Dane slammed his fists on the desk until it rattled, and Thomas cringed. "But that was my wife you put your filthy hands on, Thomas. That's the woman *I* love."

"I would never hurt Jacqueline," Thomas pleaded. "You've got to know that."

Dane ignored him. "You betrayed me, you betrayed Alexander, and you betrayed our country. All for a woman who was using you for her own purposes. A woman who planned to discard you . . . and George Holt," Dane added pointedly, seeing the shock of realization flash in Thomas's eyes, "as soon as she had achieved her own goal: French supremacy and the rise of General Bonaparte."

"What?"

"Monique never planned to send that letter to England, Thomas. She was concealing it in one of Holt's shipments to France. Not that it would have done her any good." Quickly, efficiently, Dane recounted Hamilton's plan to Thomas watching his friend grow paler with each word of explanation.

"Dane, I . . ."

"Don't." Dane shook his head adamantly. "Don't insult me by denying your involvement, nor humiliate us both by admitting it. Just say nothing at all."

Thomas's throat worked convulsively. "I assume you've arrested Monique," he managed.

"We have."

Thomas bent to remove his coat from the back of the chair. "I'm ready to go," he said quietly. He hesitated, gazing at Dane with tears in his eyes. "Would you believe me if I told you how very sorry I was?"

"I'd believe you." A muscle worked in Dane's jaw.

"Thank you for that." Thomas shook his head sadly and headed toward the door. In the hallway, he paused. "I think I'm actually relieved it's all over." He wiped a shaking palm across his face. "It was getting harder and harder to live with myself."

"I'm sure it was."

They walked in silence until they'd reached Hamilton's office. There, Thomas placed a restraining hand on Dane's arm. "Allow me this one small dignity," he requested. "Let me bear this humiliation alone."

Curtly, Dane nodded. "Very well." He turned to go.

"Dane?"

Dane paused, inclined his head.

"Heed this man you once called friend," Thomas said, his voice choked. "Go home and tell Jacqueline you love her. Then, every day of your life count your blessings, both of you. Be grateful that you found each other." He knocked on Hamilton's door, then gave Dane a mock salute. *"Au revoir,* my friend."

Jacqui was out of her chair the instant she heard the front door open.

"Dane?" She ran to him.

"Hello, *chaton.*" He caught her up in his arms, burying his face in her hair, savoring her softness.

"Are you all right?" she whispered.

"Now I am." He leaned back to look into the glowing midnight eyes that consumed his dreams . . . and defined his life. "Your father?" he questioned softly.

"Father will heal." She searched his face. "Was it terribly painful?"

"It's over. That's all that matters." He brushed her lips softly with his, hearing Thomas's advice echo in his mind.

"I love you, Jacqueline." Dane's words were hoarse, raw.

Jacqui smiled. "I love you too . . ." she replied, her heart in her eyes. "Forever."

CHAPTER
20

"From Laffey's initial reports, it appears that Alexander's strategy to combat the whiskey insurgents has thus far been successful," Dane reported, lounging in the kitchen doorway and scanning the first paragraph of Laffey's October 30th column.

"Really?" Jacqui's brow was furrowed in concentration as she completed the task of cooling her strawberry tarts . . . the first batch she had baked without Greta's assistance.

"Yes . . . really." Dane returned to his reading. In truth, he was inordinately pleased that Jacqui's words were once again in print. Perpetuating Laffey's career had taken a great deal of effort on Dane's part. First, he'd had to convince Hamilton to reward Jacqui's bravery by keeping her secret and not interfering with the writing of her column. Next, he'd paid a handsome sum to Jacqui's young contact for his sworn silence. The lad was happy to comply . . . and to retire, now that Dane himself was transporting Laffey's column each week to the office of the *General Advertiser*. Last, Dane had himself assured Bache that Laffey's credibility remained intact, despite the reporter's temporary alliance with Secretary Hamilton during the weeks preceding the arrests of Monique and Thomas. Laffey was and always would be, Dane had informed Bache regretfully, a steadfast Republican. And Bache, aware of Dane's respected position and influence in the community, had astutely agreed to allow Laffey to continue his anonymous work. If Bache wondered how Dane knew so much about the obscure Jack Laffey, he was wise enough to keep his questions to himself.

The only other threats to Laffey's true identity were Monique and Thomas. Dane had covered those avenues as well. Monique's silence was ensured: convicted of treason, she had been deported to France, never to set foot on American soil again. Thomas, also found guilty, was serving a light prison sentence, thanks to Alexander's intervention, and was determined to turn his life around. Just to be sure, Dane had paid Thomas a visit, demanding to know his intentions with regard to Jacqui's identity. Thomas had looked stunned, then distinctly amused, vowing to Dane that under *no* circumstances did he plan to grapple with Jack Laffey again.

So Dane was convinced, and Laffey was back at work.

Now Dane's eyes twinkled as he lowered the *General Advertiser* and addressed his wife. "Reading this recounting of Hamilton's expedition into western Pennsylvania, one would almost believe Jack Laffey admired our Secretary of the Treasury."

Jacqui straightened, hands on hips. "Laffey is merely reporting the situation as impartially as he can," she answered defensively. "Secretary Hamilton is equally as brilliant in execution as he is in planning, and deserves to be commended. He is leading hundreds of troops, yet not a shot has been fired. The militia's display of strength has evidently scattered the insurgents."

"Ah, but what of the farmers' freedom to rebel?" Dane teased.

"I believe in freedom . . . not civil war."

"Agreed." Dane returned to the column. Abruptly, his smile vanished, warning sparks erupting in his eyes. "What the hell does this mean?"

Jacqui inclined her head. "I presume you've reached the section I penned too late in the day for you to read prior to delivering the column to Bache, the part that deals with Robespierre's downfall and the probable signing of the Jay Treaty?"

"You make it sound as if America is using France's vulnerability to solidify our ties with the British!"

"Well?" Jacqui demanded, ready to do battle. "Isn't that why the signing of the Jay Treaty appears imminent . . . despite Grenville's uncompromising attitude? France might be celebrating its freedom . . . but it is also uncertain of its future. Therefore, hasn't our government decided that it is far more advantageous for us to further our ties with Britain?"

"Jacqueline . . ." Dane tossed the newspaper to the floor in frustration.

"Compromise, husband. Remember?" Jacqui laughed, holding up her hands to ward off Dane's threatening advance.

With an exasperated groan, Dane pulled her into his arms. "If I didn't love you so damned much . . ."

"But you do." She wound her arms around his neck and kissed him soundly. "And I love you."

Dane deepened the kiss, wishing they hadn't made plans to visit Greenhills that day.

"Dane." Jacqui broke away, her cheeks flushed. "Your mother is expecting us in two hours, and I want to finish preparing these tarts."

Skeptically, Dane glanced at the lumpy pastries. "They don't much resemble the ones Greta bakes, do they?"

"Haven't I yet convinced you that appearances are deceiving?" Jacqui defended her creations.

Dane grinned. "That you have."

"Good." Jacqui placed one steaming tart on a plate and headed toward the sitting room. "I baked them for your mother, but this first one is for you . . . since I know how you adore them. Come and taste it."

She was halfway to the sitting room when the crash from within brought them both running. At their abrupt entry, Whiskey looked up and blinked, calmly resuming his task: lapping up the contents of a shattered whiskey bottle.

Dane sighed. "I don't hold out much hope of reforming your cat. So I guess I'd best accept him."

"I'm glad to hear you say that," Jacqui said, glancing out the window as she placed the plate on the side table. Rubbing her hands nervously down her apron, she inched toward the hallway. "Because there is something I've been meaning to tell you." She opened the door, leaned forward, and gestured for whoever was outside to enter. "Come in," she invited.

With all the arrogant grace of a queen, an elegant white cat strolled into the house, her head held high. She paused, glancing haughtily at Jacqui, then looking protectively behind her. Satisfied with what she saw, she made her way toward the sitting room . . . and a proud-faced Whiskey.

It didn't take long for Dane to figure out the cause of Whiskey's pride. Hobbling behind the regal white cat stumbled five tiny kittens, ranging in color from black to white, most of them a combination of both. There was no question of their parentage.

"Surprise! Whiskey is a father," Jacqui announced proudly.

"So I gathered," Dane responded, his tone dry. Before he could continue, the ears of the last coal-black cat perked up, and the tiny animal bounded off, tripping over his own small feet, racing to his sire's side. Then, without pause, he began to furiously lap at the remaining whiskey on the floor.

Dane groaned. "Now I *know* whose kitten he is."

Jacqui smiled, a reminiscent look in her eyes. "He reminds me of Whiskey that first night you met."

Puzzled, Dane asked, "What night?"

"The night in April when I adopted Whiskey . . . and glimpsed the impenetrable Dane Westbrooke for the first time." Jacqui gave him a mischievous grin. "You and

Thomas were strolling along with your drinks, and I was returning from my Monday night excursion. Whiskey attacked your liquor just as you were announcing your premonition of danger. Thomas had you convinced that your instincts were faltering." Jacqui dimpled. "They weren't . . . I was in the trees, trying to avoid discovery."

The night in question came back to Dane in a rush. *"You* were there?"

"I certainly was. I was also terrified that you had spotted me, which, incidentally, is why I was so frightened of you when we met at Secretary Hamilton's ball."

"You thought I might recognize you," Dane concluded aloud. He stared at her in amused realization. "And here I assumed you were merely shocked by my advances."

"Oh, that too," Jacqui laughed, recalling Dane's shameless behavior that night at the City Tavern. "I meant it when I said you surpassed scandalous."

Picturing Jacqui crouched alone in the dark row of trees, Dane shook his head in amazement. "And I meant it when I said, 'So do you,' *chaton,"* he replied. "More than even *I* knew at the time."

He raised her hand to his lips, turning it over to kiss her soft palm. "Well, wife, have you any other secrets to divulge?" he teased. "Other than your dual identity, our first meeting, and an army of kittens sired by your inebriated scoundrel of a cat?"

Jacqui's smile illuminated her face. "I? How could I possibly possess any other secrets, husband? When you proposed marriage to me, did you not promise to strip them all away?"

"I did."

She stroked his jaw with tender fingers. "Then the question is a moot one."

Dane frowned. "I notice you didn't answer it, however." His dark brows drew together. "Jacqueline . . . if there is anything . . ."

A frightened squeal from one of the kittens interrupted

359

his oncoming chastisement. Perceiving the problem, Dane squatted to rescue the little fellow from beneath the arm chair, scooping him to safety upon the floor. The kitten looked about, bewildered, then caught sight of something that interested him. He scampered to the side table and swatted at it in frustration.

"I believe he wants your strawberry tart, sweet," Dane chuckled. He broke off a small piece and offered it to the kitten. "That is all you get, small one. The rest belongs to me."

The kitten appeared overjoyed, his tiny mouth open and ready. Gleefully, he sniffed at the pastry . . . and abruptly halted. He gagged, staring at the tart in utter distaste. Then, with a tiny shudder of revulsion, he wrinkled up his nose and stumbled off.

Dane threw back his head and roared with laughter. "Perhaps we'd best ask Greta to prepare a substitute for us to bring to Greenhills, *chaton*. Else we might be banished from Mother's home forever."

Jacqui looked crestfallen. "I spent all morning baking. I don't know what could have gone wrong . . . I followed Greta's instructions exactly."

Dane wrapped his arms around her and drew her close. "Your talents, darling, are far more crucial to my well-being than the baking of a superior strawberry tart." He nuzzled her hair, whispering wickedly, "The sweetest confection I consume each morning cannot be found in the kitchen."

"Dane!" Jacqui was trying desperately not to laugh. "If even a cat rejects my cooking, what hope is there for me?"

Without a word, Dane swept her up and headed for the stairs. "Now that we no longer require that extra half hour for cooling tarts, I'll show you precisely what your true accomplishments are." He silenced her laughter with his mouth. "I'm sure my mother will understand if we're late." He kicked the bedroom door shut behind them.

* * *

"Greenhills is so lovely in the autumn," Jacqui murmured, gazing out the carriage window at the exquisite array of fall colors. "I don't blame your mother for secluding herself here."

Dane sighed deeply as the carriage came to a stop in front of the great manor. "Unfortunately, love, I don't believe Mother's reluctance to join in social gatherings has much to do with the beauty of Greenhills."

Jacqui smoothed her gown idly. "You think she still misses your father?"

"I know she does."

As always, Dane's jaw set inflexibly when he spoke of Edwin Westbrooke. Jacqui fell silent, merely accepting her husband's assistance in alighting from the coach, wondering, for the hundredth time these past months, if her seeds would bear fruit.

"It's so wonderful to see you!" Lenore was rushing down the path toward them before they could take a step. She stood on tiptoe to kiss her son's cheek, then gave Jacqui a warm hug . . . a hug Jacqui wholeheartedly returned.

"Fill me in on all the news," Lenore demanded, leading them along. "It's such a glorious day, I've had a light meal set up for us in the garden."

"Perfect!" Dane said, straight-faced. "We have some homemade gingerbread from Greta, still warm. She barely had time to remove it from the oven before our carriage departed."

Jacqui shot him a withering look. "I baked my first strawberry tarts for you this morning," she explained, at Lenore's puzzled expression. "They were an abysmal failure."

"I'll tell you a secret," Lenore whispered, leaning forward. "I detest strawberry tarts."

"But I wanted to make something special for you," Jacqui said dejectedly. "And my culinary abilities are severely lacking."

"There is one gift I desperately long for . . . more than any other," Lenore confided. "And I know you would create it splendidly and savor every moment of the labor required to do so."

Jacqui looked skeptical. "And what is this gift?"

Lenore's smile was mischievous. "A grandchild."

Jacqui flushed and Dane laughed aloud. "Mother, we would *both* be happy to oblige you . . . as quickly as possible," he assured her.

"Wonderful!" Lenore clapped her hands. "Then you concentrate on that task and let Greta concentrate on her cooking. Come . . . our food is getting cold."

Over salmon, sweet peas, and rice custard, Dane and Jacqui told Lenore of Monique's deportation, Thomas's abbreviated prison term, and George's remarkable recovery.

"Your father is a strong and fine man," Lenore said. "Someday he shall meet a woman worthy of his love."

"I know," Jacqui agreed, smiling softly.

"But in the interim," Dane added with a wide grin, "George's pointed comments indicate that he is awaiting the same gift as you, Mother."

"All the more reason to indulge us," Lenore replied. She turned to Jacqui. "And what of Jack Laffey?"

Jacqui beamed with pride. "Thanks to Dane, Laffey has resumed his column."

"Yes," Dane muttered. "Thanks to Dane, Laffey is back, as opinionated and arrogant as ever."

Both women laughed.

They were sipping their coffee and munching on some gingerbread when a large carriage pulled into the drive leading to Greenhills.

Lenore squinted. "Who on earth could that be? I'm not expecting anyone today."

Dane shrugged. "Possibly someone who is lost and needs proper directions." He rose. "I'll find out."

Jacqui said nothing, only sat up straighter . . . and

waited. Her heartbeat accelerated as the carriage drew closer, revealing a sole male occupant of middle to late years. He alighted, tall and distinguished, dark hair heavily laced with gray. Jacqui clasped her hands tightly in her lap, praying more fervently than she had allowed herself in years.

The shocked gasp from Lenore was Jacqui's first clue that her prayers had been answered. Coming abruptly to her feet, Lenore's hands flew to her mouth and she stared, white-faced, as the gentleman walked toward the house.

Perhaps he heard Lenore's sharp cry, or perhaps it was merely intuition. He halted, veering slowly in their direction, staring across the fifty feet that separated them.

Jacqui saw Dane stiffen in shock.

"Yes, sir, may I help you?" Greenhills's efficient butler, Jarvis, hurried out the front door to the stranger.

With great effort, the gentleman tore his gaze from Lenore and faced the servant. "Pardon me?" he asked hoarsely.

"May I help you?" Jarvis repeated.

"Yes." He cleared his throat. "I'm here to see the marchioness."

"Who, sir?" Jarvis looked blank.

"The Marchioness of Forsgate," the man repeated, then broke off, grappling with some internal demon. All at once, he straightened his shoulders and swallowed decisively, restating his form of address. "I'm here to see Mrs. Westbrooke."

"Who shall I say is calling, sir?"

He inclined his head, gazing toward where Lenore stood, unmoving. "Her husband."

Jarvis blinked. "Her . . . what did you say, sir?"

"It's all right, Jarvis," Lenore called out. "The marquis may join us."

Dane took an involuntary step forward as though to intervene, but Jacqui lay a restraining hand on his arm. "Don't, Dane," she said softly. "Please."

Lenore took in Dane's reaction, her expression uncertain,

apprehensive as a young girl's. Much as she loved her son, Lenore knew in her heart that Dane could not be the one to advise her in this all-important decision; he could not be impartial, nor could he truly comprehend a woman's emotions. Lenore's gaze found Jacqui's, the bond that had grown between them making it natural for her to turn to the girl she now regarded as her daughter. Silently, she requested Jacqui's support as she took this pivotal step.

Jacqui smiled, slowly nodding her encouragement. "Yes," she replied to Lenore's unspoken question. "Go ahead"— her voice trembled—"Mother."

A current of communication passed between them, and Lenore's lips quivered with emotion. "Thank you, Jacqui," she whispered, turning to meet her fate.

Edwin Westbrooke walked through the garden and stopped before his wife. "Lenore."

Lenore brought herself under control with a great deal of effort. "Edwin . . . I never expected . . ." She stopped, inhaled sharply.

"Nor did I." He smiled faintly, an action that softened the harsh lines of his features from stony to disciplined. "But I found it harder and harder to stay away." Stiffly, he took her hand, his words forced out in a way that clearly showed how difficult they were for him to say. "I've missed you."

Her eyes grew damp. "It's been ten years. Why now?"

"It's taken me this long to realize what an obstinate fool I've been." His expression was guarded, his question direct. "Is it too late?"

"Too late?" Lenore dabbed at her wet cheeks. "I don't know, Edwin. I'm no longer the same woman who left Forsgate. I've changed."

"I know. Nor am I the same man. I'm older, more philosophical, perhaps, more certain of my priorities, definitely."

"And what are those priorities?"

"My family. Sharing their lives." Edwin spoke loud

364

enough for Dane to hear, although he kept his gaze averted from his son's, taking one hurdle at a time. "Lenore, I cannot promise to understand all your beliefs, but I can promise to try. Can you do the same?"

Lenore inclined her head. "I could . . . but it matters not, for we will be an ocean apart." She shook her head adamantly as Edwin tried to speak. "I will not leave Philadelphia, so do not even suggest it. This is my home and I have a life here, Edwin. I cannot simply abandon it because you will it to be so." She gave him a sad smile. "A decade changes not only people but circumstances as well."

Edwin nodded at Lenore's wisdom. "Recently, I learned a new word," he told her quietly. "Compromise. It is something totally new to me, explained by a very wise person, and I am more than willing to attempt it. Are you?"

"Compromise? How?"

"Six months in Philadelphia; six months at Forsgate. Does that sound reasonable?"

Lenore gaped. "You would spend one half of each year living in America? For me?"

"For you . . . yes." The grin he gave her was almost boyish. "In fact, if the terms are agreeable, I'd like to begin my stay immediately. All I need is your consent, and I'll have the servants bring in my bags."

Lenore's lips twitched. "Even if I agree to your arrangement, my servants will not be bringing in your bags. At Greenhills, Edwin, you are merely Mr. Westbrooke, not the Marquis of Forsgate. My servants and I work side by side . . . without class distinction. So you'll be responsible for your own bags."

He ingested that stipulation with a baffled shake of his head. "Agreed," he surprised her by saying. *"Now* . . . will you consider my offer?"

A smile erupted on Lenore's face . . . and was quickly extinguished. "I wasn't the only person who left Forsgate hurt."

Edwin allowed his gaze to travel to Dane, who stood rigidly beside Jacqui's chair. Only the tight clenching of his jaw gave any indication that he was affected by this reunion.

"Hello, son." Edwin studied the tall, powerful man that was his only child, the tension between them palpable. "You've accomplished everything you intended when you went to America: you've achieved independence, respect, self-made prosperity. Your mother's letters glow with praise for Westbrooke Shipping and its great success. You must be very proud."

Dane didn't blink. "I am." His lips tightened. "How is Forsgate?"

Edwin winced at the bitterness in Dane's tone. "Forsgate is prospering. . . . It is also, I've discovered, a mere parcel of land that cannot provide solace in one's old age." He raised his head, his words straightforward, his steel-gray eyes the image of Dane's: candid and piercing. "The same wise person who taught me about compromise taught me to know when the time comes to bid the past goodbye. It is time, Dane, time for us to reap the joys of the future without the burden of yesterday's encumbrances."

Edwin's expression softened somewhat. "And that same person taught me one thing more: that it takes a great man to admit he is wrong . . . and an even greater one to accept, to forgive, and to trust again." Edwin held out his hand. "I was wrong . . . and I'm sorry. Our beliefs will often clash, but you're a principled, intelligent man, as equally entitled to your views as I. You're also my son, and I care for you." His voice wavered, and he waited, his hand extended.

Dane stared at his father's hand, his expression unfathomable. Then he slowly looked up, meeting Edwin's gaze, reading the vulnerability in his father's eyes and simultaneously baring his own. Silently, Dane held out his hand, clasping Edwin's fingers in his. "Welcome to Philadelphia, Father."

Witnessing the raw emotion on her husband's face,

Jacqui's heart swelled with joy. Silently, she blessed the fates for realizing her most fervent prayer.

Edwin's voice was gruff. "Thank you, Dane. Thank you very much." He coughed, glancing past Dane to Jacqui. With a broad smile, Edwin gestured toward her. "Here is someone I have yet to meet."

Dane turned abruptly. "Forgive me. Father, this is . . ."

"Jacqueline." Edwin drew her to her feet and, to Dane's stunned surprise, embraced her. "You are every bit as beautiful as I knew you would be."

"Welcome, my lord," she returned warmly.

Edwin chuckled. "My lord? I hardly expected so formal a greeting. Especially after the way you lambasted me."

Dane was totally at sea. "Jacqueline is my wife," he clarified.

"Yes, Dane, I know she is," Edwin replied with a twinkle. "She's also much as your mother was . . . and still is, for that matter: opinionated, far too forthright, and utterly charming." He sobered. "And I owe her a debt of thanks I can never truly repay."

"What debt?" Dane demanded.

"Your father is mistaken," Jacqui told Dane softly, turning glowing eyes to her husband. "He owes me nothing. All I did was pen him a letter, passing on all the wondrous things I've learned from you . . . and Lenore. It was the last of my secrets, the only gift I could think of to adequately express my gratitude for all you've given me. And, just as your magic transformed my life, I knew it would transform your father's as well. So, you see"—Jacqui smiled at Lenore, who was unashamedly weeping with joy—"it was actually you who provided the marquis with the insights he just quoted, not I. You taught me the importance of compromise, gave me the strength to let go of my past, and, with the utmost patience, offered me friendship, trust, and, most important . . ." She went to stand by Dane's side. "Love." Tenderly, she intertwined her fingers with his. "The debt, husband, was mine to repay."

Dane closed his eyes, so overwhelmed by Jacqui's words, the selflessness of her gesture that he could barely speak. How could he explain to her that she'd brought something back into his life that he hadn't even realized he'd lost, made him whole in ways he'd never known he was empty?

Earnestly, he sought the means to express what was in his heart: that her love was his present, his future, the restorer of his past. Choked with emotion, Dane opened his eyes, cupping his wife's face and raising it to his. And suddenly he knew no words were necessary.

The tears glistening on Jacqui's cheeks told him she already knew.

Author's Note

The Jay Treaty, ultimately signed on November 19, 1794, was bitterly debated in the Senate for its staggering concessions to the British. It was submitted to President Washington in June 1795, yet not ratified until 1796 (when it passed by only four votes). All sources point to the fact that Alexander Hamilton, who drafted the original instructions to John Jay, would have been a far wiser choice than Jay as American envoy to England. Nevertheless, public turbulence over Hamilton's alleged (and eventually disproved) misappropriation of Treasury funds made it impossible for him to accept the appointment, and he recommended Jay be designated instead.

England received John Jay simultaneous with the news that Sweden and Denmark had asked America to join them in forming a general alliance of neutral countries determined to combat England's violations of neutrality (a development of which Jay was unaware). The fear of such a powerful allied force united against his country would very likely have influenced Lord Grenville, England's Secretary of State for Foreign Affairs, to acquiesce to Jay's terms; however, Hamilton himself inadvertently destroyed this hope by making a grave *faux pas*.

George Hammond, then British minister to the United States, was a personal friend of Hamilton's. Unfortunately, Hamilton foolishly entrusted Hammond with the closely guarded secret that America did not intend to join in an alliance against the British. Hammond, in turn, hastily and secretly dispatched the information to Grenville, eliminating Grenville's greatest concern and thus dramatically tilting the Jay negotiations in England's favor.

I found myself totally intrigued by the fact that the course of history might well have been altered by this chance forewarning. Intrigue snowballed into inspiration, and thus was born the fictional treason committed in *Masque of Betrayal.*

Alexander Hamilton is one of history's most colorful and controversial figures. Depending on the source, he is depicted as everything from a blatant monarchical dictator to a brilliant, patriotic hero. From extensive research, I determined him to be a charismatic leader and nationalist, who possessed unfailing integrity and farsighted wisdom. I hope I brought some of those traits to life.

Dear Readers:

As always, my greatest wish is for you to share my characters' emotions as they discover themselves, each other, and the magic of falling in love. I hope Jacqui and Dane brought you hours of joy, much laughter, a few tears, and a heart full of love!

I treasure all your wonderful letters, and promise to keep reading and answering each and every one! My current newsletter will transport you to Victorian England and the beautiful Isle of Wight, where Lady Ariana Caldwell and Trenton Kingsley, the Duke of Broddington, are carving their jagged niche in *Echoes in the Mist,* my next Pocket historical. If you would like a preview of their unlikely, unwilling, yet unavoidable union, just drop me a legal-sized SASE at:

P.O. Box 5104
Parsippany, NJ 07054-6104

Much love,
Andrea

SWEET LIAR

JUDE DEVERAUX

Dramatic, passionate, and deeply moving, yet filled with endearing lighthearted moments, SWEET LIAR celebrates the joy of life and love...and reaffirms Jude Deveraux's reputation as one of our most treasured authors of romance.

POCKET
BOOKS

Available from Pocket Books

The Irresistible New Novel
from the *New York Times*
Bestselling Author of *The Secret*

JULIE GARWOOD

*Julie Garwood has captivated countless
readers with her <u>New York Times</u> bestselling
novels. Now she surpasses herself in a superb
new tale of passion, mystery, adventure and
romance. Set in Regency London, <u>CASTLES</u>
is the breathtaking story of an English lord
and the impulsive princess who wins his heart.
Another winner from Julie Garwood.*

CASTLES

**Available from Pocket Books
Mid-June 1993**